THE UNKNOWN SHORE

Patrick O'Brian, one of our greatest contemporary
novelists, is the author of the acclaimed
Aubrey–Maturin tales and the biographer of
Joseph Banks and Picasso. His first novel,
Testimonies, and his *Collected Short Stories* have
recently been republished by HarperCollins. He
has translated many works from French into
English, among them the novels and memoirs of
Simone de Beauvoir and the first volume of Jean
Lacouture's biography of Charles de Gaulle. In
1995 he was the first recipient of the Heywood Hill
Prize for a lifetime's contribution to literature. In
the same year he was awarded the CBE. In 1997
he received an honorary doctorate of letters from
Trinity College, Dublin. He lives in the South of
France.

The Works of Patrick O'Brian

BIOGRAPHY

Picasso
Joseph Banks

AUBREY/MATURIN NOVELS

Master and Commander
Post Captain
HMS Surprise
The Mauritius Command
Desolation Island
The Fortune of War
The Surgeon's Mate
The Ionian Mission
Treason's Harbour
The Far Side of the World
The Reverse of the Medal
The Letter of Marque
The Thirteen-Gun Salute
The Nutmeg of Consolation
Clarissa Oakes
The Wine-Dark Sea
The Commodore
The Yellow Admiral

OTHER NOVELS

Testimonies
The Catalans
The Golden Ocean
The Unknown Shore
Richard Temple

TALES

The Last Pool
The Walker
Lying in the Sun
The Chian Wine
Collected Short Stories

ANTHOLOGY

A Book of Voyages

THE UNKNOWN SHORE

Patrick O'Brian

HarperCollins*Publishers*

HarperCollins*Publishers*
77–85 Fulham Palace Road,
Hammersmith, London w6 8jb

This paperback edition 1998
1 3 5 7 9 8 6 4 2

Previously published in hardback by HarperCollins 1996

First published in Great Britain by
Rupert Hart-Davis 1959

ISBN 0 00 649795 0

Set in Monotype Baskerville by
Rowland Phototypesetting Ltd,
Bury St Edmunds, Suffolk

Printed and bound in Great Britain by
Caledonian International Book Manufacturing Ltd, Glasgow

For Mary, With Love

Chapter One

MR EDWARD CHAWORTH of Medenham was a well-disposed, good-natured man with an adequate fortune, an amiable wife and a numerous family: he thought the world an excellent place, and he could suggest no way in which it could be improved, except for the poachers and the Whigs – they would be abolished in an ideal world, and the trout in his stream would be a trifle larger.

Yet in the present state of things, Whigs abounded, and whenever Mr Chaworth thought of them, his cheerfulness was clouded. Sir Robert Walpole's name always made him frown, and he would happily have seen the prime minister hanged, drawn and quartered: he could not bear the sound of a Whig. How much more obnoxious, then, was Mr Elwes, who was not only a Whig but also Mr Chaworth's nearest neighbour? The thought of Mr Elwes luxuriating in Whiggery not half a mile beyond the kitchen-garden filled Mr Chaworth with indignation. The earliest symptoms of this indignation were a straightening of his back and a tightening of his lips: he had served under the Duke of Marlborough, and this martial stiffening was associated in his mind with carnage, the thunder of guns, blood and the general unpleasantness of battle. Mrs Chaworth, upon seeing the beginnings of it, glanced anxiously round the breakfast table.

It was so very large a table, there were so many children round it and so many things upon it that obstructed her view – a ham, a round of cold beef, an unusually tall pork-pie, chafing-dishes with mutton-chops, eggs, bacon, kippered trout, kidneys and mushrooms, apart from the tea and coffee urns and the host of minor objects such as marmalade, toast, rolls, potted char and Sophia's bowl of ass's milk – that it took her some time to survey the whole. Anne, Charles and Sophia were behaving perfectly well, and so was little Dormer, the youngest to be allowed downstairs; but she saw with regret that Georgiana was balancing her spoon and causing its bowl to float, in imitation of her cousin Jack, who was partially concealed by the raised pie: she coughed significantly, but they were too engrossed to hear and it was obvious, from her fascinated stare, that Isabella, Jack's sister, was going to join in.

Mr Chaworth grew more and more upright in his chair as he turned the page of the letter that he was reading, and Mrs Chaworth knew that unless he found something agreeable on this new page, his right hand would go up to clutch his wig, his left thump the letter on to the table and he would cry, 'Lard, Lard, *Lard*, Mrs Chaworth!'

It was very thoughtless of Jack: he knew that Mr Chaworth was easily vexed in the morning. But perhaps Jack thought that he was no longer subject to reproof, having been away from home. She peered round the pie at her younger cousin, who, with his head barbarously near the cloth and his rapidly growing form bulging from his blue midshipman's coat, was now engaged in making a storm in his tea-cup, by blowing. Jack Byron and his sister were cousins of the Chaworths, but they had lived at Medenham from their youngest days, ever since Lady Byron had died, and they were entirely part of the household: even now that Jack's elder brother, the present Lord Byron, was living at Newstead Abbey again, there was no question of their going back there.

'Lard, Lard, *Lard*, Mrs Chaworth!' cried the master of the house, grasping his wig. She automatically put out her hand to steady the tea-urn, which was apt to fall over, parboiling her knees: but the expected thump did not come. Mr Chaworth arrested his descending hand and pointed its index finger at Jack. 'What the devil do you think you are doing?' he exclaimed. But his words were prompted less by a spirit of inquiry than by a momentary urge to be disagreeable, and without waiting for an answer he went on, 'If these are naval manners – ha, *manners*, forsooth – they were best kept for sea.'

'What is it, my dear?' asked Mrs Chaworth, waving a lace handkerchief by way of distracting his attention from Jack, whom she loved dearly.

'The stream,' cried Mr Chaworth. 'The stream. He's going to turn the stream into his top field to make an enormous vast loathsome fountain for his wedding-day.'

'Well, my dear,' said Mrs Chaworth, who had expected something very much more shocking than this, 'I am sure Mr Elwes will turn it back again afterwards, when he is married.'

'And what do you suppose the trout will do in the meantime?' cried Mr Chaworth with all the agony of a devoted fisherman. 'What do you suppose will happen to the trout, Mrs Chaworth?'

Mrs Chaworth really did not mind; she never fished, or hunted, or shot, and she secretly disliked all these creatures that were so laboriously pursued; if it were not for them the family would spend most of the year in London – a much more agreeable kind of life. However, she did not say this, but soothingly replied, 'But in that case, surely it would be much easier to take them up, my dear? You could use a little net, in the puddles that are left.'

Mr Chaworth uttered a desolate howl, but made no further reply: in twenty years of an otherwise happy marriage he had never been able to make his wife understand the sanctity of game, and now, rather than persist in the hopeless task, he seized upon the ham, and silently carved it, with as much ferocity as if Mr Elwes had been under his knife.

It cannot be denied that Mr Elwes was a troublesome neighbour: his eccentricity was the delight of the countryside; yet it is one thing to have an amusing eccentric two or three parishes away, and quite another to have him as your next-door neighbour. The person in classical mythology who fitted his guests to the bed in his spare room by means of an axe or a rack was a source of endless gossip and diversion to the neighbourhood in general, but he must have been a sad bore to those who lived within the range of his victims' cries. Mr Elwes, then, was a troublesome neighbour; and this menace to the stream was but the latest of a series of outrages. He lived at Plashey, whose venerable roof could be seen from the terrace at Medenham in the winter, when the leaves were off the trees. Plashey was the other big house in the parish, and it was much older than Medenham; its most recent parts were Tudor, and the kitchens were Saxon; it was built facing north, in the bottom of a watery dell. Mr Elwes, however, had not inherited Plashey; he had only bought it, and although he had lived there some twenty years he was still considered a newcomer. For most of these years, that is to say, until he took up politics, he had lived a retired, secluded existence, with

3

a household consisting of no more than a few vague, shiftless servants and a boy, Tobias Barrow, who was usually called his nephew.

Jack Byron and Tobias Barrow were very close friends; their friendship dated from long ago, when there had still been a fair amount of visiting and acquaintance between Medenham and Plashey, and as soon as breakfast was over Jack hurried away to find Tobias. He knew that Mr Elwes was capable of any villainy, but he also knew that rumour delighted in exaggeration (Mr Elwes' ape, at its first arrival, had been confidently reported as the Devil in person) and he hoped to learn that this appalling news was ill-founded.

He crossed the bowling-green, hurried through the kitchen-garden into the park and along his private path towards the outer paling. During his absence at sea the path had almost vanished in the grass, but he knew it so well that he could follow it at midnight without a moon. He came to the pollard hornbeam that had always served as his ladder to get out of the park: there were rounded knobs on its gnarled old trunk that allowed one to reach the pointed ends of the pales, there to poise for the downward leap over the ditch and on to the soft bank that ran along the side of the lane below – the lane that separated Plashey's land from Medenham's. Jack and his nearest cousin Georgiana had used this route from their most tender infancy; in those days the ascent of the tree had been a matter of tears, blood, barked shins and childish oaths, but now Jack swung up it with the ease of one to whom the maintopgallant masthead of a man-of-war is as easy and familiar as a pulpit to a parson, and he was just about to spring down when he saw Mr Elwes in the meadow over the way, gathering simples in a sky-blue coat and scarlet breeches. He was a man past the middle age, with a large yellow-grey face; he had a very great deal of energy, and as he sprang about the field he sang odd snatches, gesticulated, and harangued the yak that stood in the far corner. Jack shrank back into the leaves. Mr Elwes picked dittander, middle confound and stinking arrach; he picked nigwort, figwort and liriconfancy, adding thereto polypody of the oak, pellitory of Spain and herb true-love, and he offered a blade of the last to the yak as it stood panting in the shade of the ragged hedge. This monolithic beast had been imported by Mr Elwes, at vast expense, under the impression that it was the aurochs of antiquity – it was supposed to improve the local breed of cattle out of all recognition,

4

but it did nothing but lurk in the shade, gasping, and it was evident that the race of Nottinghamshire aurochs would soon die out. This was not the case with all his importations, however, and it was almost impossible to keep servants at Plashey, because of the salamanders. Salamanders in the library, salamanders that had to be rescued from the ashes of the drawing-room grate, the gentle plop of salamanders falling from stair to stair as they tried to mount to the attic to hibernate in the servants' beds, but above all, salamanders multiplying in their thousands in the cellars that were Mr Elwes' pride and joy. It was not as cellars that they delighted him, because he drank no wine, but as Saxon relics: he was a virtuoso, for whom anything old was better than anything new – anything to do with the arts, that is to say, for in other respects he was wonderfully advanced, and he farmed his land upon the newest philosophical principles, designed great schemes for the improvement of mankind, and had invented several machines, including a musical treadmill and a hydraulic rack.

But it was in the matter of education that his theories and his energy appeared in their brightest light. 'You have no conception,' he said to one of his learned friends – 'you have no conception of the amount that an infant mind can learn, if it be subjected to it for twelve or fourteen hours a day, with none of your foolish holidays. Take a boy . . .' he said, and went on to describe how the boy would learn Latin and Greek by ear, thus absorbing them unconsciously; the time saved would be devoted to logic, mathematics and physical studies; when these had been acquired the ornamental arts of rhetoric, poetry, music, dancing and singing would follow, and in a surprisingly short time there would be loosed upon the world a new wonder, an even more Admirable Crichton. The prodigy would be brought up by a dumb nurse so that it should hear nothing but the classical tongues, which its tutors would speak from morning to . . . here Mr Elwes' learned friend interrupted him and said that the plan was vain, chimerical and, in short, a mere vapour – the more so as no child's mother would ever allow it to be carried out.

'Vapour?' cried Mr Elwes, with a furious glare. 'We shall see.'

'I dare say we shall,' replied the friend, walking away.

Within the hour Mr Elwes, fired by contradiction, had begun negotiations for the purchase of a suitable male child, for this conversation took place in London, not far from the scene of his earlier activities. Mr Elwes had begun life as a surgeon, and his practice had lain on the borders of the richest part of the City and the poorest slums that adjoined it. The first accounted for his wealth (grateful patients had helped him to South Sea stock, and he had sold out the week before the South Sea Bubble burst), and the second made him familiar with whole streets of people who had far, far too many children and no money. It was not a matter of searching for a child to buy, but rather of turning away the crowds that hurried up with surplus offspring, washed and even combed for the occasion.

Before the week was out Tobias Barrow arrived by post-chaise at Plashey, done up in an old, old shawl. He was given a small bowl of black broth, for Mr Elwes intended that he should be brought up in the Spartan manner, and the Spartans liked their soup black; these dismal people also slept hard, without any bedclothes, and so therefore did Tobias, weeping sadly. The next morning his education began.

It was a remarkable education, and one that only a wealthy man could afford; but Mr Elwes *was* a wealthy man, and even if he had paid the usual price for the tutors' services he could have done so easily; like many other wealthy men, however, he was exceedingly near with his money, particularly where small sums were concerned, and his experiment was conducted on the most economical principles. He employed very poor and unworldly scholars, and he often took them for a term or so upon approval, without any definite arrangement about their salaries. They came and went: sometimes, when Mr Elwes was engrossed in some other experiment and had little time to quarrel or interfere, a tutor might stay for a year or more – Mr Buchanan did, a sad, gentle, unbeneficed clergyman who probably knew more about birds than any man in England – but usually they went away much sooner, and nearly always on foot. One young man took a horse from the stable to help him on his way, and he had almost reached the shelter of Cambridge before he was overtaken. Mr Elwes prosecuted, of course, and it was rumoured that after the unhappy youth had been hanged he bought the body from the executioner for dissection.

This was untrue, as it happened, but Mr Elwes was in fact a most accomplished dissector: whatever his character may have been in other respects, he was an unusually learned and skilful surgeon, and he taught Tobias anatomy with great success. He had a real love for his profession (apart from anything else it gave him unrivalled opportunities for experiment on his fellow men), and he never abandoned it: after he came to Plashey he formed a small practice among his tenants and servants and the local poor; and this enabled him, in due course, to bind Tobias as his apprentice and to teach him the work of a general practitioner in medicine – for at that period, and for more than a hundred years afterwards, all surgeons began as apprentices: though to be sure few began quite so young as Tobias.

By the time the first part of the experiment was over – the part devoted to useful knowledge – Tobias had absorbed a great deal of information; he was not the all-knowing marvel that he ought to have been, however, for although his physical knowledge was beyond expectation and his Latin and Greek prodigiously fluent, he was distinctly weak in metaphysics, and in spite of the most severe whipping he could never be brought to understand the infinitesimal calculus. But when the second part was to begin Mr Elwes found that he no longer cared about it: he did make a determined attempt, but by now Tobias had an entirely scientific cast of mind, and he showed a very shocking, if not brutish, indifference to the graces, as professed by Mr Elwes. From natural inclination as well as training he was entirely devoted to natural history: it had been his comfort in adversity, his solace in loneliness, his delight at all times, and he was barbarously indifferent to Mr Elwes' poetry, music, rhetoric and song. His naturally stoical temperament and his Spartan upbringing made him almost insensible to the beating and starving with which Mr Elwes endeavoured to open his mind to beauty, and in the end Mr Elwes admitted that it was useless to continue. Tobias joined the yak as one of his disappointments: the last tutor was turned off, Tobias started the first holiday of his life, and the house lapsed into a grey, damp silence from which it was roused only by the terrifying visits of the widow Ellis.

The widow Ellis was the chief reason why Mr Elwes had lost interest in his experiment – the widow Ellis and Whig policitics. He had discovered politics at the end of the first stage in Tobias' progress, and he had thrown himself into them with great enthusiasm. He had joined the Whigs, to their dismay, and he had done so through a sneaking attorney named Ellis – a fellow whom he employed very often, for he was perpetually at law. And when this person was killed and partially eaten by a performing bear at Mangonell Bagpize, Mr Elwes fell madly in love with his widow. She was an odious woman with a dark red face, black eyebrows that joined across her nose, and seven daughters. She hated Tobias at first sight, and she was determined that her first step in reforming and renovating Plashey would be to put him out of doors.

'Oh the happy wedding day,' sang Mr Elwes, adding a final stalk of bugwort to the dank swathe under his arm. 'Happy, happy wedding day.' His voice died away behind the hedge.

Jack came out of his leaves and dropped into the lane. He gave the yak an affectionate thump as he passed, asked it how it did, and hurried through the meadow to the temple of Fame, a crumbling plaster-and-rubble edifice hastily run up by Mr Elwes in a spinney to shelter the busts of Galen, Aristotle and Mr Elwes, but now forgotten and taken over by Tobias for his bats.

Tobias was not there, but Jack knew that he would come, and he sat down cautiously on the steps of the temple to wait. He sat down cautiously and with a meek, dutiful expression, because of Tobias' bees; they lived in a row of hives in front of the building, and in spite of many sad proofs to the contrary Jack still believed that if he did not provoke them they would not sting him.

Behind him and above his head Tobias' bats scratched and rustled in the darkness of their dome, faintly, shrilly gibbering as they quarrelled among themselves. A steady, good-tempered hum came from the hives, and in the sunlight that now came slanting through the spinney the bees could be seen rising and shooting away with surprising speed: Jack gazed at them with detached respect, and wondered vaguely what was keeping his friend.

It was difficult to account for their friendship. Apart from their age they had nothing at all in common, or at least nothing that appeared at first sight. Nothing could have been more different than their appearance, education and family; nothing could have been more unlike than their pursuits; but they were happy when they were together and they missed one another very much when they were apart. Jack's education had been completely normal – he had done tolerably well at school and had come away with a certain amount of Latin, a reasonable acquaintance with mathematics, and nothing more. The education of Tobias, on the other hand, might have been calculated to produce a monster, and the fact that it had not done so was rather a proof of the resilience of the human spirit than any evidence of judgment on the part of Mr Elwes.

Yet one can avoid being a monster without necessarily being ordinary: Tobias was far from ordinary. He had never been to school, and he had never known anyone of his own age except Jack Byron and Georgiana Chaworth; he had spent all his days in that strange, dark, unsocial house, with odd, unsatisfactory servants perpetually coming and going; he had been kept to his book with inhuman persistence; and he was a strange young creature, very strange indeed.

'But he is so very strange, my dear,' said Mrs Chaworth. 'So very strange. He assured me that toads were capable of gratitude.'

'Are they not, ma'am?' asked Jack.

'Perhaps they are, my dear,' said Mrs Chaworth, closing her eyes, 'but with these words he passed a very large toad to Mrs Jerningham – Mrs *Charles* Jerningham – and desired her to caress it. Mrs Jerningham was obliged to be led away and recovered with sal volatile in the small drawing-room. My dear, unequal friendships never answer, as your grandfather often used to say.'

Mrs Chaworth did not forbid the association, but she dropped a gentle drizzle of disapproval upon it, and she would have been happy to see it die away, particularly on Georgiana's account. This young creature, the prettiest of her daughters, was passionately attached to her cousin Jack and even more so to Tobias: she played cricket with them, tirelessly fielding while Tobias bowled and Jack batted, and a primitive kind of baseball; she climbed trees, whistled and shouted in a manner that distressed her elegant mother, and cherished hedgepigs (presents from Tobias) in her bedroom.

When Mrs Chaworth objected to his strangeness she referred not only to qualities that were produced by his nurture but also to some that were born in him; for example, he had a strange power with animals, however wild, and sometimes (though not always) he could call them to him over great distances; he had always handled bees without any protection, and since his earliest days he had been reputed a horse-witch. Clearly a budding horse-witch, however fluent

9

in Greek, was not an ideal playmate for Georgiana: the family intended to marry Georgiana to Lord Carlisle, and Mrs Chaworth did not wish to hear any adverse criticism from the young man's mother about Georgiana's bringing-up: she often said to her daughter, 'Lard, Georgiana, what an ill-looking fellow poor Toby has become; and will grow even worse, alas.'

And however Georgiana might snort and cry 'I do not mind it,' not even she could claim that Tobias Barrow was in any way a beauty. He was meagre, narrow-chested and stooping; his dull black hair made his white face even paler, while at the same time it made a startling contrast with his almost colourless light green eyes. To an unaccustomed eye it was a face so strange as to be almost sinister – Mrs Ellis, upon contemplating it for the first time, had been struck dumb; which is saying a great deal. It was in no way a boy's face, and no one, looking at it, would ever have expected to see it moved by a boyish spirit. And then he had so early grown accustomed to loneliness and learning that he had slipped into odd, graceless habits; he would make sudden untoward gestures, forgetting his company – he would distort his face in thought, grind his teeth, and sometimes utter a low hooting noise. He washed only when he felt need of it, shifted his linen rarely, and always wore black clothes.

Jack could see him now, a slight dark figure running towards him through the trees. Jack smiled to see him coming, put up his hand after the fashion of sailors, and hailed him very loud and clear, 'Ahoy.'

The bats instantly fell into a petrified silence. 'There you are, Toby,' said Jack; and to this valuable observation he added, 'Why are you running?' For it was a rare thing to see Tobias running.

'Jack,' said Tobias, 'I am very happy to see you. I am very glad you have come.'

'Why, what's the matter?' asked Jack, staring. It was clear to him that his friend was strongly moved: he was flushed, and he was breathing hard.

'I tell you what it is, Jack,' said Tobias, gripping his arm and looking up into his face with great anxiety. 'You must give me your advice. I am going to run away to sea.'

Chapter Two

WHEN THE LONDON ROAD leaves Mangonell Bagpize it plunges down a hill so steep that horses must be led. The bottom of the hill was a favourite place with highwaymen, because coaches coming or going were obliged to be almost at a standstill there – highwaymen with strong nerves, that is, for the more timid or fanciful were put off and discouraged by the sight of the gallows at the top of the hill, where their unsuccessful brother Medical Dick (a former apothecary's boy) swung as a silent warning in chains, carefully tarred against the weather.

Tobias had eyed Medical Dick with a professional interest that could not possibly be shared by his companion, but he had not stopped talking; and still, as they walked down the hill with their horses stepping carefully behind them, they talked on with the same eagerness.

'. . . but the final thing, the thing I could not stand, was her sending her servant to destroy my animals. That woman, that termagant, if termagant be not too warm an expression – do you consider termagant too warm an expression, Jack?'

'No,' said Jack. 'I should have called her a termagant myself, if I had thought of it.'

'– always disliked me, and I know she told Mr Elwes that my presence was an obstacle to their union. It gave me a great deal of uneasiness, I assure you; yet I felt that I was bound to stay, because of my indenture – when Mr Buchanan wrote, offering to take me to Jamaica as his assistant – to study the West Indian birds, you know – I felt obliged to refuse, on those grounds.'

'And yet my cousin said he was trying to have it put aside. My cousin was there when Mr Elwes came in front of the magistrates to have your articles undone, but they would not. *Could* not, I think he said.'

'I know. I heard him discussing it with the new lawyer, that very morning.'

'Well, at least it means that he won't be sending people in chase of you.'

'No,' said Toby: and after a pause he added, 'It was the knowledge that he was willing to be rid of me that did away with my last scruples.'

'He is an infernal scrub,' said Jack; and when Tobias made no answer he went on, 'And for that matter, I am not very well pleased with Cousin Edward, either. I thought he would have come out of it with more credit. "Hark 'ee, Jack," says he. "I can't have anything to do with it: I know Elwes is an infernal scrub," he says, looking rather like a pickpocket, as well he might, with me looking damnably scornful and Georgiana roaring and bawling, "but I can't be seen in the affair. I'm a magistrate, an't I? I can't give any countenance to such goings-on, damn it. You ought never to have told me *before* the event, Jack. I mean, if it was all over now – if he had run off a week ago, and if he was in London now, why then, that would be a *fait accompli*, as they say. It would be quite different; and then a man might do something friendly. But I can't have it said that I induced Elwes' young fellow to run away. Here's a present for thee, Jack," says he, looking at me very hard and giving me fifteen guineas in my hand – he would only have given me five ordinarily, at the best of times. It was pretty handsome, and I knew well enough what he meant; but I think he might not have shuffled so.'

'Jack,' cried Tobias, suddenly stopping, 'did you remember the lesser pettichaps?'

'Yes,' said Jack, 'I did. I opened the door of her cage before I went up with Georgiana's bat. She gave me a note for you. But don't you think we look a pretty couple of fools, with our horses in our hands?'

They had, in fact, walked right down Gallows Hill and half a mile beyond; they were now in perfectly level open country, still leading their horses with anxious care. 'Thankee,' said Tobias, taking the note and mounting. *Dear Toby*, read the note, *I shall take extreame great Care of the dear Batt. Yr affct. G. Chaworth.* 'That is an excellent girl,' he said, folding the paper carefully into his pocket. 'It does me good to think of her.'

Here the road ran wide over a common, and the horses began to dance a little with the grass under their feet. 'Come on,' cried Jack. 'If we are to get there tomorrow, we must canter whenever we can.'

There is nothing like a long sweet gallop on a well-paced horse for changing a melancholy state of mind: Jack's horse was a high-blooded dashing chestnut, the property of his elder brother, and Toby's was a grey cob that belonged to Cousin Charles. The Chaworths and the Byrons formed a large, closely interrelated tribe, and there was always some of them coming or going between Meden-ham and Newstead and London, sometimes with a servant, some-times without; the result of this restlessness was that the horses tended to accumulate at one end or the other, in droves – the grey, for example, had been left by Cousin Charles when he had gone back to London from Newstead in Uncle Norwood's chariot – and long ago a tradition had arisen in the family, a tradition of employing any means whatsoever to maintain a reasonable balance of horses in each place. It is almost certain that if a neighbour had been going up to London to receive a sentence of death, he would have been asked to ride thither on one of the Medenham horses, and to be so obliging as to leave it at Marlborough Street before he was hanged.

Mr Chaworth would not – in all decency could not – acknowledge Tobias' flight; but the opportunity was too good to be missed, and the grey made a silent appearance beside Jack's horse in the morning, tacitly understood by one and all. The two of them, then, being mounted far above their stations, had the good sense to make the most of it while it lasted, and they flew along over the smooth green miles with their spirits rising like larks in the sky. When the going grew hard again, and they reined in, Jack observed that his friend was more than usually elated; this being so he permitted himself to say, 'Toby,' said he, 'you will not be offended, will you?'

'No,' said Toby.

'I mean, you are an amazing good horseman, of course.'

'Just so,' said Toby.

'I don't mean to imply that you ride badly. But people tend to stare so – very foolish in them – and it would oblige me uncommonly if you would sit like a Christian.'

Tobias had an entirely personal way of riding upon a horse: he would sit upon various pieces of his mount, facing whichever view pleased him most, and from time to time he would stretch himself at length, to the amazement of all beholders. At this moment he was kneeling upright on the cob's broad bottom, staring fixedly backwards into a waving meadow.

'I believe it was a spotted crake,' he said. 'What did you say, Jack?'

Jack patiently repeated his request, and Tobias received it so well, promising amendment and desiring to be reminded if he should forget, that Jack added, 'And would you mind changing your slippers, before we come into Melton Mowbray?'

'Slippers?' cried Tobias, gazing first at one foot and then at the other.

'You cannot conceive how barbarous they look,' said Jack. 'List slippers.'

'I am heartily sorry for it, if they offend you,' said Tobias, 'but I have nothing else to put on.'

'Why then,' cried Jack, 'it don't signify.' But from time to time he looked wistfully at his friend's stirrups.

'Do you see that farmhouse?' cried Toby, after they had trotted another mile. 'Over there beyond the turnips. I went there once: Mr Elwes took me to see a remarkable case of hydrophobia. But I have never been farther. You could make a pretty verse upon that, Jack, could you not?'

'Hydrophobia?'

'No. I mean the passing of childish limits – launching into the great world unknown. Is that not poetic?'

'Oh yes, devilish poetic. Wait a minute . . .

What lies beyond, Muse tell us truly,
Beyond Tobias' Ultima Thule?

(That's rather neat)

The wealth of Spain? The gallows, or the grave?
The frequent guerdon of the sea-borne brave.'

'What is a guerdon?'

'It is a sort of thing – a reward. It means that you may be drowned; but I only put it in for the metre.'

Here a coach-and-four went by, jingling and rumbling and covering them with dust, and when they had spurred out of the cloud Jack said, 'Toby, if we meet any of my naval friends, I beg you will not mention my verse-making.'

'Very well,' said Tobias, in a wondering voice.

'They might not understand, you see: and I do not think it would answer at all, to have it generally known in the service.'

They rode into the wide main street of Melton Mowbray while Tobias was digesting this, and Jack led the way to a splendid inn.

'Good morning, Admiral,' said the ostler, beaming.

'Good morning, Joe,' said Jack.

'Is that Mr Edward's . . .' The ostler was going to say 'horse' when his eye, which had been travelling down Tobias' person, reached his slippers, and the word died in his throat.

'Yes, it is,' said Jack, and guiding Tobias by the elbow he walked into the inn. Men will go through fire and water for their friends; they will lend them money, if there is no help for it; but to lead an exceedingly shabby friend, who is known to have rather peculiar table manners, into a grand place of public entertainment, is little short of heroic, above all when the friend is shod with list slippers: not many would do it – you may search all Plutarch without finding a single case. List slippers are now so little worn (we have seen but one pair in our earthly pilgrimage) that it may be necessary to state that list is the edge of cloth in the piece, the selvedge, and it is woven in a particular manner to prevent its fraying; frugal minds, unable to throw the list away when the cloth was used, would form it into hard-wearing slippers, often very horrible, because of the strongly contrasting colours of the strips.

Tobias was totally unaware of what he owed his friend on this occasion, for he was as unconscious of his appearance as he could possibly be: a more unaffected creature never breathed.

'Eat hearty,' said Jack, pushing the enormous pie across the table. 'You won't get any more until we pull up this evening. And even then it won't be much – just an alehouse.'

'May I put a piece in my bosom?' asked Tobias.

'No,' said Jack. 'You may not.'

From Melton to Burton Lazars and on to Oakham and

Uppingham and Rockingham, where they baited their horses, and Barton Seagrave and Burton Latimer they rode steadily, while the sun rose higher and higher on their left hand, crossed over the road before them and crept down the sky on their right. They talked all the way, and this most unaccustomed flood of words caused Tobias to grow hoarse and, by the border of Rutlandshire, inaudible; he was usually as silent as a carp, but before he lost his voice altogether he told Jack how very much he looked forward to seeing London, how infinitely agreeable a maritime life must be, with its unrivalled opportunities for seeing seabirds and foreign countries, with wholly different flora and fauna, to say nothing of the creatures of the sea itself, and how nearly it had broken his heart to refuse his former tutor's offer. 'Though indeed,' he added, 'the assistant he did take died within a fortnight of getting there, of the yellow fever.'

Jack was by nature far from taciturn, and he had never been deprived of practice: his voice held out perfectly well all the way, and he told Tobias a great many things about his life in the Navy, his views on the conduct of the present war with Spain, and his hopes of seeing active service within a very short time. He was telling Tobias of a somewhat mysterious plan for ensuring this when he pulled up very suddenly by a lop-sided grey haystack. 'I nearly missed it,' he said, pointing with his whip. In the silence they heard a partridge assembling her chicks, and from behind the sagging rick a little darting of rabbits ran back into the hedge: the evening was coming on. Tobias looked closely at the rick, but said nothing. 'It is the lane I mean,' said Jack, 'not the haystack. If we go down there, we can take the cross road to Milton Earnest, and leave Higham Ferrers on our left. It saves two miles, and you come out on the main road again by the Fox. Cousin Charles found it, when he was looking for a way round the Irthlingborough toll-gate: and it cuts out the Westwood turnpike, too. He won't pay turnpike tolls, you know, on principle. There's something in the Bible, he says: but I think it is meanness.'

He pushed his horse down the muddy lane, and very soon they were in deep country. The trees met over their heads, the road varied from a broad green ride to a mere track between high banks, and sometimes, when it went over open fields, it vanished altogether; but most of the way it was narrow, dirty and comfortless – only the fanatical zeal of Cousin Charles (who was quite rich, and perfectly generous in all other respects; but like nearly all the Byrons he had his private mania – his mother, for example, collected little bits of string) would ever have found it out. They were obliged to ride one behind the other, which impeded conversation; moreover, Jack had reached a particularly private piece of his plan – one which had to do with confidential information, and even in the remote fields and ditches of Irthlingborough parish he could not very well bellow out the secrets of the Lords of the Admiralty.

'I'll tell you about it when we get to the Fox,' he said over his shoulder, and they rode in silence through the sweet evening, sometimes along the narrow paths through the wheat, sometimes wide over the new stubble of the earliest oats, sometimes through coppice in the twilight of the leaves, and once for half a mile over a stretch of bracken where nightjars turned and wheeled half-seen. The sky changed to a deeper, unlit blue; the colours left the fields and the trees, and were replaced by a violet haze, much darker than the sky: there was no sound but the creak of harness, the horses' breath and the soft churring of the nightjars. And now, plunging into a wood, they found themselves in the full darkness of the night, with a slippery, wet and stony path under them. 'I think we are right,' said Jack, 'because I believe this was the place where I fell with Miss Bailey's mare.'

This recollection did not cheer him very much, however, and he looked so anxiously forward for the main road into which this short cut should fall that when it appeared, ghostly in the night, he did not believe it, but took it for a stream. Yet no sooner were they on the highway, with its hard surface underfoot, than the lantern of the Fox appeared – a little, low and rather squalid ale-house, but more welcome at this time than the grandest stage-coach inn on the road.

'Well,' said Jack, pushing away his empty plate and gasping with repletion, 'that went down very well: Toby, what do you say to a bowl of punch?'

Toby was about to say 'What is punch?' when he found that his voice was completely gone: he smiled secretly, and Jack called for the landlord.

'There,' said Jack, wielding the ladle through the fragrant cloud that rose from the punch-bowl, 'that will do you all the good in the world. Now, as I was saying, the position of the fleet is this . . .'

Toby drank up his punch: he hoped that it would help him keep awake and to pay attention, and indeed it did seem to have some such effect, in that it made him gasp and sneeze: he refilled his glass.

'. . . so there they still are at St Helen's and I am still at the Nore, which is a very great shame. I protest, Toby, that it is quite disgusting . . .'

Toby was very sorry to hear that it was a disgusting shame; but he had ridden sixty-two miles that day, after a sleepless night of the greatest emotional agitation that he had ever known, and now, for the first time in his life, he had nearly a pint of strong punch glowing inside him. He was almost entirely taken up with watching the strange coming and going of Jack's face the other side of the candle – sometimes it was large and distinct and sometimes it was small, blurred and remote – but by taking laborious care he could make out sentences of Jack's discourse, now and then.

'. . . and so, my dear Toby,' said Jack's voice through the thickening haze, 'that is what I meant in the very first place, when I said "Come with me, and I will make your fortune." If all goes well, and upon my word I don't see how it can fail, we shall come back amazingly rich.'

Tobias allowed his eyes to close upon these encouraging words, and at once an exquisitely comfortable darkness engulfed him. He heard no more, except an unknown, distant voice saying, 'I will take his feet. Why, bless my soul, Mr Byron, sir, your friend has got a pair of list slippers on.'

These slippers were the first things that met his eye in the morning. Somebody had put them on the window-seat, where they caught the first light of the sun in all their violent glory, and Jack was sitting by them, looking pink and cheerful.

'Lard, Toby, how you do sleep,' he said. 'It's nearly five o'clock.'

Slowly Tobias looked from the slippers to Jack, and from Jack to the slippers. He had been very deeply asleep, and it was some moments before he could remember where he was and how he came to be there. 'I have run away: we are half-way to London,' he observed to himself. 'And I dreamt that Jack had put me into the way of making my fortune.'

'I dreamt that you said that we should make our fortunes presently,' he said to Jack, as they rode away from the ale-house.

Jack looked at him with a very knowing air, and said, 'I don't believe you remember much of what I told you last night.'

'No, truly I do not,' said Tobias. 'It is much confused in my memory – not unlike a series of dreams.'

'Well,' said Jack, laughing with wonderful good humour for so early in the morning, 'I shall tell you again. You know I am in the guard-ship at the Nore, although I was promised to be posted to the *Burford*: and the *Burford* was the flagship at Porto Bello?'

'Yes, I remember you told me that before; and it was a great disappointment to you not to be at the battle.'

'It was indeed: Admiral Vernon had promised it to my uncle, or at least practically promised it; and it was a horribly shabby thing to sail off in that manner, leaving his best friend's nephew languishing between a guard-ship and a press-smack at the Nore. The Nore is a very disgusting station, Toby.'

'I am much concerned to hear it, Jack.'

'But, however, it is probably all for the best. It is perfectly obvious that the Admiralty owes me some reparation – no reasonable being could deny that for a moment – and this secret expedition gives them a perfect chance of making all square.'

'What secret expedition?'

'The one I was telling you about – but you did not take it in, I find. It is an expedition,' he said, lowering his voice, 'that is fitting out for the South Sea, to attack the Spaniards there, where they least expect it. Lard, Toby,' he cried, 'think of Chile and Peru, and all the treasure there. Think of Acapulco and Panama and the Philippines. Pieces of eight,' he cried, in a transport of greed and enthusiasm, throwing his arms out to indicate the immensity of the wealth. He was a fairly good horseman, but his fervour for prize money was too much for him, and he fell slowly over the chesnut's shoulder.

'Never mind,' he said, as Tobias dusted him. 'It was all in a good cause. The whole point is, that I must be posted to one of these ships. And if I had gone off to the West Indies in the *Burford* I could not have been here to join this expedition, could I? Everybody who has any interest is trying to get into it, of course, but it is plain enough that I have much more right than most, having been so very ill-used.'

'Did you say it was a secret expedition?'

'Oh yes. You must not speak of it, you know.'

'Then how is it that people are trying to get into it?'

'Well, it is secret in a certain sense; I mean, it is officially secret. That is to say, everybody in the know knows about it, but nobody else.'

A single magpie crossed the road, and Jack paused to see if another would follow: but the bird was alone. 'I wish that damned bird had chosen another moment to go over,' he said. 'But as I was saying, I have a perfect right to the appointment; and what is much more important, I have got just about twice as much interest as I need to get aboard. So, do you see, I shall be able to get in with half, and use the rest to draw you in after me. Lard, Toby, I don't know how a fellow with your simple tastes will spend all the money.'

'How very kind you are, Jack: I am very much obliged to your goodness. As for a great deal of money, I don't know that I want it; but when you consider, Jack, that not one single sentient being has even remotely glimpsed the birds of the Pacific Ocean and its shores –'

'But, my poor Toby, people have been sailing round the Horn and into the South Sea these hundred years and more.'

'Only mariners, Jack: and, with respect, your mariner is but a shallow creature. I have read Narborough and Dampier and the few other voyages into those regions, and the unhappy men might as well have been blind. They saw nothing, *nothing.*'

'They saw noddies and boobies. I particularly remember that Woods Rogers said, "Boobies and noddies."'

'They saw birds that they *called* noddies and boobies; but do we know that they *were* noddies and boobies? May they not merely have resembled noddies and boobies? It is no good coming to me and saying, "Ha, ha, I have seen noddies and boobies in the Great South Sea," unless you can support your statement with the measurements and weights, and preferably the skins, of your noddies and boobies.'

This seemed a frivolous objection to Jack, and he only replied, 'Still, you would find it prodigiously agreeable to have a fortune, you know. You could lay it out in sending fellows off to Kamschatka, or Crim Tartary, to gaze at the boobies there, and measure 'em, too.'

They wrangled about the disposition of the money for some miles, and then Jack said, 'Well, you shall do whatever you please with it, Toby, if only you will sit the right way round.'

'I beg pardon,' said Tobias, loosening his grip on the grey cob's tail and swarming back into the saddle: the cob was not the steadiest mount in the world, and a tenth part of this behaviour in anyone else would have sent it into a foaming fit; but it trotted placidly along the road to Bedford, and Jack resumed his account of the secret expedition.

'There are to be five ships. The *Gloucester* and the *Severn* are both fifties, and the *Centurion* – she's the flagship – is a sixty; then there is the old *Pearl*, a forty-gun ship, a very pretty sailer and quick in her stays.'

'Five ships, you said.'

'Oh yes, there's the *Wager* – she's the fifth. *Centurion*, *Gloucester*, *Severn*, *Pearl* and *Wager*: that makes five. But the *Wager* don't count. She's only an old Indiaman, bought into the service as a storeship, because there is some ridiculous plan of trading with the Indians, and they need a ship for their bolts of cloth and beads and so on. In my opinion it is a vile job – a mere trick to get a vast deal of money into the pocket of a pack of merchants and politicians. Politics are monstrous dirty, you know, and everything is done by backstairs influence. Anyhow, it is quite absurd to call the *Wager* a man-of-war; and she only mounts twenty guns. Then there is a sloop, the *Tryall*, and that is all the King's ships; though there will probably be a victualler or two to carry things some of the way – some little merchantman or other,' he said with kindly patronage. 'Now the *Severn* and the *Gloucester* have their full complement of officers, because they were already in commission, you see; but the *Centurion* has not, and that is what we must aim for. I know some of her people – excellent creatures – and my friend Keppel is very anxious that I should join him there. I told you about him, did I not? We were shipmates in the *Royal Sovereign*.'

'The one who set fire to you, and thrust you into the North Sea?'

'Yes. Augustus Keppel: he is only quite a young fellow, but he can be amazingly good company.'

The white gate of a turnpike appeared as they turned a corner and Jack observed, 'This is the Clapham pike already.' He looked at his watch and said, 'We are doing very well.'

'Jack,' said Tobias, when the gate was far behind them, 'when you paid the man at the turnpike before this, he gave you some money. He said, "Here's your change, your honour." This one not.'

'Why, no,' replied Jack. 'I hadn't any change at the first one, so I gave him half a crown; but then of course for this one I already had a pocketful of change.'

Tobias was pondering upon this, when very suddenly he whipped his leg over the saddle, passed the cob's reins into Jack's hand and slipped to the ground. He tripped from the speed, but recovered himself and vanished into the tall reeds that stood about a marsh on the low side of the road. The horses saw fit to indulge in a good deal of capering, and Jack dropped his hat and his whip before he brought them to a sense of their duty.

He was waiting with them by the side of the road when Tobias reappeared, and he exclaimed, with something less than his usual good humour, 'Why, damn your blood, Toby, what do you mean by plunging off in that wild manner? How can you be so strange? You have been in the water,' he added, seeing that Tobias' lower half was soaked and his stockings and slippers were masked with greenish mud. 'You look as pleased as if you had found a guinea.'

Tobias rarely showed any emotion, but now his face displayed a private gleam; and when he was mounted he showed Jack a brown, speckled feather, saying, 'Do you know what that is?'

'A phoenix?'

'No,' said Tobias, with inward triumph. 'A bittern. I never saw a bittern before.' He munched silently and nodded, remembering the bittern in vivid detail: but recollecting himself he cried, 'I beg your pardon, Jack! I do indeed. You were telling me . . .' He hesitated.

Jack was never one to take umbrage; he laughed, and said, 'I was telling you about Keppel, before we passed the toll-house.'

'Yes, yes, Keppel; your excellent good friend Mr Keppel,' said Tobias, with the most concentrated attention, but secretly fondling his bittern's feather.

'Well, Keppel, you know, has a prodigious great deal of interest, and seeing that there are two vacancies in the *Centurion* – two midshipmen unprovided – he has already started stirring up his relatives on my behalf. That is one of the reasons why I am in such a hurry to be in London, because I have appointed to meet him tomorrow.' They were coming into Bedford at this time, under a threatening sky, and when they had baited their horses and set off again, the first drops were falling.

'There is another short cut of Charles's between Cotton End and Deadman's Green,' said Jack doubtfully. 'But seeing that we are in a hurry, perhaps we had better keep to the high road. It looks quite dirty,' he said, looking up at the towering light-grey clouds. Behind the clouds the sky showed black, and as he spoke a flash of lightning ripped across: the thunder followed close behind, and so loud as to drown his words. He grinned as he calmed the nervous chestnut, and told Tobias, in a nautical bellow, that it looked as though it might come on something prodigious. He dearly loved a storm; rain alone satisfied him, provided there was enough of it, but if it were accompanied by a very great deal of wind, then it raised his spirits to a very high pitch.

'Have you brought your greatcoat?' he asked Tobias. Tobias shook his head. 'What's in that valise?' asked Jack, shouting over the double peal.

'Nothing,' said Tobias, and as far as he knew this was true – he had put nothing in the valise: it had been there, strapped behind the saddle, as much part of the harness as the big horse-pistols in front, when he had mounted, and he had paid no attention to it. But in point of fact it was filled with necessaries. 'The poor boy cannot go out into the world without so much as a clean shirt,' had been Mrs Chaworth's instant reply on hearing that Tobias was on the wing. She might disapprove of Tobias in some ways, but she had a real affection for him, and she anxiously rummaged the house for things of a suitable size – Jack's were all far too big – and Georgiana, guided by who knows what unhappy chance, crowned the whole valise-full with another pair of strong list slippers, all bedewed with tears. But Tobias was unaware of this, and the excellent greatcoat behind him remained untouched: Jack therefore left his alone, and very soon both of them were so exceedingly wet that the water ran down inside their clothes, filled their shoes, and poured

23

from them in a stream that contended with the water and mud flung up from the road. The extreme fury of the storm was soon over: the thunder and the lightning moved away to terrify Huntingdon, Rutland and Nottingham, but the rain had set in for the day and it fell without the least respite from that moment onwards. However, Tobias was wonderfully indifferent to foul weather, and Jack, though he preferred a dry back, could put up with a wet one as well as anybody, so they rode steadily through the downpour, conversing as soon as the thunder would let them.

'You have often mentioned interest,' said Tobias. 'What is this interest, I beg?'

'Well,' said Jack, considering, 'it is interest, you know. That is to say, influence, if you understand me – very much the same thing as influence. Everything goes by interest, more or less. It is really a matter of doing favours: I mean, suppose you are in Parliament, and there is a fellow, a minister or a private member, who wants a bill to be passed – if he comes to you and says, "You would oblige me extremely by voting for my bill," and you do vote for his bill, why then the fellow is bound to do as much for you, if he is a man of honour. And if you do not happen to want to do anything in the parliamentary line, but prefer to get a place under Government for one of your friends, then the fellow with the bill must do what he can to gratify you. Besides, if he don't, he will never have your vote again, ha, ha. That is, he must do what he can within reason: if you want a thundering good place, like being the Warden of the Stannaries with a thousand a year and all the work done by the deputy-warden, you must do a great deal more for it than just vote once or twice; but if it is just a matter of having someone let into a place where he will have to work very hard every day and get precious little pay for it, which is the case in the Navy, why then there is no great difficulty.'

'I do not understand how a private member can help you to a place.'

'Why, don't you see? You have two votes for the time being, your own and this other man's: so when you go and ask your favour of the minister – the First Lord of the Admiralty, if it is the Navy – he knows that you are twice as important as if you were alone, so he is twice as willing to oblige you. And of course if you have a good many friends and relatives in the House, you are more important still, because if you were all to vote against the administration together you might bring them down and turn the ministers out. And then it is even better to be in the House of Lords, if you can manage it, because, do you see, a minister might decide that it was worth while offending a member of the Commons' house, for at the next election he may not come in again, but a peer, once he is in, is in for the rest of his life, and he could do you an ill turn for years and years. But it is all pretty complicated, and not at all as simple as that.'

'How do the people without interest get along?'

'They have to rely on merit.'

'Does that answer?'

'Well,' said Jack slowly, 'valour and virtue are very good things, I am sure: but I should be sorry to have to rely upon them alone, for my part.'

Tobias made no reply, and they rode for a long way in silence through the rain. Jack looked at him from time to time, and regretted that he had been quite so talkative about the squalid side of political life.

'You're pretty shocked, an't you?' he said at last.

'No,' said Tobias. 'I had always read that the world was like that. What I was thinking about was your poem which begins *Historic Muse, awake.*'

'Were you indeed?' said Jack, very pleased.

'Yes. I was wondering whether "Spain's proud nation, dreaded now no more" was quite right: "now" could mean *now*, and thus confuse the reader's mind.'

'Oh no, Toby. Think of what goes before –

'Twas in Eliza's memorable reign
When Britain's fleet, acknowledged, ruled the main,
When Heav'n and it repelled from Albion's shore
Spain's – and so on.

It was *then* that it was not dreaded now, do you see? I have composed a great deal more of it, Toby.'

'Oh.'

'Should you like to hear it?'

'If you please.'

'I will begin at the beginning, so that you lose none of the effect.'

'I know the beginning, Jack,' said Toby piteously, 'by heart.'

'Never mind,' said Jack hurriedly, and in a very particular chant he began,

'Historic Muse awake! And from the shade
Where long forgotten sleep the noble dead (I am sorry that
    don't rhyme better)
Some worthy chief select, whose martial flame
May rouse Britannia's sons to love of fame . . .'

The verse lasted until they were so close to London that the increased traffic made declamation impossible; but still the rain fell with the same steadiness, and Jack said, as they climbed Highgate Hill, 'I am very sorry that it has not cleared up: I wanted to show you London from here – you can see it all spread out, and the river winding, and millions of lights in the evening. Besides, I thought that you would like to hear some lines I wrote about the prospect while we were actually looking at it. It is in praise of London, considered as a nest of singing-birds – poets, you know.'

'A pretty wet nest, Jack?'

'Of course, it was not like this in the poem,' said Jack, reining in and peering through the darkening veils of drizzle, 'but flowery, with meads and zephyrs. Nymphs, too. But I dare say you would like to hear it anyhow, and take the view on trust.'

As Jack reached the last few lines he quietly loosened the flaps on his saddle-bow and brought out a long pistol, which he cocked: at the sound a lurking pair of shadows in the trees behind them walked briskly off.

'We had better look to our priming,' he said, sheltering his pistol as well as he could from the rain. 'There are a terrible lot of thieves about. We don't run much risk, being mounted, particularly as the rain usually keeps the poor devils indoors; but Cousin Charles got into a by-lane when he was trying to avoid the Holloway turnpike – you can just see it from here, right ahead – and half a dozen of them got about him and pulled him off his horse. They dragged him off towards Black Mary's Hole, over the way there' – pointing through the soaking twilight – 'and used him most barbarously.'

It was completely dark by the time they reached the town, and it must be confessed that Tobias was sadly disappointed with it; he had expected something splendid, definite and comprehensible, not perhaps so distinct as a walled city with light and splendour inside the gates and open country outside, but something not unlike it. As it was, they rode through a vague and indeterminate region of incompleted new building interspersed with scrubby fields and then (seeing that Jack always took the most direct line possible) through a series of narrow, dirty, ill-lit back streets.

'Here we are,' said Jack, as his horse stopped in the narrowest, dirtiest and smelliest of them all, with no light whatever. 'Jedediah! Jedediah!' he shouted, banging on the door.

After a long pause, while the rain dripped perpetually from the eaves and somewhere a broken gutter poured a solid cascade into the street, there came a slow shuffling noise from within and a gleam of light under the door.

'Who's there?' asked a voice.

'Hurry up, Jedediah, damn your eyes,' called Jack, beating impatiently.

'Oh, it's Master Jack,' said the voice to itself, and with a rumble of bolts and chains the door opened. He had been expected all day, but as usual Jedediah was amazed to see him, and holding the lantern high he exclaimed, 'Why, bless my soul, it's Master Jack. And Master Jack, you're wet. You're as wet as a drowned rat.'

'It is because of the rain,' said Jack. 'Now take the horses in and rub them down, and tell Mrs Raffald I shall be back to sleep. We are going round to Mrs Fuller's now. Come on, Toby, climb down.'

'The other young gentleman is wet, too,' said Jedediah, taking the horses.

At the beginning of the journey Jack had assumed that Tobias would stay at his family's house, but he had run up against his friend's delicacy, and knowing Tobias' immovable obstinacy in such matters, he had proposed a very simple alternative. Mrs Fuller, who had been in the family for a great many years, now let lodgings for single gentlemen in Little Windmill Street, just round the corner from Marlborough Street: she received Jack with a hearty kiss (having been his nurse at one time) and told him that he was wet, disgracefully wet.

'Wet through and through,' she said, tweaking his coat open and plucking at his shirt with that strong authority that belongs to her age and sex. 'Come now, take it off this minute, or you will catch your death. You too, young gentleman: come into the kitchen at once. Nan, come and pull the gentlemen's boots off. Good Lord preserve us all alive! he has come out in his slippers.' Mrs Fuller gazed upon Tobias with unfeigned horror. 'Where is his cloak-bag?' she asked Jack, as if Tobias could not be trusted to give a sensible answer.

'He forgot it,' said Jack.

'He left it behind, and came in his slippers? Was there ever such wickedness?' cried Mrs Fuller, who considered it a Christian's duty to wear wool next the skin in all seasons, and to keep dry. 'However will he change?'

Jedediah came into the kitchen with the valise and a white packet: he said, 'I brought the young gentleman's cloak-bag and this here: under the saddle-flap it was, and might have fallen out any minute of the day or night.' He put the folded parchment down with some severity.

'Oh yes,' said Tobias; 'I forgot it. It is my indenture, Jack, with my plan of the alimentary tract of moles on the back of it.'

It was clear to Mrs Fuller that they were both demented. The rain had soaked into their wits, and the only way to drive it out again was with warmth, dry clothes, soup, a boiled fowl, a leg of Welsh mutton and the better part of a quart of mixed cordials.

Thacker's coffee-house was the meeting-place for naval officers, just as Will's was for poets and literary men; and Jack, whenever he was free and in London, divided his time between the two. He had seen Admiral Vernon, the hero of Porto Bello, in the first and Mr Pope in the second, and it was difficult to say which had caused him the livelier delight.

He was at Thacker's at this moment, with Tobias by his side, waiting for Keppel: at present his face had no lively delight upon it, however, but rather the traces of fatigue, alarm and apprehension. The fatigue was caused by having shown Tobias the sights of London, or at least all those that could be crammed into seven uninterrupted hours of very slow creeping about shop-lined streets, tomb-lined churches, the danker monuments of antiquity and the never-ending alleys of the booksellers' booths around St Paul's: Tobias was not used to anything much larger than Mangonell Bagpize, and his amazement was now, in a fine (if muddy) summer's day, as great as ever he could have wished; but he was utterly careless of the London traffic, and the effort of keeping him alive among the carts, drays, coaches and waggons had perceptibly aged his friend. Jack had known London from his earliest days, and it was difficult for him to marvel, to stand stock-still in the mainstream of impatient crowds to marvel for ten minutes on end, at a perfectly ordinary pastry-cook's window – 'What unheard-of luxury, Jack; what more than Persian magnificence – Lucullus – Apicius – Heliogabalus.' He did marvel, of course, in order not to damp Tobias' pleasure; but it too was an ageing process. The itinerant bookseller who visited Mangonell market always gratified Tobias with a sight of his wares, although Tobias never bought any of them (this was not from sordid avarice, but because Tobias had never possessed one farthing piece in all his life) and Tobias unquestioningly assumed that London booksellers were equally good-natured: and then again, Tobias, until Jack begged him to stop, said 'Good day' to every soul they met, in a manner that would have passed without comment in the country, but which in London was another thing altogether.

But sight-seeing with Tobias, though it left its mark, was as nothing, nothing whatsoever, compared with taking Tobias to see his patron.

The Navy, apart from its administrative side, is a tolerably brisk service; those members of it who go to sea have it impressed upon their minds, both by circumstances and by the kindly insistence of their superior officers, that time and tide wait for no man; and Jack was a true sailor in his appreciation of this interesting truth. Within minutes of waking up he had sent a note to his influential cousin; the answer had come back appointing a given hour, and tearing Tobias from the belfry of St Paul's in Covent Garden, which he had penetrated in order to view the mechanism of the clock (he asserted that it was the earliest illustration of the isochronic principle) and in which he had lingered to look into the ecclesiastical bats. Jack had brushed him, thrust him into a presentable pair of shoes and had conducted him to Mr Brocas Byron's house. The head of the family was not quite as wise as the Byrons and Chaworths could have wished; indeed, he was what Jack, in an excess of poetical imagery, had termed 'potty'; and his relatives had persuaded him to leave all matters of political judgment, voting and patronage, to Cousin Brocas.

Cousin Brocas was no phoenix himself, but at that time the family was not particularly well-to-do in the matter of brains, and at least Cousin Brocas was always on the spot: he was the member for Piddletrenthide (a convenient little borough with only three voters, all of them kin to Mrs Brocas) and he never left London for a moment during the sessions of Parliament. He was rather pompous, and he stood more upon his rank than his noble cousins, but he and Jack had always got along very well together, and, having performed the introductions, Jack left Tobias with Cousin Brocas in entire confidence that they would spend half an hour in agreeable conversation while he stepped round to see whether Keppel had arrived yet, and to leave a message if he had not.

Judge, then, of his perturbation when upon his return the footman told him that 'they was a-carrying on something cruel in the libery,' and the sound of further disagreement fell upon his ears, accompanied by the rumbling of heavy furniture. He darted upstairs: he was in time to prevent Tobias and his patron – or perhaps one should say his intended patron, or his ex-patron – from coming to actual blows, but only just; and Tobias was obliged to be dragged away, foaming and vociferating to the last.

This accounted well enough for Jack's depressed appearance; but his mind was filled with apprehension, too. He had a haunting certainty that Keppel would have met with some comparable disaster in his designs upon the vacancies in the *Centurion*; and while upon the one hand he assured himself that it was better to remain in a state of hopeful ignorance, upon the other he watched the clock and the door with increasing impatience.

The great hand of Thacker's clock – a wonderfully accurate clock – crept to the appointed minute, and Keppel walked in, accompanied by his particular friend Mr Midshipman Ransome. Keppel was small, neat and compact; he had been to a wedding and he was dressed with surprising magnificence in a gold-laced hat, an embroidered waistcoat with jewelled buttons and a crimson coat encrusted with gold plait wherever it could be conveniently sewn, and cascades of Mechlin lace at his throat and wrists: Ransome was a big, leonine fellow with a bright blue eye, not unlike Jack, but heavier and older; his kind-looking face was much marked by disagreements with the King's enemies and his own, as well as the small-pox; and he wore a plain blue coat.

They stood for a moment in the doorway, looking over the big room with its many boxes: they saw Mr Saunders, the first lieutenant of their own ship, the *Centurion*, pulled off their hats and bowed very humbly; they saw a lieutenant of the *Gloucester*, a Marine captain belonging to the *Severn* and a group of black coats which included Mr Eliot, the surgeon of the *Wager* and the chaplain of the *Pearl*; to all of these they bowed with suitable degrees of humility, and then advanced to Jack and Tobias.

It took some little time to make Tobias understand that he was being introduced: and as he had the unfortunate habit of closing one eye and screwing his pursed mouth violently to one side whenever he was roused from a train of reflection, he did not make quite as favourable an impression as he might have done otherwise. Ransome moved perceptibly backwards, and Keppel said, 'Your servant, sir,' in a reserved and distant tone.

Keppel, in any case, was far from easy. 'I am very sorry to bring you the news,' he said. 'Upon my word, I regret it extremely. But the fact is – the fact is, my dear Byron, the vacancies have gone to a couple of – Irishmen.'

'Wery nasty undeserving swabs, I dare say,' said Ransome, with the intention of bringing comfort, 'if not Papists, too.' He spoke in a hoarse whisper, having no other voice left, other than a penetrating bellow, for use only at sea.

'Oh,' said Jack, horribly disappointed, but smiling with what appearance of nonchalance he could summon. 'Well, it was prodigious kind to try; and I am much obliged to you.'

'But that ain't all,' said Keppel, with still greater embarrassment, after a long and awkward pause. 'My father, d'ye see, being only a soldier, and not thoroughly understanding these things, although I have told him these many times the difference between one class of ship and another – and really you would think it plain enough to the meanest understanding; I mean, even a landsman can see that a pink is not a first-rate.'

'Far from it,' said Ransome.

'Nor even a second,' said Keppel.

Jack turned pale, and gazed from one to the other.

'Not that some pinks ain't pretty little vessels,' said Ransome reflectively, after a prolonged silence.

'But the fact is,' said Keppel, who appeared to derive some comfort from this expression, 'the fact is, my dear Byron, that my father, having once got into the matter, thought he could not come off handsomely without doing something: so when he found that he could not do what I asked, instead of waiting for my advice, he went blundering about like a horse in a hen-coop and had you – I beg you'll not take it amiss – nominated to the *Wager*.'

'Oh,' said Jack again; and then with a slowly spreading grin he said, 'While you were talking I had imagined something much worse. After all, Keppel, it does get me to St Helen's; and I am sure we can manage some kind of a transfer. I must wait upon Lord Albemarle and thank him.'

'You can't do that,' said Keppel, 'for he went off in a passion –'

'And a coach and six,' said Ransome.

'What?'

'He went off in a passion *and* a coach and six. Hor, hor.'

'– to Aunt Grooby, and he won't be back until the end of the month: and' – Keppel lowered his voice – 'we sail on Saturday sennight.'

'Saturday week?' cried Jack, whistling.

'Hush,' said Keppel, looking round.

'Oh, I'm sorry,' said Jack, 'but it leaves so precious little time.'

They fell into a low-voiced, highly confidential discussion of the means at their disposal for coping with the situation. This lasted for some considerable time, and they were roused from it only by the repeated cries and nudges of Ransome and Tobias: these gentlemen had, after an unpromising start, taken to one another wonderfully, and Ransome, having learnt that Tobias' sight-seeing had not yet included the lions at the Tower, now proposed taking him to see them. Nothing could have been calculated to cause Tobias more pleasure, and his eyes shone with anticipation; but for the moment he was pinned and immobilised, for they were on the inside of the box, and Jack and Keppel, lost in the depths of their planning, blocked the way to these simple joys.

'What is it?' said Jack impatiently.

'The lions at the Tower,' said Tobias, 'ha, ha, the lions, eh, Jack?'

'Which your friend ain't seen 'em,' said Ransome. 'Won't you come?'

'Bah,' said Jack and Keppel, who scorned the lions in the Tower.

'That fellow, Keppel,' said Jack, looking after their departing backs, 'that friend of mine, Tobias Barrow, causes me more anxiety than – worries me more than I can give you any conception of.' He outlined the situation, and went on, '. . . so I left him with Cousin Brocas, and somehow they came to be talking about the government, and parliament, and the House of Lords and all that. Heaven knows why. And I think Cousin B. must have dropped some graceful hints of what an important, high-born, clever cove he was, and what an unimportant fellow Toby was: something of the "beggars can't be choosers" nature – you know Cousin B's little ways. Not that he means any harm; but it vexes people, sometimes. Anyhow, Tobias turned upon him. "Never been so roughly handled in all my life," says Cousin B. "This dreadful creature of yours, Jack," says he, "said things to me in Latin and Greek, and attacked the constitution in the most hellish way: a most hellish Whig – nay, a republican, God help us. A democratical visionary." It seems that they fell out over the hereditary principle. "Would you employ an hereditary surgeon?" says Tobias, "A fellow who is to cut off your leg, not because he is an eminent anatomist, not because he is profoundly learned and highly skilled, but because he is merely the eldest son of a surgeon, or the eldest son of a man whose great-great-grandfather was a surgeon? And do you think the laws of the land less important than your infernal leg," says he, "that they are to be made and unmade by a parcel of men whose only qualification is that their fathers were lords?"'

'What did he say to that?' asked Keppel, with a kind of awful glee.

'Why, truly,' said Jack, 'I think they gave up argument at that point, and took to calling names. They were hard at it when I came in, and Tobias had a long round ruler in his hand, and Cousin B.

was backed up into a corner behind the celestial globe. By the time I had got Tobias away and down the stairs, Cousin B. had recovered his wits to some degree, for he Rings up the library window and bawls out *"Miserrine . . ."* but he can't remember the rest, and claps the window to. Tobias as near as dammit breaks the tow in order to dart back and make a reply, but I get him round the corner into Sackville Street: and there, strike me down, is Cousin Brocas again, at the billiard-room window. *"Mis . . . Mis . . ."* he holloes, but it escapes him again, which must have been very vexing, you know, Keppel, for I make no doubt that it was a stunning quotation – and he has to content himself with shaking his fist. Which he does, very hearty, purple in the face. Well, when they had gnashed their teeth at one another for a while – through the glass, you understand – I managed to get him under way again, and brought him fairly into Piccadilly, where he calmed down, sitting on a white doorstep, while I told the people that it was quite all right – only a passing fit. But I do assure you that some of the things he said made my blood run cold. "The House of Lords is an infamous place," he cries, "and exists to reward toad-eaters and to depress ingenuous merit. I will rise," he says, very shrill and high, "upon my own worth or not at all." Now, that is all very well, and Roman and virtuous, but I appeal to you, Keppel, is it sensible language to address to a patron?'

'No,' said Keppel, with total conviction, 'it is not.'

'And to think,' said Jack, 'that I had proposed taking him to the House to present him to your father.'

'I wish you had,' said Keppel, writhing in his seat. 'Oh strike me down, I wish you had. But tell me,' he added, 'did you not expect him to blow up all republican?'

'No,' cried Jack. 'I was amazed. Lard, Keppel, I have known him all my life, and have always considered him the meekest creature breathing. I have known him take the most savage treatment from his guardian without ever complaining. Besides, when we were riding to Town I explained the nature of the world to him, and he never jibbed then – said he had always understood that it was tolerably corrupt. Though it is true,' he said, after a pause for reflection, 'that he never had much in the way of what you might call natural awe – was always amazingly self-possessed.'

At this moment Tobias' self-possession was as shrunk and

puckered as his shabby old rained-upon black coat, for the boat in which he and Ransome had embarked for the Tower was in the very act of shooting London Bridge. The tide was on the ebb – it was at half-ebb, to be precise – and when Tobias moved his fascinated gaze from the houses which packed the bridge and leant out over the edge in a vertiginous, not to say horrifying manner, he found that the boat was engaged in a current that raced curling towards a narrow arch, and there, to his horror, he saw the silent black water slide with appalling nightmare rapidity downhill into the darkness, while the rower and Ransome sat poised and motionless. He had time to utter no more than the cry "Ark", or "Gark", expressive of unprepared alarm, before they shot out of the fading light of day. A few damp, reverberating seconds passed, and they were restored to it. The rower pulled hard; in a moment they were out of the thundering fall below the bridge; and all around them were vessels of one kind or another, rowing, sculling, paddling and sailing down and across the Thames, or waiting very placidly for the tide in order to go up. All these people seemed perfectly at their ease – in the innumerable masts that lined the river or lay out in the Pool no single man stood on high to warn the populace of the danger, and even as Tobias gazed back in horror he saw another boat shoot the central arch, and another, full of soldiers who shouted and waved their hats, while a woman, leaning out of her kitchen window on the bridge, strewed apple peelings impartially upon the soldiers and the raging flood: apparently this passage was quite usual. But Tobias was unable to repress his emotion entirely, and he said, 'That is a surprising current, sir. That is a very surprising piece of water, indeed.'

'I thought you was surprised,' said Ransome, with a grin; and the waterman closed one eye.

'I was never so frightened before,' said Tobias, 'and I find that my heart is still beating violently.'

'Why, it's a question of use,' said Ransome, wishing that his companion would be a little less candid in public. 'I dare say you never was in a rip-tide or an overfall?'

'I have never been in a boat in my life.'

'Nor ever seen the sea?'

'Nor yet the Thames, until today.'

'The gentleman has never set foot in a boat before,' said Ransome to the waterman, 'nor ever shot the bridge: so he was surprised.'

'Never set foot in a boat before?' exclaimed the waterman, resting on his oars.

'Not once: not so much as a farden skiff,' said Ransome, who was a waterman's son himself, from Frying-pan Stairs in Wapping, and who had been nourished and bred on the water, fresh or salt, since first he drew breath. They stared at Tobias, and eventually the waterman said, 'Then how do they get about, where he comes from?'

'They walk,' said Tobias. 'It is all dry land.'

'Well, I don't know, I'm sure,' said the waterman, dipping his oars and edging his boat across to the Tower stairs. He would take no further notice of Tobias: considered him a dangerous precedent, and was seen, as they went away, to dust Tobias' seat over the running water, with particular vehemence.

It was a still evening as they walked into the Tower, and although the day had been tolerably warm, the mist was already forming over the water; two or three hundred thousand coal-fires were alight or lighting, and the smoke, mingling with the mist, promised, as Ransome said, 'to grow as slab as burgoo' before long.

They walked briskly in past the spur-guard, past a faded representation of a lion and up to a door with another lion painted above it: a tiny black-haired man with a white face, the under-keeper, was renewing the ghastliness of this lion's maw with vermilion paint. 'There is horror, look you,' he said, putting his head on one side and surveying his work through narrowed eyes. 'There is gore and alarm, isn't it?' He was unwilling to leave his brush; but the prospect of immediate gain will always seduce an artist, and pocketing Ransome's shilling the under-keeper opened the door.

'I am infinitely obliged to you, sir,' said Tobias, when they were outside again and walking down to the river.

'Haw,' said Ransome, with a lurch of his head to acknowledge this civility. 'That's all right, mate: but I wish you had not a-done it. It makes me feel right poorly, only to think on it,' he said, leaning against the rail of the Tower stairs and reflecting upon the sight of Tobias in the lions' den, peering down the throat of an enormous beast that was stated to be 'a very saucy lion, the same that is eating the young gentlewoman's arm last Bartholomew Fair.'

'Up or down, gents?' cried the waterman. 'Oars, sir? Pair of oars?'

'Up or down, mate?' asked Ransome, recovering from his reverie and thumping Tobias on the back.

'Do you see that bird?' asked Tobias, pointing to the Customs House, where a number of kites were coming in to roost upon the cornucopias and reclining goddesses (or perhaps nymphs) that decorated the pediment.

'Ar,' said Ransome, looking through the misty dusk in the general direction of a flight of pigeons.

'I believe – I do not assert it, but I *believe* that it is a black kite,' said Tobias.

'All right, mate,' said Ransome, with cheerful indifference, 'I dare say it is. Up or down?'

'The tail was so much less forked. Up or down? I think, if you will excuse me, that I will stay a little longer.'

'If you want to see 'em go to roost,' said Ransome, 'you should go round behind: there's millions of 'em there. But I must drop down now, or I shall lose my tide.'

'Good-bye, then,' said Tobias, 'and thank you very much indeed for showing me the lions.'

'You'll take boat directly?' called Ransome, turning as he stood in the skiff. 'You'll know your way all right?' Tobias waved.

The boat pushed out into the stream, where it was lost in the crowd and the evening, and Tobias leant musing against the rail. Dozens of people came down the steps to take to the water or mounted them as they were landed, and perpetually the boatmen bawled 'Up or down?'

A thin, sharp child brushed against him and stole the handkerchief from his coat pocket. 'Up or down?' cried a waterman in his ear. 'Come, make up your mind.'

'Why, truly,' said Tobias, 'I believe that I shall walk.'

'And the devil go with you,' cried the waterman passionately.

'What did he mean by "round behind"?' asked Tobias in a gentle mutter as he walked away. He looked at St Dunstan's in the East, the Coal-meters' Office and the Bakers' Hall; there were pigeons and starlings, but nothing more, for kites were already growing uncommon in London, and Ransome had quite misunderstood

Tobias' remark. They were coming in to roost in their thousands, and while the day lasted Tobias searched among them for black kites; but very soon there was not a bird abroad, black or white, and Tobias stopped under a newly-lit street-lantern to consider his bearings. He had a good natural sense of direction, and with an easy mind he set out and walked through the crowded Mark Lane, crossed quite mistakenly into Crutched Friars by way of Hart Street, and tried to correct his error by going north-westward along Shoe-maker Row and Bevis Marks to Camomile Street and Bishopsgate. A good natural sense of direction is a charming possession, and it is very useful in the country; but in a London fog, and even more particularly in the crowded, narrow, winding streets and alleys of the City, it is worse than useless; for the countryman, confident of his ability, will go for miles and miles in the wrong direction before he can bring himself to ask a native for guidance. This state of affairs is not without its advantages, however; the countryman, in his winding course, is made intimately aware of the monstrous extent of London; and by the time Tobias had passed the parish churches of Allhallows Barking, Allhallows the Great, Allhallows the Less, Allhallows in Bread Street, Allhallows in Honey Lane, Allhallows in Lombard Street, Allhallows Staining and Allhallows on London Wall, he found his ideas of London much enlarged. He went on patiently by St Andrew Hubbard, St Andrew Undershaft and St Andrew by the Wardrobe, St Bennet Fink, St Bennet Gracechurch and St Bennet Sherehog, St Dionis Backchurch, St Laurence Jewry, St Laurence Pountney and St Clement near Eastcheap, St Margaret Moses, St Margaret Pattens and St Martin Outwich, St Mary Wool-church, St Mary Somerset, St Mary Mountshaw, St Mary Woolnoth, St Michael-le-Quern, St Michael Royal, St Nicholas Acons and St Helen's, which brought him back to Bishopsgate again, with at least sixty parish churches as yet unseen, to say nothing of chapels.

Here, by an unhappy fatality, Tobias turned to his right, hoping to find the river, but he found Bedlam instead, and the broad dark open space of Moorfields. He looked with respectful wonder at the vast lunatic asylum, but the new shoes that Jack and he had bought earlier in the day (it seemed more like several months ago) were now causing him a very highly-wrought agony, and he wandered into Moorfields, now deserted by all prudent honest men, to sit on the grass and take them off. After this he went on much more briskly, and determined to ask his way of the next citizen he should meet: it was some time, however, before he met anyone who would stop, and by then he had walked clean out of Moorfields northwards.

'I beg your pardon, sir,' he said to one of a group who were crossing the vague field with a lantern, 'but can you tell me . . .' With a thrill of horror he found that he did not know the name of the street where he lodged, nor Jack's street either.

'Tell you what?' said the lantern, suspiciously.

'Knock him down,' said the lantern's friend, adding, 'We've got pistols, you rogue.'

'Tell me where I am?' asked Tobias, with unusual presence of mind.

'Where you are?'

'If you please.'

'Don't you know where you are?'

'No, I do not.'

'He doesn't know where he is,' said the lantern.

'He will cut your throat in a minute,' said the lantern's friend. 'Why don't you knock him down?'

'So you want to know where you are?'

'Yes, sir, I should like to know very much.'

'Why, then, you're in Farthing Piehouse Field,' said the lantern, and by way of proof waved towards a dirty glimmer a hundred yards away, saying, 'And there's the Farthing Piehouse itself, in all its charming lustre.'

'Sir, I am obliged to you,' said Tobias.

'At your service, sir,' said the lantern, with a bow.

'You could still knock him down,' said the friend, wistfully. 'It's not too late.'

The door of the Farthing Piehouse opened easily, letting out the odour of farthing pies: it was a crowded room, and when Tobias walked in holding his shoes, they all looked up; but the farthing pie-eaters were thieves to a man, and as it was obvious to them that Tobias had just stolen these shoes – that he too was a thief – they took no more notice of him.

'When I have eaten a pie, I shall ask the way back to the river,' thought Tobias, 'and from there I shall be able to find the house, no doubt. It is most likely, too, that I shall remember the name of the street quite suddenly, if I do not force my mind to it. The mind is saturated with new ideas, but it is starved for material sustenance, and must be fed. House,' he cried, 'House, a pie here, if you please.'

'A pie for the gentleman,' called the man of the house into the kitchen, adding, in a voice meant only for his spouse, 'A rum cully what I never set my glimmers on before.'

Tobias, by way of keeping his mind from searching too hard (it was a mind that would remember almost anything if it were not worried and if it were given time, but it was apt to grow stupid if it were overpressed), turned his attention and his anatomical know-ledge to his pie. But this was a most discouraging course of study, and he abandoned it in favour of recalling the events of the day: he dwelt with pleasure upon Ransome, not only as a most amiable companion, but also as a living proof that unaided merit could rise, for Ransome had entered the Navy as an ordinary pressed seaman. 'I wish I had been able to find a moment to ask him about money, however,' said Tobias, yawning: he had intended to do so, but what with their voyage on the river, the lions and the other beasts in the Tower, there had not been time. Jack had shared his purse with Tobias, and these were the first coins that Tobias had ever owned; but Tobias' education had been such that although he could have dealt in the market places of Athens or Rome with ease, he did not know a farthing when he saw one, and he was sadly perplexed by the whole system of modern coinage. The English currency, even now, is the most complicated in the world, with its twelve pence to the shilling and its twenty shillings to the pound; but it is child's play to the time when there were broad pieces, reckoned at twenty-three and twenty-five shillings, half and quarter pieces, ninepenny and fourpence-halfpenny pieces, as well as tin, brass and copper small change, and when the shilling passed for thirteen pence halfpenny and the guinea for anything between a pound and twenty-five shillings.

To distract his mind, which would revert with a touch of panic to the question of his lost address, Tobias turned his fortune on to the table, with the intention of making what sense he could of the inscriptions. At the sound of money all the farthing pie-eaters stopped

40

talking, eating or drinking; and when Tobias, paying his host with a four-shilling piece, asked for a direction to the river, he spoke in the midst of a profound and attentive silence. The man slowly paid out a mountain of small coins, talking as he dribbled them out, and from his questions the hearers learnt that Tobias was lost, unknown and unarmed, and that this was his first day in London.

The pie-man scratched his head: he had a certain pity for his guest – even a very ill-natured brute will stop a blind man from walking into an open pit – but he also had a duty towards his regular customers. In the end he satisfied his conscience by giving Tobias an exact route for the Thames, by telling him that he ought to take care, great care, and by winking with all the significance in his power.

The door closed behind Tobias: the pie-man said to his wife, 'He never did ought to of been let out alone,' and shook his head.

There was a pause of some few listening minutes, then the door opened, and all the regular customers hurried in again.

'They never left him so much as his shirt,' said the pieman to his wife, coming back into the kitchen.

'Well, my dear,' said she, placidly wiping her hands upon her apron and looking through the door to where the regular customers were making their division, 'I hope they have not cut his throat, that's all. Or if they have, that they done it at a decent distance from the house, poor wandering soul.'

Chapter Three

JACK BYRON sat in Thacker's coffee-house, staring vacantly before
him: he was almost alone in the place, apart from the waiters, and
he sat there as steadily and silently as if he had been part of the
furniture. The clock in front of him said half-past seven, and the big
calendar beside it bore the ominous name Friday, newly changed
that morning.

The door opened, and an elderly man in a black coat and a
periwig walked in: he nodded to Jack, who bowed, although for the
moment he did not recognise him. It was Mr Eliot, the surgeon of
the *Wager*, to whom Keppel had presented Jack some days before.
'So you have not gone down to Portsmouth yet?' he said, with some
surprise.

'No, sir,' said Jack.

'Are you not cutting it uncommon fine?' asked the surgeon.

'Yes, sir,' said Jack, who was all too vividly aware of the racing
hours and the horrifying speed with which Saturday, his last day in
England, was rushing towards him.

The surgeon, in spite of Jack's short answers and unhappy face,
sat down by him, and said, 'I am up myself only because of my
infernal mate, and I shall take the mail-coach down this evening.'
He explained that he was very particular in his choice of assistants,
that he could not bear the confident, half-licked cubs that were
usually wished upon him by the Navy Office – had even paid one
to go away out of the *Wager* and transfer himself elsewhere – and
that he was now waiting for a young man who had been strongly
recommended to him as a person of a truly scientific cast of mind.
'Such a rare creature, these days,' said Mr Eliot. 'It was quite different when I was young.' Here a group of officers came in, brown-faced
men whose voices reverberated in the big room, filling it with sound;
another naval surgeon came just behind them, Mr Woodfall of the

Centurion, and he stopped by Mr Eliot to wish him good day and to tell him that Mr Anson had been to the Admiralty already.

Mr Anson, the captain of the *Centurion* and the commodore of the squadron, appeared as if by magic as the surgeon spoke his name, stood there for a moment, looking for someone, and then walked away: in spite of his preoccupation and state of dismal worry, Jack looked with the closest attention at his commanding officer, a tall man, upright, with the head of a Roman emperor, though tanned and weather-beaten – a plainly dressed man: blue coat, buff waist-coat, hat with the King's cockade and nothing more, a plain steel-hilted sword.

'Let us have a pot of chocolate together,' said Mr Eliot to Mr Woodfall. 'Hey there. Ho. Ahoy. A pot of chocolate here.' The older waiters at Thacker's were used to being called as if they were three miles off in an impenetrable fog, but the new ones were rendered nervous by it, and were sometimes obliged to give up their places. 'As I was telling our young friend here,' continued Mr Eliot, 'a decent surgeon's mate is scarcely to be found in these degenerate days.' He went on to speak of the desirable qualities of the young man who was to come: learned, even to the point of knowing some Greek, skilled, and above all interested in his profession, in its widest aspects, in its philosophical implications – qualities all too rare in the common run of modern surgeon's mates. 'Where,' he cried, 'will you find a young fellow nowadays who will purchase a dead baboon at the cost of his suppers for six months, and preserve its vitals in spirits of wine for the pure love of anatomy? Best rectified spirits of wine at eighteenpence the Winchester quart.'

'Ah,' said his colleague mournfully, 'where indeed? But have you not left it very late, my dear sir?'

'For such a paragon it is worth it,' said Mr Eliot. 'And so you would say if you had seen the fellow the Navy Office sent me last month – a very mere rake indeed. Besides,' he added confidentially, 'I though it prudent to wait until my brother-in-law and our friend Bartholomew were both on the board of examiners – it is their turn now, you know – in case of any little difficulty with this young man's qualifications. His indentures are regular, but he has not quite served out his time. I prefer to take him to the Hall myself, see him examined and certificated, take him to the Navy Office, see to his warrant directly, and so carry him down to Portsmouth, all in one.'

'Well,' said Mr Woodfall, getting up, 'I wish you joy of him. I am sure a good mate is a wonderful comfort to a man, particularly on a voyage . . .' He walked away, puffing and holding his arms wide apart to indicate the extraordinary length of the intended voyage.

'Come, Mr Byron, another cup of chocolate?' said Mr Eliot; and looking at him more keenly he asked, 'Are you feeling quite well?'

'Oh, I'm well enough, thankee, sir,' said Jack wearily; then suddenly, unburdening himself, he said, 'The truth of the matter is that I have lost my friend, and your talking about a philosophical cove dissecting things brought him so clearly to my mind, I could cry like a girl. Upon my honour I could. Toby would dissect you anything you like, a baboon, or a horse, or a mole. Anything. I sit here all day long in case he should find his way – I've left instructions at the house, of course. He had only been one day in London. Blast and crush me down,' cried Jack, wiping his eye, 'you talk about your fellow knowing some Greek: why, Toby Barrow was speaking it as quick as I speak English when he was only ten; and Latin too, like a bench of infernal bishops, rot them all.'

'Quietly now, Mr Byron; do not curse the bishops so. Perhaps I could help you, if you would tell me clearly what has happened.'

His listened attentively, and he was advising Jack to apply to the magistrate at Bow Street and to the Mansion House when a thin young man with knock knees and a cheese-coloured face was brought up to him by the waiter: this person carried a bridal posy in one hand and a letter in the other. 'Be not severe,' he said, putting the letter into Mr Eliot's hand. 'Severity were out of place,' he said, with an arch simper, and left them gazing after him.

The youth, Mr Eliot's supposed assistant, had escaped from his family's control and had married; and this was the bride's brother to bring the news that the paragon did not choose to go round the world any more.

Mr Eliot took no notice of this other than by checking an oath and saying, 'Perhaps we are as well shot of him: his father told me that he was attached to some odious wench. But as I was saying, the magistrate at Bow Street has proper officers for this kind of enquiry: I will step in at his office, if you wish, and find whether they have any news.'

44

'It is exceedingly good in you, sir,' said Jack, 'particularly when you have been so disappointed –' nodding towards the letter.

'As for that, I say nothing: it is no use running your head against a brick wall. I cannot unmarry the fellow; and by not giving vent to my vexation I shall certainly feel less of it. Did you say that your friend was properly indentured?'

'Yes, sir; his paper is still at the house. It has a chart of a mole's innards on the back of it, though.'

Mr Eliot stood for a moment in thought. 'I shall have to see what they have at the Navy Office,' he said. 'I shall have to see what they have to offer me. Though if they have nothing better than the common run of 'prentice sawbones, I shall sail without one. I've done it before, and I'll do it again,' he said, nodding very firmly and moving off. 'But,' he said, coming back, 'if your friend should be found before we sail, I may be able to serve him.'

Jack sat down again and leant back against the partition of his box; he was feeling tired and stupid, for he had scarcely been to bed these three nights past; and as well as searching the vast expanse of London he had been obliged to go down to the Nore and back. But he felt comforted by Mr Eliot's kindness, and he closed his eyes for a catnap. 'I shall take a quarter of an hour's sleep,' he said to himself. 'And I wish those infernal swabs would make less of a din.'

The infernal swabs were a party of midshipmen in the box behind him: they had been roving about all night, in a greater or less degree of intoxication, and they were still inclined to be troublesome and obnoxious. They were arguing now, interminably and without the least hope of reaching a conclusion, about the identity of certain monstrous birds that had been seen upon the Monument the day before. Storks, pelicans and frigate-birds were suggested, rocs, phoenixes and tabernacles: here they drifted off on to a profitless discussion of tabernacles, whether birds or no, and Jack began to sink down into his nap. He had heard of these birds several times already: they had perched up there on the gilt ball of the Monument for an hour or more, during the time he was coming up from the Nore in the press smack; they had attracted an immense crowd and a great deal of speculation. They were universally held to be portents; but what they portended was less certain.

'In my opinion,' said a milk-faced midshipman (whose mother

would have wept to see him, unwashed, slobbered with brandy that he could scarcely drink and smelling of tobacco that he could scarcely smoke) 'in my opinion those fowl mean a frightful prodigious ghastly disaster, which would probably be a very bad thing.'

Jack leapt to his feet as if he had been stung and ran with astonishing speed to the door, where he cannoned from a rear-admiral into a post-captain and fell heavily over Ransome's feet. They asked him what he thought he was doing, and where he thought he was going, and the admiral struck him repeatedly with a gold-headed cane from the Malacca Straits; ordinarily Jack would have resented this, admiral or no, but now he scrambled to his feet, seized Ransome by the hand and ran furiously down the street, crying out, 'Come on,' in a very vehement tone.

Coming to the river stairs, he bawled for a pair of oars. 'Give way,' he said, thrusting Ransome into the boat, and he exhorted the rowers to pull with all the force and eloquence that ever he had learnt at sea, directing them to pass straight down the river to the press tender in the Pool. At the sound of the words 'press tender' the watermen paused, and Jack cried, 'Give way, can't you? You have got your infernal certificates, han't you?' The watermen certainly had, and they could not be taken by the press-gang nor kept aboard the press tender; but, as the bow oar explained, 'It makes the blood go thin as gin in my arteries.'

'Veins,' said stroke.

'Arteries,' said bow.

'Ransome,' said Jack, 'you have heard about these birds on the Monument? Well, don't you see that they would bring Toby out of his grave, if they were to appear again? You must go ashore at Old Swan stairs, buy a couple of turkeys – turkeys, mind you, Ransome; none of your common geese – and hoist them at the top of the Monument. And I will go down to the tender – Dick Penn is in command – and bring up a thundering great party to stop every alley, once the crowd has gathered. Do you understand? Have you any money?'

Ransome struck the side of his nose with his finger to indicate comprehension, jingled his pocket to show his wealth, and remarking that Jack was a credit to his Ma, stepped on to a lighter that was moving in to the shore, and thence, in order to lose no valuable seconds, to a wherry, adjuring it 'to shove in, cully, and do the handsome thing for once in its – life,' words which the wherry recognised as its native tongue, and which it complied with, wafting the intruder ashore with all the elegance that a wherry is capable of.

Some hours earlier than this the first lieutenant of the guard-ship had told Mr Richard Penn, the fifth lieutenant (and until recently a midshipman and a colleague of Jack's) that what he, the first lieutenant, wanted was a little zeal, initiative and mother-wit on the part of Mr Penn. The first lieutenant freely acknowledged that it would be vain to look for seamanship, intelligence or beauty in Mr Penn; but at least the first lieutenant had a right, he hoped he had a right, to expect Mr Penn, when in command of the press smack, to bring back something better than crippled half-wits with certificates of exemption. Were there no idle apprentices left in the City of London, no stout, able-bodied young men? Did the entire uncertificated population resemble Mr Penn?

These harsh words were still rankling in the bosom of the press-tender's captain when Jack appeared on the river, and crying, 'Hoy, Dick,' darted up the side.

'Good morning, Mr Byron,' said Dick coldly.

'I beg your pardon, sir,' said Jack, saluting and growing quite red. 'May I have a word with you?'

'I am going below, Mr Hape,' said the captain to a dwarfish midshipman, and led the way into a kind of moist cupboard.

'Now, Jack?' he said, sitting down and waving to an empty locker.

'I am very sorry I forgot myself just now,' said Jack earnestly, 'but I am in a great taking, Dick, and I rely upon you absolutely. Do you know about those birds at the Monument?'

At the Monument itself Ransome was having difficulties that he had not allowed for: he had bought his turkeys easily enough, and although the poultryman had foisted the oldest, stringiest birds in the market upon him – birds that had proved unnaturally strong, cunning, malignant and resourceful – he had them under control by now, and he had reached the door of the Monument, only to be told that he might not bring them in.

'No turkeys. No fowls whatsoever,' said the keeper of the Monument, who, seeing that Ransome was a sailor, supposed that he was drunk. 'And no tarpaulins, either,' he added, with offensive sobriety.

'In the King's name,' cried Ransome, in a hoarse wheeze.

The keeper hesitated for a moment; but the turkeys, who were peering at him inquisitively with their little beady eyes, were too preposterous to have been brought on his Majesty's service, and the keeper turned his back. How unwise was this, how imprudent a move, and how sincerely the keeper regretted his temerity when he felt an iron hand upon his neck and found himself dashed with appalling force into the Monument.

The Monument, as the world in general knows, is a hollow column, with a spiral staircase inside it: for a brief interval this tube was filled with a whirling mass of keeper, turkey and enraged sailorman, a confused mass that ascended to emerge crimson and breathless on the square parapet under the brass knob that tops the edifice.

Ransome always carried a knife and a piece of line; he would have felt indecently naked without them. 'Now, brother,' he said, showing them to the keeper, 'you must bear a hand. Because why? Because it's in the King's name, that's why; and I swear I'll have the quivering liver out of you, else.' He tapped the keeper pleasantly in the region of his liver, and passed him the turkeys.

'Do you swear it's in the King's name?' asked the keeper in gasps, when he could fetch his breath.

'Yus,' said Ransome, spitting on his hands and eyeing the brass flames that sprang from the upper part of the Monument.

'I wouldn't give no countenance otherwise,' said the keeper. 'Have you got a wipe?'

Ransome passed him the powerful square of canvas that served him for a handkerchief, and the keeper neatly hooded the turkeys with it; the birds at once become docile and motionless. 'You don't know nothing about fowls,' he said, with surly self-approbation.

'Now listen, cock,' said Ransome from amidst the flames, 'I shall let you down this line, and you must make 'em fast when I'm atop. And then, do you see, I shall haul 'em up: and a flaming multitude will turn out: and we shall press a tidy few.' He spoke slowly, for the top of the Monument is quite unlike the rigging of a ship, and although the two-hundred-foot drop did not worry him, the arrangement of the flames did; for whereas the rigging of a ship is based upon utility, monumental brass flames are there for architectural effect – a wholly different principle.

'If you had said you was the press earlier, we could of walked up like Christians,' said the keeper sulkily. 'Three hundred and forty-five steps, run up like Barbary apes.'

'What?' called Ransome, round the curve, and perilously engaged with some artistic flames.

'Three hundred and forty-five steps,' shouted the keeper. 'Six inches thick.'

'What?'

'And ten and a half wide.'

'All hands aft, Mr Hape,' said the captain of the press smack.

The vessel was not so large that all hands could not hear this perfectly well, but they would not have considered it manners to move before the order was officially relayed. All hands, having been properly summoned, stood facing the quarter-deck, not in the stiff, wooden rigidity of soldiers, but in the easy, *dégagée* attitude of sailors – looking, it must be admitted, not unlike a band of dutiful gorillas: for these were the press-gang, equally impervious to the blows of the pressed and to the temptations of the shore.

'Listen to Mr Byron,' said the captain, whose mind was reeling with the magnitude of the design, and who did not trust himself to do it justice.

Jack explained it, to the infinite delight of the crew, and said, 'But this is the great point: I am confident that a friend of mine will be there. He was lost, by reason of being freshly come up from the country. Now here's a guinea,' he cried out, pulling one out, 'and here's a guinea' – pulling out another – 'and if I had any more I would put it down – I can't say fairer than that, damn your eyes. And the first man to clap him to, shall have them both. He is a little cove, ugly, with light green eyes and a pale face: wears an old black coat and sad-coloured breeches. Though he may have had the coat stolen off his back by now. He has an odd fashion of staring about him and jerking his head, and you might think he was simple; but he is a very learned cove indeed, and must be civilly used.'

'Deck,' hailed Mr Hape, who had taken a glass to the masthead, and who had been training it on the shining top of the Monument these ten minutes past, 'Deck there. I see two birds broke out on the top of the flaming urn.'

Tobias' dress did not excite much comment: there were too many people in London who had sold their shirts in Rag Fair or who had lost them for one more to make people stare. He was clad in a sack; it had a hole in each corner for his legs, and it looked not altogether unlike the trunk-hose worn in an earlier age: it had been a very good sack, once, but it did impede his progress – having no belt, he was obliged to hold it up all the time, and he reached Fish Street Hill (the Monument is set in Fish Street Hill, not far from Pudding Lane) in a fume of anxiety, much later than the bulk of the spectators. Between twenty and thirty thousand people had already found leisure to come and stare, and already there were some twenty-five thousand opinions on the birds.

'They are vultures,' said a thin citizen, 'a bird well known in the Orient.'

'They are halieutic eagles,' said a clergyman.

'They are common turkeys,' said Tobias.

This was not at all well received: there were cries of 'Who are you, to put in your word?' 'Ragged muffin!' 'Saucy fellow!' 'Teach him better manners,' and he was nudged, pushed and attempted to be cuffed by the thin citizen, who bore such malice that he repeatedly forced his way through the crowd to get in his blow.

'They *are* turkeys,' cried Tobias. But he was saved from the consequences by the panic-stricken shout of 'The press! The press is coming!' All the men who did not wish to serve their country in the Royal Navy (and their name was legion) instantly began to run as fast as they were able: in an instant Tobias was knocked flat in the mud and overrun by an anxious herd. 'What press?' he asked, getting up; but the only reply was, 'Run, run. Run, or you will be taken.'

A week before Tobias would not have run at the recommendation of a terrified grocer; he would have stayed to watch, preferably on a slight eminence; but so many disastrous things had befallen him in London that he was ready to believe that still worse might be to come, and he began to run as industriously as his sack would allow him.

'Deck, there,' came a huge voice out of the sky. 'Ho, deck, there,' bawled Ransome from the top of the Monument; and at the sound Tobias ran the faster. 'There he is, mate. A-making for the river.'

Tobias glanced over his shoulder, and saw two long-armed hairy men coming after him with naked cutlasses, running as fast as nightmares and crying 'Hoo, hooroo, hoo' as they came. He turned the corner of Fish Street Hill, scarcely touching the ground, raced along Thames Street and up Pudding Lane: the thudding feet were dying away behind him when from an alley to his left burst more hairy men with swords, like armed gorillas. By a superhuman effort he drew ahead of them, and turning into Eastcheap he saw the crowded street before him: as a hunted deer seeks refuge among horned cattle, so Tobias saw safety in the herd of citizens. His breath was coming short, the cries behind him louder, and he was labouring with dreadful effort: he could scarcely hear now for the panting of his own breath, and his sight was darkening; but he could make out the crowd not a hundred yards before him now, and he knew that if he could keep running for just those intervening yards he would be lost to view and safe.

'Heave to,' cried the gorillas, seeing their gold fly from them. ''Vast running, damn your eyes. Ho.'

Twenty yards to go, and he would be lost: ten yards, no more; and his sack fell from his nerveless hands, tangled about his feet and brought him thumping down under the exulting cries of his hideously armed pursuers.

'I never thought it could have been done,' said Mr Eliot, pushing Tobias up the steps of the Portsmouth coach.

'There you are,' cried Jack, pulling him up on to the roof. 'I had been staring in the wrong direction. How did it go?'

'Now then, old gentleman,' cried the guard, 'If you're a-coming, get in.'

The door slammed, the whip cracked and the mail-coach pulled out of the yard: Mr Eliot crept past the knees of his fellow inside travellers, sat down in his place, took off his hat and his wig, put on a nightcap and repeated, 'I never thought it could have been done,' gasping as he did so.

Outside, Tobias was slowly scrambling across the lurching roof, pulled by Jack and propelled by the guard, while London whirled by at a shocking pace.

'How did it go?' asked Jack again, very anxiously, when he had wedged Tobias into a sitting position, with his feet against the low iron rail and his back against the mound of luggage in the middle of the roof.

'Very well, Jack, I thank you,' said Tobias, and sat panting for a while. 'They asked me what I should do in a case of ascites, and I satisfied 'em out of Galen, Avicenna and Rhazes. And there was a civil gentleman who desired me to show him the insertions of the *pronator radii teres* on a little corpse they had at hand, which I did; the *pronator radii teres* is a very childish dissection, Jack.' He yawned, stretched and as nearly as possible plunged over the edge as the coach turned left-handed into the Portsmouth road.

'Yes,' said Jack, grasping Tobias and hauling him back, 'yes, I knew that would be all right' – he had unlimited confidence in Tobias' ability to satisfy any board of examiners whatever – 'but did they give you a decent letter, and what about the Navy Office?'

'The Navy Office was far less interesting than Surgeons' Hall, Jack,' said Tobias, and Jack turned pale. 'At the Hall, while my letter was writing, the examiners took notice of my anatomical drawings of moles – they were on the back of my indenture, which lay on the table – and one of them made some very happy and enlightening remarks about the exiguity of the descending colon in the mole. But the Navy Office was very kind, nevertheless.'

'Come, that's better,' said Jack, brightening. 'You could scarcely expect them to harangue you about the guts of a mole, but if they were kind, why, that is the great point. What happened?'

'We had to run there – Mr Eliot runs most surprisingly for a man of his age – because the conversation about moles had taken so much time, and the Navy Office was closing, to say nothing of the departure of the coach; and as we ran we passed the doorway where I used to sleep. But, however, we did not stop; I merely pointed it out to Mr Eliot as we ran, and said –'

'Now, Toby, do not be so infernally long-winded. What happened?'

'The secretary read me the letter that the surgeons had given me – it was sealed, you understand – and it said that they had examined

52

me, and that they judged me sufficient for a third rate.'

'A third rate,' exclaimed Jack, whistling.

'Yes,' said Tobias, with a frown. 'It was a reflection that piqued me, I must admit.'

'Damn your eyes, Toby; how can you be so unredeemed? Don't you know what a third rate is?'

'No,' said Tobias, 'but it don't sound very eligible. Third rate – pah.'

'A third rate,' said Jack impressively, 'is a seventy-four. Think of that, Toby.' He looked at his friend with new respect: he had always considered Toby a creature of shining parts, but he had never connected him with the grandeur of a seventy-four. 'Think of that, Toby,' he repeated, in a solemn tone.

Toby thought of that; or at least he appeared to be thinking, for he gazed into the air and munched his jaws, as he did whenever he was thoughtful. His eyes slowly closed, and he rolled in his seat. 'Go on,' cried Jack. 'What when he had read you the letter?'

'Eh?'

'What when the secretary had read you the letter? Come, Toby, don't be stupid,' said Jack, nudging him strongly by way of admonition.

'Oh, then he said that he was sorry that he had no third rate to propose to me.'

'Oh,' said Jack, in a low voice of cruel disappointment.

'"But," says he,' continued Tobias, 'with a wink at Mr Eliot – I saw something pass between them, which I suspect of being a customary present, and must remember to pay it back – "But," says he, winking in the manner that I have described, "I can offer you the *Wager*, if you will please to accept of it." And with this he shook me by the hand and gave directions for my warrant to be made out at once; and as soon as it was signed Mr Eliot fee'd the clerk and the porter, wished me joy and ran me at a still greater speed to the coach.'

'So you have it?' cried Jack, his face shining all over with joy, 'you have your warrant, Toby? I wish you joy, indeed I do. How glad I am, Toby,' he cried, beating his friend upon the back, knocking him off his balance, rescuing him as he fell, shaking him fervently by the hand and adding, 'Three times huzzay. You are in the Navy now, old cock, and glory is just round the corner, strike me down. Let me have sight of it? The warrant?'

'Yes,' said Tobias, and he felt in his pocket. A concerned, preoccupied look came over him, and he began feeling all over his coat, waistcoat and breeches. He was no longer dressed in his sack: clearly, it would never have done to present himself at the Navy Office in a partially decayed sack, and they had kept him aboard the press smack while the bosun's mate (a linen-draper's apprentice in the days of William and Mary, and still considered a judge of cloth) new-rigged him at the nearest slop-shop. The bosun's mate was stronger in goodwill than judgment; his time was limited to ten minutes and his purse to Jack's remaining twelve shillings; and the result fitted Tobias rather less well than his sack. But that was of no importance at this juncture: now the point was that the pockets were all unfamiliar, and they had to be found and searched one by one, with conscientious effort. Toby's face grew more and more preoccupied, and he began the search again, rummaging from top to bottom.

'In your hat?' asked Jack, tapping the villainous round felt dome that the slop-dealer had thrown in for fourpence and taking it off with due care that nothing should fly from it.

'Do you think they would stop the coach?' asked Tobias: but before Jack could reply, he cried, 'Mr Eliot has it. He told me that it would be better if he had it: I am almost certain that I gave it to him.'

'Toby, Toby,' said Jack, with quiet despair, 'if you go on like this I doubt you will ever arrive to any great age. Hold on to my legs, will you?' He let himself over the edge of the roof, and appeared, purpling rapidly, upside-down at the window. 'Do you have his paper?' he roared.

Mr Eliot put his hand to his ear to show that he could not hear: on being asked again he nodded violently and tapped the bosom of his coat, with that curiously exaggerated silent pantomime that is usual whenever people communicate through a pane of glass.

Jack regained his place, an elegant mulberry, but with all his calm restored. 'Now, Toby,' he said, settling himself as comfortably as the incipient drizzle would allow, 'will you tell me how you came to be in that sack?'

But Tobias had lived through a very great deal in the course of that day: he had been hunted down by the press-gang and taken, restored to his friends with surprising violence, clothed, examined by Mr Eliot, examined by the surgeons, and provided with a warrant, a ship, a career and the prospect of seeing creatures unknown to natural philosophy in the immediate future; and now, in the moments that had just passed, it had seemed that the process was to be reversed. The speed at which they had had to move – flying to Marlborough Street for money, to Mrs Fuller's for his indenture and his remaining possessions, quite apart from the racing about with Mr Eliot – had left no time for eating, and now Tobias was quite exhausted with nervous tension, hunger and emotion. He said 'Sack?' nodded for a minute, and quietly observed, 'It was a very good sort of sack, in the first place.' He then went to sleep, so utterly and completely to sleep that he was obliged to be lashed on to the luggage to keep him on the coach at all, and Jack supported him to stop him from falling sideways as the coach ran through Guildford, Godalming, Mousehill, Seven Thorns, Petersfield, all the way past Purbrook and right up Portsdown Hill, from whose height the whole vast expanse of the harbour could be seen, the dockyard, the fortifications and, far out, under the sheltering Isle of Wight, the squadron riding at St Helen's, the *Centurion*, the *Gloucester*, the *Severn*, the *Pearl*, the *Tryall* sloop and the *Wager*.

Chapter Four

THE SQUADRON did not sail that Saturday. Mr Eliot learnt that it was not to sail the minute he set foot to ground in Portsmouth, from the most authoritative of all sources, his own captain. Captain Kidd was coming out of the Crown, in company with Captain Mitchel of the *Pearl*, as the coach pulled up, and as soon as he saw the surgeon he called out, 'You might have come down by the wagon, doctor, if you had pleased, ha, ha,' with the greatest good humour.

Mr Eliot had served forty years in the Navy, and he received the news with perfect equanimity, only observing that the Admiralty would find it cheaper to cut their throats out of hand, than to kill them by sending them round the Horn still later in the year. Jack was also quite unmoved by learning that all their frantic hurry had been useless; he remarked that it would be just as well for Toby to have a decent meal and to spend the rest of the night in a bed ashore – it was always more agreeable to report to one's ship in the morning.

The morning of Saturday was as sweet and clear and blue as an English summer's day can be. Tobias had woken to the sound of gulls, and to the realisation of what yesterday had done and what today was to bring – a very vivid, sudden and delightful awakening. He found that Jack was up already, washed, dressed and fully alive, peering at Gosport through a telescope.

'Would you like to have a look?' he said. 'You can't see St Helen's from here, but if you screw yourself into the corner, you can get a charming view of the hospital.'

Tobias looked at Haslar, looked at three herring-gulls, several black-headed gulls and a shag. 'Gulls, eh, Jack?' he said, with a triumphant munch of his jaws. 'Sea-birds. I shall go out and look at 'em more closely.'

'Don't you think it,' said Jack.

'Must I not go out?'

'No,' said Jack, very firmly. 'You are never to go out, Toby, unless I am with you. Not by land, anyhow. So don't you think it.'

Tobias could not but acknowledge the justice of this, and Jack, having gained his point, instantly proposed taking a turn while breakfast was preparing.

If he had wished to display the naval might of England at its greatest advantage, he could not have chosen a better day: the vast fleet against Carthagena and the Spanish main was fitting out, as well as their own squadron, and men-of-war of every rate lay at Spithead, with transports among them, and tenders and ships' boats perpetually coming and going, their white sails on the sea answering to the scraps of white cloud that were passing easily over the pure blue sky. The royal dockyard, the greatest in the world, reared its astonishing forest of masts in even more profusion than usual, and although the day was a holiday in the civilian part of the town, the yard echoed and re-bellowed with the din of hammers. The clear, sharp air from the sea mingled with the smell of tar, paint and cordage from the dockyard and with a certain spirituous mixture of brandy and rum that emanated from the town in general.

Jack pointed out their own squadron over at St Helen's, too far to be distinguished without a glass; he pointed out the *Royal George*, a three-decker with a hundred guns, and all the other rates, from the first right down to the *Salamander*, a bomb-ketch of eight guns (and those of the smallest kind); he defined a ship of the line and a frigate, a ship, a barque and a brig, and he would have defined a great deal more had he not been interrupted by the sound of cheering. It was the *Lively*, a sloop of war, coming out of the harbour: she glided down to within a few yards of them; her gaff-topsail took the breeze, her close-hauled mainsail filled with a huge smooth curve, and she heeled away, running faster and faster, as though she herself made the wind; it was as pretty a sight as could be imagined – new paint, new canvas, gleaming decks and shining brass; her new commander's pride and joy – and the long wake straight as she sailed so tightly for the green island over the water.

'How did you like that, Toby?' asked Jack, when the cheering had died away. Tobias did not reply, but he slowly gnashed his teeth, and his white face showed a flush of delight.

On the way back to the Crown Jack pointed out a vice-admiral of the blue and two post-captains, and he thought it was well to profit by Tobias' present nautical enthusiasm to impress upon him the necessity for a due respect for rank.

'You cannot conceive,' he said, earnestly spreading butter upon his toast in the coffee-room of the Crown, 'my dear Toby, you cannot *conceive* the gulf between a captain and a mere person.' He went on in this strain, while Tobias ate four boiled eggs out of a napkin; but he doubted whether he was doing much good, and for some pensive moments he envisaged the consequences of Tobias' turning upon the commodore with reasons in favour of a democratic management of the squadron. However, his mind, saturated with buttered toast and coffee, did not dwell for long upon this, and with a sudden grin he said, 'It is infernal good luck, by the way, that we don't sail directly: you would have had to put up with purser's slops and whatever we could have bought at Madeira, or wherever it is we water. But now we can fill you a sea-chest in a decent sort of way.' Jack, like all his relatives on his father's side, was impatient of ready money; solvency, with gold jingling in his pocket, seemed to him a thoroughly unnatural condition; and few things gave him a more lively pleasure than spending. The thought of spending a considerable amount, very quickly, and upon Tobias, filled him with such an agreeable sense of anticipation that he whistled aloud. Jack had a true and melodious whistle, but it was rather loud indoors, and a yellow-faced lieutenant at the next table put his hand to his forehead and glared at them with pure hatred. 'But,' said Jack, glancing at the clock, 'we had better report first; besides, that will enable you to find out what you will need in the way of saws and knives and so on.'

They walked down to the water and called for a boat. '*Wager*,' said Jack, stepping neatly in. 'Easy,' he said, picking Tobias out of the bottom and setting him upright. Tobias had stepped in while the boat was rising, and (as it has happened to so many landsmen) he had ignominiously doubled up at the knees. 'It was the wave,' Jack explained.

'Was it indeed?' said Tobias. 'The billow? I shall grow accustomed to them in time, no doubt.'

It was a long pull, but the morning was so splendid, the fleet and its activities so absorbing, that for more than half of the way they sat silent: when the *Wager* was well in sight, Jack bade the waterman bear away for the head of the squadron, and so come down to her, she lying in the last berth but one.

'But you said go straight for the store-ship first,' said the waterman.

Jack had been thinking of the *Wager* by the same plain shameful name, but it stung him exceedingly to hear anyone else say it, and he desired the waterman very passionately to stow his gab and to attend to his duty. The waterman, who had been cursed by admirals before Jack was born, took this with provoking calm, only observing that 'it would be an extra fourpence, and twopence for the oaths.'

'Store-ship,' muttered Jack. 'Damn your eyes.' But as they came abreast of St Helen's church, where the commodore lay, and turned to pass down the line, his spirits revived: it was a beautiful line of ships, and he explained them to Tobias as they passed. 'The *Centurion*,' he said, 'she's a sixty-gun ship, do you see? A fourth rate. Damn it, Toby, that's where we should be, alongside of Keppel and Ransome. Look, going along by the hances, there's the commodore – do you see him, Toby? He is pointing down into the waist.'

'I see him,' said Toby, looking attentively at the august form of Mr Anson. 'Shall we pull off our hats, and wave?'

'No, no,' cried Jack, for the *Centurion* was no distance away at all, and he could even hear the commodore's voice. 'Give way,' he called to the boatman, and he hastily drew Tobias' attention to the *Gloucester*, the next in line, and then to the *Severn*, both fifty-gun ships. 'Who commands the *Severn* now?' he asked the boatman.

'Captain Legge,' said the boatman. 'A lord's son. The honourable Legge, as they say. You can do anything you please if you are a lord's son' – spitting virtuously into the sea. 'If I was a lord's son,' said the boatman, 'do you think as I should be a-sitting here, toiling and moiling all day long?'

'Do you moil a great deal?' asked Tobias.

'Like a porpoise, governor; and likewise toil. But was I a lord's son, I should sit a-taking of my ease in a cutter with pink taffety sails: because why? Because honest worth has no countenance these days.'

'Captain Legge was with Admiral Vernon at Porto Bello,' said Jack. 'He was in the *Pearl* then. And there *is* the *Pearl*: ain't she elegant?' She was, indeed; and she had the aura of a famous victory about her still. When Jack had looked long enough at her, he added, 'Forty. She is one of the old forty-gun ships, but she is a very fine sailer on a wind, they say – will outsail anything. Captain Mitchel has her now. The sloop lying inside her is the *Tryall*: belongs to us.'

'But you described a sloop as a vessel with one mast and a sail out behind,' objected Tobias, seeing two undeniable and very tall masts before him, and a square rig.

'Ah, she's only *called* a sloop,' said Jack. 'It is perfectly logical really – we do not mean that she *is* a sloop.' He did not elucidate this statement, but looked fixedly towards the *Wager*, which they were now approaching. 'Well, here we are,' he said, after a few moments, and he glanced anxiously at Tobias to see whether he would be disappointed: but to Tobias the *Wager* looked very much like any other ship. She was about a hundred feet long, as opposed to the hundred and fifty of the fourth rates, and she had but a single row of gun-ports; but still she was a high and beautiful ship, far beyond anything that Tobias had aspired to. Searching for something agreeable to say (for he felt Jack's eye upon him), he stared at her for a while, screwing his face hideously to one side and scratching his right thigh. 'It is wider than the others,' he said at last, 'and, I presume, less liable to be overset.'

It was quite true: the *Wager* was broad in the beam, wide and motherly; she was built to carry a large quantity of merchandise at a prudent pace, and in spite of her naval trim and Captain Kidd's lavish use of dockyard paint she had (to a knowing eye) nothing of the high-bred, dangerous air of a man-of-war. She was undisguisably a former Indiaman, a store-ship; and however worthy she might be, and however little liable to be overset, Jack thought that it would be difficult to love her.

'Well, never mind,' he said; and to the waterman, 'Lay us alongside, then. Toby,' he said, in a low but urgent voice, 'you will be discreet, I beg? You will remember not to scratch or look awry or squint when officers are talking to you? Do just as I do, eh? And manage it so that you come aboard her with your right foot first – it is amazingly lucky.'

It was amazingly lucky, too, that the sea was so calm, so unusually calm; for many a landsman going aboard for the first time has been confronted with the towering ship's side, rising and falling in nasty, cold, dangerous black water while the boat dances here and there in imminent peril of being crushed or sucked under, and he must make the journey, dry and undisgraced, over the varying gulf and up the appalling slippery height to the longed-for deck. But Tobias had merely to step from a well-behaved boat to a scarcely-moving ship and walk to the entering-port: which was just as well, for he stopped to ponder at the water-line, and had there been any hint of a swell he must inevitably have been ducked, if not washed off and drowned at the very moment in which his nautical career began.

It was perfectly evident to Jack as he went up the side and as he went from the entering-port to the quarter-deck that the *Wager* had had no intention of sailing that Saturday: she was half deserted, and although her decks were being quite briskly washed she had a comparatively somnolent air. These were momentary impressions, received as he approached the officer of the watch, with Toby just behind him, to report for duty, to announce his presence in a correct and official manner.

Mr Clerk, the master of the *Wager*, was a mild, elderly man, with a bleached, sea-washed appearance and watery blue eyes; he received them kindly, told Jack that the purser had been asking for him, told Tobias that Mr Eliot was in the cockpit at that very moment, and called one of his mates to show them the way. 'Mr Jones,' he said, in his nasal East Anglian voice, 'you will take these gentlemen below, if you please, and see them properly bestowed.'

From the poop to the quarter-deck proper, and thence to the dim light of the upper deck, where Tobias, trying to see too much at once, tripped over the handle of a swab and measured his length (five feet five and a half inches): he brought his forehead against the unsympathetic surface of a gun, and jarred it till it rang again; the master's mate picked him up, told him that he had fallen down, and that he should take care – that he should look where he was going. At the same time a fat man in a greasy black coat, a pale fat man with the face of a cellar-dweller, hurried down from the shadows and greeted them.

'Mr Byron?' he said. 'The honourable Mr Byron?'

'At your service, sir,' said Jack coldly.

'My name is Hervey – purser,' said the fat man. 'And I have saved you a cabin. May I have the pleasure –?'

'You are very good,' said Jack. 'Mr Hervey, this is Mr Barrow, the surgeon's mate, who has just joined.'

'Servant,' said the purser with a distant nod, and hurrying Jack away by a moist grip of his elbow he continued, 'I have the honour of being known to your grandfather . . .'

'Old Greasy,' muttered the master's mate. 'Come on, young Saw-bones, and mind your step.' Mr Jones spoke in this unceremonious manner not from any native moroseness or incivility of mind, but because he had taken a disgust at the purser's obsequious tone. They went on a little circuitously towards the cockpit, for part of the gun-deck was at that time shut off, with its ports netted or closed, for the better retention of the lately pressed men, who would escape if ever they could: he led the way along the deck, up and down again, and so to a hatchway that vanished into the total darkness; his voice floated up, advising Tobias to mind the cascabel, with an odd reverberating hollowness, and Tobias, whose eyes were still filled with the yellow flashing coruscations of his fall, followed him by the sound, like a bat. Presently the darkness became a little less intense, and in addition to the smell of bilge, sea, pitch and hemp, Tobias caught the familiar odour of medicaments: they rounded a canvas screen, and there was Mr Eliot, standing in the middle of the cockpit with a farthing candle in his hand and an expression of marked discontent upon his face.

'Here is your mate, doctor,' said Mr Jones.

'Thank you, Mr Jones,' said the surgeon, looking a trifle less vexed. 'And Mr Jones, if you should see that damned loblolly-boy, give him a great kick, will you, and send him to me? I sent him,' he explained to Tobias, 'I sent him half an hour ago to the bo'sun for a man to refashion your screen – a pretty simple message, I believe.'

Mr Eliot afloat was not altogether the same as Mr Eliot ashore: much more authoritative, less loquacious and companionable; and at this moment he was out of humour. His natural benignity had prompted him to come down to see to Tobias' quarters, which (as he said) few surgeons would have done, but by now a large number of little irritations had mounted up, so that he felt distinctly aggrieved by Tobias. 'Andrew!' he shouted into the echoing cavern of the gun-deck, 'Andrew! Blast that brute-beast to the nethermost bottom of Hell. Ah, there you are. Where have you been? Ah, lumpkin!' cried the surgeon, sweeping his hand in the general direction of the boy's head.

'The bo'sun says it is the carpenter's business,' said the boy, ducking.

'What a disobliging dog that bo'sun is,' said the surgeon. 'A shabby fellow – a Gosport truepenny. It is always the same, Mr Barrow: he knows the carpenter is ashore. I wished to have this screen arranged so, do you see?' he said, holding up a piece of canvas. Tobias' eyes were by now thoroughly accustomed to the murk, and he saw that he was in an enclosure about nine feet by twelve, made of canvas up to five feet high on two sides, while an immense chest with a prodigious number of small drawers closed the third side. Mr Eliot was holding a loose piece of canvas across the fourth. 'This would give you a surprising degree of privacy, could we but fix it,' he said. 'It is a magnificent cockpit, upon my word – almost a standing cabin. And look at the head-room! Even I need hardly stoop, and you can stand quite upright, at least in the middle. You should have seen the hole I started my career in. Half the size, and there were three of us, one a very nauseating companion. But we might as well make it even better, and screen you from the view of our future patients: a little privacy is a wonderful thing at sea.'

'Sir,' said Tobias, 'I am infinitely obliged to you, for your attention to my comfort.'

'And well you may be,' said Mr Eliot, 'for there's not another surgeon in the service who would do half as much.' Then, feeling that this was a little more ungracious than he had meant, he showed Tobias the medicine-chest, and offered him a draught of medicinal brandy, or a spoonful of syrup of squills, and anything that he might fancy in the way of melissa balm, Venice treacle or aniseed julep. In the course of a lifetime spent among drugs he had acquired a taste for many of them, a taste shared, to some extent, by Tobias and the loblolly-boy, and for a while they browsed among the tinctures, linctuses and throches, mixing themselves small personal prescriptions – mandragora, opium, black hellebore. 'We operate here,' said Mr Eliot, 'in time of action,' and he showed Tobias the instruments.

'This is a very fine trepan,' said Tobias, holding up a wicked machine for boring holes in one's skull.

'Yes,' said Mr Eliot. 'The last time I used that was on the second lieutenant of the *Sutherland*, a very obstinate case of melancholy. I conceived that it would relieve him.'

'Did it do so, sir?'

'He was a most ungrateful patient.'

Tobias thought it as well to change the subject, and observed, 'Here are bandages; here are needles and sutures. If we were to make a hole in this piece of wood with the trepanning-iron and pass a bandage through it, we could fasten the screen, by sewing the flaps as though it were a Gemelli's prosection.'

'Very good,' said Mr Eliot, whose temper had been largely restored by a saline draught and a blue pill; and seizing the trepan he bored the standard with a skill and celerity that reflected much upon the gratitude of the second lieutenant of the *Sutherland*. Speed is of vital importance to those who must operate without anaesthetics, and Mr Eliot, seconded by Tobias, whipped up the canvas erection as if they were racing against a stop-watch.

'It will do,' said the surgeon, snipping the last suture and standing back, as if from a patient. 'About two minutes, I believe. Now I will leave you, Mr Barrow, and I shall expect to see you at eight o'clock in the morning, abaft the foremast: the rest of the day is your own. If there is anything you want, pass the word for one of the loblolly-boys, or come to my cabin, which is on the starboard side of the half-deck, next to the master's. I dare say his mates will invite you to mess with them.' With these words he walked off, followed by his attendant, leaving Tobias in the cockpit; leaving him, too, in a state of confusion. He sat in the gloom, repeating 'abaft the foremast' in an undertone, and trying to reconcile his ideas of the healthiness of a sea-going life – unlimited fresh open air, and light – with this appallingly fetid den in the darkness. He tried to remember the way by which he had been led into the cockpit; he wondered whether it would be improper to leave it, whether he would ever be fed, and if so, where. A little later there was a strange drumming noise, followed by an unrestrained bawling and hallooing: a body of men rushed along the deck, lit now by occasional gleams and the opening of ports, and the canvas walls of Tobias' berth bulged inwards as human forms blundered past it, to vanish as suddenly as they had come, with a spirited howl.

'If I had had more presence of mind,' said Tobias aloud, feeling his way slowly out of the cockpit, 'I would have asked them the way. It might not have looked well, however: and I shall certainly find it myself, sooner or later.' He was particularly anxious not to expose Jack as the possessor of a discreditably ignorant friend; he had, without being able to define the immediate causes, been aware of Jack's uneasiness on several occasions, and although for himself he was totally indifferent to public opinion, he now, on reaching the main well-pump ladder, crept silently down it into the hold.

When he had crawled over six of the lower futtocks, he found himself against the bulkhead of the bread-room, and here he was obliged to stop, for there was no way of getting farther aft. He was entirely surrounded by vast shrouded forms, very faintly to be surmised by the strangled remnant of light that filtered down through four successive gratings: rats moved about, and the unseen bilges slopped drearily underfoot. He no longer knew which way round he was.

Immediately above him, separated by some thirty feet of perpendicular distance, Jack and the purser took leave of one another.

'You will commend my humble duty to his lordship,' said the purser, 'and if there is any way in which I can oblige you, I shall be most happy.'

'You are very good,' said Jack; and as soon as the purser had gone he wiped his hand, for Mr Hervey had been very zealous in shaking it. 'I wonder what he wants,' he thought, looking after the purser: Jack was not unduly cynical, but he was aware of the facts of life. 'Probably one of the livings,' he surmised, quite accurately, as it happened. His grandfather, Lord Berkeley (Jack was disgustingly well-connected, and there were lords in every direction, in his family), had two livings in his gift, whose present incumbents were very old; and Jack had more than once received marked civilities and attentions from clergymen and their relatives. He always accepted anything that was going in this line with a natural cheerful corruptness, and now he looked about the cabin with intense satisfaction: it was an odd, long, thin space squeezed between the wardroom bulkhead and the first lieutenant's cabin, and if the *Wager* had carried a normal complement of lieutenants it would certainly have belonged to one of them, if not to two, for it was much too valuable a space to be occupied by any midshipman, however gaudy his connexions. It had a bunk of rather curious lines, excellently adapted for a triangular dwarf, two lockers and just enough room to sling a hammock; it had no light or air, of course, except that which could make its way through the door, but it represented a degree of comfort that Jack could not have looked for legitimately for years to come.

'I must find Toby,' said he, and he hurried forward to the midshipmen's berth. Here there was an apprehensive thin youth, but no Toby. 'Hallo,' he said to the thin boy. 'My name is Byron. Have you seen the surgeon's mate? A little cove in black?'

'No, sir,' said the thin boy, standing to attention.

'Never mind me,' said Jack, 'I'm only a midshipman. If he should come in, beg him to wait for me, will you? I am going down to the cockpit.'

He drew a blank in the cockpit, although he waited there for some time; but reflecting that Tobias would probably be with the surgeon in his cabin revolving the ghastly topics of their trade, he went back to the berth: he had heard the noise of several parties returning to the ship while he was below, and he was not surprised to find two more midshipmen there. One was a big, fleshy fellow with a red face and a loud laugh, and the other was a dark, pock-marked, wry-mouthed creature with a Scotch accent.

The fat, jolly midshipman was amusing himself by interrogating the thin boy, an obviously new arrival, who was standing stiffly before him, terrified. 'Here, you,' called out the inquisitor, on seeing Jack. 'Come here and give an account of yourself. Double up.'

'Damn your blood,' said Jack mildly, sitting on a locker. 'Do you think my name is Green?'

'I suppose you are Byron?' asked the other, with a grin. 'Your chest came aboard just now: Ransome of the *Centurion* brought it – he only hooked on, and said he would see you again. My name is Cozens, and this is Campbell. I was only trying it on: for a laugh, you know. You ain't offended?'

'Never in life,' said Jack, shaking hands.

'Ye're the pairson wha's tookit yon pigwidgeon cabin,' said Campbell. From this point onwards it must be understood that Campbell spoke broad Scotch at all times, although his remarks will be put down in English; for the representation of a dialect is tedious, inaccurate and often incomprehensible. On this occasion the only part of the remark that Jack clearly understood was the unfriendliness of the tone; but he was saved from making any reply by the hubbub of all hands being piped for dinner.

66

'Who's the senior among us?' asked Jack, as they sat over the frugal delights provided for the midshipmen.

'I am,' said Cozens.

'Well then, do you mind if I bring a friend into our mess? He is the surgeon's mate, a capital fellow.'

'Bring a dozen, mate. The more the merrier, I always say,' said Cozens, laughing heartily. 'I love a crowd.'

'It is not regular,' said Campbell.

'What do you say?' said Jack to the new midshipman, whose name was Morris.

'Certainly,' said Morris.

'Well, that is kind and handsome in the mess,' said Jack. 'I shall introduce him this evening – he is a very learned cove, and excellent company. I say,' he said, stretching, 'what an amazingly spacious berth this is. In the *Sovereign* you could scarcely eat for the elbows each side of you.'

'You expect to have elbow-room in an Indiaman – she's only a cursed Indiaman really, you know,' said Cozens. 'But you wait till the soldiers come aboard – we shall have a charming great crowd –'

He was interrupted by a quartermaster, who, standing in the doorway and putting his knuckle to his right-hand eyebrow, cried in a harsh, complaining tone, 'Now, Mr Byron, sir, what about this here chest? It can't lay about on deck all day,' – winking and nodding in order to make it clear that he was not in earnest.

'Why, it's Rose,' cried Jack, recognising an old shipmate. 'How are you, Rose? I'm very glad to see you. As for my chest, stow it in . . .' and then, conceiving that it might be tactless just now to shout about his cabin, he got up, and said, 'Come along, I will show you. How do you come to be aboard, and are there any more old Pembrokes?' he asked, leading the way – the *Pembroke* had been his ship before the *Royal Sovereign*. The quartermaster had been sent into the *Wager*, Jack learnt, because he had experience of stowing a siege-train, and one of the *Wager's* chief purposes in life was to carry battering-pieces to argue with the Spaniards on the Pacific – a much more convincing argument, in the eyes of all her crew, than the bales of trade-goods, broad-cloth, beads and basins that filled the after-hold and even part of the bread-room.

'I will show them to you, if you like,' said the quartermaster, having filled the cabin with Jack's sea-chest, 'for we are going below directly, to make all fast, and it will be the last any man-jack will see of 'em until' – here he shaded his mouth with the back of his hand – 'we're in the Great South Sea.'

'Not the same as the dear old *Pembroke*,' observed Jack, as they passed along the roomy bays on the gun-deck, where the men slung their hammocks.

'Not the same by no means,' said Rose emphatically; and after he had shown Jack the hold and some of the finer points of stowing a very heavy and dangerously movable cargo, he returned to this subject. The dear old *Pembroke* might have been a pig in a cross-sea, he said, and she might have had the narrowest cruel hatches known in creation; there was certainly no room in her for a man to spit, as he might say, in a manner of speaking; she was an unhealthy ship, with mould three fingers deep on the beams, and the dear old *Pembroke* was obliged to be pumped morning, noon and night; but he would rather have the old *Pembroke* than a dozen *Wagers*, however dry and well found. Because why? Because the *Pembroke's* crew, though an ill-faced parcel of thieves to be sure, were men-of-war's men. You knew what to expect. With the people of this ship you did *not* know what to expect: he had never seen anything like it. In thirty-one years odd months of service he had never seen anything like it. 'It is not that they are pressed men,' he said – 'we are all pressed men, more or less. But I tell 'ee, Mr Byron, if anything untoward or nasty, as I might say in a manner of speaking – if anything should happen, with such a pack aboard, why, mark my words –' Here he raised the lantern to give solemnity to his foreboding, uttered a terrible scream, clawed the air past Jack's left ear, struck his head against an upper-futtock rider and fell trembling in the bilge.

'I beg your pardon,' said Tobias, just behind Jack, 'but can you tell me where the midshipmen are to be found?'

'No,' said Jack, speaking with the harsh pipe of a very aged man; 'there ain't none left, your honour, in consequence of salt being sprinkled on their victuals, whereupon they died in terrible agony.'

'Jack,' cried Tobias, with unfeigned relief, 'I could not find my way to the top floor.'

'In my opinion,' said Jack, 'you would get lost in an open boat.'

'I was trying to get back to the place where I last saw you,' said Tobias.

'What made you think that I would be crawling about the hold?' asked Jack; and when he thought of the hideous lingering end that might have come about he grew angry and said, 'Don't you know that this part of the hold is going to be sealed? What do you think would have happened to you? You would have been starved, and the rats would have eaten you.'

The quartermaster was also extremely vexed at having taken him for the ghost of his deceased wife's sister, and he wanted to know whether Mr Barrow knew the difference between up and down – a difference clear to quite unintelligent people. They both set about him: they repeatedly asked him what he thought he was doing in the *hold* – his being in the *hold* particularly exasperated them, and his inability to explain how he got there. 'Why not the forepeak? Or the bread-room? There would be some sense in that.'

When they had badgered him enough, both being impressed by the enormity of what might have happened, they undertook to explain what he should have done.

'You come out of the cockpit,' said Jack.

'Or orlop, as you might say,' added Rose.

'And there's the whole length of the gun-deck before you.'

'No, Jack,' said Tobias, 'I assure you there was not a gun there.'

'Bah,' said Jack impatiently. 'Of course not. You don't expect guns on the gun-deck of a *one-decker*, do you?'

Tobias admitted that he had thought it rather likely – that he could not otherwise see the value of the name.

'Guns on the gun-deck,' said the quartermaster, with intense relish. 'He looked for to find 'em there; hor, hor.'

'We only *call* it the gun-deck,' explained Jack. 'The guns are all on the upper-deck and quarter-deck, which is natural in a one-decker. The *Wager* is a one-decker, Toby.'

'But there are at least four storeys, or decks, as you say in your jargon,' cried Tobias, with some indignation.

'Ah,' replied Jack at once, 'we only *call* her a one-decker, you see.'

'Guns on the gun-deck; heu, heu, heu,' said the quartermaster to himself. 'Rich. Very rich, heu, heu, heu.'

'Now you come out of the cockpit,' Jack began again.

'No, Mr Byron, sir,' interposed the quartermaster, 'you might as well save your breath. There are minds that reason cannot reach, no, nor kind words persuade: they have to be drove – took by the hand and shown each halliard and brace or deck, as the case may be. And,' he added, with a recollection of beating the bounds of the parish in his long-distant childhood, 'it is best to whip them right severely when you are a-doing of it. And some there are,' he concluded, 'who can never be brought to understand what you tell them, not if it is ever so.'

It is very clear that Tobias belonged in this last hopeless category, and that he would go on looking for guns on the gun-deck out of mere ill-will and brutish stupidity to the end of his days. And as they ascended through the body of the ship, with occasional glimpses of the light of day through various gratings and ports, Tobias was inclined to agree with this harsh estimate of his abilities. It seemed to him that he would never be able to make out this maze of ladders, dank recesses and unlit passages.

Yet what will not custom do? Or, as one might say, how prepotent is not habitude? Long before the squadron sailed, Tobias knew his way perfectly well, and when, after they had spent forty days at sea, he heard the cry of 'Land ho, on the starboard bow,' he darted below for a telescope; not finding it in their cabin, he recollected that he had taken it down to the cockpit to clean the lenses with spirits of wine, and he ran down there and back without the slightest conscious thought – his feet found their own way, counted the steps from the quarter-deck to the upper-deck and from the upper-deck to the gun-deck – they brought him to and from with automatic ease, although the *Wager* was rolling with her usual heavy skittishness.

It was only a little more than a month, but already it seemed natural to him that the deck should perpetually move under his feet, that he should be sick if it moved more than a certain amount, and that he should begin his day at one bell in the forenoon watch, stationed abaft the foremast, while the loblolly-boy beat with a pestle upon a brass mortar and cried

'Pills

For all ills.'

In these forty days he had grown accustomed to the ordered routine that underlay the apparently chaotic running about and noise of the ship's work. He was no longer amazed that Jack should appear at all hours of the day or night, coming or going, according to his watch, or that he himself should be precipitated from his bed, now and then, in lively weather. And such is the force of custom that both he and his stomach accepted salt pork on Monday, salt beef on Tuesday, dried peas on Wednesday, salt pork on Thursday, dried peas on Friday, salt beef on Saturday, salt pork on Sunday, and so on in a sequence varied only by their private stores – a not inconsiderable variation, however, for their sailing had been so delayed that Jack's grandfather had had time to come down and see him, as well as two uncles and a cousin, all of whom had been pretty liberal in the way of presents; these presents had mostly been converted into food and drink (a very prudent measure), and although they had made great inroads, there still remained a coop of hens in the gangway, a contemplative pig below, and in their cabin, besieged by rats, a whole Cheshire cheese, the better part of an enormous keeping cake from Medenham, and some strong, flat, greyish objects of surprising weight, baked by Georgiana's maiden hand and decorated with calcined raisins, lovingly arranged in the form of conventional trees.

It was forty days since they had at last set sail from St Helen's, after several ignominious false starts; and for Jack at least they had been forty very full days. The *Wager*, like all the other ships in the squadron, was undermanned; not only was she undermanned, but a great many of the crew were landsmen, and they had to be taught their duty – unwilling, seasick and frightened pupils, many of them, and some uncommonly brutal in their stupidity and resentment. This would have made her voyage troublesome in any case, but as it fell out, foul weather had met them on almost every single day since the signal for their departure had broken out from the *Centurion*'s mizzen, and this had made it exceedingly laborious and exasperating. The passage to Madeira might, with a fair wind, have taken no more than twelve days or a fortnight of easy sailing; but it had taken forty, and everybody aboard was thoroughly displeased – apart from anything else, it was generally understood that if they did not reach the high southern latitudes before January, they would have missed the only good season for sailing round the Horn.

These forty days had been hard and frustrating: Captain Kidd,

71

Mr Bean, his lieutenant, and Mr Clerk, the master, were good-tempered men, but the effort of driving this new crew, and of keeping exactly to their allotted station in spite of every difficulty, had worn them to a pitch of hard ferocity that would have surprised their friends at home. But it was wonderful to see how this cloud of depression lifted from off the ship at the cry of land: it was just at two bells in the morning watch, at five o'clock in the first grey of the dawn, when one can see farthest – and although this is ordinarily a time when even the hardened mariner is feeling a little jaded, within a minute of the look-out's cry the decks were alive with the watch below, all looking as bright and pleased as the watch on duty.

Tobias was up already, although he belonged to neither watch and could have lain abed until the noise of breakfast. He grudged every waking hour that kept him from watching the sea or the sky, and at the time land was seen he was in the act of trailing a jelly-bag along the surface from the larboard cathead in the hope of catching some of the very small pedunculated cirripedes that he had found, the day before, in the stomach of a dissected procellaria. At the cry he abandoned the pedunculated cirripedes, fetched his telescope, and climbed laboriously into the foretop, where he knew he would find Jack: this was nominally Jack's watch below, but Tobias did not now have to be told that it was only *called* below, and that in fact Jack would station himself in one of the highest convenient parts of the ship.

It was doubly certain that Jack would be up there today, for it was for this particular morning that he had foretold the landfall. He prided himself on his skill in navigation – an art, rather than a science, for at that time one of the most important factors in finding your longitude at sea was your own personal judgment of the ship's way – and he had been rather more public and confident in his prophecy than was altogether wise: he had stationed himself in the foretop very early that day, willing Madeira to rise above the south-western horizon with all the power available to him.

'There you are, Toby,' he cried, hearing a familiar snorting on the shrouds. 'Have a care, now,' he said, leaning over the edge, as anxious as a hen. Toby was a wretched topman; he climbed stiffly, with pale determination, munching as he came, and he took no notice whatever of Jack's agitated warnings to take care, to mount one ratline at a time, to hold the shrouds, to wait for the roll. He had early discovered that height terrified him, and every day, seasick or not, he had, with rigid obstinacy, crept painfully up to the foretop, there to exult in silent triumph, with the view of the whole squadron before him if the foresail happened not to be set (the *Wager* came last in the line) or the great expanse of sea to the windward if it were – a sea that might at any moment disclose a whale in its bosom, or a wide-ranging sea-bird upon its surface. Jack lived in terror of the day when Tobias should decide that the top was not enough, and he threw out many hints to the effect that an ascent of the topmast would be gross folly, and an attempt upon the topgallant masthead criminal ostentation; but he doubted their utility – even now he had another example of his friend's odd kind of courage, for Tobias' head came through the lubber's hole, followed by the rest of his person and the telescope. The lubber's hole is a square space cut in the broad platform that forms the top; it is conveniently situated there, at the head of the shrouds of the lower mast, so that anyone who wishes to go up into the top may do so with comparative ease and safety: but, of course, it is never used. An old lady visiting the ship might possibly go through it, or an admiral with a reputation so well established that he could afford any eccentricity; but every-body else reaches the top by the futtock-shrouds, an uncomfortable assemblage of ropes that run from near the masthead below out to the edge of the top, so that a man climbing them must of necessity hang backwards.

'Why do you not use the futtock-shrouds?' Cozens had asked, winking round the table in the midshipmen's berth, after the first time that Tobias had been seen to go aloft.

'It would frighten me too much,' Tobias replied, adding with the utmost candour, 'I am of a very timid disposition: I am far from being so brave and fearless as you.' This last had quite dumb-founded Cozens, who had not been at all sure how to take it, and who had finished by laughing in an uncertain and particularly vacant manner.

So every day Tobias came up through the gate of ignominy: and on this day, the twenty-fifth of October, 1740, according to the old, or Julian, style of reckoning, he had the infinite gratification of seeing a remote, dark lowering on the rim of the sky, which was Madeira, the first milestone on their great journey to lands and seas unknown.

73

Chapter Five

THE CHARMING TOWN of Funchal was unusually animated, for not only were there a good many privateersmen and the crews of two East India Company's ships ashore, but also every one of the fifteen hundred seamen and five hundred soldiers of Commodore Anson's squadron who could get leave.

Jack was one of these: he sat now on the terrace of a wine-shop, sheltered from the brilliant sun by a vine, sipping a glass of the best Madeira and surveying the bay, with the men-of-war and the merchant ships and the boats that plied to and fro. There was music behind him and on either side, while before him, in the open courtyard of a tavern at a lower level, there was music again, and dancing. The scene was one of universal gaiety; yet Jack looked upon it with a dark and bilious eye – he watched the people in the street below with indifference, and he watched his shipmates dancing the pimponpet in the tavern below that with real dislike. The pimponpet may be described, according to the most accurate definition current at the time, as 'a Kind of antic Dance, when three Persons hit one another on the Breech with one of their Feet.' The three persons were Cozens and the two junior lieutenants of marines from the *Wager*, and they trundled indefatigably round and round, rising at every fifth note to kick one another, with roars of laughter: round and round they went, cheered by a motley crew of bo'sun's mates, shiny young gentlemen with curls from the lower parts of the town, and inebriated seamen.

'You may say what you like,' he said to Keppel, 'but at least the *Centurion* is run as a man-of-war and not an infernal merchantman. You would not believe the airs our gunner gives himself: it is perfectly monstrous that a gunner should be a watch-keeping officer. And then your berth may be pretty crowded – I dare say it is – but it is crowded with tolerably agreeable fellows, I believe; you do not have

74

to put up with a great oaf like that.' He nodded in the direction of Cozens, still bounding tirelessly about. 'Nor with a dismal Scotch crow, who is never content unless he is slighted or put-upon.' Draining his glass and thumping it down in a very ill-humoured way, he asserted that it would have been far better if the Lords of the Admiralty had made up their minds in the first place whether the *Wager* was to be a store-ship or a man-of-war. 'She can't be both,' said he, 'for it is against nature, and every man aboard feels it, whether he knows it or not. What is more,' he added, with the inconsequence of exasperation, 'the bo'sun is a thorough-paced villain, and our solitary lieutenant is an old woman – a pitiable creature.'

'What a foaming rage you are in,' said Keppel, looking at Jack with some wonder. 'But if you want more lieutenants, you are very welcome to every single one of ours – a parcel of scrubs, I assure you, and not a seaman among them.' This vile slander was still quivering upon the outraged air when the first lieutenant of the *Centurion* passed by in the street below, and his keen eye, turning by chance upon Keppel, seemed to pierce his being for evidence of sin. 'That is to say,' said Keppel, in a somewhat daunted tone, 'I am sure you do not have to come down on people so unholy severe, merely on account of a trifling error in steering.' Keppel, in charge of the *Centurion*'s cutter, had been distracted by the remarks of a privateer's boat at the wrong moment, and he had rammed his parent ship with extraordinary violence, which was no way to make the first lieutenant love him.

Jack was about to reply when the sound of Cozens' laugh interrupted him, a braying noise that echoed far and wide. 'Bah,' cried Jack, 'that flaming ape has begun again.' Cozens had worn out the two redcoats, and he was circling with Morris, the thin midshipman, now much attached to him, and the shiniest of all the locals.

'You are in a bad way – quite hipped,' said Keppel. 'I think you ought not to drink any more of that stuff until we have had something to eat.'

Jack very deliberately filled his glass, and looking Keppel firmly in the eye he drank it down. He would not for the world have admitted that he was either hipped or in a bad way, but in fact he was both. To begin with, he was far too hot: secondly, he had wandered about all the forenoon, and although he had very much

75

enjoyed showing Tobias sugar-cane and custard apples and bananas growing, thirty-six varieties of horse-flies, leeches and mosquitoes had bitten him; he was itching all over, and he was tired out. Thirdly, he had appointed with his friends to meet at this place for dinner, and he had now been waiting for more than an hour, intolerably hungry. Lastly, he had spent his time drinking sweet Madeira; it is a delightful wine to drink in small quantities, with cake, but drunk by the pint upon an empty stomach it has the most dismal effects.

So what with fatigue, sticky heat, irritation, faintness from want of food, unbearable itch and nausea, Jack was indeed in a bad way: it was this that led him to speak so venomously of his shipmates, for in general he never did – in general he was a very tolerant person, uncensorious and easily amused – by no means a backbiter. He felt a little uneasy, even now, and he said, 'I do not mean Cozens is a bad-hearted fellow. Not at all. Only he has such a flow of animal spirits that he is obliged to make a vast brutish noise all day and night – practical jokes every day of the week – and the least drop of brandy or rum goes straight to his head, and then we have a scene. But he means no harm, and the men love him.'

'There they are,' cried Keppel, pointing through the crowd of Portuguese, Lascars, Barbary Moors, Negroes and English seamen to where Ransome and Tobias came down the hill, riding in an ox-drawn sledge, the usual conveyance of those parts.

'At last,' said Jack angrily. 'Damn their impertinence: two hours late. This will need a great deal of explanation.' He was prepared to be offended and disagreeable, but as they came nearer, grinning all over their faces, loaded with the animal, vegetable and mineral productions of Madeira and looking thoroughly delighted, he found that his surliness vanished of itself, and he was unable to do more than curse their vitals with his ordinary benignity.

He and Keppel instantly began ordering dinner: they added O to any vaguely French or Latin word they happened to remember, and shouted very loud and clear in imperfect English when the foreign words ran out.

'You bring um soupo et pano first,' explained Keppel, 'then pisces fresco – you got um, pisces fresco? And vino blanco: not sweet, seco.'

'Me no want vino,' said Jack. 'Vino for the other senhores, com-prenny?'

'And then carno, viando. Not goat. No capricorno.'

'Oh no,' put in Ransome, looking sharp and attentive, 'no capricorno.'

The ordering took a long, long time, but eventually their meal arrived, capricorno or not, and they ate it with immense zeal. Food always had a mellowing effect on Jack: by the end of the first dish it could scarcely be detected that he had ever been out of humour; by the end of the seventh he was restored to all his usual complaisance, and beamed greasily upon the assembled company.

'What is meant by the owner of a vessel?' asked Toby, suddenly speaking for the first time.

'The captain,' they replied.

'Are you making game of me?' he asked, looking at them very narrowly. His trusting nature had been much imposed upon, and with advancing age he was growing wary and suspicious.

'No, no; I assure you that it is so,' said Keppel. 'We call him the owner, although the ship is the King's. Ain't it so, Ransome?'

'Yes, cully,' said Ransome reassuringly. 'It's a kind of joke. Hor, hor.'

'It is a joke, Toby: he is only *called* the owner for a joke,' said Jack. 'But what about it?'

'Well, the owner of the *Gloucester* is going home. He has a very obstinate marasmus.'

'How do you know?'

Toby was surprised to find his news received with such attention; he told them that Mr Eliot and the other surgeons had been called in that morning and that their unanimous verdict was that Captain Norris must return to a northern climate at once; he assured them that a recovery was probable, and he would have explained the nature of the disease, supposing that to be the reason for their interest. He had yet to learn that the strongest passion in a naval bosom is concerned with promotion, and that although none of his hearers yet had his commission they were all thoroughly imbued with the spirit of the service, and regarded the sweeping-off of a post-captain with the same ghoulish delight as if they had been lieutenants and therefore in line for an upward step. Besides, the question had an immediate bearing for Jack and Tobias, in that their captain would certainly be changed.

'Mitchel will have the *Gloucester*,' said Keppel, who was a walking compendium of naval seniority, 'and Mr Kidd will go to the *Pearl*.'

'Yes. You'll lose your captain, cock,' said Ransome.

'I had not thought of that,' said Tobias. 'I am concerned to hear it.'

Captain Dandy Kidd was an old friend of Mr Eliot's; they had been shipmates in many commissions, and, as Mr Eliot had often told his mate, the lot of the surgeon aboard the *Wager* was unusually agreeable for this reason – nowhere else would they have such liberty for philosophical experiment, nor such facilities.

'It will be Captain Murray for us,' said Jack sombrely, and in a low tone he added, 'They say the *Tryall* is not a happy ship.'

'He's all right,' said Keppel. 'It is his first lieutenant that is so disagreeable.'

'A proper – he is,' said Ransome. 'I served along of him in the *Royal Oak*. A wery spiteful cove, as loved to see a man flogged: there was a landsman, name of Murdoch – Stanley Murdoch – that we had pressed out of a Scotch smack from Leith for London: he was a passenger in it. He did not like being pressed, and he said something disrespectful. "Oh," says the lieutenant, "do you presume to say that to me? I'll serve you out," says he, "you fat dog." This poor Murdoch was heavy; not paunchy, but thick, and he wheezed something cruel when made to run or go aloft – asthma. It was "Murdoch, lie aloft," every day; and as he always kept a flogging for the last man off the yard, it was Murdoch copped it every morning. One day the poor soul tried to jump for the main topgallant backstay, to be down sooner, for he was rendered desperate, you understand; but being a landsman, he missed it.'

'Poor wretched Tryalls,' said Keppel, 'they will have to make the best they can of it, for he's the senior lieutenant, and must succeed. An't he the senior lieutenant in the squadron, Ransome?'

'Who?' asked Ransome, who had stepped away to stare better into the harbour.

'Cheap.'

'I dare say he is,' said Ransome, considering. 'He was made master and commander when they took the Salee rover with the boats, in thirty-six; so I dare say he is. God help his crew, when he comes to be captain.'

78

'Did you say Cheap?' asked Tobias.

'Yes.'

'A squat, thick-bodied, yellow-faced man with a cast in his eye? Speaks with a rude northern accent?'

'Yes. He is from Scotland, and he is no beauty.'

'Toby,' cried Jack, 'what have you been doing?'

'I only begged him to hold my serpent while I stepped into the boat: I spoke very civilly – bowed, desired him to excuse the freedom, and would he hold my serpent while I stepped into the boat? He replied with a very cynical degree of asperity, damning my eyes, damning my blood and liver, no he would not hold my serpent and who did I think he was? I told him, an ill-looking fellow, that had yet to be taught the usages of civilised society.'

'Oh dear me,' said Keppel, in the middle of an appalled silence.

'What happened then?' asked Jack.

'Nothing. The boat rowed away. But I called out after him that he need not have been so afraid – the serpent was comatose, and in any case it was a coluber. He called back in a great passion; he mentioned his name and said he would remember me; but I was resolved not to notice him and I walked off directly. The Portuguese in his boat – it was a bum-boat – were infinitely diverted by his passion: the Portuguese are a good-natured, amicable nation, as far as I can see.'

'So they are, cully,' said Ransome, 'and I would advise you to spend the rest of your days among 'em, rather nor set foot aboard the *Tryall*. Because why? Because he would learn you the usages of the gunner's daughter, that's why.'

'It is very ridiculous and illiberal, this fear of serpents,' said Tobias. 'I remarked upon it to the commodore . . .'

'Oh no,' cried Jack, with a strangled shriek of protest.

'Yes,' said Tobias. 'Mr Anson was just putting off in his boat – no, in his barge,' Tobias corrected himself, with a smile, for he knew Jack liked him to use the correct nautical terms. 'So I told him that he would oblige me extremely by carrying me as far as the *Wager*, if it lay in his way. Yet even he seemed shy of the snake, though I told him how innocent it was: but the commodore is a very polite man – he told me something of the habits of the frigate-bird, and said he hoped to see some as soon as we were south of the thirtieth parallel. He bade me keep an account of the longitude and latitude at which each sea-bird was found, as being an observation useful to sea-faring men.'

'Well, I am glad you approved of his manners,' said Jack; and turning to the others with quiet despair he said, 'You see how it is? I try day and night to teach him the difference between an admiral and a swabber's mate; I entreat him to mind his duty towards his betters, and what happens? "Just pull me across to the *Wager*, Anson, my good man; and hold this serpent while you are about it." Next it will be "Captain Murray, I will trouble you for the use of your state-room, if you please, to keep my luminous squids in." Oh damn your eyes, Toby, have I not told you a thousand times not to speak to your superiors unless they speak to you first? I don't believe he thinks he has any superiors, Heaven preserve him.'

'In Plato's Republic . . .' began Tobias.

'But you are not in Plato's loathsome vile republic,' cried Jack. 'You are in the Royal Navy, and must never speak to anyone. At least, nobody above you in rank.'

'I do not know how you can be so ungrateful,' said Tobias, 'for I told the commodore, as we rowed along, what a worthy, deserving creature you were; and he was visibly impressed by my words.'

There were a good many points upon which Jack and Tobias did not see eye to eye, apart from the desirability of chatting with captains and commodores; one difference concerned the proportion of their cabin that could reasonably be devoted to reptiles, and another was about the relative worth of their ship, considered either as a man-of-war or as a home.

Jack was very good in the matter of birds and mammals; fish he admitted without a word; even the octopus glowed faintly through the night in its bell-jar without protest from him, and the interesting Madeiran wood-slugs crept about in the company of their insect friends with no more than a silent shudder: but when a man comes down at the end of the middle watch, fagged out and ready to turn in, only to find that the scorpions have got out and are playing in his bed, together with a large assortment of serpents – why, then, in Jack's opinion, things have gone too far.

Then, as to the *Wager* herself, Jack judged her with a mind formed by a certain amount of naval experience: he had not been a great while at sea, but the service he had seen was remarkably various. In any case, it did not need any extraordinary degree of penetration to see that the *Wager* was not an ideal ship. To begin with, she had more than her fair share of rogues aboard: if the crew had been sorted out, one third would have been good, steady seamen, quite reliable afloat, if somewhat given to the bottle when ashore; another third neither good nor bad – apt to follow the lead in either direction; but the last third was made up of the sweepings of various prisons and houses of correction. There were many landsmen in this last third, naturally; but there were some seamen in it too, and among these were faces that would have looked quite natural on Execution Dock, where pirates are hanged. Jack had served on the West Indies station, and he had seen a good many pirates – hard, brutal, very stupid and profoundly disagreeable men, for the most part. She was lucky not to have more, for Commodore Anson's squadron had been manned after two admirals commanding important fleets had had their pick; and just as the squadron came after the fleets, so the poor *Wager* came after the other ships of the squadron. The Navy was used to dealing with such people, and with bitterly resentful sailors pressed out of merchant ships coming into port after long voyages; but it meant rigid discipline and a great deal of punishment, and floggings every other day do not make for happiness. And then the *Wager* was not particularly fortunate in her warrant officers, either: for the Navy, though capable of almost anything, is not infallible, and the bo'sun (who has a great deal to do with the immediate direction of the hands) was so evil-tempered a fellow – unreliable and drunken – that it was a wonder that he had ever been given his warrant; the gunner, who had been a mate in the merchant service and who kept the master's watch when the master was ill, was almost as quarrelsome as the bo'sun, and prided himself beyond measure on his ability to navigate; and the sailing-master – the man who would have been the captain had the *Wager* been a merchant ship – was old, tired and ailing. As for Mr Bean, the only commissioned officer aboard other than the captain, Jack did not know what to make of him. In a fit of spleen he had described him to Keppel as 'an old woman', but this was by no means his considered opinion; the lieutenant had a curious hesitation in his speech that sometimes made him appear uncertain, he had the peculiarity of never swearing and he was an unusually quiet, reserved man. He was old for a lieutenant – grey-haired – but there had been a long period of peace, with little likelihood of promotion for anyone, and scarcely any at all for a man without interest, so that did not necessarily reflect upon his ability. The first lieutenants of Jack's last two ships had been tremendous fire-eaters, exceedingly fierce in word, deed and appearance, and Mr Bean showed palely in contrast with them: but he was obviously a good seaman.

Tobias, however, could never be brought to see that the *Wager* was anything but perfect – 'a very happily conceived vessel, with a great deal of room downstairs, and a sick-bay better than any other in the squadron.' But, then, Tobias' point of view was entirely unlike Jack's: for one thing, he was not there to see that work was properly done, but to help make the men well if they were sick; he had no authority over them, and they looked upon him in quite a different light; and whereas Jack was not altogether enchanted with his superiors, Tobias was perfectly content with his – he was immediately subject only to Mr Eliot, and Mr Eliot suited him very well.

Mr Eliot was not entirely perfect; he could be ill-tempered and sharp, and he had a reasonable number of bees in his bonnet; but he was an able surgeon, and he was very much concerned with curing his patients. He was much esteemed aboard, very much more than his military colleague, Mr Oakley, who was there to look after the marines, and who (like too many army and navy surgeons) believed every man who reported sick to be a malingerer until he was proved to be ill.

Mr Eliot was also pretty well acquainted with malingering; he was no fool, and he had not treated some thousands of sailors without learning something of their tortuous mental processes; but, as he said to Tobias, he would rather have a dozen malingerers impose upon him than turn away one genuinely sick man. In fact, he was very rarely deceived – far less often than Mr Oakley.

One result of this was that as the ship settled down and the lower-deck began to understand the nature of the officers, marines who felt unwell would insinuate themselves into the group of sick seamen, to be treated by the naval surgeon – a proceeding which led to the most violent resentment on the part of Mr Oakley. Mr

Eliot utterly discountenanced it, for one of the first principles of medical practice is that another man's patients must never be taken from him, nor his treatment adversely criticised. But discountenancing a practice does not always abolish it, and the ship's company remained obstinately attached to Mr Eliot in time of sickness.

An instance of this arose on that very morning, four days out from Madeira: it was a Tuesday, a very pleasant, warm and sweet-tempered Tuesday, with the sun two hours above the horizon on their larboard quarter, and a steady north-east breeze sending them roundly away under all plain sail on their south-western course over the width of the Atlantic for Brazil. The squadron was sailing in close, rigid formation, with the *Pearl* hull-down ahead, looking out for the Spaniards, and for once the *Wager* was keeping her station without any particular effort: she could sail well enough with a following or a quartering wind, and it was only when the wind came forward of her beam that she turned into a heavy, awkward and cross-grained slug.

They had scarcely had a single day of quartering wind all the way until this, the thirtieth parallel, but now the *Wager* was doing very well, and as Tobias stepped on deck a few minutes after the change of the morning watch, he saw her looking at her charming best: immediately before and above him the vast spread of the mainsail reflected the sun with a splendid whiteness on to the already whitened deck, left scrubbed and spotless by the departing watch, and under the steady thrust of the wind the lower edge of the huge sail swept in a pure, unchanging curve above the waist of the ship; the shadow of the mainsail, with this same curve repeated, fell across the foc's'le, above which the foresail made the same strong arc; on the foresail itself, as Tobias could very well see from the gangway, lay the shadow of the maintopsail and the crescent of blinding sunlight that shot between the topsail and the mainyard; and so throughout – a brilliant impression of enormous parallel curves, the strong lines of the yards across and the intensely blue and luminous sky. The *Wager* was running easily, making a good eight knots, and the long Atlantic swell came from the north – a following sea that passed under her nobly carved stern-gallery, where Captain Murray sat drinking coffee in a coffee-cup and admiring the glorious royal-blue ocean, under her counter to give her a long easy lift from behind;

the whole ship was alive, and the wind sang in her rigging. Her easy pitch was one of the rare motions that did not make Tobias sick: he walked forward champing with delight.

There was a good deal of animation on deck, quartermasters roaring, anxious seamen running and rope's ends flying, for the new captain had changed the *Wager* from a ship that kept watch and watch to a three-watch ship; the hands were not used to it yet, and the duller landsmen could not understand it at all. They blundered about in every direction, so Tobias made his way forward but slowly. Kindness and consideration had suggested this change: under the three-watch system a man may sometimes turn in for the whole night instead of never having more than four hours of sleep; and all the thanks the captain had was to be wished to the bottom of the sea 'with his new ways, damn 'un . . . not what we are used to.' They had been barely six weeks afloat, but custom had already grown very strong, almost immemorial: there is nothing like the sea for conservatism, and Tobias felt it as much as any; three months ago he had never seen a pair of trousers – seafaring garments unknown a mile inland – but now he wore them to the manner born, a working pair made of the strongest canvas known to man, by the sailmaker.

In this immemorial garment, therefore, he paced to the foremast, where Andrew awaited him with the great brass mortar; here he turned about and took up his immemorial position three paces to the starboard of the galley grating and five paces forward of the *Wager's* bell, while Andrew beat on the mortar and uttered his immemorial cry.

There were three cases of chronic indigestion, one sad toothache – remanded to the cockpit for extraction later – and then John Duck, able seaman, presented himself. He was a big fellow, rosy, powerful and in shining health; in a fine strong voice he proclaimed himself 'right poorly within, if you please, and no stomach for his meat.' He described a number of symptoms that he could not possibly have had, with a bare-faced mendacity that made Tobias stare: they were symptoms, however, that were entirely compatible with an attack of dysentery, and Tobias, not knowing what to say about it, said nothing for the present, but considered within himself. These public consultations on the foc's'le were very popular, sailors as a class being fascinated by disease, and there was a tendency on the part of the patients to exaggerate their sufferings, from vainglory: but it was rare that a hand should invent a malady altogether, particularly with such skill. Tobias looked at John Duck, who wore an expression of glazed and simpering innocence: he glanced at the onlookers, and noticed that their faces were unnaturally wooden.

'Why is John Duck telling such monstrous lies?' he asked himself: he looked up to the sky as he reflected upon this problem, and there between himself and heaven he saw Jack, casually suspended from the main topmast stay. He watched Jack as he walked over the yard and vanished behind the sail into the shrouds, where he and his party were setting up cat-harpings – the new captain's recipe for making the *Wager* sail closer to the wind. Looking away from this, Tobias brought his gaze to the ship's bell, which hung under an elegant little arch. 'Does he think that we shall believe him?' he wondered, and he peered through the little arch to the quarter-deck, where Mr Eliot was taking his half-dozen turns, a very recognisable figure in his black coat and full wig: behind him there were two of the marine officers – two splashes of red – and the blue of the officer of the watch. Mr Eliot always took a certain number of turns at this time, to show his independence of set hours and duties; when he had demonstrated this to his own satisfaction he invariably came to the foremast to see if there were anything interesting and to receive Tobias' report.

As Tobias watched him he turned short in his walk and stepped to the gangway, where Joe, the senior loblolly-boy, stood in expectation of his coming.

'John Duck,' said Tobias, 'stand aside. Good morning, sir.'

'Good morning, Mr Barrow,' said the surgeon. 'Do not let me interrupt you.'

'Not at all, sir. We have here a case of hypertrophy of the sollertia.'

Mr Eliot listened to Duck's tale, pommelled his sturdy frame and took his pulse; and then suddenly said, 'When did you say it began? It is of the first importance.'

John Duck, quite flustered by now, sought anxiously among the bystanders until he found a sad, wan marine, who held up three fingers.

'Three days, your honour,' said Duck.

'Three days? Are you quite sure?' The marine nodded: Duck

nodded. 'In that case,' said the surgeon, 'you may drink rice-water and eat nothing for three days; then you will find yourself much improved. Rice-water, my man, but without a grain of salt. One grain of salt and you are a corpse, a cadaver, a subject for dissection, food for the gentleman over the side; the late John Duck, A. B., formerly of the Royal Navy, amen. Sometime of his Majesty's ship *Wager*, his hash was settled by a grain of salt, in latitude 30°N., much regretted by his comrades.'

'Aye-aye, sir,' said the seaman, in a faint voice; and some of his shipmates, infinitely impressed, murmured 'Amen.'

'We must have him out this afternoon,' said Mr Eliot, walking over to the side and looking down through the clear blue water to the shark that swam under the curve of the bows, conveniently placed for anything that might be thrown from the galley. 'We must have him on deck, and I will show you what I mean about the piscine heart. What was that noise?'

'That metallic crash, sir, and the shrieking?'

'Yes.'

'We are immediately above the midshipmen's berth, sir.'

'That is Mr Cozens, doctor,' put in the ship's barber, who tended to presume upon the ancient association of barbers and surgeons. 'It is his joke. He empties water on the other young gentlemen, for a joke, ha, ha.'

'Mr Cozens and his joke,' said the bystanders, with benign approval. 'He loves his joke, ha, ha.'

'But there is the whole upper deck and the galley between us and the midshipmen's berth,' said the surgeon.

'Mr Cozens is wery fond of his joke, sir,' they told him.

He shrugged his shoulders, and the morning's consultation being done he walked away aft with Tobias, explaining the mild duplicity of John Duck.

'Yes, sir,' said Tobias, 'I thought as much. But I do not understand you in the article of salt. I speak under correction, but I cannot conceive that the marine would perish from a grain of salt – from ten grains of salt – from a peck of salt.'

'Can you not, Mr Barrow?' said the surgeon, looking at him side-ways. 'Can you not? Well, we have twenty minutes before we go into the sick-bay, so perhaps we may consider the physical nature of salt, and the metaphysical nature of salt, in my cabin. I say its metaphysical nature, Mr Barrow.'

Tobias made no reply, but gazed earnestly into his chief's face, and followed him along the quarter-deck, under the break of the poop, where stood the wheel with its two solemn quartermasters: one of these was Rose, and he winked secretly as Tobias passed, at the same time imitating the agony of one who has been bitten behind, by way of acknowledging Tobias' attention to a wound that he had received at Madeira.

The surgeon's cabin was against the bulkhead of the coach, on the starboard side; it was spacious, comfortable and particularly well lit. Waving Tobias to a seat, he said, 'If I am never better lodged than this, I shall die content. Now salt, Mr Barrow, has physical properties, as we all know; and it may have metaphysical properties . . .'

Mr Eliot held that nothing cures like faith: he held this very strongly and he could bring many examples from his own experience and from books to confirm his doctrine. He divided diseases into three sorts: those which could be treated by the knife, and which belonged to the chirurgeon; those few which would yield to drugs, and which fell to the physicians (a pompous, fanciful set of men in general, Mr Barrow), and those, the most numerous class, which were to be healed by the imagination – which were to be attacked through the imagination of the patient himself. Among these he ranged melancholy, dyspepsia, seasickness (whatever you may say, Mr Barrow) and, extraordinarily enough, scurvy.

'I have seen men within twelve hours of their death from scurvy who have been roused from their lethargy by the cry of a sail: that was in the year of Vigo, when we were cruising upon the Spaniards, much as we are doing now. I hope that this cruise may show you the same effect, from the same cause; for at Vigo, Mr Barrow, we took a million pieces of eight, which was pretty handsome, I believe. But that is nothing, they say, to the treasure that is waiting for us round the Horn – Chile, Peru and Panama . . .' He lapsed into a reverie for some minutes, and at the same time glided a guinea from the back of his hand to his palm, and from his palm away into his sleeve – an habitual gesture with him, performed with wonderful ease and celerity.

87

Mr Eliot took a harmless delight in conjuring, and by a happy coincidence his pastime and his profession could be practised together, the one helping the other; hitherto he had been shy of opening himself up on this subject to Tobias, because the practice was not only far from orthodox but it also had a certain remote hint of – his mind would not, even silently, pronounce the word *quackery*, but that was the expression that an enemy might have used.

'Let it be supposed, Mr Barrow,' he said, 'that Martha Smith comes to me, complaining of a headache, and I find that this headache is of the immaterial, or imaginary class. I can bleed her, of course, and cup her, and apply Spanish fly; but unless I can play upon her imagination (the soul of the trouble) her head will ache still. Do you follow me, Mr Barrow? Tobias Barrow, do you pursue my line of reasoning? Yes. Now it may very well be that this young lady supposes that an earwig has gained an entry to her brain, and is feasting upon it: a very usual idea, Mr Barrow. We may tell her that she is mistaken, that physically speaking she has no earwig and no headache at all; but will this make her feel any better? No, my dear sir, it will not. But if we syringe the young lady's meatus auditorius (always use a warm lixivium, Mr Barrow), and if in the bowl we find a fine brisk earwig? Eh?'

Tobias began to understand the reason for the existence of an old, worn, partially bald, very familiar white mouse, and of a grass-snake, a small eel whose water was surreptitiously changed from time to time, and a toad, all of whom led a very private and secluded life in a recess of the surgeon's cabin, together with the more legitimate leeches.

'To revert now to your seaman and his salt, Mr Barrow: certainly he may eat as much salt as the next man, and so may his dysenterical friend, the marine. But the man must drink his rice-water, and he must not eat. We cannot see him dosed, nor can we ensure that he will starve: how then are we to impress the importance of our recommendation upon his mind? Why, by coupling it with a surprising, an astonishing prohibition that will impinge upon his leaden, clownish imagination. And the more extravagant the assertion, so long as it remains just within the bounds of credibility, the better; for man has a natural gust for marvels, and he loves to believe that his complaint is cousin to a marvel – a very rare complaint. What do you say to that, Mr Barrow?' he asked, with an affectation of indifference.

'Sir,' said Tobias, 'I honour your penetration.'

'You are an honest fellow,' cried the surgeon, shaking him warmly by the hand; and as if to underline his words the number one quarter-deck gun went off with its usual unholy bang about six feet from their ears: it was followed by the other quarter-guns, and then, one after another, by the nine-pounders of the starboard broadside, so that in a moment the whole ship was vibrating and so filled with sound, from the high shriek of the recoiling carriages to the deep reverberation of the beams as they took the impact of the recoil, that it was quite impossible to elaborate the moral point at issue.

The bald mouse, a man-of-war's mouse, born in a nest of oakum, moved as fast as its old limbs would carry it towards the surgeon's spence, a triangular cupboard in which particular delicacies were kept, and whose door had been known to open of itself in time of gunfire.

Mr Eliot looked at his watch, went through the motions of saying 'We must go along to the sick-bay,' nodded with great meaning, and changed his wig for a nightcap. They walked into the sharp smell of powder, and descending the companion-way to the upper-deck they picked their way cautiously through the acrid smoke to the fore-hatch – cautiously, because the guns were firing indepen-dently, not in broadsides, and each gun, as it fired, sprang back; Mr Eliot had treated the results of carelessness, and he walked behind the guns with as much attention as if they had been so many ill-tempered mules.

It was a remarkable spectacle, this long deck swirling with smoke; the brilliant sun came in through the gratings and the gun-ports, and its beams, sharply defined in the smoke, were all shaped by the squares that let them in. The gunner hurried up and down the deck, from crew to crew; the powder-boys ran behind the guns, flitting in the gloom; there was water, wet sand and wet sawdust everywhere, and in barrels by the guns the slow match burnt portentously, with the particular crackle of saltpetre. Mr Eliot stopped by number seven: the captain of the gun had laid it and he was waiting for the roll of the ship to bring the sight up to the mark, a raft of barrels that had been thrown out for the *Wager* by the next in line ahead, the

Severn. The ship rose on the swell, up and up; the layer glared along the barrel of his gun. With a grunt he clapped the linstock to the touchhole: there was the smallest conceivable pause, then the bellowing roar. The gun shot back under the arched body of the layer, whipped back past the crew kneeling on either side of it, until the breechings brought it up – ropes fastened to strong rings, that gave a great deep twang as they tightened. The square of the port was darkened with smoke and pieces of the wad; then the wind cleared it and they saw the ball hit the water near the mark and skip on with three gigantic bounds. Without more than a moment's pause the swabber doused and cleaned the gun, they charged, loaded, wadded and rammed it, and ran it up to the sill of the port, primed and ready to fire again.

It was a beautiful sight, in its way; but Mr Eliot had seen it so many times in the last forty years, and Tobias was impervious to this kind of beauty; they walked on, thinking only of the number of casualties this gunnery practice would bring them.

Early in the voyage, when the new hands were quite green, every exercise with the great guns had brought crushed fingers and toes down to the cockpit. There had been a great many, for the commodore ordered practice on every possible occasion: any morning might show a superior Spanish force to the windward, and with his ships undermanned and overloaded (in spite of the two victuallers that accompanied them, the squadron had to carry so much that at this stage the two-deckers could scarcely open their lower gun-ports, and their decks were much encumbered by stores), he could only hope to equalise the contest by superiority in gun-fire. The Spaniards, of course, having ports on the other side of the ocean, were not obliged to carry the same overwhelming burden of provisions. To begin with there had been many casualties, but today no one was hurt except an enthusiastic boy – one Diego, who had stowed himself away under the *Wager's* yawl when they were in Funchal, and whose natural curiosity had now induced him to put his face so near the mouth of a gun that his hair had been burnt off in patches and his wits sent all astray.

Yet if there were no casualties to fill the sick-bay there were nevertheless several regular inmates swinging there in their hammocks: they were very old men, worn out in the King's service, many of them with inveterate wounds, and the history of their coming aboard was discreditable to all who were concerned with it. The administration, unable or unwilling to put an adequate number of marines aboard the squadron, had seized the Chelsea pensioners (who were subject to military law) and had sent five hundred of them down to Portsmouth; half of them had deserted, but enough remained for twenty-seven to fall to the share of the *Wager*. This was typical of the difficulties that had beset Mr Anson from the beginning – the long-winded hesitations that had destroyed all hope of reaching the Horn by December and had probably done away with all secrecy, so that the Spaniards might be waiting, anywhere along the course fully prepared and heavily armed.

It was a depressing thought that the ship was to carry these poor old men away from their homes, south across the equator and both the tropics, through the great heat down to the southernmost extremity of the known world, round it and up into an almost unknown sea, there to fight for their lives – if indeed any of them survived so far. But on the other hand it must be admitted that on that particular day the invalids presented an excellent example in support of Mr Eliot's theory on the power of imagination. The smell of powder had reached the sick-bay, and the roaring of the guns could not possibly be kept out of it: the old gentlemen were much enlivened by both; they piped away in their high old quavering voices about battles long ago, they prated about their knowledge, experience and wisdom, and wondered what would be for dinner with a vivacity that would have been remarkable in a pack of boys.

'What will be for dinner? What indeed?' said Mr Eliot, as they left the sick-bay. 'Sea-pie, perhaps. That cook, old Maclean, is eighty-one, to my certain knowledge. Did you know that, Mr B? It is a comforting reflection, is it not? He makes an excellent sea-pie; an admirable sea-pie. There is no sea-pie like Maclean's.'

Chapter Six

BLOOD, BLOOD in the scuppers, blood tinging the sea, blood all over the deck, blood everywhere, blood under the tropical sun. Buckets of blood. There had been four buckets full, to be exact, carefully filled and set aside until the next should be brimming and ready to join them: Mr Eliot made it a fixed rule to bleed all the men in his charge the moment they passed beneath the tropic of Cancer, and the operation was now taking place on the foc's'le. There had been the usual number of faintings, and a carpenter's mate called Mitchel, perhaps the most savage and vicious man aboard, had chosen to pass away into, upon and among the buckets that Mr Eliot and Tobias had preserved, for philosophical purposes: this accounted for the shocking appearance of the deck and for the look of vexation upon the surgeons' faces. Some of the *Wager*'s people positively liked being bled, because they felt better after it; some did not mind it; but some, though reasonably courageous, manly and resolute, turned greenish-yellow at the sight of the instruments, and, without being touched, collapsed like so many maidens. And there were some who were terrified by the whole proceeding: Moses Lewis, Nicholas Griselham and George Bateman were discovered trying to hide themselves in a perfectly inadequate triangle of space between the cutter and the booms. They belonged to Jack's watch and division, and he was responsible for their appearance; he adjured them 'to come out of there as quick as they liked, the swabs', and then, less ferociously, he assured them 'that it was nothing at all – did not hurt in the least – all over in a moment'. And to encourage them still further, he said that he would go along with them, although the officers were pierced in decent privacy.

'Come along,' he said, 'and we shall all be bled together. You will see, there is nothing in it.'

As it happened, Jack did not know what he was talking about;

although it was so common, he had never been bled and he had never seen the thing done. Now, standing there under the blazing sun and watching, he wondered how he had come to speak so lightly of it, and how people could say, with such indifference, 'Was you let blood? – There is nothing like a little blood-letting, for the good of the system.'

Two stools were there, and the victims came in pairs, sometimes with unstudied calm, sometimes with ostentatious bravery, sometimes with reluctance bordering upon mutiny. Tobias took the larboard man, Mr Eliot the other; the patient sat and presented his arm, the surgeon turned a handkerchief tight about it, picked a vein and lanced it, while the loblolly-boy held a basin. Mr Eliot used a large horse-fleam, Tobias a thin lancet; but there was no difference in the grave, detached zeal of their approach. Jack wondered at it: there was something inhumanly authoritative about the way Tobias seized an arm, considered it and then with the utmost equanimity cut into the living flesh. Repulsively unfeeling, thought Jack, looking away. There was a great deal of joking between those who were standing about with their arms bent to close the vein and those who had not yet been done; Jask thought the laughter very much out of place.

He looked at other things, to divert his attention – the foresail hanging without enough air to round it, for the expected north-east trade wind failed them day after day. He looked at the glazed hat of the bo'sun, who, having quarrelled with the gunner and the carpenter, kept very much among the hands forward, trying to make himself popular; he was the only warrant-officer on the foc's'le. Just beyond the bo'sun's hat there was the sinister face of the man Sirett, who had escaped the gallows only by informing on his own brother – a face that was now turning horribly pale.

A reek of butchery rose upon the still, hot, damp air. Jack swallowed hard, gave Griselham, Lewis and Bateman a smile, a ghastly smile that was meant to keep their spirits up, and looked studiously away, far away, to the leeward.

There, wallowing along under the protection of the men-of-war, were the two victuallers, the *Anna* and the *Industry*, pinks that had been chartered to carry stores for the squadron as far as the tropic. They were merchantmen, of course, and by naval standards they sailed along in a very haphazard sort of way, as if they had their hands in their pockets, shabby, with washing hanging out in incongruous places; but they were always there, and sometimes they were in their proper stations. Jack fixed the *Industry* with his eyes: if he did not concentrate, something dreadful would happen.

The *Industry* was a family concern, from the West Country, and the family was a whiggish, nonconformist, Hanoverian sort of a family: most of the crew were called George or William.

'What do 'ee make 'un, George?' asked the swabber of the first mate.

'But thirty-nine, I doubt,' said the first mate, lowering his quadrant.

'You'm not holding of 'un right,' said the cook, coming out of the galley and wringing a piece of wet salt pork as he spoke.

'Now then, our George,' cried the mate, quite vexed, 'if so be you mind your pot as good as I mind my latitude . . .'

The captain of the *Industry* came out of the round-house, where he had been figuring on his slate. 'What do 'ee make 'un, William?' asked the swabber.

'What's five nines?' asked the captain.

Here followed a very long, slow and ill-formed family wrangle, at the end of which the *Industry* decided that she had probably reached 23° 27′ N., that she had fulfilled her agreement, and that she would signal the commodore to that effect.

A flag mounted uncertainly on the *Industry*'s signal halliard: when it was broken out it proved to be upside down, and it stated, with great emphasis, I AM TAKING GUNPOWDER ABOARD.

Jack saw this: he knew that the *Wager* should repeat the signal to the *Centurion*, and he knew that as soon as the look-out hailed the deck with the news of a signal flying, it would be his duty, as midshipman of the watch, to run aft and cope with the repetition. But the look-out was a morbid creature, fascinated by the scene below, and although he now and then looked at the *Centurion* (the only probable source of signals) and gazed around the horizon, he devoted most of his time to peering down through the rigging at the bloody deck.

'Next,' said Tobias, and to his horror Jack saw that there was nothing between himself and the stool, although indeed Nicholas

Griselham stood beside him. 'Go on, Griselham,' he said; 'go in and win' – smiling very hypocritically.

He glared up at the masthead, and there was the look-out leering down at him instead of minding his duty: Jack shook his fist at the fellow, but it was no good. Griselham's faint gasping shriek reached his ears, and Jack closed his eyes: then suddenly everybody was roaring out 'Mr Byron, Mr Byron', and his neighbours were nudging him and saying 'Quarter-deck, sir. Mr Bean is passing the word for you.'

Passing the word was a faint expression for the lieutenant's clamour: he had seen the signal and he now wanted to know where the midshipman was; and Jack, with a speed and a devotion to duty rarely paralleled, raced aft to satisfy the lieutenant's curiosity.

'You may not like phlebotomy,' said Tobias, 'but where would you be without it?'

'Where indeed?' said Jack, rather vaguely, for his attention was taken up by the curious yawing of the *Wager*'s barge. The squadron was lying-to, taking in stores from the *Industry*, and the boats were plying to and fro over the still face of the sea: it looked very much as though the barge and the *Gloucester*'s longboat were going to collide, but at the last moment they ran past one another with their oars shipped and rude words flying free – Cozens' voice came very loud and plain over the water, followed by a bellow of laughter from the barge.

'When I went aboard the *Centurion*,' continued Tobias, 'their sick-bay was so full that the men's hammocks were touching, and the other surgeons made the same report – fevers, calentures and agues, and scurvy, in every ship but the *Wager*. And we are the only ship to use phlebotomy. I really must insist upon opening your vein this afternoon: come, Jack, it is a very mere trifle.'

'It is not your infernal splashing about in blood that makes the difference,' said Jack, 'it is that they cannot open their lower ports, and we can, being higher in the water. Did you not notice the vile rank smell as soon as you went below? Keppel says that there is some very extraordinary scheme afoot – some idea of making the men wash, every day. It will never do, however.'

'I did notice the smell,' admitted Tobias. He could scarcely have missed it: the *Centurion* had more than five hundred men aboard and most of them were crammed into the gun-deck, which (she being a two-decker) also had to find room for two dozen huge twenty-four pounders; she was so deeply laden, being victualled for a voyage no less than the circumnavigation of the whole world itself, that the sills of her lower gun-ports were nearly awash, and the gun-deck was therefore quite unventilated, although the heat down there was enough to make a man choke, whether he was used to the tropics or not. The heat also enabled vermin to breed very fast, and the *Centurion* was much infested; but she was not unique in that, by any means – every ship in the squadron had her cargo of parasites, and the *Wager* was amply supplied with fleas, bugs and lice.

'But,' continued Tobias, 'they are to cut holes in the deck, to let in sweet air.'

'Scuttles, Toby; surely it was scuttles? They could not have said holes.'

'I had understood them to be holes, indeed: large square gaps, with canvas funnels leading down.'

'Yes. Scuttles. I thought so.'

'Are they not holes, then?'

'Oh yes, they are holes, in their way. But we call them scuttles. Not holes.'

'Very good. We are to have them too, and Mr Eliot is talking about the one for the sick-bay with the carpenter at this moment.'

'The hands will not like it,' said Jack. 'Any change makes them uneasy. I tell you what, Toby,' he added, moving along the rail to the shadow of the maintop. 'I wish it would snow. Or blow. I do not give a rap for foul weather, so long as we are not on a lee-shore, but this sticky heat undoes me. I do not know how you can bear a coat – to say nothing of that vile hat,' he said, looking with distaste at the yellowish-white woollen nightcap of Portuguese origin which Tobias had worn, upon philosophical principles, since latitude 25°N.

'Was you to be blooded,' said Tobias, fingering a small lancet in his pocket, 'you would feel cooler directly.'

'How you do go on,' cried Jack, moving a little farther off. 'You are exactly like a flaming horse-leech. Now there's a fellow that needs your attention. Look at him. He'll have the boat over if he carries on like that.' Cozens was weaving the barge about in a very extraordinary manner: the *Wager*'s cutter was alongside unloading at that moment, and Cozens was profiting by the interval to hinder the progress of the other boats, in a most jovial and hilarious way.

The cutter, with Campbell in charge, lay hooked on at the main-chains, with a pyramid of barrels carefully arranged in it, and from the yard-arm swung a tackle. With mechanical regularity the tackle descended, raised a barrel, swung it inboard, lowered it into the main-hatch and reappeared empty; everyone who was not on duty watched this with close attention; all the heads followed the descending tackle down into the cutter, saw the two loops put about the barrel, heard the cry, saw the barrel rise vertically, rotating slowly, until the inhaul party drew it over the hatchway, and vanish to more cries of 'Easy – handsomely now.' The movements were all the same; the shouts never varied; the hot, still air was heavy with the smell of rum. It was rum and little else that they were taking out of the *Industry* – the remaining stores were to stay aboard the *Anna* pink, and she to keep in company while the *Industry* went off on her own occasions. No ship in the squadron could find space for any more flour, biscuit or beef, but they could all make just enough room for their full share of rum, although it meant great discomfort in the crowded 'tween-decks; they would make sure of the rum, at any event.

Now the cutter had discharged its load and was pulling away for the pink again, and the barge took the cutter's place. Cozens' big red face was turned up to them as he sprawled in the stern-sheets; as a general rule it was not a very attractive face, being exceedingly coarse and somewhat hairy, and now its charm was further dimin-ished by crimson blotches and a staring, almost lunatic expression. The redness was shared by the barge's crew, and it was perfectly evident that they had all been getting at the rum. The steadier men in the barge were trying to cover up the midshipman's state, but their efforts were spoilt by his activity: he would keep trying to fasten the tackle, and he would not be quiet – had not sense enough left to be quiet. Jack looked anxiously over his shoulder, but the officer of the watch, Mr Clerk, was at the fife-rail of the mainmast, shouting through the hatch to the deck below. Mr Bean was in his cabin, writing letters that the *Industry* was to carry over to the West Indies, and although Mr Hamilton, the senior marine lieutenant, was watching from the poop, he was a redcoat, and did not count. And the captain was aboard the commodore, so perhaps it would pass off well enough.

But Cozens had not had time to cut one more elephantine caper before the voice of the look-out floated down, quite conversational in the calm, 'Deck oh! The yawl is pulling away.' Captain Murray had left the *Centurion*, and in a few minutes he would be received aboard his own ship with the proper ceremony, the shrilling of bo'suns' calls and the dutiful attendance of the officers: captains come up the starboard side, and it was on the starboard side that the barge was unloading. There was no possibility that Cozens' state would remain unnoticed.

Already there were stirrings, the preparatory orders and hurrying about; the yawl was in sight, coming across the line of the bowsprit. Jack swung over the side into the chains; he stood there an instant, whispering to Tobias, 'Get him below – anywhere below,' and then jumped down into the boat. 'Come on, now,' he said to Cozens; 'one arm in here, and one in there. Way oh; haul away. Roundly, there.' Cozens, looking very stupid and aghast, rose in the air on the tackle.

Tobias, who was not devoid of mother-wit, pinned him as soon as his legs were above the rail and called out, 'Stop. Belay. Avast. Pull no more, there. Let it go. Sunstroke – this is a very sudden sunstroke.' They let him down with a run, and Cozens, still altogether amazed, squelched down on deck. 'Carry him downstairs,' cried Tobias, waving his opened lancet.

'What is this? – Clear the way – get forward, the idlers – what is this?' exclaimed the master, pushing through the crowd as two men of Cozens' watch hurried him out of sight.

'It is the effect of the sun, sir,' said Tobias, 'and I shall dose him below.'

'The sun, Mr Barrow?' said the master. 'Mr Snow, clear me those men to the foc's'le. When is the side to be dressed, bo'sun? We do not have all day.'

'I suggest that hats should be ordered to be worn,' said Tobias, plucking Mr Clerk's coat to draw his attention. This was the first lie of his life, and he thought he might as well make the best of it. 'Such a stroke, my dear sir,' he said, leering at the master and nodding emphatically, 'such a stroke would never have occurred without the head was too lightly covered, eh?'

Mr Clerk would have replied, but his words were cut off by the howling of calls as the captain came up the side; he composed his face to a suitable expression of complaisance and stepped forward, while Tobias nodded and becked behind him, with infinite enjoyment.

'Who is the midshipman in the barge?' asked the captain, after he had taken a turn on the quarter-deck with the lieutenant. He said it in a tone of considerable displeasure, and he answered it himself, for going to the side and leaning over, he looked into the boat. 'Byron,' he said, 'I am surprised at him. There has been too much tom-foolery, Mr Bean: playing the merry-Andrew before the whole squadron. The barge has been making a Jack-Pudding of itself. It will do that young man no harm to be brought down to his proper level, Mr Bean.'

When Jack next set foot on deck it was just before dinner-time; in fact the hands were being piped down as he made his appearance. For a long time he had heard this tuneless up-and-down shrieking before meals, and the result was that whenever he heard the piping-down he felt hungry; not to put too fine a point upon it, he slavered. But today his wreathed smiles of anticipation were wiped off very quickly. A most unexpectedly sour Mr Bean asked him what he thought he was doing on the quarter-deck in shirtsleeves and why he considered himself privileged to play the ape in the barge, making the *Wager* despicable in the eyes of the whole squadron, with mer-chantmen looking on, to make it even worse.

The answer to the first question would have involved a compli-cated explanation, and the second was not really answerable at all, so Jack bowed to the storm, looked meek, begged pardon – did not intend to offend – would do so no more – and hoped that it would soon be over. But it was not soon over; meekness was not enough, and presently Jack found himself on his way to the masthead.

He went aloft with the melancholy but calm philosophy of one who regrets his dinner but who knows that injustice is inseparable from human existence, and most particularly from the existence of mid-shipmen. He had not been mastheaded before on this voyage, partly because everyone who knew the difference between a sheet and a tack was too valuable on deck during the early days, partly because of the equable temper of the lieutenant, and partly because he had not transgressed the law. Not that the last had a great deal to do with it, for the young are often punished because their elders are peevish; as he climbed, Jack was inclined to attribute his fate to Mr Bean's digestion. Rum, in hot weather, is as dangerous to handle as gun-powder, because of the fumes; for the last two days, therefore, the galley fires had been out – and cold victuals did not agree with Mr Bean.

'I wish he may burst,' said Jack, with an uncharitable glance at the distant quarter-deck. But his spirits were not really much affected, and he alternately admired the view and carved his initials upon the topmast cap. The view was a circle of the purest blue some thirty miles across, the full deep oceanic blue, without the shadow of a single cloud upon it; and in the middle of this glorious disk there was the squadron, brilliantly white from above, gathered in a comfortable group – he was going to say 'like ducks'; but his sense of poetic fitness as well as a due reverence for the service made him substitute halcyons, as being grander, and more classical.

One of the disadvantages of being called Byron is that B is a difficult letter to carve: however, by a course of long practice Jack had almost overcome this handicap, and the most recent of his Majesty's ships in which he had served before the *Wager* was sprinkled with JBs of an almost professional excellence. The first lieutenant of that vessel was a man of great independence of spirit; he would never have it said that he was influenced by important connexions, and he had come down upon Jack's slightest faults with ferocious rectitude. At that time Jack had often wished that either his grandfather had never been First Lord of the Admiralty or that Mr Toke had less greatness of soul: good came out of it all, however, for not only was he now able to carve his initials quite beautifully, having had so much practice at the masthead, but the frequency of the punishment made him take little account of it.

This was not the case with Tobias, however. When he had finished with Cozens – bleeding, purging and a strong emetic – he went along to the midshipmen's berth for dinner.

'Yes, he will do very well,' he said, in reply to their questions. 'Where is Jack?'

'Mastheaded,' said Campbell, helping himself to the last of the Madeiran cheese.

'Old Bean sent him up,' said Morris.

Tobias ate biscuit for some time in silence and then said, 'Masthead.' There had been such a very great deal to occupy his mind since they sailed that he had not taken very much notice of the working of the ship nor of naval discipline. He had seen the many floggings, of course, they being solemn occasions, with all hands piped up to witness the punishment; besides, it fell to him to treat the sometimes shocking wounds that a severe flogging entailed; but Morris or Cozens might have been sent to the masthead fifty times without Tobias paying any attention to it.

'What is he doing up there?' he asked. 'I should have supposed him to be hungry.' He took a weevil out of his biscuit and looked keenly at the little creature's proboscis.

'I dare say he is,' said Campbell, with a prim smile; and he explained the meaning of the term.

'Oh,' cried Tobias, pale with fury. 'Is that the case? What an unprincipled abuse of authority. To send him up there – that most dangerous eminence – infernal tyranny – public ignominy.' Tobias became incoherent, and sprang about in a high state of rage and excitement. 'Mr Bean, was it? The proud satrap, the man of blood. I shall bring down his vile presumption.'

Morris and Campbell seized him as he darted out and confined him to the berth until he had stopped foaming. 'If you were to say a rough word to him,' said Campbell, 'much less lift your hand, do you know what it would be?'

Tobias breathed hard, but did not reply.

'Mutiny,' said Campbell.

'There is only one punishment for mutiny,' said Morris, imitating a hanging man.

'Your friend may be able to command cabins and all manner of irregular favours,' said Campbell, who meant well enough by Tobias, but who did not love Jack, 'but his grand relations could not save you from a court-martial. He would be involved too, I dare say,' he added.

'You are quite right,' said Tobias. 'I shall be calm, prudent. Pass the biscuit, if you please, and the pork.' He took off his neckerchief, spread it out and very firmly carved a picnic into it: he hurried to their cabin for a piece of the remaining cake and so came on deck.

He passed close to the lieutenant, and Mr Bean, turning in his pace, received a very implacable and malignant glare which (being so unexpected) quite upset him. At the end of his next turn Mr Bean noticed Tobias again, creeping up the shrouds, and he could almost have sworn that the surgeon's mate had been shaking his fist at him, or at least in the direction of the holy quarter-deck. Mr Bean was on the point of calling him down, but he hesitated: Mr Barrow could never have been so abandoned, so wanton; Mr Barrow was known to be sober, grave, unusually learned; Mr Barrow also had a particularly happy turn of the wrist, and Mr Eliot delegated all the *Wager*'s dental business to him. The lieutenant's teeth were none of the best, and any day Tobias might have him hideously at his mercy. To call such a person down to explain what probably never happened, decided Mr Bean, would be the height of folly.

Jack had finished his initials, and with an Olympian detachment he was watching the last boats crawling over the sea from the victualler; the unloading was almost done; soon they would be making sail. From time to time he stared at the *Centurion*, trying to make out whether the figure at the mizzen masthead were Keppel or not: the *Centurion* was a very much stricter ship than the *Wager*, and there was somebody at the main as well.

'It is probably one of the ship's apes,' he concluded – the *Centurion* had bought every ape on the Madeiran market, being ashore earlier than anyone else – and he frowned, because there was a curiously familiar noise that he could not locate. 'It is almost exactly like a bulldog,' he said, 'or Toby, when he is coming up into the foretop.' A sudden doubt came into his mind. He looked down, and with a thrill of pure horror he saw Tobias' nightcap not five ratlines below him.

The shrouds, with the ratlines across them, form a kind of ladder; they are spread out to as wide a base as is possible at the bottom, because their chief function is to support the mast, but as they are made fast at the top to the mast itself, so of necessity the ladder that they make becomes exceedingly narrow for its last dozen rungs – narrow, and difficult to climb, because so many ropes converge. Furthermore, the roll of a ship is more and more perceptible the higher you are. A ten-degree roll is nothing much on deck once you have your sea-legs, but by the time you reach ninety feet (the *Wager*'s main topmast crosstrees were about a hundred from the water) a little roll like this will send you through fifteen feet of lateral distance each time. The silent rush through the air is refreshing in the heavy atmosphere of the doldrums, and the constantly changing effects of the earth's gravity, now pressing your face on to the tarred rope of the ratlines, now plucking you backwards as the swing is reversed, are an additional delight to an inquiring spirit; but it is as well to have a head for heights and to be used to the behaviour of the upper rigging before you go swooping to and fro so near the sky.

Tobias had begun fairly well. From the deck to the maintop (which was the highest point he had reached before) it had been fairly easy, and the first half of the topmast shrouds had not alarmed him much; but from then onwards the swing had been so much greater, and his ladder so much narrower, that his parcel hampered him sorely. Now he was mounting only between long rests; he hooked his arms right through the ratlines and hung there during the backward roll, and then as the *Wager* came slowly up and her masts approached the vertical he transferred his parcel to his teeth, grasped the next ratline with both hands and hauled himself up with a convulsive movement. Then he threaded himself into the web again, took the parcel in his right hand and closed his eyes while his steady aerial motion bore him out beyond the deck below (how small and far) out over the sea and back again. Sometimes it took him two rolls or three before he could arrange his feet properly for the next upward scramble, and sometimes he had to wait for a long time to recruit his strength, for this was a very laborious way of going aloft – worse than that, it was based upon a misapprehension, for although at the lower stages the space between the shrouds was amply wide enough, it was now so narrow that he could scarcely get his arm through, and after the next step, where the cat-harpings drew the shrouds in tight, he would not be able to do so at all.

'Toby,' called Jack softly, so as not to startle him, 'I'm coming down. Just stay where you are.'

By way of answer Tobias shook his nightcap, surged up one more step and hung there, breathing hard. Jack ran down the starboard shrouds to the height of the cat-harpings and peered round the mast into Tobias' face, which was candle-pale and glistening.

'How are you, old Toby?' he asked. 'Give me that thing, will you?'

The *Wager*, at this moment, was reaching the limit of her starboard roll: Tobias cautiously held out the parcel, but he mistook and let it go just before Jack's hand was there. It fell, down, down and down; then there was a little white splash in the blue water well out from the side, and while they watched a great long shape glided fast from under the stern, and they saw the white gleam of its belly as it turned so far down there in the clear sea.

'Come now, Toby,' said Jack, 'this will never do. You must run straight up to the crosstrees. Wait a minute.' He swarmed round the cat-harpings to the larboard shrouds just under Tobias. 'I will take your shoes off,' he said, doing so. 'Now put your feet here and here, and grip with your toes. Now up you go – quick, hand over hand.' He ran Toby's feet up, pushed him on to the crosstrees, writhed round him and above to get the other side of the mast and hauled him into a sitting position, talking busily all the time, adjuring him not to look down, never to worry, to look lively and to go easy there. He judged it very well: by the time the mast was upright Tobias was sitting firmly on the crosstrees with his feet on the huge fiddle-headed block of the topmast stay, his right hand on a topgallant dead-eye and his left arm round the masthead itself, as firm as a limpet. 'There you are,' said Jack. 'What an intrepid topman you are becoming, Toby, upon my word and honour.'

'I have got up,' said Tobias, and this remark seemed to satisfy him for some time. 'But I regret your dinner,' he said at last, 'and if you wish I will fetch you some more.'

Jack was infinitely obliged, infernally grateful, but it so happened that he had no appetite: it had suddenly left him, he said. They sat for some time, while the sun declined on the right hand and the *Wager*'s shadow grew on the smooth sea: it was smooth, with hardly a ripple upon it, but the long slow swell from the south was increasing.

'It is most significant, Jack,' said Tobias, peering round the mast, 'most significant that I am not at all seasick. The motion is very great – it is becoming greater – but there is no nausea, no vertigo.'

'I am heartily glad of it,' said Jack, 'and I dare say it is uncommon significant. But what of?'

'It signifies that Mr Eliot may be right – that seasickness may be in some degree a creature of the imagination. I am too much preoccupied by terror to be sick. Query: are the timid less seasick than the bold, as being more readily distracted?'

'I wish you were safely down below,' said Jack, who had no philosophy to spare. 'I do indeed.'

Down below the boats were being hauled in, hoisted up by tackles on the yard-arms and brought inboard to be stowed on the booms: the blue watch was on duty, and it had its full share of men who hauled stupidly, at the wrong moment, or not at all; this was a piece of work that called for exact coordination at any time and now it was complicated by the heavy swell. When Jack heard, among the roaring and the fending-off, that a back-stay had parted, he felt sure that all hands would soon be called. A glance round the squadron made him surer still. The signal to make sail was flying aboard the *Centurion*; the *Severn* already had her fore-topsail shaken out, and, as he looked, her main-topsail fell white from the yard and was sheeted home directly; everywhere in the squadron canvas was breaking out. The *Industry* was already under way, flying a signal that said I HAVE SOMETHING IMPORTANT TO COMMUNICATE, but its intention was generally understood to be Farewell, or possibly Merry Christmas. Only the *Wager* was still blundering about with the longboat, later than everybody else, as usual.

'Listen, Toby,' he said, 'we must get you down. I shall have to go on deck in a moment, so let us put you on this preventer-stay at once, and send you down to the foretop. You will not mind climbing down from the foretop.'

'What stay?' asked Tobias, looking alarmed.

'This,' cried Jack, kicking the block under Tobias' feet so that the stays vibrated again: there were two, running straight and taut from the main-topmast head to the foretop at an angle of about 45°, and as the staysail was not bent they made an excellent road. 'Come now, give me your belt. Hold on here. Hook your leg round the stay.' Jack passed both their belts round Tobias and the stay: as he was fastening them the watches below were called, and there was a general bellowing of 'All hands on deck. All hands to make sail.'

'You are as safe as the ark,' said Jack, 'but don't go too fast.' With these words he vanished, leaving Tobias hanging under the stay, attached to it by his hands and legs somewhat in the manner of the Brazilian (or three-toed) sloth, except that the sloth would never have been supported by a belt and in general would have been calmer in its mind – the sloth's bosom would have been less agitated by conjecture and doubt.

'What did he mean by too fast?' asked Tobias of the sky. 'What is considered a moderate speed, in these circumstances?' He loosened his cataleptic grasp a little and allowed himself to slide a few feet before gripping again: the experiment pleased him, for it proved that he could start and stop. He now had complete confidence in his suspension, and as his face was turned upwards he had no impression of petrifying height, but rather a sense of being pleasingly afloat. He let himself go a little further, and smiled; then further, in a steady glide.

'This is capital,' he said aloud. 'Before we reach the equator I shall accustom myself to the upper rigging; and before we cross the tropic of Capricorn I shall (sub Deo) climb to that ball,' – nodding to the distant truck of the main-mast, which looked like a ball from below – 'and put my nightcap upon it.' So saying he let himself go a little faster, and then faster and faster until at length with a shrill whizzing sound he shot, amazed, feet first into the foretop, scattering its unsuspecting occupants like ninepins.

Chapter Seven

WHO SHALL DESCRIBE the crossing of the equator, with Neptune dispensing the traditional ordeals to all who had not been south of the line? Cozens, with a seaweed beard was Neptune, and it would take a great deal of space to describe the merriment and the jollity, the way everybody was soused, covered with tar, made to drink bilge-water. Tobias did not think it worth describing, but Jack, who had been as nearly as possible drowned – Neptune bawling, and weeping with laughter the while – was not of the same opinion. He had worn the necessary grin throughout the licensed Bedlam and the violent horseplay, but he was still privately indignant, and meditated a satirical poem.

'You may say that I am not a Pope,' he said.

'My dear Jack,' said Tobias, 'I am sure of it. A Pope, ha, ha.'

'Oh, very well,' said Jack in something of a huff; but in a moment he said, 'I mean Mr Pope, you know: not the gentleman in Rome.'

'Oh?'

'Mr Pope, damn it, Toby: the one I hoped to show you at Will's, only he was not there. Strike me down, I don't believe he even knows who I mean.'

'Yes, I do, Jack. The poet. You have often mentioned him, with approval.'

'Well,' said Jack, who was easily mollified, 'you may say that I am not a Pope and that my piece would not be a Dunciad; but I reply, that there is the same disproportion between the subject of his poem and mine – which is pretty well put. What was that?'

'Six bells. If you do write it, you must not omit the flying-fish.' He looked out over the sea in case there should be another flight – there had been thousands of flying-fish that afternoon and a good many doradoes. 'I can conceive nothing more poetic than a flying-fish, unless indeed it is the pelagic loxodrome.'

Jack leaned back with a faint sigh: in spite of the breeze it was too hot to try to make Tobias understand poetry in the correct, or Popish manner. They were sitting in the weather mainchains, which was about the pleasantest place aboard, though damp: strictly speaking they were not aboard at all, for the chains were outboard, they being the very strong projections from the ship's side that hold the chain-plates and the immense dead-eyes of the shrouds. It was a kind of shelf that they sat upon, and if the *Wager* had been on an even keel they would have been suspended about half-way up the side, six or seven feet from the water and six or seven feet from the rail; but the east-south-east wind was blowing steadily over the *Wager*'s quarter, and with every possible sail set and drawing she heeled so as to raise them much higher from the sea. Even so, spray and sometimes solid water reached them now and then, for the wind was across the current and it chopped the surface into short, steep waves; it was very welcome, the coolness of the water, and it did their clothes no harm, for they were dressed in the simple elegance of calico drawers and nothing more.

'There is Old Spots,' said Tobias. In spite of the waves the sea was astonishingly clear, and the dolphin was plainly to be seen: it was a rather large fat dolphin with a protuberant forehead, a contented smile and a particular arrangement of light patches on its shoulders that distinguished it from the others. The *Wager* was making a good ten knots, but the dolphin had leisure to turn half over and scratch its back on the ship's side before running up to play in the bow wave, to pass down the lee, to cross the wake with divers leaps and bounds and to reappear under their feet with an air of simple-minded joy.

The smile on the face of the dolphin was also to be found on board the *Wager*; this was delightful sailing at last, with the wind so steady and true and the braces untouched day after day: in this weather the watch on deck was occupied with beautifying the ship or preparing gear for harder times ahead, and the watches below really were watches below – that is to say, that they were not roused out the moment they had turned in by piping of all hands for some emergency or other. The watches below took their ease: in the last dog-watch they would often sing and dance to the squeak of the barber's fiddle, and at other times they would spread abroad for repose and meditation. This was one of the reasons why Jack and Tobias were sitting in the chains – there was no room anywhere else. The *Wager* was about a hundred feet long, and her people numbered two hundred and twelve; she was not what would have been called a crowded ship, by naval standards, and at all ordinary times the hands loved to huddle into the smallest possible compartments, there to smoke and to work up a truly staggering fug, which left room enough for those who like to breathe; but now the 'tween decks was untenable even for the whaler's men (the most devoted to fug) and everyone sought a place in the breeze and out of the sun. Even the sick were on deck, and a short row of hammocks swung in the waist of the ship – the pensioners and a few new cases of tropical calenture, but nothing that disquieted Mr Eliot. In the other ships this was not the case: the *Severn*, next in line, had sick-bay hammocks as far as the catheads, and the *Centurion* was as bad, in spite of the commodore's scuttles; it was difficult to see into the other ships, for they sailed in so precise a line, two cables' lengths apart, that the *Gloucester* and the *Pearl* were obscured by the white cloud of sails.

The delight in the weather had many agreeable results, and it tended to make for general civility: Campbell, who was a morose fellow in ordinary weather, had been both friendly and communicative for some time; he too had suffered from Cozens' hilarity (Tobias had had to sew the top of his left ear on again) and he regarded Jack as a fellow-victim; he and Jack also had this in common, that they both liked navigation, and took a keen pleasure in amplitudes, right ascension and azimuths. Campbell was not an ideal shipmate even now, but he was far less disagreeable than he had seemed to be earlier in the voyage: and at least some of his unattractive ways were due to the fact that he was Scotch, and that he felt slighted and put upon because of it. He had some reason for thinking so, for the Scotch were widely unpopular in England at that time: living in a poorer country, with an even more disagreeable climate, they were obliged to work harder, to live on less and to accept hardship without complaint; this tended to make them offensively virtuous. They were industrious and hardy; they despised the English as being idle and soft; and this alone was enough to make them disliked. But in addition to all this they were said to be rude, dirty and grasping.

Perhaps the lowland Scotch were somewhat coarse in their manners, but as for dirt, there can have been no very strong contrast, seeing that the average Englishman's washing went no further than his neck, if indeed it reached so far, and the word bathroom had no meaning in domestic architecture. However, when nations are determined to dislike one another they do not let justice or veracity stand in the way, and Campbell, having found out early in his career that his nation was a disadvantage to him, resented the discrimination most bitterly. His cast of mind was dark, unhumorous and grudging, and he exaggerated the villainy of the world. He was also of an ordinary family, which had no interest. The result of this was that if a block fell on his head he was instantly certain that it had done so because he was a Scotchman in the first place, and because he was poor in the second. He often laboured under a sense of grievance, which made him a tedious companion; but at other moments he could be quite human; and at no time could it be denied that he had valuable qualities – he was attentive to his duty, seamanlike and conscientious.

'Will you make room there?' he said, swinging over the side.

Jack and Tobias made him a place, and presently he and Jack were deeply engaged on a plan to find out the longitude by watching the moons of Jupiter, while Tobias fixed his gaze upon a very large dirty bird in the distance. It was brown and blackish, with an immense wing-span: yet it was not a sooty albatross. Could it be the giant petrel, the *Procellaria gigantea* of Mumpsimus? He would have to see its beak to make sure, the bony nostrils so typical of the petrel family: Mumpsimus particularly mentioned the point. He pointed out the bird to his companions, who gave it as their opinion that it was a pretty large sort of bird, a sea-bird, no doubt, and went to fetch his telescope from the cabin.

The door offered a slight resistance; Tobias pushed hard, and down came the usual bucket, soaking him and the books that were open on the locker. The iron rim hurt him cruelly, but the pain of seeing water all over his drawings was so much greater that he took no notice of it. There was the usual bellow of laughter from Cozens and the imitative cackle from Morris as they saw the success of their joke. Tobias knew that he must not resent it; Jack (who was a better preacher than a practicer) had told him many and many a time that it was only a joke, that they meant no harm, that one must take a laugh against oneself; so he closed the door and began to mop the water off his books. He was too late to save the wash drawing of the flying-fish's muscular processes – many hours' exact labour – but he was able to preserve some of his notes; and no doubt he would soon have another flying-fish to dissect. The need for putting up with barbarity was something he could not understand, however. He took Jack's repeated assurance that it was so, but he had never been to school nor mixed with people of his own age, and the whole thing remained incomprehensible and sad.

Yet Cozens, lout though he was, had some seamanlike virtues, prompt decision being among them, and some days later when Moses Lewis, trying to spear a bonito, fell off the starboard bumkin into the sea, Cozens flung a hen-coop at him from the middle of the gangway so quickly that it struck him as he swept by. That is to say, Lewis had travelled from the bumkin to the middle of the *Wager*, some forty feet, at a rate of ten knots, by the time the hen-coop reached him; so Cozens had had a trifle over two seconds in which to roar 'Man overboard' and to act.

It is true that the coop not only drove Lewis far below the surface but also caused him to impale himself upon his fizgig, or trident. But this was a small price to pay for being kept afloat until he could be picked out of the sea, and it was generally thought that Moses Lewis should be very grateful to Mr Cozens, for his readiness of mind. Lewis was handed up the side with the fizgig still implanted in his bosom, and he was carried straight down to the cockpit in this interesting condition, looking (as the bystanders remarked) like something out of Foxe's *Book of Martyrs*.

'Moses Lewis,' said Mr Eliot, 'put out your tongue.' He said this almost automatically, it being his manner of gagging his patients and preventing tedious complaints: there was not much need to silence Lewis, who was still in a dismal and waterlogged condition as he lay there, with the trident's handle held up in the air over him, but Mr Eliot said it out of habit and went on with his examination.

'Very well,' he said at last. 'You will have to cut it out, Mr Barrow. It is the barbs that hold it so. It is of no consequence – you will not find the pleura affected, no, no. Oh no: the cartilago ensiformis and pectoralis major, that is all; and we need not be overtender of the pectoralis major. Use the great French scalpel, Mr Barrow, or even our dismembering catlin, if you please – it is of no consequence – as you please – I leave it entirely in your hands. Now Moses Lewis, Mr Barrow will kindly perform an ablation of the fizgig: you must not move, you know. If you was to move, the scalpel would slip, and I dare say it would put a stop to your earthly career. Should you like to be held, Moses Lewis? Yes, I think he would like to be held; he would be very sorry to move and spoil Mr Barrow's professional reputation. Andrew, my compliments to Mr Bean, and may I have two of Moses Lewis' messmates to hold him?'

Two very strong and eager messmates hurried in, and they pinned him at once (for his own good) with such force that the breath was squeezed from his body in a groan.

'Now don't you start a-bellowing,' said one. 'What will the doctor think of you, mate, if you start a-bellowing while he is only a whetting of his knife?'

'Fi, Moses Lewis,' said the other.

At all ordinary times Lewis would never have borne such liberties, but now they assumed such an overwhelming moral superiority, he being sick and therefore by tradition much the same as a child or a half-wit, that he could only gaze piteously from side to side. This, of course, could not be allowed: each seaman moved his shoulder inwards to clamp the patient's head, which took on a compressed appearance, not unlike a lemon.

'I do not suppose that you would have sharpened it so, if you had known where it was going to,' said Tobias, snipping the last fibres from the nick of the fifteenth barb and disengaging the fizgig.

'He says if you hadn't of sharpened it, it wouldn't of gone in so far,' said the messmate on the right, in a voice calculated to reach Lewis's muffled hearing.

'You don't want to go sharpening them nasty fizgigs so, he says,' said the other, in a virtuous tone: the squeezed lemon gave a faint nod, instantly suppressed.

'There,' said Tobias, 'you can let him go now.'

'It's all over, mate. We've got 'un out,' they told him, in a kindly bellow. 'There, there, you can lay easy now. What a horrible state of dread you was in, to be sure, ha, ha. Didn't he sweat, mate, when he see the knife a-coming? But it's all over now, mate,' they said, bending low over him, shouting in his ear and patting him heavily. 'Ah, you've missed it all, Mr Byron, sir: we got 'un out five minutes ago.'

'Well,' said Jack, 'I came down to see how he was. How is he?'

Lewis had been in Jack's division before Captain Murray's changes; he smiled to see the midshipman, for whom he had a kindness, but he thought fit to answer Jack's inquiry by the words 'Oh, oh, oh,' in a gasping, fluttering voice. This was a point of manners: if the sick are being visited it is only decent that they should be sick, however well they may feel. A little conversation followed about sharpening fizgigs, edged tools and those to whom they may safely be entrusted; and the general opinion was, that you ought to be very careful; that you don't want to go a-falling in the sea like that – which there might not be a hen-coop at hand another time, nor such a handy young gentleman as Mr Cozens; and that a bonito, or any other fish that might be named, was not worth being drowned for. An albacore was not worth being drowned for, not a barracuda; and if Moses Lewis thought a flaming dorado was worth being drowned for, he was wrong, mate, wrong.

'Now,' said Tobias, the seamen having gone, 'I think that I shall bandage him with a cingulum colchicum: hold that end Jack, I beg.' Tobias wound the bandage round and round his patient. 'How did you come by this wound?' he asked, looking at a remarkable scar on his back.

Lewis hesitated, but the impulsion to tell the truth to a medical man is very strong, and when he was the right way up again, he replied, with a blush, 'that it was a ostrich, sir, if you please.'

Tobias nodded, and went on with his bandaging. There was a short silence.

'What I do not understand,' said Jack, 'is how a cove can be such a muffin-handed slob with a rope, and yet be so handy with a bandage.' The cingulum was as neat as basket-work, and Tobias patted it with some complacency.

'Which it was a cock-ostrich,' said Lewis, who had a painful feeling of being disbelieved. 'A wery tall old bald one.'

'You shall tell me about it directly,' said Tobias. 'But we must prop you up first, and give you a little rum to fortify the tubes. Can you take rum, Moses Lewis? It is not unpleasant, and it will improve your general condition, if you can get it down.'

In a faint invalid's voice Lewis (Old Sponge among his friends) thought that he might manage to swallow a little, to oblige Mr Barrow; and as soon as the tot was gone he said, in his usual strong rumble, 'It was when they laid me off of weeding in the Emperor's garden.' He was feeling quite well again now, expansive, benign and communicative, and upon being desired to begin the history of his wound at the beginning, he delivered himself of it thus: 'It was when I was in the old *Trent*, Captain Burton, and we left the Cove of Cork in November for to convoy some store-ships and transports down to Gib and to see the India trade on their way as far as the south of Goree, along of the *Suffolk*, seventy, the *Exeter*, sixty, and the *Diamond*, forty – Captain Anson commanded her in his time, as my sister's husband could tell you, being he was cox'n of the gig – my brother-in-law, as you might say. The swab.' Lewis stared and snorted, moved by some remote villainy of his brother-in-law, and it was only with some pains that he could be brought to continue his voyage, to leave the transports bound for Gibraltar off Cape St Vincent and to stand to the south-west in dirty weather that grew dirtier with the December moon. 'But we was all right, being she was a tight ship,' he said, 'and I remember thinking that before I turned in, I would have a little bit of toasted cheese. I said to William Atkins, who was outside me on the yard, "I will have a little bit of toasted cheese, before I turn in." He was in the starboard watch too – a Plymouth man, and a wheelwright by trade. Well, we had the first watch, and it turned out very black – wind veering north-west and plenty of rain. The captain come on deck when it turned squally, but he soon went below, only telling the master to make what sail he could and not to lose sight of the commodore, no not if he carried all away. But about six bells it come on cruel and we laid aloft to hand the main tops'l: we was under our courses by the end of the watch, and so was the commodore, we reckoned, because he was right ahead, bearing south and the wind west-south-west blowing hard, but his light did not gain, as I said to William Atkins as we went below.

'It was not long after that, which I know very well because only one side of my cheese was toasted, that we struck. Cor love you,' he exclaimed, with the old amazement renewed in his mind, 'we could not tell what it was. The *Suffolk* run foul of us, or what? Because we was a hundred miles off of the land, we thought. Then she struck again, went over to port, almost on her beam ends, and you could hear her driving over the rocks like thunder. I got on deck, and when I got there she struck for good. You could make out the rocks two cables' lengths away, and she was lying with her broadside to windward and the sea making a breach over her: and between us and the shore it was all white water. The masts went by the board, she beat so hard, and all the ship's people were main anxious, I do assure you: but Captain Burton told us it was all for the best. "Ha, ha," says he, in his hailing-trumpet, "it's all for the best. Don't you see as how we're sheltered from the sea? Bear a hand there, and get everything over to the larboard, or she will heel off else." So we got everything over, and the cant of the deck sheltered us, do you see? But God' a mercy, what a sea it was. It come up green over her broadside, curling up there the height of the to'garn crosstrees, and it come down fit to split her. Dear Lord save me from such a lee-shore again.'

'Amen,' said Jack.

'Well, after a time some of the starboard watch begged leave to adventure for it in the cutter – no, I tell a lie: it was the jolly-boat. And though they was told no boat could swim, they would try: and they went down before they could even shove off. Eight of 'em. All the other boats was stove in, so when we saw she was stuck fast, no hope, we made a raft with capstan-bars and gratings and what spars we could come at: but most of the people were drunk by then, and it was a sorry old botch of a raft.'

'Drunk?' cried Tobias.

'In course we was drunk,' replied Lewis, looking at him with surprise.

'They had struck, you see,' said Jack, as if that explained everything: but seeing that Tobias still looked blank he explained that once a ship had gone aground, and when everything that could be done to bring her off had been done, then it always happened that the crew would get to the spirit-room and start every barrel and bottle there, to die drunk if die they must.

'And they put on their best clothes,' added Lewis. 'It is the custom, like putting pennies on a dead man's eyes, or dressing a corpse up pretty. I had a spotted nankeen waistcoat and a round beaver hat. And when I woke up, stone-cold sober, I was still there and it was the next day: the sea had gone down a little, and them as could swim was a-swimming, because there were Moors standing there on the black rocks waving to them to come ashore, as who should say, "I'll help you ashore, mate." So I laid hold of a piece of the starboard trailboards – she was going all to pieces for-ard – and chanced it on the back of a wave, and the minute I come ashore a fellow in a nightshirt hauls me up the rock before the sea can pull me off. Well, I make as if to thank him, and he whips off my neck-cloth. "Avast, brother," says I, quite surprised, and he whips off my spotted nankeen waistcoat. And when I look displeased he shows me a dagger at my throat, while an old party in a blue frock and veil (his grandma, I believe) trips me up by the heels to get at my shirt. They were doing it all along the shore, and nobody had the spirit to resist 'em, being so cold and wet. They stripped us naked every one, and would not allow us more than an old piece of sail that came ashore to make a tent from the cold and the rain.

'When the tide began to make the sea grew worse again, and the ship ran all to pieces, pounding and beating most horrible to see, and about high-water she broke. The fore-part turned keel up, and the midships went all abroad; but the after-part of the poop held fast for a while. About thirty men there were for'ard, and they all went, but for a few people we could pull ashore; and they mostly died from the beating of the surf. On the poop there was the captain and close on a hundred and fifty more, and every time a big sea come up fit to sweep 'em off, the Moors all laughed and capered. We looked to see them go any minute, and once the fife-rail carried away with five or six men; but they held, and when the tide was at half-ebb, the sea grew a morsel less, and the armourer, name of Coleman, well-nigh the only man left aboard as could swim, came ashore with a line – touch and go, but we haled him in when he was nearly spent. So we got a rope fast to the rocks, and they began to warp themselves ashore. But the captain would not come, there being some hands as were either still dead-drunk or too fearful to venture on the rope; and the officers called out to him, that it could never hold, once the tide of flood began to make. But come he would not, not until the cox'n of the barge crossed back and in a manner of speaking obliged him to warp ashore: which was very hard, seeing the captain could not swim and was so wore out that he could scarce hold on neither. So he came ashore, and we was right pleased. The flaming blackamoors looked for to strip him too, but that we would not abide, not the captain; and presently they sheered off.

'We had a fire, and the purser served out the drowned turkeys and hens, which was the first thing we ate in four and twenty hours; and we turned in all in the one tent, sitting up close, with the captain in the middle, it being judged warmer there. The next day the wreck was gone, broke to pieces and not another soul left alive. Then an officer of the Moors, called a bashaw, came with a troop of horse and marched us all off: and there were camels – very strange. We never rightly knew, the lower-deck, what was to do, but there was a Danish gentleman settled in those parts, a merchant, as sent us some blankets – we was naked else – and a French doctor as dressed the wounded, and right handsome it was in him, we all said, seeing how we had set about to vex his nation. Some said the king of those parts, the emperor, or sultan, as they say, was at war with King George, and we should all be slaves, like the poor swabs captured by the Algerines; and some said it was not so. But howsoever, this bashaw marched us off, with camels, for days and days, and on the way we fell in with the crew of the *Tartarus*, which had been wrecked too, the same night; so there was close on four hundred of us, counting three women belonging to the *Tartarus* and a baby one of them had brought ashore, holding its clothes in her teeth. And all the way whenever there was a village the Moors threw stones and dirt, and spat in the water they allowed us: we grew mortal tired of being made game of. And when at last we come to the city where this sultan was they set us to work, while he made up his mind whether he was at war with King George or no. The captain was very busy, as we did understand, with interpreters and letters to the Governor of Gib, and he often came to the place where we was kept to tell us to keep our hearts up, we should be took care of, and he would not leave us in the lurch: but for the work there was no help for it, and they set me and William Atkins to weeding. Some of the people was set to building up a huge old wall that had fallen down, and some to cleaning the camels' stables, and some to carrying water to make a pond where four of our midshipmen rowed about in a wherry, with the emperor sitting on a velvet chair, a-watching of 'em.

'But we was set to weeding: and one day we was in a little court with walls all round, a-weeding of it and talking, when suddenly a voice says, "Now, cully, what are you a-doing of?" We were quite at a stand, because it was in English, as good as you or me: presently I find that it come from a lattice window, so I makes my duty towards it, and says, wery civil, "Weeding, ma'am, if you please." And I says as how we was took prisoner and brought up to this city and set to weeding.

'"Would you like a nice cup of tea?" says she, and hands a little brass cup through the lattice. So we passes the time of day, and she turns out to be the queen of Morocco. Or one of the queens. For rightly speaking the Moors have many wives.

'She was the daughter of an English renegado, and she had kept Christian tastes and a liking for a chat: she was quite old, but spry and well-disposed, though sharp at times. "Are you happy in your work, my good man?" she asks. "No," says we, "we ain't." "Why is this?" says she, and we tells her as how the black quartermaster, or head-gardener or whatever, comes down on us cruel hard if so be he finds a weed, or if we touches a plant; and we, being sailormen, cannot tell the little weeds from the little plants, so we are banged and thumped like a couple of drums, every day. "Tut-tut," says she, "ain't you got no more sense that you can't tell weeds from plants, damn your eyes?" "No, ma'am," says we. "No more than you could tell a davit from a dead-eye." "Well, what a precious pair of loobies you must be, to be sure, ha, ha," says she; but when William Atkins, who is not a married man, chafes at this and says he does not care, or damn their old weeds, or something disrespectful like, she flies out wery sudden. "You stow your gab, William Atkins," says the queen, shrill and high, "damn your blood, you wall-eyed scrub – prating to your betters day and night with your davits and your dead-eyes, strike me down." But I told her he was wanting and foolish in his mind, and presently she calms down and says perhaps she can do with a man or two, to look after the poultry . . . did you hear that?'

It was the deep, unmistakable thud of a distant gun that came down the scuttle on the fresh air, and Jack was out of the sick-bay before Tobias had changed the current of his mind from the Emperor of Morocco's poultry yard to the question in hand. He reached the quarter-deck rail in company with Campbell: Cozens and Morris were already there, being on duty. Two miles over the sea to windward there was the little high-masted *Tryall*, whose station was outside the line, and as they watched the signal broke out and the gun was repeated. Morris was already on his way aloft with a glass and now he hailed the deck: the signal was the numeral twelve.

'Ay,' said the gunner, as if he personally had arranged it. He was the officer of the watch, and stepping up to the captain he touched his hat and reported, 'The *Tryall* signals soundings, sir.'

'Very good, Mr Bulkeley,' said Captain Murray. 'We will set the deep-sea line going at once. The Abrolhos: I had not expected them today.'

'I had, sir,' cried the gunner, wagging his head complacently, 'and to the very hour I was right.'

Tobias appeared on deck, blinking in the blaze of the sun. It had suddenly occurred to him that perhaps the Spaniards were upon them – that the gun was the first of a bloody combat – and he remembered with a mixture of exhilaration and alarm that Jack had told him many a time that it would be most unfortunate if they were forced to fight this side of the Horn, that they were too laden to give a good account of themselves until they were in the Pacific. Jack had also told him many a time not to gossip with people on duty, not to accost them, even; but he still found it difficult to tell those on from those off, and now he hesitated, slowly grinding his nightcap round and round on the top of his head.

'It is only the *Tryall* saying that she is in soundings,' said Jack, detaching himself from the rail and steering Tobias pleasantly along to a neutral space out of the way.

'The soundings of Brazil?' cried Tobias, taking him by the arm.

'Well, it is the Abrolhos Shoal, as I take it; but it is much the same thing.'

'How can you be so provokingly calm, Jack?' cried Tobias, in strong agitation. 'The New World, Brazil, another continent! The home of the jaguar, the tapir, the capybara, the vampire – the true, the genuine vampire, Jack . . .' – gazing earnestly at the western horizon as he spoke.

'I don't care what you say, Toby,' said Jack, steadily insisting upon the point although Tobias flowed on, 'but I will not have vampires in the cabin.'

'. . . the boa-constrictor, to say nothing of the three-toed sloth.'

'Nor a flaming boa-constrictor either.'

'I cannot wait to tread the Amazonian field,' exclaimed Tobias.

'Well, you will have to,' said Jack, leading him reluctantly away, 'for there are sixty leagues of water between us and Brazil.'

Chapter Eight

FAR, FAR TO THE SOUTH of the River Plate, a thousand miles and more, the desolate coast of Patagonia stretches down towards the bottom of the world. It is a land of cold plains, rising one behind the other to the cold interior; and sometimes there are rounded hills, or downs; but everywhere the land is made of shingle, unimaginable stretches of cold dry stones, with a little whitish naked earth among them. Here and there wisps of wiry brown grass bend and whistle under the dry cold wind, and sometimes a few low thorny shrubs are to be found in the most favoured places; but this is not enough to take away from the impression of desolate sterility – a vast, unending, silent emptiness. In places the naked ground shows snowy white with the efflorescence of saltpetre; and where the rocks stand bare, in inland cliffs or by the sea, they too show the harsh colours of chemical deposits, almost the only vivid colour in a sad, bleached, sterile world. Even the few rivers that flow over the empty pampas from the west are sterile too, clear and lifeless.

Far down this coast, in almost fifty degrees of southern latitude, and far from any summer, there is a folding-in of the shore which makes a natural harbour: it is called St Julian's. The first man ever to come there by sea, Magellan, built a gibbet on the shore and there hanged his mutineers; and Drake, coming there nearly sixty years after, did the same. So the creatures of this lost, ill-omened shore were used to strange things, whenever ships came in: the occasions were rare enough, for in the two centuries that separated Magellan from Mr Anson only a score of ships had touched there; but now St Julian's had no less than six at one time. The whole squadron was there, with the exception of the *Pearl*, which had parted company a month ago in a howling tempest, a full gale mixed with an inexplicable fog.

In this same storm the *Tryall* had lost her mainmast, and now she was alongside the *Wager*, receiving out of her a spare main-topmast: the refitting of the *Tryall* had already taken a week, and all the carpenters and the carpenters' crews of the squadron were there, hammering and sawing and banging day and night. The inhabitants of St Julian's had not been so thoroughly disturbed since Sir John Narborough spent the winter among them, seventy years before. For animals there were, although the country seemed not only devoid of life but also of anything that could ever support life: there were the guanacoes, the wild llamas, and each herd (there were several in the neighbourhood) had its sentinel on a height, watching the motions of the people by the sea; there were rheas, called ostriches by some, and they, like the guanacoes, had the long necks of creatures that must for ever be on the watch; there were pumas, tawny lion-like beasts almost invisible against the dun terrain, the destroyers, the cause of the hereditary anxiety and the long necks of the guanacoes; there were agoutis, rather like hares; and there were armadilloes. All these, except the placid armadilloes, were in a perpetual state of extreme watchfulness: there were not a great many of them – there could not be, in such a country – but they watched with the keenest attention, and they rarely missed anything at all. And when the creatures of the land did miss anything, it was certainly observed by one or another of the rapacious birds that sparsely lined the pallid sky – huge condors, hideous vulturine carranchas and chimangoes. They missed nothing, ever.

The sum of what they saw was little less than the entire refitting of the squadron, as far as it could be done without actually heaving down the ships. All the standing rigging was re-rove, all the chafing-gear renewed, preventers were sent up and storm canvas was bent against the rounding of the Horn; the holds were rummaged and restowed, and everything that was susceptible of it was oiled, greased, painted or tarred. All this was done at the greatest possible speed, for every day brought the southern winter on; and every captain did his best to see that nobody, anywhere, had the briefest moment for ease, reflection or the contemplation of the landscape; but even so there were some tasks that were less arduous than others, and one of these was the collection of salt.

Nearly all the running water in those parts is brackish, and nearly all the pools are salt – that is to say, when there is any water in them at all it is brine (guanacoes drink it, nevertheless; which is very strange). But the pools are nearly always waterless, and in the place of brine there is salt, shining and perfect, in immense crystals. This was the case when Sir John Narborough was there, but it so happened that when Jack and Tobias were riding through the rain from Bedford to London, rain also fell in south-western Patagonia, so that now, when they were sent with casks from the *Wager* to gather salt, they found a deliquescent black ooze surrounding an unlovely saline sludge, and instead of being able to cut it out as neatly as an Eskimo cuts snow blocks for his igloo they were obliged to spade up unsatisfactory dollops and set them aside to drain.

At this particular time there were several midshipmen squatting in the fetid mud, taking their ease about a handful of smoky fire (all Patagonia would not yield a blaze of honest wood – no trees at all) and waiting for their salt to drain: they spent their leisure in complaining of their lot, as seafarers so often do.

'Oh,' cried Tobias, in a great heat of reminiscent indignation, 'you may talk about your hard duty, your disagreeable quarters, your rude commanders. You may say what you please, but how would you like to be a surgeon's mate? Brazil, another universe, and I saw nothing of it – within a stone's throw of the largest rodent in creation, to say nothing of the epiphytes, and I am penned up in a hospital tent in order to tend a series of commonplace diseases – not so much as an amputation among them – mostly caused by voluptuous over-eating. People belonging to other ships, the greater part of them,' he added, glaring in what could only be considered a personal manner at P. Palafox, of the *Centurion*.

Mr Palafox was an Irish gentleman, and as such impatient of any disobliging remark; he had battered his shipmates for much less, but he was a grateful, affectionate soul, and now he only replied, 'Why, your soul to the devil, old Barrow, my dear, and did we not regale you with the great bat of the world?'

'Yes,' said Tobias, mollified, and bowing towards him, 'and I am infinitely obliged to you. But what base and lumpish mind induced the vampire, nay, *compelled* the vampire to leave the cabin? For I am persuaded that the vampire would never have left of its own accord, being a prodigious affectionate bat.'

Jack affected a high degree of unconsciousness and lack of concern, but he was not very convincing, and the arrival of a boy from the *Centurion* with loving messages from the first lieutenant and his assurance that if the salt were not aboard in exactly three minutes there would be the very deuce to pay, was quite welcome as a diversion.

'Has she come in yet?' he asked the boy. He was speaking of the *Pearl*, which had been seen in the offing the day before; the *Gloucester* had been sent for her, but with the light and contrary wind she had not yet made the harbour.

'No, sir, she's still working round the point,' said the boy, 'but her cutter has pulled round aboard of us.' The boy hesitated, but he was too big with his news to contain it, and speaking behind his hand he said, 'She's lost her captain, and she has seen the Spaniards – two seventies, two fifties and a forty.'

This news instantly swept the fate of the vampire into total insignificance, and with unbelievable rapidity the salt trundled down to the shore and the boats as all hands hurried to learn more if more was to be learnt, and to confirm what they had already heard.

It was true enough: the *Pearl* could not have miscounted, for, deceived by the Spanish admiral's signals, she had let them come within gunshot, and she had had plenty of time to number the ports of the enemy during the long chase that followed. It was clear that Admiral Pizarro had had exact information about Commodore Anson's squadron, for not only did his force outnumber it in guns and weight of metal, but he had even been able to fabricate a commodore's pendant so exactly like Mr Anson's that it foxed the officers of the *Pearl*, although they had seen the real one hundreds of times. It was clear, too, that the Spaniards were ahead of them, ready and prepared, with a superior force, on a coast familiar to their pilots for more than a hundred years, but untouched by the English since the high buccaneering days of Dampier and his disreputable friends – untouched, and unknown except for the certain knowledge that no coast, no storms and no seas were worse than those which lay before them.

And Captain Kidd was dead: that was also true. All those who had known him were heartily sorry for it, he having been a good man, cheerful, capable and very much esteemed in the squadron; but death was so usual in the Navy and at sea that it was much less noticed than it would have been by land. They had left rows and rows of graves behind them in Brazil, and they had expected to do so, for they were used to seeing scurvy, fevers and the ordinary perils of the sea carry off at least a tenth of their shipmates in a reasonably long commission, to say nothing of those killed in fighting with the enemy; and therefore without being particularly hard-hearted or callous they turned their attention more to the living than to the dead.

The Wagers had particular reason to pay attention, for they were to change captains again. By the unbreakable laws of seniority Captain Murray would succeed to the *Pearl*, and in his place the *Wager* would receive Mr Cheap, an exchange that made every man aboard very thoughtful. But however thoughtful they might be they had little time for gossip, and little for bemoaning their fate, for now the guns that had been struck down into the hold earlier in the voyage, partly to make room for more provisions between decks and partly to ease the ship in heavy weather, were laboriously roused up again into their proper places, against a meeting with the Spaniards. The guns were heavy, awkward brutes, and they had to be brought up with very great precaution; if a gun should slip it would plunge through the bottom of the ship, to the destruction of one and all, so it was understandable that the work of getting them up should call for something extra in the way of roaring, oaths and blasphemy. There was a steady bellowing throughout the squadron, for nothing can ever be done at sea without it, but aboard the *Wager* the noise was greater by far: the *Wager*'s crew was still far less of a united, skilled body than the crews of the other ships; her officers were fewer, and, in the case of the gunner and the bo'sun, far less efficient.

All this work was done in their last days at St Julian's; it was continuous, backbreaking toil, and they had no leisure for making up their minds about their new commander. He threw himself into the work; it was obvious that he was a hard driver and that he would spare nobody; and it was clear that he could talk in a very rough and savage fashion. But at this juncture any captain would drive his crew, without the ship's people holding it against him, for it was all part of getting his ship ready for sea in time.

'He means no harm,' they said, and they hoped it was true, because the captain of a man-of-war is a man with extraordinary powers; if he cannot make life at sea a perpetual picnic (the elements stand rather in the way) he can at least make it into a lively imitation of hell – he can flog, starve and hang at his own sweet will.

'He probably does not mean it,' said Morris nervously, picking at his biscuit.

'He had better not,' cried Cozens, with a devil-may-care expression. They were standing out of the bay – a light wind, though fair, and a cold grey forenoon – and the remembered heights behind the harbour were sinking into their accustomed solitude. Captain Cheap had signalised their departure by a harangue in which he had compared the Wagers unfavourably with the men of the *Tryall*, and had assured them that he would improve their speed in setting the topsails even if he had to rip out the living heart of every man aboard. He had also rebuked Mr Bean in public; he had ordered three hands for punishment for a fault in catting the anchor; and he had sworn that Morris would be disrated before he got round the Horn.

A midshipman is an officer only by courtesy; he has no commission until he is made a lieutenant. His legal status is that of a man appointed, or rated, by the captain – he is rated a midshipman on the ship's books, just as he might be rated a sailmaker or a butcher, and he is in fact no more than a petty officer. He is below the warrant officers such as the gunner, the carpenter or the bo'sun, who were at that time appointed by the Navy Office, and he can be disrated, or transformed into an ordinary seaman, at the captain's pleasure. And once he has been turned before the mast he can be flogged or punished in the same way as the rest of the lower-deck – a terrifying threat in a captain's mouth at any time, and even more so when there is the prospect of a very long voyage still to come. Morris was an inadequate midshipman, a lazy and ignorant fellow who was too stupid to try to improve himself, but on this occasion he had not really been at fault. He had been sent aloft to improve the appearance of a piece of chafing-gear – a piece of seal's skin wrapped round a rope that was likely to be frayed by another – and by the time he came down the seal's skin was hanging in disgraceful ribbons. A chimango, a bird something between a kite and a vulture but more passionately disagreeable than either, had ripped off the strong leather and had flown away with the greater part of it. This is the sort of unfortunate thing that can happen to anyone in the high southern latitudes, and in some circumstances it is best borne with a sigh and no more. But Morris was no judge of time and place, and he answered in a pertinacious, foolish manner. Nothing could have been more unwise, unless perhaps it was Toby's gratuitous intervention: hearing Morris's stuttering explanation about a bird, a sort of large yellow bird, and seeing that it gained no credit, he had stepped forward, and laying his hand on the captain's sleeve at once to calm him and to attract his attention, had assured him that there were indeed such fowls – had often watched them – probably of the polyborus family and not connected at all with the kites, though deceptively like them – destructive birds. Mr Eliot had walked him off before the end of his remarks, but not before Captain Cheap had recognised him and had said, with an ugly, sinister look, 'I shall look after you, my friend.'

Mr Cheap had the highest possible notion of the rights and dignity of a captain; but even if he had been as mild and sweet-tempered as Captain Murray he would not have relished being addressed with such freedom by a midshipman and a surgeon's mate, least of all on his own quarter-deck. As it was, he seemed to think that there had been a deliberate attempt at making game of him, and consequently of the essential discipline of the Navy. It was all most unfortunate, and it cast a heavy gloom over the present meal. Cozens was fairly talkative still, and he said, with many variations, that he would not stand for being pushed about, no, not by anyone – let them try. And he said that it was a cursed thing to have changed everything that they were used to: the new captain had ordered the ship back to the system of two watches. Morris was too uneasy about his fate to eat: Jack was plunged in thought – he ate silently, whistling at intervals and staring into vacancy while he chewed: Tobias was feeling too queasy even to look at the table, and he only sat there to keep Jack company. He was always seasick when it was rough, and even when the sea was calm, as it was now, he would be disastrously ill if he had spent even a few hours on shore. Campbell was on deck: but he had early given it as his opinion that Captain Cheap was the best seaman in the squadron, that it would do the hands a world of good to have less southern softness and feeding with silver spoons, and that if there were more like him in the Navy it would be a far better service. Furthermore, Captain Cheap was of a fine respeckit family of Gowk in Weesums, well known both to Campbell and to Mr Hamilton of the marines, wi' mony and mony a guid elder of the Kirk to his kin.

It so happened that Campbell and Captain Cheap suited one another, for as well as being acquainted and from the same part of the world, they were both devoid of humour, touchy, suspicious of insult or encroachment, deadly serious, hard and conscientious; each recognised the virtues of the other and ignored the vices; and Campbell, therefore, was satisfied with the change. But his satisfaction was not very widely spread aboard the *Wager*, and when Tobias, the dismal meal being done, went forward to the carpenter's cabin, he found the gunner there, in the act of expressing very strong views about it all.

'. . . I keep my watch and navigate, the same as Bean, and should be treated equal,' he was saying, in a high, querulous voice, 'and if this Cheap . . .' He broke off as Tobias came in, and stood about for some moments, balancing to and fro with the motion of the ship, as if wondering whether it was safe to go on; evidently he concluded that it was not, for he went away without finishing his sentence; and Tobias was glad to see him go. Mr Bulkeley was not a man Tobias could like; yet Mr Cummins, the carpenter, was particularly attached to him, and here was one of the contradictions that happen so often in life, for Tobias esteemed the carpenter highly, and was happy to be in his company. This, however, was not a social call, but a visit in the line of duty. The warrant officers were not required to present themselves at the foremast when they were sick, far from it: they were important beings, and they were treated in their cabins. Mr Cummins was a large, fat, pale man, apparently phlegmatic but in fact nervous and easily upset; he was the most skilful ship's carpenter in the squadron, and he had been much in demand during the recent re-fitting of the *Tryall*'s masts, so much so that he had quite worn himself out, working too long and too late, and he had finished by giving himself an ugly great gash with an adze.

Mr Cummins was one of those who preferred smoking his tobacco to chewing it, and as his enforced idleness called for more tobacco than usual, he could scarcely be seen through the unbreathable air. Tobias dressed the wound, and peered hard at it through the fog.

'The gash is coming along very prettily, Mr Cummins, very prettily indeed. Laudable pus, proud flesh, everything that could be desired. If there are not many sick, I shall come in the forenoon and take out the tent.'

'Tomorrow? Tomorrow, Mr B?' Tobias nodded, and the carpenter shook his head. 'Not tomorrow, you won't, Mr B,' he said, 'not if you have any bowels of compassion. Don't you know there is sixteen men ordered for flogging, in consequence of the remarks passed about the penguin? The penguin served out instead of pork? Said, "Damn the purser and damn his old penguins; they wanted their pork as they had a right to, by law." Ain't you never heard of it?'

'I did not think the captain meant it,' said Tobias.

'Well, he did,' said the carpenter. 'And if you have the bowels of a Jew, you will spend your forenoon patching of 'em up again, poor souls. And Mr B, I hope you will look to young Oram. You know young Oram, one of my crew? He is ordered up for answering saucy, though I put in my good word and said he was only a poor young fellow from the colonies, where they speak so strange, meaning no wrong.'

'Yes, I know him. But he told me he came from Philadelphia.'

'That's right.'

'In Asia Minor.'

'No, in the colonies – our colonies.'

'Oh. That is why he look so concerned when I asked him whether he was a Cilician or a Lydian, and spoke to him in Greek. So there is a colony called Philadelphia, Mr Cummins? In the New World, I presume?'

'Yes, indeed: though rightly speaking I think it may be a village in the colony, as who should say Piddinghoe in Sussex, Sussex being the county, and not Piddinghoe, if you take my meaning. Nay, for that it may be quite a town – I recollect my uncle Jones speaking of several houses in a row: made of mud and branches, no doubt, but quite a town for those parts. We must not expect a great deal from the colonies, Mr Barrow.'

'Must we not, Mr Cummins?'

'Poor barren things, I fear; and they can never come to good. And why is this, Mr B? Because was they other than poor barren things, would we have found nothing but a parcel of naked savages creeping about in the first place? No: there would have been reasonable people going about their occasions in fields, and dressed suitable, as is right and proper. But what did we find, Mr B? A parcel of naked savages, as before mentioned: which proves that nothing is to be expected from the colonies. Take poor Oram, for example: he has contracted such a rum way of speaking, what with running about with the heathen of those parts – for they are heathens there, I am sorry to say – that now he is ordered to be flogged, along with Execution Dock and John Hart, which makes three of my men in one day.'

'Why do they call him Execution Dock?'

'Mitchel? Why, because he was a pirate, in course. We always call pirates Execution Dock, or Black Flag, or the like, by way of allusion, as I may say, to their trade.'

'But is it not very monstrous to have a pirate aboard?'

'Oh,' said the carpenter mildly, 'you have to take what you can get, do you see: and if the man knows enough of the sea to reef and hand and steer, so much the better, let alone if he has enough of his craft to be carpenter's crew. Execution Dock was carpenter's mate in the *Bloody Mary* – turned King's evidence, said he was forced to it – which is all my eye,' said the carpenter, dragging down his lower eyelid with one finger, in a very hideous manner, by way of showing his disbelief, '– and so saved his neck, as many of 'em do. But as for its being monstrous to have him aboard, why, was I a commander, I should press Beelzebub into the service directly, if I thought he could hale upon a rope. Have you any clear view of the shape and abilities of Beelzebub, Mr Barrow?'

'Yes,' replied Tobias, 'a thick grey-skinned being, covered with coarse, translucent yellowish-red hair or bristles – a variable number of small thick limbs – unformed, amorphous, bulky trunk, gross and heavy – an almost human face. The head and face are almost human, Mr Carpenter.'

'Not unlike the purser, Mr B?'

'Very like the purser, Mr Cummins.'

In the long, long history of the Royal Navy there may have been a popular purser; but Mr Hervey was not this sport of nature. Pursers, at that time, regularly cheated the men in the amount and quality of their rations, in the price of the slops that the men were obliged to buy from them, and they had a way of embezzling any money that was not actually nailed down: their rapacity was so general and widespread that even the *Centurion* whose company was chosen with particular care, had a sad knave aboard – he was found to have appropriated a hogshead of tobacco and an unbelievable quantity of biscuit, when the ship was in longitude 80° W, and it was too late to do anything about it by a thousand miles and more. But to these little failings Mr Hervey added a greasy obsequiousness to those above him and an insulting haughtiness to those below, which made him quite actively disliked: he was at present currying favour with Captain Cheap, and he was said to be very thick with Plastow, the captain's steward, who had brought a fine reputation as a tale-bearer with him from the *Tryall*.

In the pause that followed their remarks about the purser the carpenter gazed at Tobias; he sighed and shook his head behind the smoke, but he said nothing.

'Apart from the tent,' said Tobias, returning to the matter in hand, 'there is nothing else to do: but you should take no beef or mutton, Mr Cummins, until this day week; and seeing that this is leap-year, that will be March the fourth – no beef or mutton until March the fourth, if you please.'

Tobias, leaving the carpenter, with mutual expressions of civility and good will, turned upwards at the break of the foc's'le and came out on to the gangway. Jack, Mr Eliot, Mr Jones (a very kindly master's mate) and several other friends had all strongly advised him to keep below and out of the captain's sight for a while, but the prodigious density of the atmosphere in the carpenter's cabin had made fresh air more important than anything else. Fresh air, thought Tobias, might keep him from being actively sick; and besides, there was a great deal of canvas between him and the poop, the breeze being so light – he would not be noticed.

He bumped straight into John Duck, who, with a delighted grin, pointed over the side. Tobias looked, and in an instant his nausea was forgotten: the sea was crimson, almost scarlet, as far as the eye could see, a lake of blood.

The squadron had not yet worked out of the great bay: low on the starboard the land lay black; far ahead a remote dark cape ran out into the crimson water, and close-hauled to weather this cape the squadron stood to the south through a sea in which their very wakes were red. It was an astonishing sight, and the strangeness of it was enhanced by the silence on deck – nothing but the quiet wind in the rigging, the faint creaking of the gear, and the solemn voice of the leadsman in the chains – 'By the deep four. By the deep four. Five fathom.'

The squadron was skirting the edge of shoal water, and the *Wager*, never a weatherly ship, had dropped away to the lee, as usual, where the water was shallower still: there was a very strong likelihood of her running aground, and everybody on deck paid the closest attention to the man with the lead – everybody except John Duck, who was hopelessly volatile, and Tobias, who did not know what was afoot and whose whole being was taken up with the spectacle of millions of millions of shrimps, incalculable myriads of shrimps, that were staining the sea, shrimps as red as if they had been boiled.

'By the mark three,' called the man in the chains.

'All hands – turn up all hands to bring the ship to an anchor,' ordered Captain Cheap, and the cry ran instantly through the *Wager* – all hands, all hands on deck, all hands to bring the ship to an anchor.

'Are the anchors clear?' said the captain.

'All clear.'

'What water have you in the chains?'

'*Shrimps*,' exclaimed Tobias, who had just realised what they were.

'Silence, there. What water have you in the chains?'

'Eight, half nine.'

'Keep fast the anchors till I call you, Mr Bean.'

'Aye-aye, sir; all fast.'

'No ground with this line,' called the leadsman.

'Pass along the deep-sea line.'

'Aye-aye, sir.'

'Are you ready there? Damn you, are you ready there, with the deep-sea line?'

'All ready, sir.'

'Heave away, watch, watch, bear away, veer away.'

'No ground, sir, with a hundred fathom.'

The ship seemed to let out her breath; it had been an anxious, a very anxious quarter of an hour, and now it was over people turned and smiled at one another: but the smiles were quickly abolished by a furious roaring from the poop – a calling out to know who that was who had presumed to cry 'Shrimps' and a demand that he should come, or be brought, without the loss of a moment. But even in such a scratch crew as the *Wager*'s, with an unfair proportion of fools and evil men, there was no one to deliver up the criminal, and fortunately a change in the breeze, with the necessity for trimming sail, diverted the current of the captain's mind. Tobias felt an oppressive weight of guilt, however; he hurried away, bent inhumanly low, with his eyes partially closed, by way of making himself invisible; and by various cunning detours he reached the shelter of the cabin undetected. He knew that he had cut it pretty fine, as Jack would say; and by way of conciliating fate he sat down to write up the sick-bay accounts in a fair hand, taking the utmost pains to make them neat.

'There you are,' cried Jack, in a loud, accusing voice, when he came below at the end of the watch. 'You are cutting it pretty fine, Toby, I can tell you, with your prancing about all over the ship, roaring out "Shrimps" like any infernal old fish-wife. Shrimps, forsooth. It will be cockles and mussels next. What were you thinking of, to make such a horrible din, at such a time?'

'I was amazed by the shrimps,' said Tobias. 'Had I reflected, I would not have called out: but you will admit that it was an extraordinary sight.'

'Prodigious,' agreed Jack gloomily, 'and a very pretty omen, I am sure. We set sail on a Friday, which is a very cheerful sort of a beginning, and we sail straight into a blood-red sea. If the commodore had asked my advice, we should not have sailed until tomorrow.'

Most of the people under Mr Anson's command would have given him the same advice, in the likely event of his asking them; and it is possible that the great man himself would not willingly have put to sea on a Friday (if only because of the despondency it spread among his more superstitious shipmates) had the urgency of his mission not pressed him so, and the lateness of the season. Superstition was a weakness from which Tobias was totally free – he was devoid of poetry, poor soul, but he was devoid of its dark, perverted shadow too – and he at once fell to proving that there was no connexion between shrimps and Friday, and none between Friday and misfortune.

'My dear Jack,' he said, 'do but consider how illiberal, how unphilosophic it is to suppose . . .'

A week later, to the very day and hour, he was reasoning with Jack in the foretop, with just the same eagerness, and with just the same amount of success.

'Do you not see that it is wholly unreasonable – contrary to experience – contrary to logic?' cried he. 'Where, for example, are your dismal forebodings of last week? You must confess that they have come to nothing: the weather is charming – see how cheerful the penguins are.'

'Yes, it is all very well,' said Jack, looking up into the cold blue sky, 'but I wish you would not say so, Toby. It is not that I mind a blow. Strike me down, I *love* a good blow. But nobody that has ever been to sea wants to find himself on a lee-shore.'

At this moment the squadron, having run down its southing in thick, cloudy weather, was lying off Cape Virgin Mary in a calm, clear evening, with the captains all aboard the commodore for a council, and the seals, sea-lions and penguins of the Straits of Magellan (the cape marks the entrance to this interesting channel) hurrying up in droves to view the ships.

'I am glad, at any rate, that we are not going through there,' said Jack, nodding towards the Straits, whose northern boundary was clearly visible from the foretop. 'Once you were in that passage, you would have a lee-shore whatever happened, unless the wind was foul or well abaft the beam.'

'Jack,' said Tobias, in a confidential voice, 'pray tell me about this lee-shore, and why it is so often mentioned with dislike.'

Jack gazed at him for a moment. Had it been anyone else, Jack would have kicked him out of the foretop, for trying to make game of him. He knew that Tobias was capable of sailing half-way round the world without noticing the number of masts that propelled him, but even so he found it hard to credit such a very monstrous ignorance as this.

'Well,' he said, looking warily at Tobias to see whether really after all he were not joking, 'you know that the lee is the side the wind is not blowing on?'

'Yes,' said Tobias, with good faith evident in his plain countenance.

'Well then, a lee-shore is a shore under your lee – and with the
wind blowing from you to it.'

'I see. Thank you very much. But what is so disagreeable
about it?'

'Why, don't you see, blockhead?' cried Jack. 'If it blows strong,
and you have no sea-room, you are going to be driven ashore.'

'But you can tack, and sail along in that ingenious diagonal
manner that you explained, Jack.'

'Yes, you can beat up amazingly, in a moderate steady breeze,
with a kind sea and a stiff, weatherly ship: but the stronger the wind,
the more your leeway. Look, we can come within five points of the
wind,' he explained, sliding his hand through the air as if it were
the *Wager*, 'and we can keep there in a topgallant breeze, only losing
one point in leeway – I mean, by being pushed sideways as well as
along. But as soon as the topgallants have to come off her, that's
another point, which makes seven. And when one topsail goes, that's
another point, let alone the other two. So under your courses you
cannot sail nearer than eight points, which is ninety degrees off. You
may be pointing up into the wind nearer than that, but your real
course, the course you really travel, is eight points off it. That means
you are sailing at right angles to the wind at the very best – when
you are as close-hauled as possible, you still move at right angles to
the wind. So, don't you see, if there is a stiff wind blowing straight
on to the land, all you can do is to run along the shore, parallel
with it. Because you cannot beat up into the wind, do you see? You
cannot make any way into the wind, however much you luff up: do
you follow, Toby?'

'Yes, I do. I see that you would have to run along the shore in
such a case: but would that be very bad?'

'Not at all, if the wind stayed at only that strength, and if the
shore were charmingly straight and even. But what if it began to
blow really hard, and what if right ahead of you, on your course
parallel with the shore, you saw a vast great horrible cape? You
could not go about on the other tack, because she would not stay
in such a wind: you could not wear, because that would mean falling
directly down the wind, towards the shore, for a great way before

you could bring her up again. Anything you could do would only bring her nearer the shore. And anyhow, if the wind had increased by only a little, your course would not have been parallel with the shore at all: you would have been edging down towards it all the time, in an old unweatherly tub like this. Besides, the waves would have been heaving you in all along, to say nothing of the tide. No: you would end up by letting everything go, in the hope that your anchors would find a hold and that you could ride it out, and everybody aboard would grow uncommon pious all of a sudden. But it would not answer, you know, for your anchors would drag, and your cables would part.'

Toby said nothing: he was never one to show emotion, but he looked with a certain wistfulness at the loom of Cape Virgin Mary.

'Whereas if you had sea-room,' continued Jack, 'you could lie to.'

'How much sea-room would you consider sufficient?' asked Toby, 'and what do you mean by lying to?'

'Oh, a hundred miles of offing should make you tolerably happy,' said Jack. 'As for lying to, I will remember to tell you when we are doing it. From all I have heard of these waters, it will not be long. Toby, look over there, will you?'

To the westward the sweet afternoon was clouding, but clouding with a strange rapidity, not in layers or white masses, but in a black boil of angry storm that lit itself up from within, dull purple, by lightning. The darkness was growing fast over the land, and although the sea was still calm, the water had an unnatural light and transparency: the penguins, as they came up for air, leaping clear and going straight down again in one curve, showed far under the surface, darting with wonderful fish-like ease, accompanied by a silver train of bubbles. A cable's length away the *Anna* pink (which showed a most offensive partiality for the *Wager*'s neighbourhood, as though they really belonged to the same service) was already taking in some sordid underwear from the rigging as a necessary preparation for reducing sail.

'Well, I don't know,' said Jack, 'but I think you ought to go below and make all fast. The last time it came on to blow the squids got mixed up with the spare blankets – most unpleasant. I would give you a hand, but as soon as Sawney comes aboard we shall be precious lively.' He nodded towards the *Wager*'s barge, which was shooting towards them, with Captain Cheap looking disagreeable and important, but also much concerned, in the stern-sheets, with Campbell beside him. 'Go on, now,' said Jack, urging Tobias through the lubber's hole, 'and I shall come after you as soon as I can.'

That was not very soon, however: by six o'clock they had taken in their close-reefed topsails, and at the very end of Jack's watch it was all hands again; so instead of swinging easily in a warm hammock, with comfortably arranged pillows under his head, Jack found himself handing the foresail, lying aloft on a yard that groaned with the strain of the wind, while a south-wester, hurling itself in irregular squalls over the mountains of Tierra del Fuego and through the gap of Magellan's Straits, did its powerful best to throw him off. He made a brief appearance in the cabin to fetch his tarpaulin hat and jacket, remarked, with a grin, that 'it would be coming on to blow quite hearty, soon – growing precious cold,' and vanished, while a surge of sea-water slopped through the door as he opened it.

It seemed hours before he reappeared – hours of stupendous darkness filled with noise, huge innumerable noises that merged into one overwhelming clamour. 'Haven't you turned in yet?' he exclaimed, seeing Tobias sitting wretchedly on the edge of his bunk. 'I say, Toby,' he said, sitting down by him, 'you ain't uneasy in your mind, are you?'

'Yes,' said Tobias, 'I am very much alarmed, and could wish to be put ashore. But I am not terrified, I find. I went downstairs to see how the sick-bay was faring, and when I gave old Bull his drops I found that I could count and pour them perfectly well, which surprised me. But tell me, Jack, is this not a very dreadful storm?'

'No,' said Jack, 'it ain't. You will not think anything of it when you have been at sea for a year or two. But it is freshening, that's true enough, and we have just been preparing for a proper gale of wind. We are lying-to under a foul mizzen stay-sail, and when it is light I will show you what it means to be lying-to – nothing so exciting, when you have plenty of sea-room. And we have put spare gaskets to every sail that is bent – I am quite fagged out. Why don't you turn in, Toby? It will be dawn in an hour or two.'

'I do not want to alarm you, Jack,' said Tobias, 'but I am afraid that I must tell you an unpleasant fact: the sea is traversing the sides of the ship. Some has got into my bed.'

'Yes, it will do that,' replied Jack, yawning. 'Whenever a ship works as much as this, water comes in through the seams; but it don't signify. Would you like the hammock? I am used to the wet, you know – rather prefer it, indeed. Come, you shall try the hammock for once.'

'No, thank you very much, Jack. I do not mind it, I assure you,' cried Toby, lying down immediately, with a sudden squelch. 'It is perfectly comfortable,' he said, controlling an involuntary gasp. 'It was only that I supposed that the condition was abnormal – that we were about to sink.'

'What a din those guns make,' said Jack, after a pause, and speaking very loud over the screeching, 'although we double-breeched them all.' With each roll the guns, first on the one side and then on the other, strained their tethers to the utmost and then shot back again, each making a pig-like screaming as it did so and a thump as if it would force its way through the port. 'Then,' said Jack, closing his eyes, 'we got rolling tackles upon the yards, squared the booms, made all the boats fast, set tarpaulins and battens to the hatchways, got the topgallant masts down upon the deck and the jib-boom and spritsail yard fore and aft – we nearly lost Cozens and the bo'sun doing that – should have been sorry to lose Cozens – Lard, Toby, how sleepy I am. But never worry; she is as snug as can be – all the searoom you could wish – not the least danger or inconvenience in the world, so long as the *Pearl* don't fall aboard us – you will think nothing of it. Nothing at all – nothing . . .'

Chapter Nine

'YOU WILL THINK nothing of it,' Jack had said, long ago: he had been right, and now, in a sea that outran all description, Tobias balanced between the swinging hammocks of the sick-bay without consciously noticing the tremendous roll. The motion of the ship was less down here, but even so the hammocks swung so wide that the men were obliged to be lashed in, and the lantern threw so wild a light, and so uncertain, that he made his round mostly by touch.

He moved with the cat-like wariness that he had learnt in months of storm, the worst storms in the world, and he went steadily from hammock to hammock on his round – a long round, for the sick men stretched far away into the madly tossing shadows. There was little he could do for most of them. Ever since the scurvy had started to be really bad much of his care was nearly useless; but they did not know this, and the formula of taking their pulse and asking how they did at least showed them that they were not abandoned. Besides, there were the surgical cases, the men who had been injured on deck or hurt aloft – there were life-lines rigged in plenty, but, for all that, men were continually being hurt; men who had been at sea all their lives could not keep their footing in these storms, and there were broken collar-bones, stove ribs and three broken arms for him to attend to at present, as well as sprains and dislocations.

He covered the face of a seaman at the end of the row and nodded to Andrew, who hung a mark upon the hammock: that was the third today. But death was so familiar in the sick bay of the *Wager* that it was accepted without any surprise: so many had died. Ever since they had come into the Southern Ocean the scurvy had been with them, and growing every day, so that now more than half the ship's company was either so ill as to be laid up altogether or at least so kitten-weak as to fall down after five minutes at the pumps. And there was scarcely a man among those who were reckoned sound who was not affected in some degree; so that by a private calculation Tobias reckoned that unless the crew had some refreshment in their diet within seventeen days there would not be enough of them left to work the ship.

It was all a question of diet; everyone knew that. Men cannot live indefinitely upon salt beef, salt pork, dried peas and biscuit: they have to have something green and fresh, or they will eventually die. But how was greenstuff to be provided for a voyage in the far south, where for months you never see land but what you fly from it with all the sail you can bear? Mr Eliot had tried an experiment with cress and with sprouted grain; but that was in March, and his trays and seed-pans had stood no chance against the terrible seas since then – they had been destroyed by the fury of the Pacific long ago.

They were still just in the Atlantic when he and Tobias had planted them on that memorable day when they made the passage of the Straits Le Maire, and they had kept breaking off their gardening to run up on deck to see, on the one hand, the terrifying desolation of Tierra del Fuego, and on the other the shocking precipices and the dead-white snow of Staten Island, while a tide like a mill-race swept the whole squadron through the twenty-five mile channel in two hours' time, the wind fair behind them and the sky a brilliant blue. The ship had been alive with pleasure and anticipation, and although the night before had been spent in bending a whole new suit of sails – the strongest storm canvas – the watch below lined the sides to gaze at the astonishingly horrible land and to look for the sea at the end of the strait, the Pacific, the Great South Sea upon which the Spanish galleons sailed. They knew that round the corner of Cape Horn and a few hundred miles up the other side of the mainland there lay Chile and Peru, the golden treasures of Baldivia and Callao, Panama and Acapulco and beyond – all plain sailing in an open sea.

Even Captain Cheap was cheerful and obliging; he spoke civilly to Captain Pemberton of the marines, although they had not been on speaking terms since his second day aboard, and pardoned two defaulters. The bo'sun chatted in a friendly and animated way with the gunner and the carpenter, all grievances forgotten, at least for the time. Mr Eliot and Tobias planted their seeds and invited Mr Oakley to drink a bowl of rum-punch with them to the success of their sowing and the voyage. It was a delightful morning.

But the seeds had never even sprouted green before they were awash with salt water. The foremost ships of the squadron had barely cleared the strait before the wind backed with unbelievable suddenness into the south-west (the direction in which they had hoped to sail) and blew in tremendous squalls that laid the ships right down before the topsails could be taken in; and at the same time the tide turned, to run with even greater force than before and to sweep the hindmost ships, the *Wager* and the pink, towards the black cliffs of Staten Island and the half-sunken jagged reefs, all spouting with white foam. It was then that Tobias learnt what a lee-shore was; and as the *Wager* was driven slowly closer and closer, until at last a biscuit could have been thrown from the poop into the surf, he had had time to consider it, and to feel that Jack's passion for sea-room was not unreasonable. But in those days they had well over a hundred men capable of going aloft, and close on two hundred to work the ship: the *Wager* was stout and well-found then. They had weathered the point of Staten Island, profiting by a little shift in the wind, and they had saved themselves, if not Mr Eliot's flowerpots.

After that day in early March there had been a series of storms, one after another so close that it was not the storms that were remembered, but the rare intervals of calm between them. It was in one of these calms, a day of drifting fog, when the masts vanished upwards into nothing, and men who had sailed in the Greenland whalers swore they smelt the loom of icebergs, that they lost Mr Eliot – not by death, as they had lost and were to lose so many of their shipmates, but by his going aboard the *Gloucester* to help in an operation upon the fourth lieutenant, cruelly mangled when the huge main-yard broke in the slings. The *Wager's* carpenter had also been ordered across by the commodore to help in the repairs, and so, when the worst weather of the whole voyage struck them, they were without him. It was a westerly storm that raised a sea so enormous that a man could scarcely bear to look up at the waves, a mountain high and black, and it lasted for four nights and three days. Hour after hour the wind increased, hour after hour, until on the third night it seemed to have reached the highest point that could be borne: but those who thought so were wrong, for on the

141

third day it rose higher still, and the spray that filled the racing air began to freeze: it coated the masts, the yards and the rigging, and it accumulated in frozen grey masses on the deck. The *Wager*, burdened by the ice, rolled gunwales to; and, as she rolled, the wind's shriek in her rigging varied – highest when she was in the middle of her roll, lowest when she was down – so that it made a slow, dreadful ululation. Suddenly in the fourth night it changed: in one moment the whole note changed, for the mizzen-mast had gone. The chains to the windward had broken: the whole massive assembly had yielded, not only the dead-eyes and lanyards, but the irons too. The mizzen-mast had gone, and with it the main-topsail yard. The main-mast was tottering, and the standing rigging, afore and abaft, was a senseless tangle.

Then, when the ship could have been dismasted altogether, broached to and destroyed, the wind died to no more than a steady gale; they had a few hours' respite to knot and splice, and although without a carpenter aboard there was little enough they could do to deal with the masts, they managed to survive another week, and even to keep company as the squadron beat to westward: a day calm enough for a boat to swim came at last, and they had their carpenter again. But Mr Eliot stayed aboard the *Gloucester*. He had been knocked down by a block falling from the rigging (a very usual accident) and he was obliged to stay in the *Gloucester* until the next opportunity – an opportunity that never came.

Mr Eliot had always insisted that scurvy was to be classed among the diseases of the imagination; and certainly in the last few weeks there had been three striking facts that supported his theory. A little after the loss of the *Wager's* mast the *Pearl* and the *Severn* vanished – they parted company in rain and sleet so thick that you could not see the ship's length, and they were never seen again. Secondly, when the squadron had been beating to the westward for so long that the navigators reckoned themselves at least ten degrees of longitude, or three hundred and fifty miles west of Tierra del Fuego, in spite of the strong current that set against them, orders were given to steer north; the larboard tacks were hardly aboard before the news spread through the ship – they were bound for the warm, calm waters of the true Pacific; the rigours of beating up in snow, ice and hurricanes were over. Then at two bells in the middle watch, the

Anna pink fired every gun she had; the moon, shining for a few providential minutes through the racing clouds, had showed her the appalling spectacle of Cape Noir right ahead, with the surf rising a hundred feet up its side. Providentially, again, the wind that was carrying them right on to the land, shifted into the west-north-west, and they came safely off. But the whole wretched task of making their westing was still to be done – they had not allowed enough for the current and for their own leeway. Thirdly, after a still longer reach to the south west and another turn northward, the squadron was scattered by still another appalling storm, and from that day on the solitary *Wager* had plunged northwards through a black and lonely sea, so utterly alone and in such a sea that men doubted the reality of things, and half suspected that they were already dead and condemned to a sailors' hell.

Each of these three happenings had been followed by an increase on the dead-list that Tobias gave to the captain and the purser; and the coincidence of extreme disappointment and death from scurvy was so striking that Tobias was almost convinced. Yet on the other hand he did not consider himself a fanciful creature; a less imaginative one was not to be conceived, in his opinion: but he knew that he was entering the third stage of the disease himself. He had seen it too often in others to be mistaken. The symptoms were many and various, and although blotches growing and spreading, swollen legs, bleeding nails and gums, teeth going were usual, they were not inevitable; but the third stage, difficulty in breathing, followed by extreme weakness and prostration was, in his experience, invariable. He had seen it so often – a man at the pumps or the halliards would drop sometimes as suddenly as if he had been struck down, but more often slowly, staggering away a few steps and crumpling up; and his mates would carry him below to his hammock. No one who had reached that stage had ever come out of his hammock, except to go over the side; at least, no one aboard the *Wager*.

And the idea that this disease, as well as the seasickness that had haunted him so long, should be set down as in any way connected with his mind, nerves or imagination, was inexpressibly vexing.

'How can it be classed among the diseases of the imagination?' muttered Tobias, frowning and clapping his hand to his forehead.

'Eh?' cried Andrew, holding up the lantern.

'Andrew,' said Tobias, after staring about for a moment to recollect where he was and what was to be done next, 'Fetch the sweet oil, if you please. I must go to see the master.'

Mr Clerk had been injured when the starboard shrouds of the foremast parted, and in addition an old wound, healed twenty years before, had reopened – a usual consequence of scurvy – and he needed tender handling: but during these months of almost continual crisis, with all ordinary rules and customs gone by the board long since, Tobias' waking hours had been spent either in the sick-bay or at the pumps, or hauling on a rope, or even lying aloft in some emergencies, and his hands were as hard and horny as a seaman's. They were quite unsuitable for the work he was to do, and as he went aft to the master's cabin he rubbed the sweet oil in to make them a little softer.

He passed Jack, who was hurrying on deck still half asleep, and they passed the time of day; they rarely saw one another now, for when either was not on duty he turned in, dead to the world, however great the noise. Jack looked anxiously after him as they parted, but Tobias went steadily on to the master's door and disappeared. Jack ran on deck, and judging the roll to a nicety, he stepped straight over to his usual place at the break of the poop. The *Wager* was standing to the north-north-west, and for once the wind had shifted out of the west and south-west and had come into the east-south-east, blowing in over the *Wager's* starboard beam – a strong wind, three parts of a gale, with occasional squalls of sleet, and she was making about six knots under her courses. Ordinarily she would have been showing her topsails, reefed or perhaps double-reefed; but with her masts so frail she had spread no more than her courses these many days. Besides, there was scarcely a sound piece of storm-canvas left in the ship: the topsails that were now bent to the yards were the last they had, and they were so worn that they could not be relied upon in a blow; but even if the sail-room had been full of new sails, there were not enough upper-yard men left to use them.

Jack was a little before his time. Mr Bean and what remained of the starboard watch were still on deck; the lieutenant, one of the master's mates and Cozens under the lee of a tattered strip of weather-cloth, and the hands forward, huddled in the shelter of the gunwale, looked wretched, blue and surly. Jack was feeling blue as well, for the cold, although it was not quite freezing, was of a peculiarly penetrating damp nature, very disagreeable before breakfast; but he was better able to withstand it than most, being surprisingly fit and well; apart from a great weal across his face; where a lashing strip of topsail had nearly blinded him, he was in excellent condition. This topsail was one of the many that they had lost: it was furled up tight to the yard and kept there not only by its gaskets but by a whole doubled set of storm gaskets as well, and yet the wind had found means to work into the folds, to balloon the sail out, to burst its bindings and so to loose it to the full, whereupon it split in every seam and thrashed about so as to endanger the yard, the top and all the rigging near it. It had to be cut free, and that was a desperate task, on a black, black night off the pitch of the Horn, with the sea running monstrously high and the shrouds and yards all coated with ice: they had lost four men, at one time and another, doing this, and a fifth was so injured that he was in no way to live.

Campbell came on deck, looking yellow and exhausted; he nodded to Jack, and as he did so, eight bells struck. In these times many naval ceremonies slipped out of use – for example, Jack was dressed in a curious hairy garment called a grieko, which made him look not unlike a bear, and beneath it showed a foot or so of crimson waistcoat, chosen for warmth rather than uniform appearance – but many were so firmly rooted that they would stay as long as the shattered vessel held together. The watches succeeded one another in due order, the quartermaster handing over the helm repeated his course with the traditional solemn exactitude, and now in a minute the gunner would relieve Mr Bean as the officer in charge of the quarter-deck. The watch on deck went thankfully below to what cold comfort they could find, and a new set of men took up their stations.

Precious few of them, reflected Jack; and those few difficult to work with. They had never been the same since the commodore had been lost to sight. Mr Anson was held in great respect throughout the service, and it seemed as if his presence alone, somewhere within the bounds of the horizon, had kept the men to their duty; certainly they had been far less biddable since the *Centurion* went.

But what kind of example did they have? The gunner had been openly criticising the captain's orders these weeks past. Every time he relieved Mr Bean he said, 'Well, sir, and what do you think of a lee-shore with the ship in this condition?' – it was becoming a sort of unwholesome ritual. Bulkeley, the gunner, and the other inferior officers, were certain that the ship ought to be carried to Juan Fernandez: the master was of this opinion, and the master's mates, but Bulkeley was the only one to say it publicly on the quarter-deck. And anything said on the quarter-deck was retailed below, on the gun-deck, within a very few minutes: no wonder the men were not in good heart.

'Well, sir,' said the gunner, in his high, complaining voice, to Mr Bean, 'and what do you think of a lee-shore with the ship in this condition?' He cast a look up at the low torn clouds, and bit his nails.

'Oh, I cannot tell,' said the lieutenant in a non-committal tone, and he went below.

The fact of the matter was that the gunner, ever since they came into the southern ocean, had been suffering from fear, self-importance and wounded vanity; but above all fear. It was natural enough; the circumstances were very frightening indeed and everybody aboard had spent a great deal of the time in a state of alarm – a state bordering upon terror. But in the gunner it had the unfortunate effect of making him loud-voiced and talkative: he was convinced that he could handle the ship and navigate her better than anyone else, and no considerations of decency, respect or modesty (they being overcome by fear) prevented him from saying so, in a high, persistent, nagging shout.

'The captain did ought to consult his officers,' said Bulkeley, meaning that Mr Cheap should submit to his guidance, particularly in the article of steering away from the coast of Chile and making for the safety of Juan Fernandez.

It was a grave reflection upon Captain Cheap that things should have reached this pitch. This was his first experience of command (apart from a little while in the *Tryall*) and he had tried to impose respect by ferocity towards the men and haughty reserve towards his officers; but he had not been consistent in this attitude, and at times he had allowed and even encouraged liberties which even a very easy-going captain would never have permitted. He had also been very much out of order – painfully ill at times – and this had made him more offensive than he might have intended.

In the course of their navigation he had naturally consulted with the navigating officers about the ship's position; that is to say, he had taken notice of the observations of the lieutenant, the master and (in this unusual ship's company) the gunner. But he had made the great mistake of sometimes allowing a difference of opinion over their longitude degenerate into an argument about their destination, which was nobody's business but the captain's. It was generally believed aboard the *Wager* that Juan Fernandez, an island some five hundred miles to the west of Chile, was to be the squadron's rendezvous in case of separation. This was an inaccurate rumour, however, for the last council of war aboard the *Centurion* had decided upon a meeting-place off the island of Socorro, in order to attack the Chilean town of Baldivia; and it was only if the ships should fail to meet there within a certain time that they were to bear away for Juan Fernandez. This decision was secret, of course: the orders that were given to the captains were not shouted from the maintop but delivered under seal.

Yet so persuaded was the gunner of the truth of the rumour about Juan Fernandez (and that remote island seemed wonderfully attractive after they had been beating round the Horn for a few weeks) that he scarcely believed it when the captain, in the course of one of these undignified wrangles, said that his orders directed him to Nuestra Señora de Socorro, in 44° South. Bulkeley had then begun to talk about the captain's discretionary powers: Captain Cheap had the right to vary his orders, because to sail for Socorro would carry them all the length of the coast – the winds, tides and currents all set in towards the mainland – they would be on a lee-shore all the way – it was madness to attempt it with the ship so shattered – they could do nothing even if they got there – would be of no use – any captain had the right and the duty to vary such orders, for the good of the service, and all the officers would agree . . .

Captain Cheap did not choose to be told his duty and he felt that in any case the talk had gone far beyond tolerable limits. He silenced the gunner, but in doing so, and after he had done so, he never referred to the whole point of the rendezvous as a gathering-point for the attack upon Baldivia. It therefore appeared to the gunner that the captain was standing in with the coast either out of pig-headed obstinacy and ignorance or out of a furious desire to reach it before the others, to have the earliest chance of prizes and the first hand at the Spanish treasure.

This was the gunner's opinion, and he made it widely known. The captain was already unpopular for his brutality and for his habit of listening to tale-bearers and favourites; but now he was represented as an incompetent navigator as well, and as a commander who was careless of his ship and the lives of his crew. Many people believed the gunner, and the *Wager* sailed northwards towards Socorro in a wretched, discontented, distrusting and fearful state of mind – a condition that made the inevitable hardships even harder and the daily perils even more dangerous.

Jack had heard of the plan for the attack on Baldivia (not all the officers of the squadron were as discreet as Captain Cheap) and he saw the vital importance of carrying the *Wager* to the rendezvous – you cannot conduct military operations against a fortified town by land without field-pieces, siege-guns and the like, and everything the squadron possessed of that kind lay in the *Wager's* hold – and he honoured the captain for his determination to be at the appointed place. It was a most respectable determination, he thought: though natural enough, in all conscience, aboard a real man-of-war – if you were ordered to Sodom or Gomorrah you proceeded thither under all sail conformable with the weather, and you either arrived there or perished on the way; and at no time did you consult with the various members of your crew to make sure that your course was exactly to their liking. That, at least, was the simple philosophy that Jack had learnt aboard the ships in which he had served hitherto, and it still seemed sound enough to him. Suppose, he thought, they were now to sail off to Juan Fernandez and after that to tell the rest of the squadron that they had not chosen to bring the artillery to Baldivia, because the sea was rough and the coast unkind . . . the supposition was so monstrous that he snorted, flapped his arm, and walked over to the rail.

'But for all that,' he said to himself, fixing a torn raft of seaweed with his eye to judge the speed and leeway of the ship from its movement on the heavy western swell, 'for all that, I wish he would keep more of an offing until we are at the height of Socorro.' They had been seeing patches of weed for the last two or three days, as well as some birds like comorants; and in general these are never seen far out in the open sea.

'Hey, Mr Byron,' shouted the gunner, over the roaring of the wind. 'You have young eyes. What do you make of that?'

Jack followed the gunner's outstretched arm, and balancing to the great rise and fall of the deck he looked into the thick leeward clouds just long enough not to be too uncivil. 'A cloud, sir,' he said. The gunner was always seeing land, and Jack was not going to gratify him by flying into a panic. The quartermaster, Rose, was clearly of the same opinion: not that he said anything, nor made any contemptuous motion; but his stone face spoke volumes.

'Keep her –' began Bulkeley, but a double crash forward and a huge flapping cut him short. The fore-yard was down and the sail was billowing away over the larboard bow, wrapping itself about the bumkin, catching on every projecting remnant of the smashed rails and timbers of the head. The stupidest man in the watch knew that the sail must be saved, and they flew to bunt it to the shifting yard – they bundled it up, clewed it up as best they might while the yard, loosely held by the starboard lifts and the yard-tackles, ground heavily to and fro over the deck. Jack knotted his gasket tight and skipped out of the way as the hulking great yard lurched over to pin him: at the same time he saw the gunner, waist-deep in the leeward foam, whip a turn about the yard and the cathead, making all fast so quickly that he was back inboard before the ship pitched again. It was all very well done, and now they could secure the yard without much danger – Bulkeley could act in a seamanlike manner in an emergency. It was when he had time to think that the gunner was so unpleasant, and now he had scarcely discovered the cause of the disaster before he was complaining again. 'The jeer-blocks, the strops of the jeer-blocks is broke. It is the end of everything – I never seen the like – a proper hulk we are now, along of this carrying too much sail.'

The captain was there, looking wretchedly ill, with Mr Bean behind him. The din had brought every able-bodied man on deck – a thin company now, for where the waist of the ship would once have been crowded as thick as bees on a comb, scarcely a dozen hands stood gazing at the wreckage, and away aft no more than three of the soldiers showed their pale faces. For a moment the captain looked distraught and haggard, as if the breaking of the jeer-blocks were more than he could encompass: then he said, 'They must be new-stropped. Have it done at once, Mr Bulkeley.' Before the gunner could reply, he turned away and hurried below.

The falling yard had done a great deal of damage, and there being so few men in the watch it was hours before the foc's'le looked in any sort of order; but at last the yard lay trimmed on deck, and the jeers were ready to be rove: Jack, the gunner and the master's servant were in the foretop to deal with the upper block, and it looked as though the task would soon be done. They did not intend to sway the yard up, but to get it ready to be raised when the damaged mast and rigging should have been repaired to some degree. The day had been clearing as they worked, and it had grown colder; by cruel experience they knew that this often meant a harder blow – in those regions almost no change was for the better – and during a pause Jack looked up into the sky and round the horizon in a search for portents. The green light that foretold a storm was there, surely enough, but it was not the light that made his blood run cold. It was the line of high land, black and topped with snow, that lay right under their lee. The land stretched away far to the right and the left, and it bore north-west of them on the larboard beam: it was impossible that land should be in that quarter. By the charts it was impossible that there should be any land to port. And yet there it was, and the ship was driving bodily upon it.

The gunner was peering down and directing the work below, the passing up of the jeers and their tackle, and between orders he kept up a running grumble – he knew what it would all come to, and always had – and it was a shameful sight, the officer of the watch working like any common sailor – some people there were who kept their beds. 'Pass that parrel-line,' he said to Jack. 'Do you have flannel ears?' he cried angrily; then, seeing what Jack was staring at, he cried out 'Oh my God,' and hurled himself down a rope to the deck.

A moment later the bo'sun's mate was piping all hands. The captain came running forward, and as he reached the after-ladder he tripped; the head of the ship was right down in the trough of a wave at the moment he fell, so he pitched far and hard – an unlucky fall. Getting up he shouted 'Sway up the yard and set the foresail. Wear the ship.' And with this effort he fainted away for a moment, for he had dislocated his shoulder and then in rising had twisted and wrenched the joint most shockingly.

Tobias, running up towards the jeer-capstan, stopped to help him, but Captain Cheap roared out an order to get forward and thrust him away.

'You will do yourself a mischief,' said Tobias, as the captain staggered against the fife-rail and nearly fell again. 'Here, Mr Oakley, bear a hand, if you please.' Between them they carried him to his cabin, and the army surgeon (being the senior) tried to force the arm back; but he could not manage it, and they were obliged to leave him, wedged into his bunk, half insensible with pain.

Slowly the capstan turned, and at long intervals the pawl went click: this was the ratchet that prevented the capstan from turning back again, and often Jack had heard it ticking as fast as a little loud clock. But now instead of three men to a capstan bar there was only one between two, and it was so hard to turn that Jack feared their strength would give out before the yard was up. He found that the only thing to do was to pay no attention to anything else, but to lean forward on the outermost end of the bar with his head down and his eyes closed and concentrate entirely on getting a good grip with his bare feet on the deck, so as to keep a continual pressure with all his force on the bar. There was a distinct difference as Tobias and Mr Oakley added their weight to the thrust, but Jack did not look up; it was essential to set the foresail for they could not wear the ship without it, and it was essential to set it at the earliest possible moment. Slowly they went round and round, and the pawl went click, click, click; very slowly the heavy yard rose on the mast, swaying wildly with the increasing roll of the ship, while inadequate parties at the yards and braces tried to steady it.

Round and round: with one part of his mind Jack counted the strokes of the pawl, each one a little victory, and with another he tried to account for their situation. The land to the north-west made no sense unless the ship had come so far to the east of her intended course that she now stood right in with the shore, and that she had somehow entered a vast uncharted bay or gulf whose northern arm was that land on the larboard beam – some cape or peninsula that trended far away into the west. That was the only explanation: the current had set them to the east, the variation of the compass had done the same (they had not been able to take an amplitude to check it for weeks) and their underestimated leeway had done the rest: they were entangled with the land and embayed. Their only chance, on this uncharted coast, was to turn about and try to get away by the way they had come in. To do that they must wear the ship, and to wear the ship they must set the foresail: he thrust on and on.

Somebody was banging him on the shoulder. He looked up stupidly and found that the yard was home.

The land was clearly visible from the deck now, the headland with snow on it that he had first seen was there to the larboard, and now a dark line loomed right round the northern horizon and joined a distinct mass of land on the starboard side. From the yard, as they set the foresail, they could see the vast white mountains of the Cordillera, filling the whole of the east. Far over there, to the east, the sky was clear: to the westward, darkness was gathering fast.

With the foresail set the *Wager* plunged on at a great pace. They wore her at once: she wore easily – it was her one good point – and came up with her head to the south-south-west just as the light of day was fading. She would come up no closer to the wind than that; but if the wind stayed true, and above all if it would allow them to set their main-topsail, they might very well make a comfortable offing by the next day.

'It all depends on the wind,' said Jack. The cook, a very old but indomitable man, had somehow managed to give the midshipmen's berth a hot mess of beef and beans, and stuffed with this Jack was turning in. Tobias, who now lay on a piece of grating between his chest and the bulkhead – the bunk was perpetually awash – still sat up, soaking a biscuit in a mug of their last Madeira: he could no longer chew biscuit, because some of his front teeth had come out with the scurvy, and the others were unsure.

'It always seems to depend on the wind,' he said. 'An uncomfortable dependency, Jack, I believe?'

'Yes. But we cannot do anything about it, you know,' said Jack, 'and in my opinion it is far better to sleep while you can.'

'Just so,' said Tobias.

At midnight Jack woke suddenly and completely. The hands were being turned up for the second watch – the graveyard watch – and as he came on deck he was met with a stinging packet of water that was driven on by a stronger wind by far. The big tarpaulined form of Cozens blundered into him, and said, 'It's blowing up, mate. It's blowing up.' It was indeed: by the light of the top-lantern Jack could see that they had set the fore, main and mizzen staysails, and he wondered they had dared to do it, for the *Wager* was lying down, and the shrieking of the wind in the rigging was higher than he had ever heard it. She was up as close to the wind as ever she would come, and a wicked cross-sea kept hammering her a little aft of her larboard bow; the torn spray and the rain drove in sideways so thick and hard that the poop-lantern was no more than a dim white blur. She was shipping a great deal of water; the waist of the ship was swirling deep, and it seemed to Jack that she was much heavier, much longer in coming up from her roll.

There were two men at the helm, trying to master the kicking wheel and to keep her from falling off under the thrust of the sea; and by them, under the shelter of the poop, Captain Cheap stood lashed to a stanchion: his face showed ghastly by the binnacle light.

The lieutenant's watch did not leave the deck, and minute by minute the wind grew louder. There was a prolonged struggle with the staysail sheets, which had to be hauled farther aft, and then the watch regained the shelter: they all, without a word, stood with their backs to the weather staring into the leeward darkness, trying to pierce the thick, black night.

An hour passed: two hours. From time to time the captain gave an order for the trimming of the sails, and the lieutenant relayed it. During the course of the night, as the wind increased, so it veered south and then south-west: it was blowing so hard towards the middle of the watch that a man could scarcely stand the whip of the rain in his face, nor breathe without making a shelter for his mouth. But still they stood, listening with strained attention.

They were all of them listening for a sound that was not the wind, but the roaring crash of breakers. Presently they heard it, and one after another their faces turned to the captain as they were sure of the sound.

'Mr Bean,' said the captain, 'we will throw out the tops'ls.'

'Aye-aye, sir,' said the lieutenant. It was their only chance to claw the ship off.

The *Wager* staggered as the topsails filled, staggered and laid down until the lee gunwale was far under the foam: a still more shocking blast laid her farther still. 'She's gone,' cried Jack, clinging to the yard. But with that the topsails split, flew out cracking in ribbons, and were cut away. The ship righted herself slowly and surged on through the terrifying sea.

Jack found himself on deck again, scarcely knowing how he got there. Many more people had come from below and were standing on the quarter-deck, the marine officers and the purser. The steadiness of the binnacle-light, the helmsman's face lit from below, grave, intensely serious, but in no way terrified, entirely wrapped in his task – these things were a comfort, something solid in a dissolving world. The captain had evidently given orders, for the carpenter and his crew were there with broad axes ready.

Half an hour passed: the wind grew higher, and as it mounted the rain stopped; the moon had risen behind the thinning cloud, and the night grew less impenetrable.

He felt a nudge, and there was Cozens next to him, saying, 'We shall claw off yet,' joining his hands in a trumpet by Jack's ear.

Jack nodded. He asked 'Do you know the time?' for he was longing for daylight.

Cozens held up four fingers: and at that moment she struck.

The first was no more than the blow of a very strong sea, but the next wave raised her and smashed her down on her beam-ends, right down, and the sea made a fair breach over her.

Now that they were in the white water, the faint light increased, and they could see breakers all round, huge and mounting, a white boiling sea. Every man who could move in the ship was now coming on deck, at least to die in the open: and the deck was canted like the steep roof of a house. The captain was down; the lieutenant had gone forward to cut away the sheet-anchor.

A great thundering sea came roaring in, lifted her up and drove her a long way inshore; she struck with a terrible crash and smashed off her rudder, but she floated – heavy, half settling, but free of the rock, she floated now.

'Does she steer?' shouted Mr Jones, the mate of the watch.

Rose, the quartermaster, carefully tried the wheel, then replied 'No sir, if you please, she don't.' But he remained there, grasping the spokes, for he had not been relieved.

'Come,' roared Mr Jones to the disorganised mob on the quarter-deck. 'Don't be downhearted. Have you never seen a ship amongst breakers before? We can push her through them. Come, lend a hand. Here's a sheet – here's a brace. Lay hold. I don't doubt but we may stick her yet near enough to the land to save our lives.'

His cheerful, confident words brought men to the sheets and the braces at once, and now, through a white sea of destruction, they steered in a break-neck course for a faint gap in the breakers, easing the main sheet as she came to and hauling the fore-sheet aft as she fell off. The ship hurtled through the sea for five minutes, ten minutes more. It was impossible that it should last and yet it seemed to go on for ever: the orders came from the quarter-deck and with perfect co-ordination the men hauled, sometimes smothered in spray, sometimes blown half off the deck, but always there for the next command, as if they were all in a dream, and indestructible.

A huge rock loomed up on the larboard bow, black and sheer: there was another the size of a church to its lee. The captain was on his feet again, holding on to the mate, and pointing, and now the *Wager* ran for the space between the rocks. She reached it, and struck. She struck there, bilged and grounded. The carpenter instantly cut away the foremast and the mainmast, they let go the sheet-anchor, and there she lay under the shelter of the rock, beating terribly, but upright. Men stared at one another as if they had come out of the grave, and there was a sort of hoarse vague cheer, strangely audible now that some of the wind was cut off by the rock.

The day had begun to break, and there, a few hundred yards away, was the shore.

'What do you make of it? Take my glass,' said Captain Cheap.

'Fairly sheltered, sir,' replied Jack. 'Some surf, but a boat could land.'

'Report on the boats. Ask Mr Bean to come aft.'

The boats were in very fair shape, but to launch them over the gun-wale now that the masts and yards were gone was a long piece of work; and all the time the ship beat so hard that she might go to

pieces at any minute. They accomplished it, however, and the barge
went off first, and Mr Bean in the yawl after it. 'They have landed,
sir,' reported Jack. 'But they are finding it very hard to put the boat
through the surf again.'

A very long wait followed, and in this time the scene on deck
changed totally: someone had staved in the head of a barrel of
brandy, and in the waist of the ship, where Campbell and Cozens
were trying to get the cutter over the side, there was a confused
roaring, a shouting of contradictory orders and a bellowing song.
Jack saw the bo'sun, who had not been on deck for three weeks,
springing about with an insane vigour, laughing as the ship beat on
the rocks. The gunner went by, scarlet in the face and smelling like
a distillery, and with him a little silly man, capering as if he were at
a fair.

The barge came alongside: immediately afterwards the cutter was
launched: the officers did what they could to get the men decently
into them. The disorder grew, not only in itself but because
the steadier men were all going out of the ship as the boats plied to
and fro.

'Andrew,' cried Jack, seizing the loblolly-boy by the arm as he
went to go over the side, 'where is Mr Barrow?'

Andrew pointed to the shore, said something inaudible, and fell
bodily into the cutter.

On the quarter-deck the remaining officers stood watching the
captain: in the trough of each wave the *Wager* beat her keel upon
the rock and at each stroke the deck jarred shockingly beneath their
feet. All this time Captain Cheap had kept Jack beside him to report,
transmit orders and describe what was going on: now Jack stepped
forward and said, 'If you please, sir, that is a hundred and seventeen
men gone ashore. The rest will not leave the ship while they can
stand. Will you step into the barge, sir?'

Captain Cheap had refused before. He refused again – he would
be the last man off. In the lee scuppers two seamen and a cooper's
mate, who had drunk themselves insensible, washed to and fro; they
would be drowned presently, and already they looked entirely dead.

'There is no bidding the men, sir,' said Jack. 'They will stay while
there is any drink.' It was obviously true: there was a howling, rioting,

smashing noise in the cabins. Captain Cheap paused for a long moment, nodded, and walked slowly to the side.

The barge ran in through the surf, and they hauled it up the beach: the feel of solid ground was inexpressibly moving.

'Do you know where Mr Barrow is?' asked Jack, pushing through the cold, wet crowd at the landing-place and seizing the first intelligent and sober man he could find.

'No, sir. He ain't come ashore,' said the seaman, with complete certainty.

Mr Bean said, 'I have not seen him.'

'But the sick-bay was reported clear,' cried Jack.

'Yes,' said Mr Bean. 'Perhaps he came ashore in the cutter – I may have missed him.' He passed the word for Tobias, and half a dozen men called out very loudly for the surgeon's mate; but there was no reply.

'I seen him aboard,' said a heavily-bandaged seaman, who was lying on the ground. 'I seen him aboard not two boats ago. We was aft of the sick-bay, Joe and me. He cut me out of my hammock and shoved me up the hatch and then went back for Joe. But I think Joe was dead by then. There was four or five feet of water down there, gaining fast.'

Jack, two men of his division and Rose pulled the yawl out in the teeth of a sudden fresh squall of sleet. They searched with furious haste, and there in the echoing thunder they found him quite soon, floating between-decks, buoyed up by some jars that his arms still clasped. He was breathing, but only just; a hatch-cover, dislodged by the beating of the ship, had struck him so cruelly that it scarcely seemed worth handing him down into the boat.

'But at any rate,' said one of the men, passing him through the wrecked companion-way, 'we shall be able to give him a Christian burial.'

Chapter Ten

WHEN TOBIAS WOKE UP he could not tell where he was. He had come from a very deep sleep, floating up to the surface, as it were, from the bottom of some dark profundity, far, far down; now he lay quite still, expecting his recollection to come to him in a minute. But it did not. At the end of half an hour he was still looking upwards, motionless, wondering where he was, who and even *what* he was: there was some fundamental change in his being; or perhaps in his surroundings. He could not say what it might be, but it filled him with a vague uneasiness. He gazed fixedly at the ceiling. As far as he could make out in the grey light, it was made of blue serge – a most unusual substance for a ceiling. Between him and cloth floated thin layers of smoke, and outside there was the steady drumming of rain.

The nature of the fundamental change came to him very suddenly: the world was no longer in motion – it no longer heaved, rolled or pitched. The bed was as fixed and unmoving as if it had been bolted to a rock. This was horrifying. 'She's struck,' he cried. 'Oh dear me.'

'Never mind,' said Jack's voice from the shadows; 'she will float when the tide comes in.'

'I am *amazed*,' said Tobias.

'I dare say you are, old cock,' said Jack placidly, and added, 'I wonder if I can get a little pap into him.'

'This is not the ship,' cried Tobias. 'This is dry land.'

'Not so dry as you might think,' said Jack, stirring busily. 'His Majesty's ship Wet-as-Hades, Captain J. Byron, R. N., commander. Come, drink that, like a good creature.' With these words he seized Tobias' nose in a seamanlike manner, causing his mouth to open, and slid a warm, semi-liquid spoonful in.

'What are you thinking of, Jack?' cried Tobias indignantly, when he had done choking.

'Well, you know my name today,' said Jack, as if he were speaking to himself. 'That's an improvement. But I dare say I shall be Artaxerxes or Eupompus tomorrow. Shall I wash his face? You are very much beslobbered, you know, Toby.'

'Do you mean to make game of me, Jack?' asked Tobias, quite vexed. 'I think it a very great liberty, to pull a man by the nose, without provocation.' He tried to get up on his elbow, but could not, being strongly lashed to his bed.

'Upon my word,' said Jack, 'you would swear he was perfectly lucid. Damn these drips,' he said, looking upwards. 'I cannot get them to run off outside.

What walls can guard me, or what shades can hide?
They pierce my thickets, through my grot they glide,
Coming in particularly from the outside

as well as the bottom.'

Tobias lay back, suddenly exhausted by his indignation and his struggle to get up, and Jack droned gently on, sometimes quoting Mr Pope at length, at other moments stirring something over a little red heap of embers and desiring it to bubble – double, double, toil and trouble, fire burn and cauldron bubble – and then again reciting lines of his own. 'Lalage, Lalage,' he murmured, 'if only there were a rhyme to Lalage, what a capital thing that would be.'

'Hypallage,' said Tobias.

'Old Truepenny,' said Jack. 'He sounds almost human. And who may your Hypallage be, my poor friend?' he asked, with a kindly chuckle.

'It is not a person, blockhead,' cried Tobias, 'but a grammatical term, a term in rhetoric. When I say "He set my nose to his impious hand" instead of "He set his impious hand to my nose," that is hypallage. How came you to do such a barbarous thing, Jack?'

Jack did not reply at once, but came and looked earnestly into his face for a minute before asking whether he were in his right senses, by any chance?

'My dear Toby,' he said, 'how very glad I am. You have been out of them this age. How are you? How do you find yourself?'

'Very well, I thank you.'

'How happy I am to hear you speak like a Christian, Toby. And do you really tolerably well? How charming. You were monstrously ill – raving, roaring out like a Turk, ha ha. I will cast off your lashings – you would like to sit up. Handsomely, now,' he said, easing Tobias up in bed and propping him there. 'That incompetent rogue Oakley said you were past praying for – comatose, moribund, scuppered, not worth feeding. How are you, Toby?'

'A little strange, upon my word.'

'I should think so, indeed: you must be infernal weak after all this time. Have some – have some of this,' he said, advancing the spoon. 'It will strengthen you amazingly.'

'What is it?'

'I will tell you when you have eaten it,' said Jack: then, feeling that this was not really the most encouraging reply, he adopted a very false air of enthusiasm and said, 'Veal. It is delicious veal, ha, ha.'

'Well,' said Tobias, putting down the bowl, 'that was very strange. So is this,' he said, gazing about him. The ceiling was, in fact, made of blue serge, and so were the walls. The room was something like a large four-poster bed with the curtains drawn, and what light there was came through a slit in the far end, which was screened by still more serge. 'Pray tell me what has happened, Jack,' he said.

'Lard, Toby,' said Jack, sitting on the edge of his bed, 'such a vast deal has happened. Where shall I begin? There was the wreck – do you remember that? No? Well never mind: we were wrecked, I assure you – ran aground off this island, as long ago as the middle of May, a great while since. It is astonishing how you have lasted, Toby: like one of the Seven Sleepers, or the cove in Ovid.'

'Which cove?'

'Perhaps it was not Ovid. But anyhow, we were wrecked, and counted ourselves precious lucky to come off alive.'

'I have no recollection of it at all: how remarkable. Yet clearly I must have come ashore. How did I come ashore?'

'Oh, as for that, they fetched you in the yawl. The sick-bay was reported clear, but they forgot that you had had a couple of hammocks shifted aft, until somebody on the beach – Bateman, I think it was – said that you had gone back there.'

'Ah, yes,' said Tobias, and after thinking for some time he asked after several of his patients: some were alive, but most were dead.

'There were a hundred and forty-seven who came off in the boats, counting the soldiers,' said Jack; 'and now there are ninety odd. It was mostly the sick who died, of course.'

They fell silent for a while. Two hundred and twenty men had set sail from England, and now there were ninety. Eventually Tobias said, 'If we had been another week or two at sea, there would not have been so many left alive.'

'Toby,' said Jack, suddenly starting from his meditation, 'I have to go on guard now. Take a little more dog and drumble, and then go to sleep. I will bring back some wine.'

'Wait a minute,' cried Tobias, 'where are we, Jack?'

'How do you mean, where are we?'

'Are we among the Spaniards? In civilisation?'

'Oh no. We are on a sort of wet island, in forty-eight south. But never fret – I shall be back very soon.'

'Forty-eight south,' reflected Tobias, 'forty-eight degrees of south latitude. That must be some five hundred miles below Baldivia – scarcely any way up the coast at all. I am lying on the west coast of Patagonia, in forty-eight degrees south, on dry land: what a delightful reflection.' He then examined himself with some care. His head was heavy, painful and misshapen, but he could feel no broken bones. 'Concussion – coma. See Artemidorus and Baptista Codronchus: by no means unusual.' He called to mind what Dithmarus Bleskenius had to say of a nineteen months coma in Iceland in the year 1359, and by way of seeing whether his faculties were impaired he repeated the whole chapter verbatim. Satisfied with the state of his wits, he turned to his person, and found, to his very great surprise, that there was scarcely a trace of the scurvy left upon it. Unblotched, unswollen, it appeared to be quite sound, though weak; his remaining teeth, standing like isolated tombstones, were firm where they had been shaky. He gnashed them for a while, observed, 'It is a question of diet,' and went quietly to sleep.

'Jack,' he said, waking suddenly at the sound of flint and steel, 'What did you mean by "dog and drumble"?'

'Oh,' said Jack, blowing upon the spark in the tinder, 'it is just an expression, you know.' He raised a flame at last, lit a candle and surveyed Tobias. 'How are you now?' he asked, as if expecting him to have lapsed into idiocy.

'Perfectly well, I assure you. What have you been guarding?'

'The store tent,' said Jack, sitting down by the bed. 'The truth of the matter is,' he said confidentially, 'we are on precious short commons here and the people keep trying to get into the tent to steal food. So we have to guard it.'

'Is the food so short, then? I had imagined from your speaking of veal that cattle must abound – the guanaco described by Meropius, or some bovine as yet unknown.'

'The veal,' said Jack, looking at the ground, 'was rather hyperbolical veal – in the poetic line. You did not dislike it, Toby?'

'Not at all.'

'Well,' said Jack, 'it was dog. But I imagined that you might not relish it very much, just at first; so I called it veal.'

'Dog. Very good. Dioscorides, Crato and Polidor Virgil all commend dog: and Riccius the Jesuit, *Expeditio in Sinas*, book 23, chapter 9, states that the physicians of the Emperor's court prize dog's meat above all. Ludovicus Vives, Pomponatius and the rational Peter of Wye agree: I say nothing of Cornelius Agrippa, Jack – nor Paracelsus. Far be it from me to cite Paracelsus.'

'I am very glad to hear it, Toby. It was old dog – the last – but not very old. I pound it up with scrooby-grass and spoonwort and mire-drumble.'

'They are all sovereign for the scurvy, but above all mire-drumble. Mr Eliot always cried up drumble. But, Jack, I beg you will go back to the beginning, and tell me what has happened.'

'I ought to have kept my journal; then I could have told you everything in order. As it is, I shall probably forget a great deal, and set things out of line.' He reflected for a while, and then went on, 'The first few days were the worst – the first night particularly, because everybody was worn out and we had nothing to eat and no shelter. It came on to blow and rain, infernally cold, with ice and a wind to make you wish yourself dead. Mr Hamilton found a sort of half-ruined wigwam in the wood behind the beach, and they carried the captain into a dry corner of it. Everybody who could crowded in after him, and those who could not find room sat tight round a tree outside, all packed together for warmth. We were so starved and wretched we had not the spirit to do anything else. Two of our people were dead by the morning under the tree, and old Mr Adams of the invalids in the wigwam. The next day we did get a fire lighted, which was a comfort, and somebody found the scrooby-grass and the wild celery growing. There had been a little bag of broken biscuit and crumbs brought ashore – Heaven knows why – and we made a kind of soup out of that and the greenstuff. It very nearly killed us all, because it had been a tobacco bag, and the soup was full of shreds of it. We all lay about in the streaming rain, puking our hearts out. Oh, it was a dreary day, Toby: you were well out of it. We stowed you in the end of the wigwam, in a bag.

'Then the sea began to run very high, driving right up the beach, and you could hear the poor old *Wager* beating. Some of the fools who had stayed aboard were sober enough by then to know that she would probably go to pieces, and they began to put out signals for a boat. When we did not send one they fired at us with one of the quarter-guns, and the ball went just over the wigwam. When the sea went down enough to let us get a boat through the surf we fetched them off, and I must say I thought the captain behaved very well. He came down to the water's edge, looking half dead and his arm in a sling –'

'Did Mr Oakley reduce the dislocation?'

'No. The barber did it, more or less. He was down there, with Mr Hamilton and Campbell, leaning on his cane, and when the bo'sun came ashore, dressed in a gold-laced hat and somebody's fine laced coat, with pistols and a sword, still three-parts drunk and looking nastier than you would believe, Captain Cheap knocked him straight down with his cane. All the other fellows were disarmed, too. One of them had got my gun, and I was glad to have it back again – the one Uncle Worcester gave me when he came down to Portsmouth.

'After that things grew a little better. We had been frightened of Indians up to then – thought they were watching us out of the trees and waiting to attack – but now that we were armed we wandered about and shot a few birds. And we hauled the cutter to the edge of the wood and turned it keel up, with props to hold it, which was a much better shelter than nothing at all. Then when the sea went down we began to find shellfish at low tide, limpets and huge great mussels – famous mussels, Toby, and as soon as there is a decent day you shall have some. They weigh half a pound apiece. But you have to have good weather at low water, which is very rare; and all the easy ones have been eaten by now. We tried to get some stores out of the ship too, but at first we could make little of it; it was only when she had beat rather more that the casks began to make their way up, and then we did manage to bring some of them ashore – flour, peas, beef and pork, a good deal of it half spoiled with the sea, but more rum, because it floated better. All the casks were brought to the store tent, and at that time the hands behaved very well; if only we had not saved so much rum they might still be under proper command, but I don't know . . . Then we brought up a vast great deal of the trade goods. You would hook a cask (we scuttled the decks and used hooks on poles to claw about with below) and get it up with infinite pains and then find it was full of clocks or basins or some nonsense of that kind. They were pretty clocks: but you cannot eat a clock; and our rations were half a pound of flour and one piece of pork among three, which leaves you precious hungry. There was cloth, too; miles of it, and hats and breeches. Beads, looking-glasses, all that sort of thing. So when some Indians came into the bay we were able to give them presents. Lard, Toby, you would have laughed to see them with a looking-glass: they darted round behind to see who was the other side, with such a face of suspicion and anxiety – dumbfounded. These ones were harmless, good-natured creatures, and they gave us mussels and pieces of seal and dogs, which they carry about with them to eat, it seems. They were more or less naked, with a sort of little thing made of feathers that they wore on their shoulders and shifted according to the wind, with strings. It was pitiful to see them in the snow, but they would not put on the breeches we gave them, and preferred coloured ribbon any day. We could not understand them, and they could not understand us – knew no Spanish – nothing. They came back later with a whole tribe of their friends and relations, and they were going to settle down with us, which would have been prime, they being such knowing fellows in the woods and along the shore, and we should have come to know their meaning pretty soon. But then some infernal stupid knaves among the crew got drunk and started to play the fool with the women, and the next morning they were all gone. There were some other Indians later, but they were of a different kind: they did not like us. Nothing-for-nothing kind of people – they would not yield so much as a limpet without you gave them some blue ribbon or a button, although we had made them all sorts of presents before. But they were only passing by, it appears, and we have seen none since.'

'Have you seen any of the birds or animals of these parts?'

'Nothing much. You cannot walk about, because it is all either swamp or woods so thick you cannot get through – you would never expect it in such a cold climate. Or else it is very steep mountain, like Mount Misery over there: we had to cut steps to get to the top. But I was trying to get through the woods once when I heard a creature snuffling, and saw its traces – feet as big as a soup-plate with claws all round. I ran faster out of the wood than I went in.'

'Oh Jack, did you never wait to see its face, even?'

'No sir, I did not. Had I been made of brass I might have done so; but I did not. I ran away as fast as ever I could, trembling like a hare. And if it had come after me I dare say I should have run round the entire island.'

'It is an island? Yes, you said so before. Is it far from the main?'

'No. We thought it was all one at first – you can see the Cordillera of the Andes as plain as can be from some parts. But it turns out to be a pretty big island. The coast seems to be much broken up into islands and peninsulas here. And no wonder, when you think of the seas that come pounding in.'

'How are we to get off it, Jack?'

'That is the question,' said Jack, frowning. 'At one time I thought it clear enough – we were to lengthen the long-boat and sail north to Chiloe or Baldivia and cut out a Spanish ship there, to take us to Juan Fernandez, which is the second rendezvous. We have the long-boat on the stocks, but nothing seems to get done. Days go by, weeks go by, and nothing happens. The trouble is, Toby,' he said, sinking his voice, 'we are all at odds – half a dozen different factions, and I don't know whether the captain can command them any more. There was one time when I thought they would come back to their duty, just after all the Irishmen deserted in a body – they were going to blow up the captain and the purser, by the way, with half a barrel of powder; but Buckley, one of the quarter-gunners, persuaded them not to light the train. The men were in reasonably good heart then, or most of them, and would have obeyed orders cheerfully, but there were no orders to obey. The captain shut himself up. He felt the loss of the ship very much, I believe, and at times he seemed almost out of his mind. It was then that discipline went all astray – oh, there were dozens of causes, the quarrelling over things found and the rations, not enough to eat and too much to drink – half a pint of rum a day on an empty stomach. And then somebody spread the tale that the officers had no legal authority, once the ship was gone. But the worst of it was the different parties, the land officers, except for Mr Hamilton, not speaking to the captain, the gunner and the carpenter and their friends saying that the ship was cast away for want of attention, the bo'sun and his set of blackguards, the master – oh, it's all a very discreditable business, Toby, and I wish we were well out of it. Cozens will horse around, though I beg him not to.' Jack paused, and shook his head. 'The captain is trying to take matters in hand again now by coming down very hard: he ordered a couple of men six hundred lashes each on Wednesday.'

'Six hundred!'

Jack nodded. 'They were caught stealing from the store tent. They would have been hanged at home; but still . . . He had Cozens put under arrest yesterday for a rude answer. Cozens was tipsy, of course – he had just come from the gunner's place. Nobody has dared to disobey the captain to his face yet, but how long it will last I do not know. I believe everything would be all right if once we could get afloat again.' Jack stopped, and reflected for some time, stroking his chin. 'Poor devils,' he continued, in a low voice; 'they never asked to come – the pressed men, I mean. But I doubt if there are many who would break into open mutiny, particularly now that the worst of the lot, Mitchel and some more, have gone off to join the deserters. If only we could get the long-boat fitted out, decked and rigged, I think it would be well enough: the rules of the service seem natural at sea, but no one likes them ashore. Then if we could get to Juan Fernandez, we should be distributed among the other ships, and you and I might get into the *Centurion* at last – ha, Toby, do you remember . . .'

But Tobias did not remember: he was fast asleep. Jack crept silently about, spreading out his bed by the warm embers on the hearth-stone; he had no watch that night, and he intended to sleep right through until dawn – an uncommon luxury for a sailor – but for a long time he could not go off. Hunger had something to do with this, for it is difficult to sleep when your stomach is calling out for food, but a general uneasiness of mind had more; he was haunted by a presentiment of misfortune.

The town in Cheap's Bay on Wager Island had seventeen dwellings, ranging from the gunner's house, a big square thatched erection with room for twenty men, down to the little brutish tabernacles huddled together by the men who preferred to live alone but who had no idea of how to set about it. Jack's lay somewhat away from the rest, away up the slope and in the shelter of the trees: it was not as trim as the carpenter's construction, but it was not as ramshackle as Sloppy Joe's; like all of them, it was thoroughly well lined with broadcloth, serge and even damask, from the cargo.

From the doorway of the hut Tobias surveyed the bay, the wreck out there on the inner side of the reef, and the beach. For once the day had dawned clear, frosty clear and still, and from the rise he could see the *Wager* very plain: only her poop and foc's'le were above the water, but her shape was perfectly distinct – it was not an anonymous, battered, unrecognisable wreck, but the wreck of the *Wager* and no other. The sight of what had been his home for so long lying there abandoned was very painful: those decks, canted now to a wild degree, with gaping holes cut roughly in them, were once gleaming white and as orderly as a medicine-chest; and there, where the stump of the mainmast washed to and fro in the cold grey swell, he had lain the long night through, while the sweet trade-wind hummed in the rigging, and above the complicated patterns of ropes and sails rose the southern stars, Canopus, Antares, Achernar and, low down, the Southern Cross – long tropical nights when they sailed through a phosphorescent sea as warm as milk, across the middle Atlantic to Brazil.

This melancholy train of thought was broken by the sight of a condor: the huge bird passed straight across the sky without once moving its wings, until it was hidden by the headland that formed the southern limit of the bay; and it was followed by another, then another, all gliding with unhurried speed straight down to some remote scene of carnage – perhaps a stranded whale: conceivably another wreck.

The bay was a deep inlet, with high land running out for a mile or so on either side: black cliffs and tumbled rock everywhere except at this end, the bottom of the bay: and everywhere inland thick trees crowded upon one another, the living pushing up among the dead. It was obviously a very wet place, for there were yellow-scummed runs of water down the cliffs, and wherever there was ground unoccupied by trees, rank, sad green things grew very tall – a monstrous giant hairy rhubarb, where there was shelter from the wind, and wild celery as high as a man. Although the day was cold there was a general smell of decay upon the air: rotting wood, rotting vegetation and huge deep banks of sea-weed rotting on the high-water mark.

'What do you think of it?' asked Jack. Tobias shook his head. 'It is like the country that runs east from the Land's End, in Cornwall,' said Jack, 'only worse. My grandfather took me down there when he went to see after some dirty parliamentary business at St Murrain, and I thought it was the most horrible coast in the world – could not believe that it would be repeated. That is the store tent down there in the middle, do you see? And this' – pointing up the slope on which they stood – 'is Mount Misery. Pretty steep. The mainland looks quite close from the top; and when you are up there you can make out a cape away to the north, about fifty miles away. It runs straight out from the mainland westwards, straight into the wind – the wind is always west here, with a little of north or south in it. So if we had not run aground here, we must have done so there, which is a great consolation. But if ever we do get away to the north, we shall have to weather that cape; and it trends away a great distance to the west. There might possibly be a channel through it, however. Do you see the long-boat? Behind the square house. Mr Cummins has sawn it in two, and it is to be lengthened twelve feet. Beyond the long-boat, where the rocks begin, used to be quite a good place for limpets and a green weed you can make soup of, but they are all gone now; and beyond that there is the cove where I found a large fish with its head crushed among the big pebbles, after a blow. A pretty sea, where even the fish cannot venture inshore. We are protected by that line of rocks to the west, so it must be far worse in the offing. There is the purser going to the store tent, do you see? He will be serving out the rations directly – I will go down.'

The news of Tobias' recovery had spread quickly: there were several people moving about, and many of them stared up to the hut and waved. When Jack returned he brought with him not only a mug half full of grey flour and a wizened little knob of horse, their ration, but a tallow candle and two small clams, gifts for Tobias from the carpenter and one Phipps, a bo'sun's mate. 'This is one of the most valuable things going,' said Jack, holding up the candle. Tobias looked attentive, but said nothing. 'It is tallow, you see,' said Jack, 'not wax. We fry seaweed in it, which is uncommon wholesome and refreshing. Unfortunately the lunatics who put the trade cargo aboard sent many more wax candles than tallow. You cannot eat wax, it appears; at least, not with any profit.'

Their breakfast consisted of the last of the dog and a little flour and water thrown on a hot shovel, so that it clung together, charred slightly, and received the name of bread; and when the feast was over Jack went down to take the yawl across to the wreck. The boats were continually employed in probing the wreck for provisions to add to the all important sea-store; all hands agreed that they must have two months' minimum ration before they could put to sea, and for daily use they had nothing but damaged casks and what they could find along the shore. It was Jack's turn of duty now, and he hoped, if he fished up a cask of anything edible, to be indulged with the use of the boat to go after the birds that were sometimes to be met with, or at least to bring in some shellfish from the outer rocks.

Tobias sat outside the hut, and presently Campbell and Morris came up to shake his hand and wish him joy of his recovery; they were thin – thinner than Jack – and grey and quiet, and they left soon, because the tide was ebbing, and if they did not search the rocks at low water they would find nothing. They were obliged to profit by every minute of calm low water, for unless they could add to their rations they could barely live. Cozens, who came up after they had gone, was more changed by far – shockingly changed. He had been a fleshy young man, but now his face had fallen away and it was unevenly blotched from drinking; he was dirty; he smelt; and he looked quite old. But he was surprisingly cheerful, and he had brought Tobias a case-bottle of brandy. 'Drink it up, mate,' he cried, clapping him on the back; 'there's plenty more where it came from.' And he gave Tobias to understand, with nods and winks, that the gunner had a keg hidden, and that he could have as much as he liked: then, speaking much more seriously, he gave Tobias a rambling, disconnected account of how the captain was invading the seamen's privileges; how the captain and his little band of favourites, the purser, the steward and a few others, had double rations; and how he, Cozens, was resolved to stand up for the sailors' rights, and not submit to tyranny; and how he wondered that Jack should have turned so like a preaching parson. 'He ought to come into the square house and mess with us,' he said. 'We have all the best fellows in the crew – all the men with any independent spirit. Now, Sam?'

Samuel Stook, AB, had been hailing 'The hut, ahoy,' for some minutes. 'I come up,' he said, in a strong shout, 'to see the doctor – heard he was better – brought him a crab – ha, ha – not at all.' A friend of Mr Stook's falling sick on the West Indies station, had recovered (a rare thing in naval experience) with no ill effects other than the loss of his hearing. Recovered invalids were therefore deaf, as like as not, and Stook roared away with the unimpaired force of his lungs; the effect, combined with Cozens' way of thumping his back to emphasise a point, was shattering indeed, and when they proposed carrying Tobias down to the beach for a little company, he had not enough energy left to resist their kindly-meant importunity.

They set him on a barrel by the side of the sea, and as the rising tide drove the men from their perpetual hungry searching of the shore, he received a great number of visits. He learnt that all hands were discontented, that many were almost out of control and that some were armed. He also learnt that a sick medical man is not an omniscient pontiff any more: none of his former patients scrupled to suggest remedies, to advise him to take care, to eat more, to eat less, to sit out of that nasty draught; they told him of former cases in their experience not unlike his – the death of relatives and friends from high living, blows on the head, gout that settled in the vitals, and taking cold. They gave him edible seaweed (good for him: would strengthen the tubes), limpets and four splendid mussels, the last a gift from Bosman, a gigantic sailor whose wisdom teeth Tobias had extracted to the deafening roll of a drum on successive Sundays.

When it came on to rain, as it did just before the serving out of the rations at noon, they carried him into the square house, and there Cozens and the carpenter invited him (Jack being still at sea in the yawl) to eat with them. It was a big mess, a score of men who ate in common, and if it was not very well provided with victuals, at least it was rich in wine and spirits: Diego, the Portuguese stowaway, hurried down the long plank table clapping a pint pot before each man, either filled with wine or half filled with rum; and the whole place had a pleasant taverny smell.

'Not Taffy Powell,' said the boy, putting an empty mug before a seaman of that name. 'Purser damn your eyes, idle dog.'

Powell was strongly moved by this, and his eager examination of Diego drowned all conversation, because as Diego was a foreigner, with very little English, it was necessary to shout very high and clear to make him understand. After a great deal of bellowing, interference and cross-questioning, it seemed to the company that the purser had stopped Powell's allowance, either at the captain's order or perhaps of his own mere motion.

'I am knocking off her head, isn't it?' cried Powell. 'Yis, yis.'

A good many people called out that the purser was a beast, a swab, a thief; and in the clamour the gunner, passing quickly behind the bench, whispered in Cozens' ear. Cozens started up, grasped Powell's mug and swore he would get it filled or know the reason why. Powell cried out, 'No, no,' the carpenter shouted to him not to meddle and several of the men clutched at him; but he would be going, and he went.

'What a spirited young fellow he is, to be sure,' said the carpenter, wagging his head. 'He had a regular set-to with one of the land-officers the other day – it is only his fun. The captain was vexed to a very savage pitch, Mr Barrow; but it was only his fun. He will be argyfying with the purser now – ha, ha, ha. Take a little piece of thrumbo, Mr B; it will rectify the humours, being, as I may say, a deep-sea weed, and very suitable for the vagrant humours. Though if you take more than a little in a day, you will bring it up again, Mr B. Mr Byron will be getting some, if he takes the yawl beyond the point: I fancy that must have been him – two shots. Did you hear? Perhaps he has shot a race-horse: if he should have shot a race-horse, how happy he will be.'

'Is it likely that he will shoot a race-horse, Mr Cummins?'

'We only *call* it a – what?'

The lieutenant was in the door calling all hands. 'All hands to the captain, all hands.'

And at once the news flew round: the captain had shot Cozens down for mutiny.

'This will bring it all to a head,' said Jack, in the privacy of their hut. He was right, but he was right with a strange delay, for it was weeks and even months before the death of Cozens had its full effect.

At the very first moment, when an open mutiny might have broken out, Mr Bean, the master and his mates, and the marine officers all stood armed behind the captain: the men were overawed – they were brutally reminded of a captain's legal powers. Yet soon the ugly caballing began again. The gunner, at first timidly and then with more confidence, pursued his busy undermining of the captain's authority: his plan was to persuade the whole crew to vote for going home – to make for Brazil by way of the Straits of Magellan. At the same time the purser intrigued with the deserters in their camp on the other side of the swamp below the bay, supplying them with rum in order to buy their support. There were parties for going north; there were parties for going south; and there were some who were for wandering off on wild adventures by themselves. Most of the men were thoroughly disturbed and uncertain: but there was not one who dared defy the captain to his face, and they went no further, the most rebellious of them, than sending messages and committee resolutions through Plastow, the captain's steward and prime favourite, insisting upon a double ration of spirits. The habits of the service clung hard; the word *mutiny* still had a dreadful ring, and the shadow of the English gallows stretched out half across the world. None knew this better than the gunner – there was safety in numbers and in numbers alone: if the whole crew could be brought over, the captain would be persuaded, and no one man could be blamed. It was essential for the gunner to implicate as many as he possibly could, to cajole or frighten them into signing or putting their mark to his papers – legal-looking documents with 'whereas' and 'above-mentioned' and 'these are to certify the Right

172

Honourable the Lords Commissioners for executing the Office of Lord High Admiral of Great Britain', all over them.

The gunner was not a very intelligent man, but fear of the northward journey and hatred for Captain Cheap lent him powers that he would not otherwise have possessed. His chief point in favour of a return by way of the south was that as they had had foul winds all the way to this point, the same winds would be fair for carrying them back again: but more than that, he had cunning political sense enough to profit by the ill-feeling between the soldiers and the sailors. It seems that two services can never agree for long, and it was certainly so in the case of the marines and the seamen of the *Wager*: apart from the natural dislike between the two bodies, the marines, acting as sentries, stole the stores more often than the sailors could, and they were very much hated for this. No less than nine at one time were detected: the marine officers were bitterly reproached for their men's wretched discipline, and the alliance between them and the captain was finally broken. Bulkeley drew Captain Pemberton over to his side, and although he could not reconcile the soldiers with the sailors, he removed their support from the captain.

Now it only remained to persuade the captain that resistance was useless, and to induce him to sign a paper agreeing to go away to the south – a paper that would protect them all against future accusations. It had taken weeks and months to reach this point, but in spite of the gunner's zeal he would never have succeeded so far had it not been for Cozens' death. Cozens had been very much loved by the men; they loved his gaiety, courage and good-natured bounding energy, and they did not count any of his vices against him: in killing him Captain Cheap had killed all the affection the hands might ever have had for him, and nearly all their loyalty.

This unsavoury business had taken time, a long season in which Jack and Tobias searched the shore, the nearer woods and swamps and even (thanks to a vessel made of empty barrels) the rocks within a mile or two of the coast; for they were much more interested in staying alive than in the politics of the camp – and if you did not find something more to eat you starved, for rations were down to a quarter of a pound of flour a day. For his part, Jack said that he was thoroughly disgusted with everybody concerned: he was convinced that it would all right itself as soon as they got to sea; but until then, he said, he would have nothing to do with any of them – none of them, for the captain's loudest personal supporters, apart from his countrymen, Campbell and Hamilton, were toad-eaters, favourites and tale-bearers, the purser, the steward and a few others of that kidney.

In this long period, then, while the plot was hatching and the long-boat was slowly turning into a schooner, Jack and Tobias became intimately acquainted with the unpromising coast of Wager Island, every cove and almost every rock. Tobias, as he grew stronger, sorted out and classified the few available birds, which ranged from the condor to the humming-bird, the greatest wing-span to the least. He did not believe his first sight of the tiny bird, no bigger than a hawk-moth, nor his second, for their name alone evokes the tropics, not a dismal, half-frozen, dripping swamp; but he was obliged to yield to the evidence in time. Yet he candidly confessed that all the humming-birds in creation did not interest him so much as the fowl that they called a race-horse: it was a huge loggerheaded duck that lived on shellfish, and, being much better equipped for the task than the shipwrecked crew, it grew fat on them. A good one would weigh over twenty pounds – a delightful unctuous roast, an honour to applied ornithology; but unfortunately very rare and rapidly becoming rarer, because the bird was unable to fly. The race-horse could only splash away with wings and legs, thrashing and running over the surface of the water, and although it moved very fast, the ravening mariners moved faster still.

Tobias also resumed his duties: there was very little for him to do, for although they had fished up some of his instruments, the medicine-chest was gone; and apart from that nearly everybody who had survived to this point was healthy. But there were a few sprains, broken bones and agonising teeth to be dealt with, and he moved about among the men, kindly received by all parties, the perfect neutral. When the long-boat was nearly ready he told Jack that there was a new plan in motion, a scheme to arrest the captain: Captain Cheap had proved obstinate beyond all calculation – he would yield to none of their solicitations – and the new scheme was to arrest him for the murder of Cozens and carry him aboard. There were some who still hoped that he would embark of his own free will, and go for the south under oath and with strict limitation of his command; but the plan of placing him under arrest was gaining favour very fast.

'I know,' said Jack, 'but to tell you the truth, Toby, I don't care how they get him aboard. Once we are at sea there will be a prodigious change, I assure you. There are a good many who think as we do, and who only go along with the herd to avoid wrangling. I am sure Mr Bean does, although he says nothing, and I will answer for Rose, Buckley, Noble and plenty more. You will see, as soon as we have made a decent offing. Once we are well out to sea we shall turn everything the right way up again, and set course for Baldivia or Juan Fernandez. I do not love the captain any more than you do, but at least he is determined to rejoin the squadron. Let them arrest him, I say, and so much the better, if it means less delay.'

So, when the time of delays was done at last, and the long-boat was launched, victualled and ready to sail, Jack and Tobias went aboard quite calmly, in spite of the torn and ominous sky, and in spite of the spectacle of the marines drawn up on the beach to conduct the imprisoned captain aboard.

There were fifty-nine in the crew of the long-boat, now transformed into a schooner, twelve in the cutter and ten in the barge; they were so crowded that there was scarcely room to work, and aboard the schooner many people were obliged to go below. They weighed; the sails mounted billowing and fluttering, and they rounded at once as they were sheeted in; the schooner and the boats heeled to the western breeze and stood close-hauled for the southern point of the bay.

The movement, the feeling of life in the deck under his feet, the confused cheering and the wonderfully familiar sound of water rippling along the lee made Jack feel suddenly happy – absurdly happy. The schooner had got under way very fast and she was already making six or seven knots; it looked as though she might weather the point without having to tack, although the wind was stronger out there. Jack looked back to the bottom of the bay, to judge how much lee-way they were making: and there, which made his heart miss out a beat, he saw Captain Cheap and Mr Hamilton standing motionless on the silent beach, marooned.

Chapter Eleven

'THIS WILL NEVER DO,' said Jack to himself. He looked quickly round, and he realised that some of the men had been in the secret – all those who were now exulting in the stern – and that some had not. There were strange looks, frightened and as it were ashamed: men saw what had happened, but dared not say anything against it; they looked down quietly, pretending not to know. The gunner, the bo'sun and some of the strongest allies were conspicuously well armed, and in spite of their excitement they were keeping a very sharp watch on the deck. Mr Bean, Campbell, the master and his mates, and many others Jack had relied upon were nowhere to be seen; they had come aboard early – they had been manoeuvred aboard before the others – they had gone below, and they were still there.

The southern point of the bay lay three points on the port bow, and it was coming nearer at a spanking pace. Already they were out of the lee of Mount Misery, and the gusty wind was laying the schooner down.

'Up sheets,' came the order, and immediately afterwards the furious shout, 'For'ard there, start that sheet. Mr Byron, get off that foresheet. Byron, get off that – sheet, you –' The gunner came rushing forward, tripped in the confusion and fell, bawling still, as the schooner came up into the wind with her canvas shaking and rattling. 'There, look what you done,' he shrieked, pointing to the foresail, split in every direction and streaming out in ribbons. 'Oars, oars, out oars,' he shouted, and hailed the cutter for a tow, for they were drifting rapidly towards the point.

In a howling medley of cries and counter-commands (for many of the gunner's friends thought themselves entitled to give orders too) the schooner scraped by the point and bore away for a sandy bay on the mainland, where they dropped the anchor and took stock of the damage. The arguing about what should be done took a great deal of time: some people were inclined to solve the whole difficulty by blaming Jack, but William Rose said, 'I won't have him abused: it is because he don't understand a fore-and-aft rig. Because he's young, that's why.' The quartermaster emphasised his point with blows of a belaying-pin on the deck and glared round for contradiction. 'There is only one thing for it,' he said, with the faintest possible wink at Jack, 'and that is to put back in the barge and bring the spare canvas. As never should of been left,' he cried, with a triple thump.

The mutiny of the *Wager* may have started as a quarter-deck mutiny or something very like it, but it was fast growing to resemble one of the ordinary, or anarchical, kind. Every man thought himself as good as the next, and as none of the leading figures had the gift of command, everything was decided in a very democratic, very parliamentary fashion, admirably adapted to keeping the schooner in one place for ever. In the end, when many of the disputants had gone off fishing, the remainder agreed that new canvas was the only answer, and Jack, whispering Tobias to keep close, stepped into the barge: Rose and Noble followed quickly, and Plastow, the captain's steward, came after them. Jack saw the purser at the side, and looking significantly at him said, 'Do you wish to come, Mr Hervey?' But the purser feigned not to hear, and moved away. His namesake, William Harvey, a quarter-gunner, and Buckley, another quarter-gunner, jumped down into the boat.

'We don't want you, stinkard,' said Noble to Matthew Lively, who came next.

'Why not?' cried the gunner's mate. Noble, an old and experienced quartermaster, was used to dealing with awkwardness: he made no verbal reply, but in a moment Lively was in the schooner again, rubbing himself. Two more seamen came down, Bosman and Church, and as they were shoving off, a single marine.

'Give way,' said Jack, with the tiller under his arm. 'Toby, take your hands off the gunwale.'

'There is Mr Campbell, sir,' said Rose, at the stroke oar.

Campbell had suddenly appeared on deck, and he was signalling desperately. Jack turned the barge in a tight curve and brought it under the schooner's rail. Campbell jumped down and the barge set off again. 'We shall not be able to do that twice,' said Jack, listening to the noise behind him. There were many voices, some merely bellowing, some reminding them just where the spare canvas lay, but louder than them all the gunner's voice in a hailing trumpet ordering them to put back at once.

'He has smoked us at last,' said Jack, nodding. 'You had better pull uncommon hard.' The barge moved faster and faster through the water: nothing makes one pull harder than a suspicion that people may be pointing muskets at the boat. But presently they were out of musket-shot, and they rested upon their oars.

'I take it we are all of the same mind in this boat?' said Jack.

Some said 'Yes,' and some said 'That's right,' and some jerked their heads and laughed. The rain had come on again, the wind and the tide were against them, but these things only made pursuit – which was never likely – virtually impossible: they pulled steadily for the southern headland of Cheap's Bay over a reasonable western swell, and once they were round the point they set the barge's sail and ran down to their old landing-place.

Captain Cheap stood not at the landing-place, but near it: his face was as nearly expressionless as he could make it, for he did not know their intention, and he would not appear to be waiting for them with any hope; nevertheless it showed traces of the most acute anxiety. Jack felt a certain embarrassment at the situation, and he busied himself with the mooring of the barge while Campbell hurried up the beach to report for duty. In the extremity of his relief the captain shook Campbell fervently by the hand and came forward with the intention of saying something pleasant to the men; this was not a way of speaking that came naturally to him, however, and the words tended to stick in his throat. Still, he did say that they were very welcome, that he was glad to see them and that he would not fail to mention their conduct to the commodore. He said that he was glad, for their sake, that they had understood their own interest well enough to return to their duty. He began his remarks in the tone of a man who has been suddenly and unexpectedly relieved from a very ugly situation, but a returning sense of his office and its importance filled him as he spoke, and he finished with all the condescension of a post-captain addressing mortals.

He invited Campbell, Jack and Tobias to take a little supper with him and Mr Hamilton, and after this slender meal he told them (for he was more expansive than they had ever known him) that his plan was to go north to the island of Chiloe, the most southerly Spanish settlement, there to cut out a ship, and that the best time for the voyage, seeing that it must now be made in open boats, would be somewhat later in the year, after the solstice. The mutineers – he spoke of them with shocking virulence – had left him the yawl, but it was in a sad state of repair and it would need a good deal of time to make it seaworthy: they had also left provisions at half allowance for the deserters (for this was a mutiny that paid great regard to legal forms) and at full allowance for the captain and Mr Hamilton. Each had two pieces of pork, two pieces of beef and thirty pounds of flour; and this was ten weeks' ration. Ten weeks' ration for one man, if he were desperately frugal; Captain Cheap leant heavily upon this point while they were eating, and although this threw something of a damp upon the party, he was unwilling to leave it alone, in case he should be misunderstood, and before they parted he repeated in the clearest terms, that he had no food that was not essential for his own preservation, and that what they had just eaten was upon a footing of favour, not to be considered as a right nor as a precedent.

'It is a great pity,' said Jack, as they walked, bowed under the icy rain, through the silent village to their hut, 'it is the world's pity that people who are in the right are so often disagreeable, and that it is impossible to like them.'

'That man is in a very bad way,' said Tobias. 'His liver is chronically disordered; I remember that Mr Eliot spoke of him as an example of a bilious temperament aggravated by cirrhosis, as far back as Madeira, and he must be suffering cruelly from his shoulder. It looks to me as though he will lose the use of that arm: it has started to tabefy. He has grounds for being disagreeable, and he will have more, unless we can come at some medicines very soon.'

'I never thought we should see the old tabernacle again,' said Jack – they had reached their hut. 'But,' said he, groping about inside, 'I wish we had not been quite so free in stripping the cloth, and carrying away our beds.'

'There are the sacks, however,' said Tobias; and, as something fell on his feet, he added, 'Here is your gun. Had you meant to leave it?'

'I was obliged to, we lying so close; but I am very glad of it now. For I tell you what, Toby, we are going to find it hard to scrape a living off the shore. There is not so much as a limpet left for miles on either hand, and if we can shoot a cormorant or a kite we shall be uncommon glad of it, let alone a race-horse.'

In the morning Captain Cheap spoke to them about the deserters. He said that it was but just that they should have a chance to return to their duty, and he said that Tobias was the most suitable person to speak to them: he would thank him, therefore (a very high piece of affability), to do so at eleven o'clock.

It was not a difficult task. Tobias had been several times before to the deserters' camp, he knew all the people there, and he was welcome. There were only eight of them left now that the boldest had gone over to the mainland on rafts of their own making, and these eight were very happy to be assured that they would be pardoned and fed if they returned. They had had a miserable life of it, not having the wit or resource to make themselves passably comfortable even at first, when the coast was rich in shellfish and other delights. They were the fag-end of the *Wager*'s crew, two landsmen, two seamen and four marines, of whom three had taken the King's shilling rather than be transported.

He brought them back in the yawl, looking sheepish and (though the terms are in apparent contradiction) hangdog as well, and on delivering them to their proper officers he learnt, with unmixed dismay, that Jack had gone off in the barge to see whether the long-boat would deliver up their share of the provisions to the men who chose to stay. That is to say, he was landed on the mainland with the intention of walking down to the bay where the mutineers were lying, for the barge was not to be trusted within their reach.

Tobias found this profoundly disturbing: he did not believe that there was the least hope of success, and he feared that Jack would almost certainly be kept, for if the mutineers wished to protect themselves they could not do so better than by implicating someone with a great many influential connexions. This ran through his mind continually. He told Campbell of it, and spoke with Mr Hamilton;

he was on his way to Captain Cheap with a plan for a rescue when Jack reappeared, empty-handed, scratched, lame and utterly tired out. Having reported his failure, he went straight to bed. 'You cannot imagine, Toby,' said he, 'how hellish it was, plunging through those swamps. It was impossible to get along the coast most of the way because of the rocks and the cliffs; and inland it was all wood, where you had to creep under the undergrowth, it was so thick and high; or else it was so plash that you went in knee-deep, waist-deep in black mud. And sometimes it was both together, like that piece of country behind Mount Misery. But it was worth it. They might have given us our share – after all, we fished most of it up – and I think they would have, if most of the decent men had not been away fishing. But now we have done all we can, and I would rather know that than curse myself afterwards.'

He stopped speaking to listen to the wind; and still listening to it, he went to sleep. The weather had been surprisingly kind for these last three days – it had allowed all this activity by land and sea – but now, as if to make up for lost time, it came in dirty from the north-west, a great bellowing gale laden with rain, hail and slush, that worked up a dreadful overgrown hollow sea. By the morning they had to talk loudly to be heard over the thunder of the surf, even at that distance from the beach; but it did not go down with the daylight nor with the sunset, and the next day the towering waves were beginning their breaking run half a mile out from the shore, and the wind whipped their crests off in long white streamers that tore along before them. The sea had no surface, and the air was filled with flying water. This was weather they had often known off the Horn, and Tobias, though he was faint with hunger (the shore, their only larder, was entirely closed), munched and gnashed his teeth in private delight at the thought that he was not afloat.

Now the lean days began. Both Jack and Tobias had thought they knew a great deal about hunger, but now they found that their former pangs were but the gentlest hint of real famine. Day after day the gales succeeded one another; and even when there was not wind enough to keep them in, the pounding surf made the rocks impossible. The wild celery and the mire-drumble had all gone long ago: they ate the weed called slaw, which, eaten alone and in hand-fuls, made them very sick. It was at this time that three of the former deserters made a stupid, easily detected raid upon the stores, the little treasure of flour that the captain had set aside from the common stock for their forthcoming voyage. One escaped: the others were sentenced to be flogged and then to be marooned on a barren rock, without so much as a flame of fire to comfort them.

But now and then a fine day would come, and on one of these Jack and Tobias were in the yawl with Rose and Bosman, poking about the remains of the *Wager* at the extreme ebb of the spring tide. They had no hopes from the wreck – the upper works were all gone and the hull was fast merging with the sea-bed – but there were sometimes crabs to be found there; besides, they had a tendency to haunt the place where food had once been plentifully found, much as bees will come day after day to a place where they have been fed, although the honey is there no more.

'What is the mark on a beef cask?' asked Tobias, who, chewing a piece of sea-tangle, had been watching an iridescent holothurian creeping over the touch-hole of one of the guns far below him in the cold clear green water.

'Broad arrow in red,' said the quartermaster. 'Lovely great red broad arrow, and then a number.'

The holothurian crossed the touch-hole and proceeded along the encrusted barrel towards a mass of kelp, into which it vanished. Five minutes later Tobias said, 'Well then, there are three beef-casks under the ledge of rock down there. You can see them if you follow the pointing gun and look sideways under the kelp.'

It is a curious fact that everybody contradicted him at once – there were no casks there – it was an illusion – they were empty, staved – and that at the same time everybody trampled upon him mercilessly in order to prod the kelp with the oars and the boat-hook.

But they were barrels of salt beef, heavy, sound, unstaved barrels that loaded the yawl until it was almost level with the water. It called for the most finished seamanship to get them to the landing-place, prodigies of strength and address, but no one was going to trust the beef to the rising tide for another hour, no, not even for the time that it would take to return with the barge and the other men. They brought the beef ashore and willing hands – Lord, how willing – rolled the casks up to the store house.

'So long as you have enough to eat,' said Jack, that evening, 'you have little to grumble at: and if you have a fire and a roof over your head you have nothing to murmur at at all, but are an ungrateful dog.'

This recruitment of their stores raised the spirits of the men to a high degree: they began to agitate for their departure, and on a day when the captain's temper seemed unusually mild, Campbell ventured to tell him that the people were growing restless. Strangely enough, Captain Cheap did not resent this, but desired Rose and Noble, as representatives of the men, to accompany him to the top of Mount Misery; he bade Jack and Campbell come too. From the height they surveyed the sea to the northward and the huge distant arm of the mainland that reached out into the west – the cape that seemed to form the upper limit of the gulf that contained Wager Island and a hundred more. The captain, having looked long and hard with his glass, observed that the sea was very high outside, and passed his telescope round. But the wind was fair for the far-off cape, being for once a little east of south, and the general opinion was that they should try for it – that they should try to run straight across the whole width of the gulf and pass the western headland in one determined effort.

'Very well,' said the captain. 'Mr Byron, take the bearing of the cape. Mr Campbell, run down and see that the boats are launched directly, or we shall have to wait on the tide.'

'You haven't any money on you, sir, I do suppose?' asked Noble in a hoarse whisper, as he and Jack climbed down behind the captain.

'I have not had a penny in my pocket these six months past,' said Jack, 'or you should have it. Would it be any good to you?'

'It is John Allen over there. I thought I would put a couple of pieces on his eyes. For to tell you the truth we never did bury him fit and proper, and a couple of pieces might serve, for want of better – I doubt we shan't have time to do rightly by him now.' Allen had been murdered in a drunken quarrel by one of the earliest deserters, a violent brute nicknamed Execution Dock, who had thrown him down in a chaos of rocks just off the path they were now following: the burial-party, battered by the wind and the snow, had not done its duty. But still the idea that a man should be decently laid away was strong in his shipmates' minds, and had it not been for the procrastination that afflicts seamen ashore, Allen would have had a proper tomb long ago. Yet, as Noble said, it was too late to do rightly by him now, for an enthusiastic noise from the beach showed that Campbell had set about the launching of the boats.

Twelve in the barge; eight in the yawl. With their precious sea-store, three half-barrels of powder, their weapons and their very few personal belongings they were tightly packed and deeply laden. Jack steered the barge while the captain conned it: Campbell steered the yawl. The wind, a stiff breeze, was almost astern, and the miles slipped by. The dreadful coast of Wager Island sank down and down until only Mount Misery was to be seen, while beyond it, on the mainland the far peaks of the Cordillera reared up snowy against the sky. Tobias, sitting in the stern sheets opposite the captain, went to sleep.

He woke up with a feeling of horrible nausea, and collecting his wits he saw that they were no longer running before the wind, but had hauled the sheet aft. In fact the wind had veered right out of the east and it was now blowing in increasing gusts from the west-south-west. They were holding their course, but they were now reaching the edge of the unsheltered high-running sea, and it was a question how long they could keep the head of the barge to the cape, with the wind blowing more and more with the swell, working it up into an ugly hollow sea, with white water flying.

He leant quietly over the side, cold and sick, and when he had recovered a little he watched the yawl, rising and falling, running diagonally along the trough of the swell and climbing its side slantwise. Beyond the yawl a giant petrel sailed as easily as an albatross, scarcely moving its wings, utterly indifferent to the growing menace of the sea below it.

Jack was having an increasingly difficult time: the barge had always been a pig to steer, and now that it was so heavy it would not answer the helm with anything but a ponderous deliberation that could not have been more out of place than on this afternoon. The sheet and the tiller were in perpetual movement as he calculated the thrust of each wave, the continually varying force of the wind and the slow reaction of the boat: his mind and body were so much taken up that he was the least concerned person aboard; he scarcely noticed the sheets of spray that flew across, nor the biting cold.

The gusts were growing more and more frequent; more and more they came from the west, heeling the barge so that the lee gunwale barely cleared the sea. In the yawl they were baling hard, and while Tobias watched them at their work the barge shipped a sea that half filled it: water swirled about shin-deep, and from that time on Tobias scooped it out as fast as he could.

Then quite suddenly the wind settled in the west, due west and a full gale. They already had three reefs in the sail and all the people who could be spared from baling were sitting close on the weather-side to keep the seas from breaking aboard and filling the boat: the sky had darkened with a more terrible darkness than the end of the day. A rip of violet lightning split the clouds from the south to the north, and at last the captain gave the order to run before the wind. It was clear to everybody now that they were in for a great western storm: they had seen too many to be mistaken.

By this time they had run some twenty miles of their course for the cape: they were about half-way across the gulf, and away to the leeward, perhaps fifteen, perhaps twenty miles, lay the unknown coast of the mainland, with islands and reefs between them and it.

At first the boat was very much eased and scudded happily enough under a little scrap of a foresail, steering east-north-east; but the wind grew, and the sea grew – the wind and the sea passed beyond all measure, and after an hour the barge was tearing through a roaring desert of water more appalling than anything they had ever seen. The waves were running now at the most terrifying height: when the boat was in the trough of the sea there was nothing to be seen but the great grey hill of water ahead half-way up the sky, and behind, racing towards them faster than they fled, a still greater mountain, green and curling towards them with its head torn away forwards by the wind, threatening to overwhelm them from the height of an enormous cliff. And when they were raised to the height of the roller, with the water, the live water boiling up to the gunwale and the great wind pressing the boat down into it, their horizon was jagged all round with the crests of innumerable monstrous waves.

Sometimes in the gathering darkness they caught a glimpse of the yawl, raised vertiginously up, or so far below them that they could see right down into it. More and more of the huge overgrown seas were curling over and breaking as they ran, now, because of the movement of the tide below them; and Tobias could see no reason why an open boat should live much longer. He saw, with horror, that his shipmates, from the captain downwards, were of the same opinion. The boat laboured terribly: it had not buoyancy enough to recover from the blows it received, nor to bear the great weight of water that was perpetually flying in. They were so near to foundering, and they knew it so well, that they parted with everything – they were glad to be able to lighten the boat by any means. One after another the barrels, sacks and stores went over the side; each time the lightened barge responded, but each time the growing sea called for a new sacrifice. Tobias, with death in his soul, helped to throw out the last cask of beef: the very anchor itself went overboard, and as it went the rising wave showed them the shore, a broad zone of white breakers, a most prodigious surf.

They were in the white water: there was a line of tall black rock ahead, a cliff, with the waves breaking to its head. The wind and the sea were taking them against the cliff at the pace of a running horse – five minutes more, if that. Captain Cheap gripped Jack's shoulder, pointed at an opening in the cliff: Jack nodded, and put down the helm. All the men without an order or a word leant out to windward: if anything gave they were lost; if the worn canvas split they were irretrievably lost. Through the breaking water and on the foam the boat raced straight through the gap, and it was over. They had passed through an opening not twenty yards across and they were floating on the calm water of a round, tranquil, pond-like cove: and there was the yawl, already lying there in the middle.

It was a very solemn moment: the quietness, immediately after the immeasurable roaring outside was like a hallucination and the men sat there without speaking. They paddled quietly to the edge to find a landing-place, but finding none in this steep-sided crater they climbed on to a black rock, shining with the rain, secured the boats as well as they could, and composed themselves with thankful minds to take what rest the night afforded them.

This was the end of the first day of the voyage north. If the wind had held true, or if they had started one tide earlier, they might have passed the western headland; but now, as they judged it in the morning, they were at the eastward end of the great arm of land that barred their way, and they must coast along it, all the way into the teeth of the prevailing wind, unless perhaps they could find a passage through to the other side – that is to say, unless what appeared to be continuous land should prove to be an island, or several islands, separated from the main by narrow strips of sea. On such a coast it was not impossible, and it was known that there were many such vast islands in Tierra del Fuego, all about Magellan's Strait.

The wind dropped before the dawn, and the frost whitened their wet clothes, giving them a curiously piebald appearance. The sea was still running high outside their cove, but it was just possible to force a boat out through the breakers and into the smoother swell beyond: it was hard pulling and dangerous, but it was better than starving in the rock-bound cove, which had no food, no fuel and no way out but a climb of two or three hundred feet up sheer rock. All day they laboured at their oars, running along a broken, indented coast, mostly lined with sheer-to cliffs or great jagged reefs, and towards nightfall, the sky being full of evil promise, they hauled ashore on a little island, the only one of a group that had an accessible beach. It proved to be a mere swamp, but it was too late to find another place, and they passed a second night in the open, in the rain, with no fire, no food and with nothing dry about them but the powder in their powder-horns.

This was hard living: it could scarcely have been very much harder. But in the morning, in the first grey of dawn, Tobias, unable to sleep for the cold, wandered off with Jack's fowling-piece in his hand, and he found both fuel and something to cook upon it. He had, deeply ingrained, the poacher's and the naturalist's habit of peering cautiously into any new field, dell, dune or clearing, and now, looking over a rock into a little sheltered place he saw a huge loggerheaded duck sitting upon a mound of driftwood. He had never been so well received in his life as when he returned with his burden, nor so much caressed by all hands: the race-horse, cut up, yielded a pound of solid meat for each man, besides its bones and skin; and it was as well that they had it, for the wind was roaring again, and by sunrise the sea had mounted so high that they could not leave. The storm lasted three full days, and the fourth day saw them rowing on a sea still so furious that nothing but extreme necessity could explain their presence. It was a day that promised great things, however: over on the main the land ran down low to a sandy point, and between this point and a range of hills to the westward there appeared to be nothing but water. They pulled over to this opening and found that the water ran northwards out of sight: it was possible that this would be a passage right through the headland, and they rowed along the marshy shore until the afternoon. But then they found that they were only in a narrow bay: there was no way through. The swamps on either hand offered neither shelter nor the least promise of anything to eat, not even shellfish; and they were obliged to row back again, with the grey rain sweeping down.

At least their resting-place that night provided them with some mussels, limpets and a fire: they called it Redwood Cove, because their fuel was all as red as cedar or mahogany; and the next day, with a favourable wind, they set out in better spirits to follow the coast, which here trended away to the north. The wind held fair all day, and although it died to the faintest breeze in the evening, yet it brought them as far as an island where they could land; this island was covered with magnificent tall trees, mast-like and straight in spite of the terrible winds, and the captain named it after Montrose. They lay dry that night, for once, packed round a great driftwood fire, cedar that snapped and flew in sparks so that the whole circle smelt of singeing cloth; and in the morning – calm, but with a huge western swell – they pulled steadily along the coast, still northwards here. Clinch, one of the boatkeepers (two stayed in each boat at night, by turn), said that he had seen sea-lions by the moonlight, and they travelled in the liveliest expectation, with Mr Hamilton, the best shot among them, in the bows with a loaded musket. But their hopes were all disappointed; they saw no sea-lions, and they found that once again they had rowed to the marshy bottom of a bay. They were obliged to haul away to the west once more, following the coast in all its tedious windings; and when, towards the evening, an offshore breeze sprang up, tempting them to risk the crossing of the next bay they reached from headland to headland (for there were hills at the bottom and obviously no passage), they were very soon persuaded that in these latitudes such a thing was almost impossible. The tempting breeze turned into a growing storm, and they were glad to put back while there was yet time; they put into the only sheltered place they could pitch upon, a very little cove with a safe anchorage, but with no more than a rocky ledge on one side of it with scarcely enough room for all of them; and here two of the men, who had moved off to a place under an overhanging cliff, were as nearly as possible killed by a landslide. A huge width of cliff came thundering down a few paces beyond them, half-burying them with earth. This weighed heavily upon the spirits of some of the people, particularly the crew of the yawl: they felt that both the land and the sea were against them now, and they were not to be saved, whatever they did.

The whole of the next day they rowed into the eye of the wind across the bay, but when they came to the farther horn they could find no harbour, and they were forced to wear out the hours and hours of the black night lying on their oars, keeping the boats' heads to the roaring wind and baling out the spray and the very heavy rain. It was in the course of this night that Jack and Tobias ate the shoes off Jack's feet: they were shoes made from sealskin bought long ago from the first Indians to come to Wager Island.

Some people said that the day after this was Christmas; it may have been the case, but for the boats' crews it was a day of hard pulling, nightmarish hunger, exhaustion and continual danger from the sea; and that night again they could not land, but lay at sea, racked by the most extreme hunger they had yet known. But for all that they were in quite good heart, for in the evening they had had a sight of the western end of the land. It was lost again in the low clouds and rain of the next morning, but as the day cleared there it was, some ten miles to the west, a tall black promontory with no land beyond it. They found a bay with a sheltered beach and put ashore there for a while, to find shellfish and to mount their strength a little by a fire, and then they hurried, with a kind of despairing eagerness, to double this portentous cape. They were sure that once they were round it the wind and the sea would be less terrible: and in any case, round it they must, if ever they were to get away to the north.

They were quickly aboard, and they pulled out hour after hour until they were abreast of the cape and one mile to the south of it: they could actually see beyond it to the north. But the wind was rising, the incessant western gale, the men had very little strength left, not enough to make the extra mile or two of offing into the wind before they could dare to attempt the cape. They lay staring at it for a few minutes as the boats rose and fell on the rollers, and then with one accord turned for the bay they had left that morning. Before they could reach it darkness had fallen, however, and they spent another night lying on their oars, unable to get in until the morning.

Now the weather grew very bad, so bad that they could not leave their bay for the open sea: but this had its advantages, for being confined to this bay they explored it in every direction and found lagoons at the far end – shallow lagoons, some muddy and brackish, with fresh water draining in from the interminably rain-soaked swampy land, some sandy, divided from one another and protected from the main sea by sand bars and long spits. Here there were clams, various fish (if only they could have caught them) and much more important, a number of very large and very fierce sea-lions.

Mr Hamilton was the first to discover one. He fired upon it at short range as it lay upon a sand-bank, and it came straight for him, roaring, a beast fifteen feet long with a hairy mane, very nimble. But the soldier was not accustomed to give way: he fixed his bayonet with the utmost speed, and meeting the sea-lion with an equal ferocity he thrust the bayonet and a foot of the barrel down its throat. The sealion bit it through, turned and flung itself into the sea; it swam off, leaving the men in an amazement. This was a discouraging beginning, and indeed they never did have any success with the big maned creatures, but they shot several of the common small seals, and ate them with brutal eagerness.

The sea abating, they put out again; and pulling much more strongly this time they reached the cape by the middle afternoon and continued westward until they could see that the cape was formed of three separate mountainous heads. Now they turned north, and with an hour's hard rowing they passed the first of the three: the barge was steering strangely, and Jack, who by now felt the touch of the tiller as if it were part of his body, knew that there were some very strong currents setting in towards the chaotic mass of boulders that lay after the first head of the cape; but he was not prepared for the horrifying race that came southward round the second. It was narrowest just under the cape, a white-lined tide-rip that swirled out to sea, broadening as it went, and obviously of the most fantastic strength. A branch from the main current, clearly defined by lines of scum and drift-weed, curled in towards the tumbled reefs that edged the land. He looked nervously at the captain, who said, 'We must try to edge across.'

This was the only course; but when they came nearer to the rip the sight of it was quite appalling. The water ran sharply downhill from the edge towards the middle, and in the strongest central stream it rose again, a high, continually revolving whale-back of racing water. A tree-trunk came towards them, a huge tree-trunk running at an unbelievable speed, and as it came abreast of the barge it was swirled towards the middle of the rip, where it vanished entirely, sucked down and never seen again.

'Pull now,' cried the captain, and the barge slipped from the slack water down the side: instantly it was twirled about and hurried vehemently southwards. For a few minutes they were able to force it across the stream, but as soon as they came to the main strength there was no hope of doing more than escaping from it alive. The big heavy boat was tossed up and down, spun and twirled like a straw; and by the time it was over, when the tide was wholly ebbed and the tide-race had therefore stopped, they were far away below the first headland, far out to sea, and happy only in the prospect of a known shelter for the night, some hours' toil away, in the place they had left at dawn.

The wind had not been too troublesome that day, but the next day (which they spent hunting for seals and resting from their exhausting pull) it backed from the west into the south, and by night into the south-east; this was the one direction from which their anchorage was not sheltered, and the wind blew straight into the bay. It fell to Jack and Tobias to be boat-keepers that night: by the time they took their place the sea had not worked up to any extent, however, and they stepped in quite easily over the yawl, which lay inside of them, guarded by Rose and Buckley; Jack then hauled the barge out to where it should ride at anchor – for they had fashioned a kellick to replace the grapnel that they had lost the first day out – made all fast, and then, lying down between the thwarts, he went straight to sleep.

He woke suddenly in the brilliant moonlight: Tobias was shaking him. The sea had grown immensely, and he seemed, in waking, to have heard a shriek. As he stared he saw the yawl canted high on a breaking wave, bottom up: the breaker, roaring back from the shore, left not the boat but a man, a man hurled head down in the sand – his head and shoulders buried in the sand and for a moment his body upright. The waves were breaking outside the barge, and any one of them might fill it. Jack leapt to heave up the kellick, while Tobias held the oars ready. With the anchor up they pulled for their lives, urging the heavy barge out slowly, with huge effort, beyond the breakers. They reached the dark water before they were utterly exhausted and let the kellick go, praying, without much hope, that it might hold. It dragged slowly for a few yards and then took a firm grip, so firm that they rode there all night without driving at all, and the next day too, for the wind and the sea would not moderate. This was one of the coldest days they had had, and the sight of the fire on the shore made it seem even colder to the soaked pair in the barge, starving as they were. The men by the fire were eating seal, and when four and twenty hours had gone by and the sea (though it still would not let them land) had gone down a little, Jack veered out enough line to bring the barge within throwing distance of a jutting rock, and from there the men ashore threw them some food while the surf foamed round the barge's stern.

They seized the meat and hauled the barge back into the unbroken water. It was the liver of a seal, roasted, and Jack and Tobias ate it, engulfed it at once, like dogs. It satisfied their craving hunger for a short while, and then it began to make them so strangely ill that in a few hours' time they were neither of them in their right wits. They managed to get the barge into the shore at the turn of the tide, but that was all they could do. They lay stretched by the fire, taking little account of anything, while one of the most painful decisions that can be imagined was made by the others, at the same fireside. The yawl had been destroyed: the barge could not hold more than fifteen men, and there were nineteen sitting there.

It was not a decision that could be easily made or quickly reached, and it was not until the next day that they came to it. By this time they had buried poor Rose, drowned with the yawl; and by this time Noble had recovered from his smothering in the sand. Jack and Tobias had also recovered, for their sickness went as soon as it came;

but afterwards they lost every scrap of skin that covered them.

The decision was that four of the marines should be left behind; and although it was true that those four, like some of the others, were so worn out and disheartened that they scarcely cared, and although they were left with arms, some ammunition and present food, yet still the hearts of the men in the barge misgave them as they pulled away. The four marines stood upon the beach, gave them three cheers at their parting, and called out 'God bless the King'.

They were last seen helping one another over the mass of black, slippery boulders that formed the back of the little cove.

In order to double the cape the captain had calculated their arrival off the first headland to coincide with the last half hour of the ebb; this would give them the whole time of slack water to run past the second cape and the worst of the race. And although the wind was worse than at their last attempt and the swell much heavier, the extra hands aboard brought them there in time: but the sight that met them off the first headland daunted the most courageous of them all. The swell was from the north and the wind was right across it; this, together with the race and the strong permanent current, had worked up a sea so vicious that no seaman would willingly have rowed into it, no, not to save his life, even in the best-found boat, let alone the shattered, much overloaded barge. Yet they pushed on through it: many of them were so wretched now that they did not mind what happened: they had been chilled and starved and soaked too long; and they felt that there was no blessing on them, because they had left their shipmates behind, in such a country and under such a sky.

The boat pushed on, surviving minute after minute, and slowly the cliffs went by on the starboard side. It looked as though in spite of all they would force a desperate victory, until they came level with the second cape, farther than they had ever been, and opened a vast bay to the northward. Here was a sea worse than that which had wrecked the *Wager*: here the black shore received the full unbroken force of the swell, and the enormous breakers began half a mile out to sea.

The men looked at this, lying on their oars, No one spoke, and the barge, inert on the waves, was heaved in towards the smoking rocks with each long thrust of the sea. Jack thought that everybody aboard intended to let the boat drift and finish everything: he looked across to Tobias.

'If you want to save yourselves,' said the captain, 'you must pull for it, now or never. And you may do as you please,' he said, bowing his head on his hand.

Noble at the stroke oar, caught Jack's eye, and nodded. 'Give way,' called Jack, and mechanically the oars dipped at the familiar command, the men pulled, and the barge steered again.

It was difficult to say how they brought themselves out of those waters; but after some hours of confused struggling they were free of the capes and of the tide-race, and they stood back in the darkness and the rain for Marine Bay.

For once, Captain Cheap spoke with the voice and opinion of all his men, when, breaking some miles of silence, he cried out, 'We shall never get round that cape. We must go back to Wager Island: at least we have some shelter there.'

Chapter Twelve

WAGER ISLAND, and the cold rain driving hard from the west: they were back again, two months after their leaving. They had the shelter they had so longed for, but in their absence the short summer had passed; the green things had nearly all died down, the exhausted mussel-beds had not been replenished, and the men roamed the familiar shore in vain: they had little prospect of surviving the winter.

'I could not find anything dry,' said Jack, putting down a faggot of dead and spongey branches, 'but there is a piece of driftwood in the middle that might do for tomorrow. Did you have any luck?'

Tobias shook his head. 'I am sorry,' he said. 'I went as far as Heartbreak, but by then the tide was in.'

'They are talking of drawing lots again,' said Jack, after a pause.

'I know,' said Tobias. 'Joseph Clinch asked me whether I had my instruments still.'

It was impossible to say who had first suggested this: it was never called cannibalism or man-eating, but just 'drawing lots'; and it was in the air after every bad spell, when the weather was too harsh to allow them out. Now, at the very nadir of their fortunes, it was openly discussed, more and more insistently. There was no living on the pitiful yield of the sea, and their last resource by land, the wild celery, the one thing that had sprung again while they were away, was withering under the frosts that now came every night; it had out-lasted nearly all the other things they dared to eat, but it would not last much longer.

'What are they shouting about?' asked Jack, raising his head to listen. They looked at one another with a moment's horror, but then there was the cry of 'All hands', the sound of people running, and Campbell's voice shouting 'Come on', outside.

'What is it?' they cried, running fast through the rain.

'Hamilton – beef,' answered Campbell, labouring to keep up.

The lieutenant of marines, ranging very far to the south, had found several pieces of beef thrown up on the high-water mark. The cask must have been floating about and only very recently stove in, for it was not only edible, but it had not yet been eaten – scarcely touched – by the turkey-buzzards and vulturine hawks that haunted the coast: and Mr Hamilton, with a magnanimity that not all men would have shown, shared it out.

His bony raw face with its red whiskers was usually grave and reserved, but now it had a smile upon it – a very rare thing in those latitudes and in that company. 'Mr Byron,' he said, handing Jack a scrupulously measured portion.

'Sir,' cried Jack, with a bow, 'sir, I am infinitely obliged to you, sir. We are both infinitely obliged. Come, Toby,' he whispered, 'where's your leg?'

Through all these vicissitudes Tobias had retained his Portuguese wool nightcap: recovering his presence of mind he pulled it off, made his leg, and returned thanks in the most polished manner that he was capable of.

'Plastow,' called Mr Hamilton to the captain's steward, 'my compliments to the captain, and beg he will accept of this beef.'

'I honour him,' said Jack, as they hurried off. 'I shall never call him Sawny again, nor make game of his nation. He could have kept it all, hidden away somewhere.' This was true enough: the days of served-out rations were long past, and now it was each man for himself and Devil take the hindmost.

'So do I,' said Tobias, 'and I doubt whether I could have found it in me to do as much. The captain will not like it, however.' This also was true: Captain Cheap regarded the sharing-out by Mr Hamilton as a reflection upon his own authority. He had grown even more conscious of rank, and even more difficult; he spent much of his time shut up, seeing nobody but Plastow and sometimes Mr Hamilton, Campbell or Jack, whichever was in favour.

But they had little time to worry over that now. The question of how to cook their beef, how much to eat and how much to save, filled their minds to the exclusion of all else. It was horrible beef, grey, frayed out into loose fibres where the sea had got at it, but Lord, how well it went down!

'Lord, how well that went down!' said Tobias, leaning back and gently belching. This was only the second time they had eaten meat since the dreadful day when the yawl was lost, and they ate seal's liver. Their bodies called out for meat all the time: it was an obsessive need. 'I would give a year's pay to be allowed to finish all that at once,' he said. 'Jack, do you suppose that we shall be paid, when it is all over? I should like to make Mr Hamilton a present.'

'You will be, as a warrant officer,' said Jack. 'I shan't. My pay stopped the moment the ship went aground, and I dare say they will charge me for the ship's stores I have eaten since then. The officers' pay goes on, but the men's pay is stopped. Don't you remember they were always talking about it at one time? Those two who were wrecked in the *Bideford*, Shoreham and East, spread it abroad: it was one of the things that made them want to mutiny. No pay, no orders, they said; and you must admit there's something in it.'

'Oh,' said Tobias vaguely. 'Well, in any case, if we come out alive – why do you laugh?'

'I was thinking how delightful it would be to come out alive. One would never complain at anything again.'

'Just so. In that happy event I shall make him a present of an ox, an enormous ox, with a wreath of myrtle about its horns.' He yawned. 'I believe we shall sleep tonight; they may say what they please about suppers, the malignant influence of suppers – *más mató la cena que curó Avicena*, say the Spaniards, which is to say, suppers have killed more than ever Avicenna healed – but in my opinion there is nothing like a full belly for roborative slumber.'

'I did not know that you spoke Spanish, Toby?'

'Not I, upon my word. I can stumble through a voyage or a medical book with a dictionary, but no more.' Food had made Tobias unnaturally talkative. He gave Jack a brief summary of Don Pedro Mendizabal on *renal calculi* and of Ramón Gonzales on phthisis, and then went on to explain why he had not slept the night before. 'I kept thinking of those tombs at Marine Bay, and of the nailed-up door of the cooper's hut,' he said.

At that unhappy time when, returning from their last attempt at doubling the cape, they had searched in vain for the four men left behind, Tobias had stumbled upon a cave, partly natural and partly hollowed out: in the middle of it there was a platform, upon which lay the mummified bodies of Indian chiefs, some, as he could see from the light that filtered in from the top, quite recently dead. The cave, with its long narrow passage (he had had to crawl to get in) was upon a desolate coast, hundreds of miles of swamp and barren rock, and nowhere had they seen the least sign of human habitation, not so much as the frame of a wigwam on their whole journey: that a burial-place should be there at all was strange enough and difficult to account for; but there was a further difficulty. Everything about the catacomb showed that it had been made by people who were unacquainted with metal, which agreed perfectly with the behaviour of the Indians who had been to Wager Island; they had no notion of trading anything for nails or metal tools – did not value iron at all. And yet when the barge came back into Cheap's Bay, the first thing they found on coming ashore was the door of the cooper's hut nailed up, and inside a heap of iron, carefully preserved and extracted with great pains from pieces of the wreck. This contradiction was particularly vexing to a logical mind, and it occupied Tobias whenever he had the leisure to reflect.

In a little while the answer to the contradiction arrived at Wager Island. But by that time Mr Hamilton's beef had all gone; there had been no further supply, and in the starving encampment there was not a man whose mind was not perpetually turned to food – no leisure at all for reflection.

They had been too far gone in privation for any small kindness of chance to have a lasting effect: they had been living upon their reserves so long that some men had exhausted theirs, and in spite of this brief spell of plentiful eating Buckley died, and was buried in the same dank hollow as Noble, who had not survived the return above three days. They had inaugurated this cemetery the day after coming back, in order to put poor murdered Allen to rest; for they attributed their misfortunes, not so much to any malignance in his unresting spirit (which they had all of them heard shrieking out of the sea by night) as to a natural doom that they incurred by their neglect.

In short, things looked as grave as ever they had when, on a calm morning after the new moon, the first men on shore saw two Indian canoes standing in. One contained a set of Indians who were grave, thickset men, with their faces painted grey with white stripes over their cheekbones, and these took little notice of them, scarcely more than if they had been shadows, and would not trade for the few things they had to offer – ring-bolts, a hatchet or two – and made no account of iron. The other canoe held two unpainted men who were eager for the ring-bolts and hatchets, and who were obviously those who had piled up the metal in the cooper's hut. What was far more important, the elder of these two carried a silver-headed baton with the royal arms of Spain, and the words which he spoke to the captain were an attempt at Spanish.

He was a cacique, a chief recognised by the Spaniards, and he came from the tribe or the place called Chonos, some days south of the most southerly of all the Spanish settlements, Chiloe. All this appeared, with more or less certainty, in the course of long interviews with the captain – there was little certainty, because Tobias, who interpreted, had no ready command of the language, and the cacique, although he chattered fast enough, often spoke without any meaning and always with a deformed and barbarous accent that obscured the meaning when there was any. He was a thin, middle-aged man with yellow small eyes as shallow as an ape's, set close together and in the same plane, on each side of a thin, jutting-out nose; he scratched himself perpetually as he talked and he very often laughed with a high thin cackling noise: he was filthily dirty, in spite of the frequent rain. He said that he was a Christian, and that the slave who accompanied him had also been baptised, by the name of Manuel. He was uneasy, nervous and changeable: when first he came, not sure whether the captain were a Spaniard or no, he had cringed; then he had grown more confident. The captain issued the strongest possible orders that the Indian was not to be in any way displeased; he also privately desired the officers to use more than ordinary ceremony towards himself, as this would engender a sense of their importance in the Indian's mind, he having some knowledge of the Spanish punctilio.

The men, who also saw in the Indian their only chance of salvation, obeyed their orders to the letter, and the cacique, with a quick, monkey-like intelligence, understood his importance and grew arrogant. The captain, however, with his better clothes, the respect that was shown him by all hands and his forbidding face impressed the cacique, who early took the view that the captain was the only person of importance, and that all the others were slaves – a view that the captain's conduct at no time denied.

'Let him know, Mr Barrow, that our intention is to reach some of the Spanish settlements,' said the captain, 'that we are unacquainted with the best and safest way – the way most likely to afford us subsistence on our journey. And tell him that if he will undertake to conduct us in the barge, he shall have it and everything in it for his trouble.' Captain Cheap said this in a polite and conciliating tone, which sounded very strange.

The talk went on and on. It was impossible to know what the cacique understood or what he said or what he intended to do: he did not appear to have ordinary human reactions and there was no spontaneous mutual comprehension; at times he seemed to be in a state of strong excitement, and sometimes he laughed after every few words with a high metallic chattering. Nothing could have been more unlike the grave grey savages, who scarcely ever spoke, even among themselves, and who resembled the cacique only in their total indifference to the crew's sufferings.

It was a wearing, unsatisfactory negotiation: but suddenly, for no apparent reason, it was over; the cacique had agreed, and with a ridiculous pomp he took his place in the barge, in imitation of Captain Cheap. Grinning, he thrust Campbell out of the way with his stick and his foot, and as Captain Cheap said 'Humour him, damn you' – for Campbell looked ugly for a moment – he went 'Hee-hee-hee, humour him, damn you,' exactly as if he understood the words.

Now for the third time they rowed along the coast: once out with great expectations, once back in deep despair, and now out again with a mixture of anxiety, weariness and hope. And in the evening they fell again to their desperate former way of finding a shelter, securing the barge with hands trembling with fatigue and weakness, lighting a fire and searching for food. There was not one of the men, even John Bosman, once the strongest man in the squadron, an amiable Hercules, who was fit to pull on an oar for a morning in a pond, let alone the whole day long in a strong cold swell: their exhaustion in the evening was pitiable to see. The Indian had food, carried by Manuel in the canoe, and he gave the captain a little;

but the crew were obliged to make do with the warmth of the fire.

And so it went on. Life appeared to consist of two kinds of nightmare: in the one they starved slowly in the shivering silence of their half-deserted settlement, and in the other they starved fast under the strain of perpetual cruel activity. The two dreams alternated; they were now in the second, and the horrible unreality of it seemed to be made stronger by the inhuman callous heartlessness of the Indians, who did not count the shipwrecked men as human beings – disregarded them entirely, both the grey Indians, who in their much larger canoe were going the same way as the cacique for a few days, and the other two.

The hunger was real enough, however. Tobias, who by habit of mind, education and temperament was better formed than most to put up with it, had never felt the gnawing, all-absorbing pain of extreme hunger so much as the night when they ran to the west of Montrose Island and had to lie on their oars until the morning. The cacique gave Captain Cheap some seal: Tobias sat so near that he could smell the meat, and he was obliged to turn his head away and to bite his knuckles, to keep his mind under control.

In the morning after that the cacique brought them to a bay, where in a featureless wasteland, scoured by the wind and the sleet, there stood a wigwam that contained an ill-favoured woman and – what appeared unbelievable in such a place – a toddling child and another of running age. The cacique thought his wife of little importance or none, but he caressed the smaller child, and gave it a piece of raw, rancid blubber, which it ate at once.

At this place they stayed three days, doing their best to scrape together enough food – shellfish and the like – not only for their needs but to put by a little store, for the cacique gave them to understand that a hard stretch was coming, with no likelihood of food: it was also to be hard in some other way that he could not or would not explain. For his part he went hunting seals in his small, nimble canoe with his slave, and he must have had some success, for when the whole party came aboard for the departure, the Indians had some lumps of meat wrapped in seal-skin, and the captain carried a piece, boiled, in the length of canvas that he used as his bed. The men had nothing. Jack and Tobias had done a little better than most, for as well as some limpets they had found a rock-crushed fish.

They rowed along the coast and into a small bay that they had crossed last time because it had seemed to offer no passage: a river flowed in at the head of the bay and the cacique said that they were to go up it. The young Indian in the canoe crossed the bar in front of them, ran across the rapid stream and worked his way up the river in the very shallow slack water at the edge. The canoe, with nothing but the Indian kneeling in it, drew no more than an inch or so; Jack could not follow it in the heavy, deep-laden barge, and although he put the boat into the best path that he could make out, still the current was so strong that they made little way.

'Pull, pull, pull,' called the captain, urging them to make an effort, to pull like men – it was the ebb of the tide, they would soon be over it – the current would be much less soon – the river would broaden presently – he hoped they were not faint-hearted, to be afraid of pulling, now that they had a chance of pulling for home. The cacique grew over-excited and shouted at them too.

They pulled, and they pulled: men closed their eyes and gave up their whole beings to pulling in time, in – out, in – out, in – out. The banks scarcely moved, and at the least slackening the barge dropped down the stream; but they had gained nearly a mile when Clinch, catching a crab, fell backwards. There was confusion for a moment, and the last thing that Joseph Clinch heard in this life was the captain's oaths as the barge swept downstream.

'Take his oar,' ordered the captain, shifting into Jack's place at the tiller.

'He's dead, sir,' said one of the men in the foresheets.

Captain Cheap made no answer to this, but called, 'Pull, pull, pull,' in time.

The hours went by, slowly, slowly, one after another, but the promised lessening of the current never came. Still they must pull, pull, pull; and any weakening now would lose all the heartbreaking effort that had gone before.

John Bosman, next to Jack, dropped under the thwarts and lay there motionless. Campbell slipped into his place: and presently Bosman, recovering a little from the stupor of ultimate exhaustion, said that he was sorry, he was main sorry, and that if he might have but a bite or two of something to eat, he would pull again. He was not faint-hearted, he said; but he believed that he would die soon, if he could not have something to eat.

Bosman had been particularly unlucky in his last two days' searching; but so had most of his companions, and when he begged them (already wandering in his mind, for conscious he would not have asked it), when he begged them to relieve him, they looked steadily at the captain, leaning there on his canvas parcel: and the captain as steadily ignored them, calling, 'Pull, pull. In – out, in – out,' and adding, with automatic malevolence, 'Pull, or I'll have your backbones flayed, you – s.'

Jack's store was in his left-hand pocket, five dried shellfish; and he put them, one by one, into Bosman's mouth. 'Thankee, mate, thankee,' said Bosman, in a voice of loving gratitude; and in an hour or two he died.

The bitter labour of the day was all in vain. By evening they came to a narrow run of water where it was impossible to make any progress at all, and in spite of the cacique's anger they ran down to the sea again, losing all their distance in less than an hour.

The shore was sandy here, and in the sand above high-water mark they buried Clinch and Bosman, with a marker each and their names and the year. There was six of the men left now; one was a marine and the other five were seamen whom neither Jack nor Tobias knew well – they were men who happened never to have been treated by Tobias nor to have served in the same watch as Jack. Two of them were reclaimed deserters, naturally surly fellows, and their surliness was inflamed to a white heat against the captain now: in spite of their exhaustion they had enough energy to feel undiluted hatred for him in the evening, as he sat eating with the cacique.

'He has not tugged at an oar all day,' they said.

'He makes very sure that he will not starve.'

'He let the Indian blackguard us.' They resented this most bitterly.

'Why should we break our hearts to carry him home?'

'Damn his blood,' they said.

The next day, moved by some unaccountable whim, the cacique said that he was going down the coast in the canoe with his family to hunt seals, that he would be gone three or four days, and that he would leave Manuel to show them where to find mussels. In half an hour he was gone, with the woman paddling, a little pot of fire in the middle of the canoe and the children as motionless as reptiles in the bows.

The men straggled away along the deserted shore with the young Indian, and Captain Cheap, less ravaged with hunger than the rest, stayed to check the meagre stores that remained in the barge. He called Jack to help him, and they turned over the muskets and weapons, four or five flasks of powder, the few musket-balls, to be used with great economy, doled out one by one, the azimuth compass, some rope and scraps of canvas, their few spare clothes and the little things they had saved. The captain had a horror of theft, and continually suspected it.

'Sir,' said Jack, having keyed himself up, 'I must tell you that the men will not be driven any longer.'

The captain made no reply for some time: he twirled and twirled his fingers in the side of his beard – he had let it grow since the first boat journey – muttering to himself.

'He is not in his right senses,' thought Jack. But then in an ordinary, careless voice the captain said, 'You mean well, Mr Byron. I hear what you say.' He said nothing more (this much was already an extraordinary condescension), and presently they walked away to join the others along the beach. Jack was carrying his gun, and when they had gone a hundred yards he remembered that he had meant to ask for a couple of slugs, for he had none left: but the captain was talking to himself at a great rate, too preoccupied for interruption.

The Indian had led them to a cove beyond a point of rock, where the peaty earth and the shelly beach intermingled; here, quite a long way back from the sea, where certain remnants of stalk appeared, tubers about the size of a walnut could be found. Some of them were rotten and viscid, but some were firm. There were not a great many. 'In my opinion,' said Tobias, showing a dozen of them, 'these are a sort of little potato.'

'So long as you can eat them,' said Jack, 'that's the main thing, eh?'

They scraped and dug until they had exhausted the patch, and then went to see another kind of root that Campbell and Mr Hamilton had found.

'The Indian will know,' said Mr Hamilton, tasting it cautiously and looking round for Manuel. 'We had best carry one with us, and catch them up.' Several men had been made violently ill by eating poisonous roots on Wager Island, and one of them had died.

They walked slowly back towards the encampment and the fire, looking carefully for any more potato-haulm as they went: the captain and Mr Hamilton, Campbell and Tobias; and Jack, in front by a few yards, was the first to walk round the point. There, with a shock of total horror, he saw the barge pulling fast from the shore, with the six men in it and the Indian a prisoner in the bows.

'On the other hand,' said Tobias, 'it is a comfort to reflect that we have nothing left to lose – that we are in the lowest possible condition – that nothing can be worse.'

'No doubt,' said Jack uneasily, 'what you say is very moral, Toby, and uncommon philosophic; but I wish you would not make such damned unlucky remarks. I can think of half a dozen ways in which we could be worse off.'

They were sitting in the lee of a rock, watching the great waves break upon the beach: their thunder made the whole air tremble, and the shattered spindrift wafted from the sea like smoke, for although the wind was quiet now the heavy swell that had set in from the west on the day the barge had gone was still running high, and the canoe far out at sea could only be seen at rare intervals.

'He will be making for the cove beyond the potatoes,' said Jack, referring to the returning cacique. 'The reef will protect him there. You may say what you please,' he added, although Tobias had not spoken, 'but that fellow is a wonderful seaman. He is a horrible creature – have never seen a nastier – but he does amazing things at sea.'

'It will be difficult to explain everything to him. It will be harder still to persuade him to serve us. I wish I had paid more attention . . .' Tobias broke off, and mentally rehearsed the more-or-less Spanish phrases that he had composed for the occasion. His head was often light, now that they were hungry all day long with an extreme and painful hunger, even after they had eaten, and he could not always succeed in keeping the Spanish from turning into Latin. It was difficult to collect his ideas and it would be difficult to convey them, as well as dangerous.

His forebodings were justified. The cacique was convinced that they had murdered Manuel: he grew false and foxy, agreed to everything, spoke civilly and nodded and smirked, all with the sole idea of getting away, safe out of their hands. Like most stupid men, he was barely capable of listening and he had little idea of what had happened until, by a very pretty stroke of luck, Manuel himself walked in, in the middle of a tedious, futile negotiation. He had left the barge the first time it touched land, and in the intervening days he had walked back along the coast: he was born to the country, but the journey had marked him sore.

His arrival changed the face of things. It fortunately happened that the cacique numbered the most eager covetousness among his vices, and his eyes had often dwelt upon Jack's fowling-piece, a handsome weapon, silver-mounted and damascened: no Indian of his tribe had ever owned one, nor was there a single firearm among the infinitely superior settled Indians of Chiloe, to the north. For this and a few other things that they still had about them he undertook to conduct them as before. But, he said, after a pause, his canoe would not hold them all.

Tobias fell silent: the last time that he had heard this expression, the last time he had thought *there is not room for all*, was very strong in his mind. He leant his forehead on his hand; but after a moment he was forced from his thought of Marine Bay by the shouting of the cacique, furious that the interpretation should have stopped.

'What does he say?' cried Captain Cheap, shaking him by the shoulder.

Tobias listened again, and replied, 'He says that it will be necessary to go two days' journey. There are some other Indians: they have more canoes and will take us all. He says that you and Mr Byron should go with him. He will leave his wife. The Indians will come here, and then everybody will go north together. He says that the canoes will be carried over the land, but when or how I do not understand.'

Jack was used to most sea-going operations by this time, but paddling a canoe was new to him and he did not do it very well: he did not even paddle as well as a woman, and this increased the cacique's angry contempt for him. For the first few hours the Indian shrieked at him every few minutes, and throughout the day he threw handfuls of water at the back of Jack's head; and Jack, concentrating on the way he was to dig his paddle into the sea, murmured, 'If I had you to myself for ten minutes with a rope's end, my friend . . .' He thought of the paddle as something he was thrusting into the cacique's vitals, and the canoe went along fast, if not gracefully.

Captain Cheap sat in the middle, by the pot of fire. His shoulder would have made him useless as a rower even if he had not had such notions of what was due to his rank, but the cacique did not resent this: he was impressed by what some would call the captain's unbelievable and monstrous selfishness, and favoured it. There seemed to be some sympathy or fellow-feeling between the two, and at the close of the first day he voluntarily gave the captain as good a piece of seal as he ate himself. Jack had a hunk of gristle on that occasion, but the next day he had nothing.

It was his birthday, as it happened, and he spent it from sunrise to sunset kneeling in the bows of the canoe, watching the send of the sea, paddling with the utmost attention and growing fainter and fainter with hunger and cold. The utmost attention was scarcely enough, in one not born to a canoe, for the thing was frail, sensitive, narrow and so easily overset that time and again a cross-wave's lapping nearly had them down: for those who had time to regard it philosophically it was an interesting craft, being made of five planks shaped with fire and oyster-shell scrapers, sewn together with long, tough creeper and caulked remarkably well with the pounded bark of the same creeper, a plant called supple-jack; but, having no thwarts, it had to be propelled by men kneeling upright – a position that is intolerably painful after a little while to those whose limbs are not trained to it from childhood. Towards the end of the second day Jack began to wonder whether he could possibly last out another hour, another ten minutes. They passed through a shower of hail that to some degree refreshed or at least enlivened him, but when the light began to fade in the icy drizzle that followed the hail, he found that his courage was failing. The top of a wave came in, and they shouted out in fury behind him: he looked round the darkening sky with a haggard face, and it seemed to him that it would be very easy to die. They were out of sight of land. He had no idea any more of their direction and little memory of their purpose, and he would have thrown down his paddle if he had felt slightly less dislike for his companions. But you cannot behave shabbily before those whom you despise, and hatred alone kept him paddling, not ten minutes longer, but two interminable hours after the sun had gone down; after which time the cacique guided the canoe straight in from the offing into a bay where half a dozen wigwams stood.

The cacique took the captain up the beach from the landing-place and into one of the wigwams: Jack was left outside in the rain-filled darkness. The bitter cold invaded him now that he was no longer in continual movement: he stood there shivering for some time, automatically emptying the water out of his pocket – he had made himself a sail-cloth lining, in order never to lose anything valuable, such as a limpet or one of the little insipid half-potatoes, and it held water like a bucket.

There was a glow under the wall of the wigwam, the glow of a fire: he bent to go in, but then straightened up again. If he were to be thrust out, which was quite likely, it would be more than he could bear. Even in this extremity he would not submit to humiliation in front of Captain Cheap at the hands of the cacique and his friends.

There was a glow from the next wigwam, too, and he walked towards it, while the dogs that had been barking all this time redoubled their noise. He thought of the spears that the Indians always carried, of the perpetual ill-temper and brooding passion in which these unhappy people seemed to live; but all this amounted to less than his loathing of humiliation, and going down on his knees and hands he crawled into the tent.

Two women were sitting by the dying fire, dressed in feather cloaks; one was old and very ugly, the other young. They stared at him through the smoke in amazement, and when, with as polite a bow as the lowness of the wigwam would permit, he advanced towards the warmth, they hurried silently away, darting through the hole like rabbits.

'Well, it will be charming while it lasts,' said Jack, huddling his frozen body to the little fire. A few minutes later there was a noise outside and he held himself tense; but it was only the women coming back, in great good humour now. They seemed thoroughly amused by something, and it occurred to Jack that the sight of a face with amusement on it rather than anxiety, hostility or wolfish starvation was almost as good as a meal. He sat easy again, rubbed his hands to show that he loved the fire, nodded and smiled; they also nodded and smiled, and addressed long observations to him, presumably of a humorous nature, for both laughed very heartily at the end. Presently the old lady fetched in some wood for the fire, and Jack, finding that his pride made no objection to his lowering himself before these kind souls, pointed earnestly to his mouth, and rubbed his stomach.

In the back of the wigwam there was a tumble of old pieces of bark, and after rummaging about among them and turning most of them over, the young woman, who appeared to be the housekeeper (and a most indifferent one), came up with a handsome gleaming fish, a kind of mullet, that must have weighed four pounds. She brought it to the fire, scraped the ashes aside, and grilled it, after her fashion. The smell of the fish was a painful delight; the delay while it was lightly scorched on either side was nearly intolerable; and when it came, passed on a piece of birch-bark, a lifetime's training in civility deserted him – he seized the fish without a word or a smile and ate it, head, fins and bone and skin. Only towards the very end did a returning glimmer of decency prompt him to express his obligation with nods and greasy smiles, and even to offer the dish, holding it out towards them (but not very far). They had watched him intently all the while he ate, and now they laughed, harangued him in a very cheerful manner, and laughed again.

The heat in the wigwam was now quite extraordinary: Jack was warm right through to his spine, his clothes were dry, and for the first time in months and months he did not feel hungry; he gazed at the Indian women as they squatted there in their feather cloaks, and smiled most affectionately upon them. They seemed to waver in the rosy light of the embers as his eyes closed of themselves. He swayed as he sat, and, three parts asleep, he assured them of his infinite good will.

The old woman arranged him a soft platform of birch twigs, and lying down he said, 'My dear madam, I wish I had some token of my esteem to offer you – I wish . . .' But here a huge, mounting, irresistible sleep interrupted him, cut him off and bore him down.

When he woke up he found that they had covered him with their feather cloaks, light, and as warm as a bird's nest (though smelly). The old woman was tending the fire; the young one was talking quietly to some thin, sharp-looking, smooth dogs that had come in during the night. The dogs were painted with blue, dull red and ochre spots: Jack registered this fact, and at the same time became aware that he was prodigiously hungry, so hungry that he could not forbear telling the women about it at once. They seemed to find this perfectly natural – as natural as their having to go out into the wet and the cold with the spotted dogs to catch his breakfast. Presently they came back, streaming wet from head to foot but as cheerful as ever, and cooked him three more fishes, laughing as they dripped.

It is wonderful what a good night's rest will do, and a full belly. Jack walked about the wigwams in the morning, looking at them with the liveliest interest, whereas the day before he would not have turned his eyes to see a double-headed phoenix, had the phoenix not been edible. The camp was full of women and children – no more than two men, and one of them lame – and Captain Cheap, on appearing with the cacique, said that, as he understood it, the men were to come back in two or three days: they were gone to make war or to say their prayers or something that he could not make out.

Jack would have been happier to hear that the men were all gone for ever, but as the day was almost pleasant, for once, with a little watery sun and no wind, he determined to enjoy himself as much as he could while he might. There was a stream running down to the shore, and here, by way of a particular indulgence, he washed his shirt and cleaned his grieko by thumping it with a stone, killing hundreds at a blow. Jack was not unduly fussy about dirt or vermin, but now he found it a wonderful relief not to have so many creatures crawling on him, and to be clean for once. If only Tobias had been there, equally well fed, Jack would have asked for little more.

While his shirt was drying, he took a turn upon the rocks above the stream, and from there he saw, to his dismay, that the women were dismantling the wigwams, unfastening the curled strips of bark and carrying them down to the canoes, which were now all at the water's edge. He ran for his shirt and hurried down after them. They were only going fishing for a day or two, said his two particular friends, who divined his anxiety: they pointed to a couple of untouched wigwams, where Captain Cheap and the cacique would stay, and he understood very well what they meant. But they seemed perfectly willing to take him with them, if he had a curiosity to see their fishing, and they gave him a paddle.

A dozen canoes worked out beyond the white water; there were children in many of them, little, naked, amphibious things that fell into the surf quite often during the preparations and the departure, and were either spooned out by their mothers with paddles or left to extricate themselves as best they might: children who could scarcely walk upright would come creeping out of the vicious roar and drag of a breaking wave with as much calmness as if they had been seals. And when the canoes had come out into the quiet swell beyond the reefs and the scattered islets the fishing began: the young woman (whose name, in the face of all probability, appeared to be Maudie) handed her feather cloak to Jack, took a basket between her teeth and slipped over the side. The spotted dogs watched over the low gunwale with their pricked ears brought to bear on the splash: the splash subsided, and time went by. Still it went by, and Jack looked anxiously at the old woman; she seemed quite unmoved, but more and more time passed, and it became increasingly obvious to Jack that no one could stay under that long. The first sign that the young woman might still be alive was a gentle thumping of the dogs' tails; they all brought their ears still more to bear, and a moment later a black head broke the surface. Maudie handed in the basket, filled now with sea-urchins, breathed hard for a few moments as she held on to the side, and then plunged to the bottom of the frigid sea.

This went on and on, while the old lady told Jack that she had been accustomed to staying down twice as long, in her youth, and to diving twice as deep; modern young people, she said, sought nothing but a life of ease and luxury. Jack said 'Yes, ma'am,' and 'No, ma'am,' and 'Upon my word, ma'am, you do not say so?' at decent intervals and watched the sea-urchins pile up and walk slowly about on their purple prickles. At length the young woman climbed back in: her natural colour was brown, but with the cold she had gone a dismal purple, and her lips were bluish grey; she trembled violently, uncontrollably, and for some time she was too perished even to smile. The old woman chuckled tolerantly, slapped her with a paddle and they rowed off towards the east after the other canoes. In a quarter of an hour the young woman was quite recovered, and she talked away with never a pause until noon, when they all landed on a low, sheltered point, where the sea ran into various shallow creeks. Here they set up their wigwams. At one time Jack had esteemed himself reasonably good at withstanding the cold and the wet (he already had the nickname of Foulweather Jack in the Navy), but the young woman's performance had disabused him of this idea: and he had once thought himself tolerably handy, but now the old woman's expert erection of the wigwam set him right again. He tried to help, but it was no good: they gave him a couple of sea-urchins to keep him quiet and made him go and sit among the dogs: he had rarely felt humbler. Indeed, the dogs were far more useful than ever he could be, for presently the entire body, dogs and all, moved off to a sandy inlet; the dogs knew very well what was afoot, and when the women had all walked in about neck-deep, so that a line of them held a net across the narrowest part of the water, the dogs with one accord dived in at the far end – dived, like so many otters – and drove the fish that were in the creek towards the net. From time to time they came up, yapping, to breathe and to take their bearings, and, with extraordinary intelligence, they combined their efforts to beat the entire shoal into the extended net. It was an unusually numerous shoal, and it was an unusually fortunate day; they left barely a fish in this creek nor in the next, and before sunset they had taken as many as they could carry.

The Indians did not understand salting or smoking (perhaps neither would have answered in that sodden atmosphere), and they were obliged to eat everything within a day or two. It was a delightful interlude, a time of steady, unrestrained eating, and talking and laughing. Jack recited verse to his women; they seemed favourably impressed, and harangued him in their turn with what might have been a metrical composition, but was more probably a cooking recipe – the word for fish coming in again and again. He knew several Indian words by now, all of them to do with food: after a few months of starvation one begins to understand that one is primarily a walking stomach, and that the satisfaction of its needs is the great and fundamental pleasure of the world.

But it could not last. The skies clouded, and with them the faces of the women: the canoes were run out into the rising sea, and they had no sooner reached the bay where the cacique and the captain had remained, than the men of the tribe appeared in the offing. When the men landed, all gaiety left the encampment; the children and dogs retired to a certain distance and the women came forward with anxious, downcast expressions and dutiful greetings. Jack's two friends were the property of the chief, a burly savage who had painted his face navy-blue, although nature had made it repulsive enough in the first place: something the young woman said did not please her husband, who snatched her up in his arms and threw her down on the rocks; he threw her down again and again, but, not content with that, he beat her, snorting and gasping like a beast with the force of his blows.

If Jack had been a hero of easy fiction he would have knocked the fellow down; but being no more than a half-grown mortal, still weak with starvation and exposure, and unarmed in an armed camp of the chief's own relatives, he turned away, his heart filled with impotent hatred – hatred not only for the chief but for all bullying and domineering and for the whole brutish tradition whereby men, in order to show how manly they can be, affect to despise all pleasant-ness, kind merriment and civility, and concentrate upon being tough, as inhuman as possible, with the result that their lives are nasty, short and brutish, wholly selfish and devoid of joy; and not only their lives but the lives of all around them, particularly the weaker sort.

Now life resumed its former aspect, gloomy, unhappy and danger-ous. After hours and hours of talk between the cacique and the blue chief it was decided that they should return, that the main body of Indians should follow them in a few days and that they should then all go away to the north together. In those parts of the world where it is as difficult to live in one place as it is in another people undertake voyages, even huge migrations, very easily: the cacique had no sooner said his last word to the blue chief than he walked down to his canoe, followed by the captain and Jack, and in half an hour they were out of sight.

It was a better voyage than the journey out; the wind was behind them and the sea was somewhat calmer; Jack, for one, was a good deal stronger, and he was handier with the paddle now. When they had been going for five hours a seal blew a little way ahead of them, rolling black under the wave: the Indian dropped his paddle, whipped up a spear and crouched as tense and glaring as a cat. He cried 'Pa-pa-pa-pa,' high and shrill, and the seal put up its head to look. In one sliding movement, incredibly fast, the Indian threw his spear: it pierced the seal's head from eye to eye. This was between twenty and thirty yards over a heaving, glancing sea, a fantastic piece of skill; but the cacique, paddling furiously and shrieking at Jack to grapple the seal at once, did not seem to think a great deal of it. It put him into a reasonably good humour, however, and when his family came down to the water to greet him he picked up the smallest child and tossed it into the air, laughing like a Christian.

In Jack's absence Tobias and the others had done very poorly. The cacique's wife was a woman entirely unlike Jack's friends, and she had given them no more than a few sea-urchins, and those bitterly grudged. Sea-urchins are delicious appetisers, but as they are almost all hollow, they cannot satisfy except in enormous quantities. Jack's fish, therefore – the fish that he had carried in his bosom, having no other container and being unable to trust his companions – was more welcome than can easily be expressed, although it was pink with the dye of his waistcoat and only just good enough to be eaten, even by the standards of extreme hunger.

'How I wish you had been there, Toby,' said Jack. 'It would have set you up for a week, the smell alone. No, I assure you,' he said, turning his head away from the offered piece, 'I ate very well before coming ashore. Gormandise while you may, for Heaven knows when we shall have a bellyful again.'

This was sound enough, for in the days that passed before the other Indians joined them everybody went short of food, even the cacique. Like most people who live on the edge of starvation, the Indian and his family were capable of eating huge amounts at a sitting: they ate the whole of the seal, apart from a little that they gave to Captain Cheap, in a very short time, and then in spite of the unpropitious weather they took to the sea again.

It was upon his return from one of these fishing expeditions that the cacique gave an almost perfect exhibition of savagery and the cult of toughness carried to its logical extremity: he and his wife had one basket of urchins, no more, from a whole day's work, and on reaching the shore the cacique passed this basket to the smallest child, who, not having yet learnt caution, had come down to meet the canoe. The child slipped, let the basket fall in the surf, and the urchins were lost. The cacique leaped out, seized the child by an arm and a leg and hurled it with all his force against the naked rock.

The killing of this child was the most shocking thing that Jack had ever seen in a life not rare in terrible sights, and it left a weight of horror on his mind that would not go. It was scarcely alleviated by the coming of the other Indians, with the canoes that were to take them northwards and, for a time, his two kind women, with their cheerful faces. But even though they were there, within a few yards of the wretched wigwam that Mr Hamilton, Campbell and Tobias had botched together, they might almost have been in Asia, for the blue chief was as jealous as a Turk – the women were either at work on the sea or they were kept rigorously within. They nevertheless, and at the risk of their lives, contrived to pass some victuals out through the back of the tent to Jack – a boiled cormorant, a seal's head, two half-eaten flippers – and it was with strong regret that he and Tobias saw them go: several of the women were sent off, with most of the fishing dogs, some days before the main body began their journey.

This voyage was begun neither happily nor with any good omen. The whole movement seemed to be part of a tribal migration: these Indians, who were called Min-Taitao, were travelling upwards to their northern limits with the approach of mid-winter; they were not going on account of the *Wager*'s people, whom they regarded as nuisances, very much in the way, hangers-on who were too contemptibly soft to feed themselves, incompetent fools; and the taking of the white men was an irritating hindrance to their progress. They put them into separate canoes so that they would be less trouble, and on a lowering morning, with a strong west wind, they set out on a rising, angry sea and began to work along the coast towards the remote, miserably barren country of Marine Bay.

In time, and after drenching and freezing days at sea, they reached a place where, in a maze of sand-bars and subdivided channels, a river seeped into the head of a deep, wide bay. The barge had been here before, but they had taken no notice of the fresh water; it had not seemed practicable for the boat, and indeed it was not. The

Indians unloaded the canoes, carried them over the sand and launched them again in a fresh-water lake, or wide swelling of the river. Paddling across this, they came to a stream with various branches; the branch they took grew narrower all day long, and far stronger. Towards the evening it seemed to Jack that this was to be a repetition of the appalling time when John Bosman died, and in fact it was so hard that even the comparatively well-fed Indians were drawn to the utmost of their endurance. They lay that night under the pouring rain in a naked swamp, without putting up their wigwams, because there was not a single pole to be found, and these Indians never carried poles with them but only the pieces of bark.

The next day resembled the first, but the day after that brought them far up into a dripping forest, where the river turned away to the east: in these three days they had nothing whatever to eat, except for some bitter yellowish roots. Here they hauled out, and in the morning the Indians took the canoes to pieces; it was simply done, by cutting the creeper that sewed the planks together, and in theory it was then simple to carry the canoes, thus divided into convenient loads, across the country until another river, flowing northwards, should take them in the right direction. But this was a wicked country, the deepest forest that they had ever seen, and the trees stood in ground so interspersed with bogs and half-hidden pools of mud that it was difficult to understand how so many could find enough firm ground to hold themselves upright. A great many did not, and were either supported, slanting, by their neighbours, or lay flat along, sometimes growing in that position, but more often dead; and these falling trees in their crash broke many others, and their stumps stood long after, often covered by undergrowth, jagged, splintered stumbling-blocks every few yards along the miles and miles of march. Everywhere there were wind-fallen branches, white and rotting, and in the windless bottom of the forest cold fungus stood dying under the winter frosts.

By this time Captain Cheap was growing very weak: Mr Hamilton was sadly reduced too, but he could still walk and manage his load, which was a plank. Captain Cheap could scarcely get along at all, however, even at the beginning of the day, and he was obliged to be helped by Tobias and Campbell, who also carried a full burden each. Jack, who was in the last canoe to be dismantled, had a putrid lump of seal wrapped in the captain's piece of canvas. It had been given to the captain by an Indian who did not think it worth carrying over the long portage, and the understanding was that it would be shared in the evening, when a fire would make it edible.

The canoe was very long in taking apart, because these Indians preferred to clear the holes of the caulking now rather than when they came to sew the planks together again – the more usual practice – and by the time it was ready the others were far ahead. The planks were delicate objects; a fall would break their perforated edges; and the Indians, having weighed Jack's load, added nothing to it, but set off after their companions, carrying the whole of the canoe.

'It is just as well,' thought Jack, scrambling up a muddy slope behind them, 'for I do not believe that I could carry so much as a paddle more.' The canvas was an awkward burden, painfully heavy and apt to slide; he carried it on his neck and shoulders, with a line across his forehead, after the example of the Indians, because he needed both hands to get along and to keep up with them. They made their way through a long valley, which must have become dammed at its lower end within the last few years, for although the mud and swamp lay waist-deep in places, yet the broken stumps still stood in the firmer ground below. Jack had no shoes (he had eaten them long ago), and although his feet were quite hard they were not as hard as the Indians', and soon the blood was running under the black ooze that covered his legs.

Hour after hour they went through the forest, and the Indians, full of meat and born to the country, kept drawing ahead. Sometimes they were slipping away through close-packed saplings, which waved above them; sometimes he could hear them pushing through tall undergrowth; sometimes as he emerged at one edge of a yellow-scummed mire he would see them disappearing at the far side of it, the open black mud showing where they had passed. They had no intention of waiting for him. With ever-increasing anxiety he hurried after the Indians through the gloom; his legs would scarcely bear him, and the pace was killing: he dreaded losing them – dreaded it beyond words.

Now there was a long slough between tall trees; there was no trace of the Indians, no marks in the mud, but he could hear them in front of him, in the trees beyond the slough. A very tall beech had fallen, and it lay out across the surface of the standing water; his way probably lay along its trunk, he thought, and he hurried out along this natural bridge. Half-way over his feet slipped on rotten wood, the trunk gave a turn, and in a moment he was in the slough, struggling wildly, with his head under the surface, pressed down by his burden. There was no ground under his feet, and his clawing hands met only mud. With a tearing effort he wrenched his head back and, turning, snatched a breath of air; there was a branch within reach, and before it broke he managed to pull himself upright. He could not reach the trunk again, however, and he stood there for some moments, with only his head above the water and his feet in yielding mud. His weight was pressing him deeper: he was forced to move, and with a heavy, floundering, swimming motion he urged himself forward. The slough was shallower; the mud was only up to his chest. With each step it was less, and in ten minutes he was on solid ground on the far side.

But his strength was almost entirely gone and he scarcely had the energy to be glad of his escape. Indeed, *glad* was not a word to use in connection with him at all at that time. One can bear a great deal, but there is a limit to human endurance, and suddenly it seemed to Jack that he had reached his limit. He sat, bowed right down, and indulged in the weakness of despair. But in fact he had not reached the end of his powers, as he knew very well after a minute or two; and when he had collected himself a little the haunting fear of being left quite filled his mind again: he was carrying no part of the canoe, and there was no material reason why the Indians should wait for him.

'It is no good,' he said aloud, looking at his burden: and with a vague notion that it would be wrong to leave it lying there on the ground, he stowed it neatly in the crutch of a tree. Even without it he could barely get along at first, but presently he came to a small, clear stream, running in the direction that he should go – or thought he should go – and here, when he had washed the fetid mud from his mouth and face, he felt better; a few minutes later he saw the traces of the Indians, and, knowing that he was on the right track, he hurried on, leaving blood at every step, but less wretched than before.

For a good hour and more he followed this stream, and then quite suddenly it flowed out into a vast lake, huge and grey, with the Cordilleras on the other side; and on its muddy shore there were the Indians, reassembling their canoes. The others sat at a little distance. They seemed to be completely done up, and for some time nobody said anything; they, knowing that the Indians were not yet ready, had felt no particular anxiety; and no one who had just made that march could be expected to care for anything but his own fatigue.

'Where is my canvas and the seal?' asked Captain Cheap at last.

Jack explained. He was exhausted, but he was not beyond the prick of shame, and the low-voiced, bitter, heartfelt reproaches that met his explanation pierced him.

'I would not have believed it in *you*, Byron. I had conceived you more of a man – a braver man.'

'I would have carried the seal myself,' said Mr Hamilton, 'but I thought it was in the best hands. It was a poor thing to do. It was poorly done.'

'After all this, we are to have nothing to eat, because you left it in the wood,' said Campbell. 'Another night with nothing to eat.'

Jack rose painfully, and turned back into the forest. 'I will come with you,' said Tobias; and when they had gone some way up the stream he said, 'You must let me look at your feet, Jack. They are in a bad way.' They sat down, and he searched the cuts and scratches for splinters. 'Tell me where you left the bundle,' he said, drawing out a jagged piece of wood, 'and I will fetch it: I am remarkably fresh.'

'I never could tell you for sure, Toby,' said Jack, with a sort of smile. 'Go back now, there's a good fellow – it would oblige me most, upon my honour.' But he made no protest when Tobias walked on with him, and it would have been useless if he had.

It took something more than an hour to reach the place where Jack had left the seal and the canvas: on the way they talked very little, and now that they sat down under the crutched tree they said little more, being too weary; but the feeling of companionship was there.

'That was where I fell in,' said Jack, showing the slough. Tobias nodded. 'If we can find a sound branch,' said Jack, 'we can sling the load between us.'

'There is a puma on the other side,' said Tobias. Jack made no reply; Tobias had pointed out two dull little birds on the way up and as there was one flying about now, making a noise like the yapping of a small, silly dog, Jack thought (as far as he could think at all, through the dullness of exhaustion) that that was what he meant.

'We must go,' said Jack, 'or it will be night before we get back.'

'Allow me two minutes to walk to the other side.' Tobias walked across the shallower mud, vanished into the bushes and then returned with a pleased look on his pale, thin face.

'I believe you would creep out of your grave to look at a flaming bird,' said Jack. 'Come, take an end.'

'A puma is not a bird,' said Tobias, after a hundred paces. 'It is a kind of cat – felis concolor. You may see it soon: it is moving along with us, on the right.'

The word *cat* brought nothing into Jack's mind but a fleeting image of a shabby, brownish-black little creature called Tib that disgraced the drawing-room at home, and he plodded on in silence. Every hundred yards or so they changed shoulders, and during the third change there was a coughing noise to their right, a series of coughs, huge, deep, throaty coughs, that culminated in a shattering roar, unimaginably loud.

'Not a bird, Jack, you see,' said Tobias.

'How big?' cried Jack, vividly alive now, with terror coursing up and down his spine.

'The size of an indifferent lion,' said Tobias. 'You can see him if you bend and look under the yellow bush. He is tearing up the earth, and biting it.'

'Can he climb?'

'Oh, admirably.'

'Toby, what shall we do?'

'Why, unless you wish to go and look at him, we had better go on. It is getting late. But do not hurry so, Jack, nor make jerking movements. If he should come out, take no notice of him, or look at him kindly – do not provoke him. He is not a froward puma, I believe.'

Naked fear is the keenest spur of all; in spite of Tobias' placid assurance, Jack was terrified, and his fright carried him down the long stream to the lake in such a state of nervous tension that he noticed neither his wounded feet nor his famished stomach. Fear enabled him to do what he could not have done unterrified, and it needed all Tobias' fortitude and all his remaining strength to keep up with him.

They came out into the open at the beginning of the twilight, as the rain started to fall. Many of the canoes were already on the water, and as they hurried down several more were launched: the cacique was chattering with impatience, holding the stern of the canoe with Captain Cheap in it. They carried the bundle to the water's edge; the captain and the cacique seized it and threw it in. There were three other Indians in the canoe.

'Wait,' said Captain Cheap, waving them back, and the cacique interrupted with a flow of words. The remaining canoes were launched on either side of them, and the cacique's canoe floated out from the shore. The Indians began to paddle – all the canoes were paddling now, with the blades flashing and the water white behind.

Jack hailed: they both cried out together, and over the widening water came a confused, vague answer, half-heard and interrupted by the cacique. 'You can wait ... other Indians ... no room ... another canoe.'

They stood there silent on the bank. No shouting would bring back the boats; and they watched them over the water until they disappeared in the darkness and the rain.

Chapter Thirteen

'Toby,' said Jack, turning towards the deserted shore with a ghastly attempt at lightness, when his aching eyes could no longer see anything on the lake, 'you said that we could not be worse off when the barge left us. Don't you wish you had held your tongue now?'

'It was a thoughtless thing to say,' replied Tobias in a steady voice. 'It smacked of hubris – of insolent security.' And after a few minutes he said, 'Let us go down the shore, where the trees are thicker, and see whether we cannot find a little shelter. If we can sleep, we shall be able to think more clearly in the morning, what to do.'

They wandered down the grey edge of the lake, and the sad waves came lapping in on the yielding mud; they looked for a tree with a thick enough trunk to give them a lee and tolerably even dry ground below it, but the darkness was coming on fast, and they could find nothing that protected them more than a very little. The roots of the tree which they had chosen (a kind of beech) would not allow them to lie down; they crouched, huddled together for warmth, in a half-sitting position, shivering with cold and hunger; nevertheless, they went to sleep – lapsed into a kind of stunned unconsciousness.

Jack awoke in the black night, cramped and twisted with hunger, still partly entangled with a vivid dream of those beautiful days in the women's wigwam, the smoky wigwam, the warmth and the fish sizzling on the pink embers: when he had gathered his wits for a few minutes he said, 'Toby? Are you awake? Do you smell it? There is a smell of fire; I swear it.'

The wind had died to a breeze that eddied along the edge of the forest, and from time to time it brought them a whiff of smoke. 'Yes,' said Tobias. 'It is smoke.' They set out towards it, often stopping like dogs to sniff: there was a little suffused light from the east, and the white frost helped them as they blundered through the trees. They had not gone far into the most sheltered part before they saw a wigwam, lit from within and smoking at the top: there were loud, harsh, furious voices inside.

'It sounds like one of their religious . . .' began Tobias.

'I don't care if they are raising the Devil,' said Jack. 'Wait for me here.'

Tobias heard the noise redouble, and in a moment Jack returned. 'They kicked me in the face as I tried to crawl in,' he said, 'but at least they know we are here.'

A triangle of light appeared in the low entrance of the wigwam and an old woman peered out, beckoning. Going into an assembly of unknown savages, defenceless, on hands and knees, might very well be a matter for some hesitation, and it was a measure of their desperate state that they hurried in at once. There were several Indians, men and women; and on the ground near the fire lay a naked chief, as thin as a man could be, and he was plainly dying.

Jack and Toby sat silent, motionless and inconspicuous: the shouting went on – it seemed to be ritual, for sometimes two men shouted together, with the same words. At dawn the old woman took a piece of seal, and holding it stretched between her teeth and her left hand, sliced off pieces with a shell; she passed it raw to the Indians, but for Jack and Tobias she put it to the fire, spitting liquid blubber from a piece she chewed upon the slices until they were done. They did not understand the significance of this, nor of many other things; but they ate the seal.

Shortly after this three of the men, more brutal than any they had yet seen (their cheek-bones were slashed with parallel, raised scars, and their faces were scarcely human at all), went out, motioning Jack to go with them. Although they were not part of the tribe that had joined with the cacique, they too had carried their canoe over the watershed, and they now began putting it together. Tobias had picked up a certain amount of the Indians' language by this time, but he found, when they would answer him at all, that these people spoke a different dialect: few of the words were the same, but at least it was clear that they were going to the north – that much could be learned by pointing – and it was probable from their manner that the Indians expected them and had been told about them. But this was not sure: the Indians' lack of surprise might come from mere indifference. The only certainty was that these Indians, even more than the last, looked upon Jack and Tobias as nuisances, if not worse.

The lowest savages have little curiosity. There are some who are unmoved by things outside their comprehension – metal, cloth and ships do not interest the most primitive of all. The survivors of the *Wager* were of consequence only to the cacique, whose comprehension was comparatively enlarged and to whom their remaining possessions were of value. These Indians knew nothing of firearms, had no notion of connecting whiteness with power and wealth and disbelieved what the cacique told them. They thought the cacique a fool and his protégés a troop of effeminate, uninteresting buffoons.

And what is more, men with different-coloured skins have different smells: the Indians (whose scent was very keen, which made it worse) thought the white smell perfectly disgusting. The white colour, too, was loathsomely ugly, in their opinion – corpse-like, and probably produced by a discreditable disease which might very well be infectious. Still more important, it was obvious to the dullest Indian intelligence that many powerful gods hated these people. Why otherwise should they be so driven up and down, despised and wretched? And some of this hatred might be transferred to anyone who befriended them: their ill-luck might rub off. Lastly, it was clear to the Indians that these wretched people had no religious sense, no sense of piety; they knew nothing about the various beings who were to be appeased by ritual words and gestures; they did not even understand the simplest propitiation of the earth and sky. They were best ignored.

Some faint notion of all this had been seeping into Tobias' mind for a long while, and as they sat a little apart, watching the Indians at work (the Indians had angrily rejected Jack's help, and when he brought them a fine length of supplejack they threw it into the water), he told Jack of his suspicions.

'You may be right,' said Jack, 'particularly about the smell. I have always noticed how they hold their noses when we are by. I had thought it was the captain; but they do it still, I find.'

The Indians were ready. They renewed the ridges of their tribal scars with ash, and they stood there, dull blue with cold, shifting the little square of fur they wore to cover their windward sides; their deep-sunk eyes were bloodshot and rimmed with scarlet from the night-long smoke in the wigwam, and they all seemed to be on the edge of a furious rage. An old woman came from the tent: she was a person of some distinction, it appeared, for they neither kicked nor struck her, and she wore an ample cloak made of vultures' skins with the sparse feathers still on. Jack and Tobias stood in the most anxious hesitation: angry shouts asked them why they did not get in, the fools? And, half-comprehending, they scrambled aboard.

All day long they paddled over the lake, and all day long the snowy Cordilleras retreated from them: in the evening they came to the outflowing river that drained the lake northwards, a fast, white-flowing stream, and here the Indians put into the shore. They put up their wigwam, but they would not allow any blasphemous, smelly, unlucky lepers in it (who would?); nor would they feed them. Jack and Tobias understood the general purpose of their remarks – it could not have been mistaken – and withdrew to an overhanging rock, which, by a very happy chance, had a deep pile of dry drifted leaves under it for a bed, and, more than that, the leaves had protected the still-edible stalks of some plants of rhubarb. They slept so well here that the Indians were up before them – they saw to their horror that in another five minutes the canoe might have gone, leaving them in that desolation.

The night had been fair, but the day was as foul as could be: rain and snow from the north-west, a furious river to contend with, long, thundering cascades, whirlpools and spray that put out the pot of fire amidships. They hurtled down the river with destruction on either hand, at a terrifying, lurching speed that brought them to the sea that night. The Indians hauled up on a stony beach and vanished into the woods, no doubt to an encampment that they knew. It was too dark to look for any food, and as they dared not wander away from the canoe, Jack and Tobias lay by it, on the stones under the sheeting rain. At about three in the morning Jack made an attempt at joining the Indians by the fire that they had at last succeeded in lighting – it glowed through the trees – but this gave great offence, and they kicked and beat him away.

The dawn came, after a hideously protracted night, and the Indians put out into the northern sea. At last Jack and Tobias had come into the water that they had laboured for so long; but whether they alone of all the *Wager*'s crew they could not tell; nor could they tell where they were going now, whether they would rejoin their friends or whether, perhaps, they might be kept as slaves. At low water they came in to a rocky cove and landed to gather shellfish; it was an excellent place, and it was a very great relief indeed to Jack and Tobias. But they were so afraid of being marooned that they dared not stop to eat; they filled their pockets, Jack's hat and Tobias' night-cap – in a vile condition now – and as soon as they saw the Indians turn towards the canoe they ran for it. Jack made as elegant a bow as the circumstances would allow (he was standing on slippery rock) and presented the handsomest of the mussels they had found to the old woman. She looked amazed, but she took it, and when she had washed it a great many times she ate it.

They now headed straight out to sea, steering north-east with a moderate wind, and after a while Jack, putting his battered old hat beside him (it had once been a marine's) began to copy the Indians in front – between the long, powerful strokes they held the paddle in one hand and took a limpet with the other and ate it.

'Capital limpets, Toby,' he said, over his shoulder, tossing the shell into the sea. But instead of a civil reply there was a shrieking Indian voice, screaming out in a terrible passion. In an instant the canoe was arock with violence. One Indian had Jack by the necker-chief, twisting it hard, another had him by the ankles, taking a grip to throw him overboard: Tobias hampered the rear man, and the old woman lashed about her with a spear, howling with fury. By some fantastic chance the canoe did not overset, and in a few moments the old woman quelled the tumult. She harangued them, and although they still looked very ugly, the men set to their paddling again, but not without turning from time to time to threaten Jack and to point to the bottom of the canoe. Jack, three-parts throttled and entirely at a loss, stared back at them stupidly.

'I conceive,' whispered Tobias, 'that they had rather you did not throw the shells into the sea.' It was quite true: each Indian had a little pile of shells by him – a simple act of politeness towards Plotho, the limpet-god, obvious to a child of three.

'Damn your eyes,' said Jack, loosening his neck-cloth and taking up his paddle, 'I shall not eat anything until we are ashore and they cannot see me.'

In the late afternoon, when the canoe came in with the land again and they steered for a little, sheltered, tree-grown island, the Indians, as soon as they had hauled out the canoe, picked up their limpet-shells and carried them carefully beyond the high-water mark; Tobias and Jack meekly did the same. This met with a certain surly approval, and when, a little later, Jack was seen with a bunch of purple berries, on the point of eating them, an Indian dashed them out of his hand, and by a pantomime of death in agony, showed that they were poisonous.

This, however, marked the highest point of their good relations with the Indians. This tribe, like all the others, had an elaborate code of religious behaviour that governed all their waking moments; they were continually propitiating a host of malignant or at least very short-tempered spirits, and their guests were as continually offending them. It did not look as though a human sacrifice to the outraged deities could be long delayed: in the meantime the Indians drove them very hard and gave them nothing whatsoever from the two seals they killed.

It was some relief, therefore, when, at the end of a day of infernal hunger and toil, the canoe rounded a headland and suddenly opened a little cove all lined with other canoes and dotted with men. They could see Mr Hamilton's red coat – pink rags now – at once, and this was obviously the meeting-place.

It was some relief, but not very much: they were too tired to feel any strong emotion. In this stormy, cold, wet, rocky world the chief idea was self-preservation, even among those born to it; among strangers there was little room for any other thought. Campbell and Captain Cheap were sitting wretchedly under the inadequate shelter of a streaming rock: neither side was particularly pleased by the encounter – nobody seemed pleased. They were, in fact, reduced to a state not far from the last indifference.

At this place the cacique had a very large canoe – how it came to be there no one asked or cared: they were as incurious as savages now – and as the Taitao Indians were at that time going no farther, except for one small canoe that would go some way on in a week's time, he intended embarking the whole party in it and pursuing his journey alone. Mr Hamilton, however, was a man in whom proper pride had outlasted starvation and exposure, and he would not consent to travel under the insolent rule of the cacique. He would take his chance in the Taitao canoe that would go next week, and he would make his own way after that, if he could; he hoped with all his heart that they would meet again, and he would pray for them each night, as he hoped they would pray for him. They left him, not alone, it is true, but among a tribe of brutish savages who scarcely came up to his shoulder as he stood there on the beach, an erect, soldierly figure in spite of his rags.

The big canoe was monstrously heavy: it was heavier than anything they had ever seen among the Indians, and it needed a strong crew, six or eight men at least; but all the crew it had was the cacique's slave, Jack, Tobias and Campbell. The captain could not work, and the cacique would not; he squatted there, with his hideous wife and the surviving child, chattering sometimes, and grinning. His unbelievable vanity seemed stronger even than his desire to stay alive, for he would not bear a hand when for want of it they were almost sure to be lost, in overgrown seas, tide-rips and the thousand dangers of coasting the worst shore in the world. Still he sat, like a huge monkey. Yet in general the weather was not so extreme as it had been when the barge made its attempt: the cold grew stronger every day, but the full gales were rarer, and it was just possible for four paddles to work the canoe up towards Chiloe.

Chiloe: the cacique often boasted of his relations with the Spaniards there, and asserted that he knew five, ten, fifty of the Chilotan Indians – could always walk into their houses, and they would give him sheep, potatoes, anything, they loved and esteemed him so. Nobody believed him; nobody took any notice of his flow of words, which alternated with hours of affected gravity, when he would not answer a question. He usually addressed himself to the captain, who spent most of his time in silence, lying in the bottom of the canoe, weaker and iller every day. Nobody believed him; and as the days dragged by, they scarcely believed in Chiloe any more. It seemed that life was to consist of this for ever, an unnumbered series of days in which they urged the lumbering canoe through miles and miles and endless miles of water, often angry, always cold – hard labour the whole day, while the inhuman cacique squatted prating there; and every evening the feverish search along the darkening shore for something to eat, anything, dead or alive, to take the extreme anguish from their hunger; and then the dreadful night, lying under what shelter they could find.

April merged into May, and in that month, as they crept through the tangle of islands in the south of the Chonos archipelago, the cacique twice killed more seals than he could carry; and therefore made a general distribution – at all other times the rowers fed themselves or went without.

In the horrible repetition of days throughout the month of May these were the only two occasions of relief: in June there were none. The snow came more often, and thicker; the captain was now wandering in his mind almost all day long; his legs were hideously swollen, as if with scurvy, but his body was desperately thin. He was shockingly verminous. He no longer knew their names – called Tobias Murdoch – 'Murdoch, you villain: five hundred lashes,' – but he kept his seal-meat with unvarying caution, and when he slept it was with his head upon the seal: his hair and his long beard were matted with the blubber.

At about the day of the solstice, mid-winter's day itself, they found themselves on a cape in the most northern island of the hundreds they had passed in the archipelago: far away to the leeward there was the cacique's tribal home, a very squalid place, and to go from there to Chiloe, he said, they always came to this cape. The crossing was shortest from here, but even so it was a desperately long voyage for an open boat: the cacique looked at the roaring sea and crossed himself. He looked at it with horror and moaned and chattered for hours together.

It was impossible to say what determined him to set out, but it was quite certain that they had not gone a mile before he regretted it. But by then there was no remedy: the wind was strong behind them, and the canoe ran at a furious speed under a little, messy lug-sail made of bits of skin, blanket and the remains of the captain's canvas, sewn together with supplejack and suspended on a tripod of wigwam poles. Once they were out of the shelter of the cape the wind increased to such a pitch that they would have broached-to at the slightest attempt to alter their course; and shortly after this became evident, the bottom plank of the canoe split from stem to stern. The water rushed in, but the canoe did not fall apart; it held together by the fourteen stitches of quartered supplejack at each end, and, with all hands baling madly, it just kept afloat until Campbell managed to pass a twisted net about it and draw all taut with a tourniquet. This gave a certain amount of support, but it did little for the leak; with each rise and fall of the long canoe the split opened and the water from below joined the water that poured in over the side. The hardest baling could never get her clear, but so long as they never slackened for a moment the canoe would not sink. Hours and hours went by, and steadily the wind increased, driving the half-foundered boat on from wave to wave: at about four the sky darkened with a leaden darkness, and then the snow came hissing down on the sea – it fell so thick and fast that it settled on their shoulders as they worked, for ever baling with all their might, and often the canoe showed all white before the spray wiped it off again. The snow deadened the sea and the wind a little and this was fortunate for them, for it gave them fair warning of the thunderous surf right ahead in the darkness of the early night.

The cacique could swim like a seal: in his terror he set the canoe straight in for the shore through the breakers, trusting that he would survive, whatever happened. But Jack could not see it like that: disobeying orders for the first time, he plucked the cacique from his place, struck him into the bottom of the canoe, kicked him down and steered along the coast until they found smooth water behind a reef, so that they could run ashore safely on the snow-covered coast of Chiloe.

'Why, ma'am,' said Jack, 'if you insist, I must obey.' He took another mutton-chop piping hot from the grill, and with a courteous inclination of his head engulfed it. 'Campbell,' he cried, above the hum of voices, 'may I trouble you for the ale? Toby, do not keep the bread entirely to yourself, I beg. Bread,' he repeated, with an unctuous tear running down his crimson visage, 'bread, oh *how* I love it!'

They were seated at a table in a long, low-ceilinged room; Captain Cheap lay on a pile of sheepskins by the fire, dozing, with a half-emptied bowl of broth by his side; the room was filled with Chilotan Indians, men and women – clean, handsome creatures in embroidered ponchos, who gazed wonderingly at their guests, with expressions of compassion. The news of their arrival had spread by now, and a stream of newcomers came tapping at the door, each of the women bringing a pot, with mutton, pork, chicken, soup, fish, eggs – an uncountable treasure of food.

'Egg,' said Tobias, leering in his uncouth way. 'Egg. Ha, ha!'

Campbell said nothing, but struggled still with the remnants of a noble ham: the pleasure on his face was so acute as to be very near to excessive pain – for a nothing he would have wept. He ate and ate, staring straight before him at his bowl with bolting eyes.

Their first night in Chiloe had been terrible; they had come ashore in an entirely uninhabited, uninhabitable part – the usual rock, swamp and impenetrable forest – and at one time they thought that Captain Cheap had died in the cold. The next day, when at last they were able to get afloat, they paddled up the coast, ten weary miles and more, with the small hope they ever had fading fast with the evening and the certain prospect of another storm: and then, quite suddenly, on the far side of a rocky creek, there was a field.

It was an almost unbelievable sight, this most southerly field in the world, on the very edge of the barbarian wastes and under the same monstrous skies; but there it was, the unmistakable rectangle of civilisation, with the furrows showing where the snow had blown across them. Then there were houses, a little village with lights. The cacique, demanding his pay, the gun, crammed in the last charge of powder that they had and asked how to fire it. Campbell (a revengeful spirit) showed him how to rest the butt on his chin and bade him pull the trigger. The gun went off, the kick knocked out the cacique's four front teeth and hurled him into the bottom of the canoe, and at the noise men came running down to help them in – good-looking men, wearing top-hats, with their hair done up in neat buns behind, breeches, ponchos and woollen gaiters – and at last they were out of the canoe; they were done with the vile thing for ever, and they were led up into a real house and installed by a beautiful fire.

The cacique (who took his injuries very much for granted, and valued the gun rather more for its malignance) sank into an obsequi-ous, cringing object, and his prating was done with for good: the Chilotans allowed him into the house only because he was, at least nominally, a Christian – but even so, he was not admitted beyond the outward porch.

The Chilotans had been converted by the Jesuits, that often-maligned Society, who had liberated them from the burden of ghosts and demons which oppressed their southern neighbours, and had taught them the nature of charity, the duty of kindness. Some of the later padres had been perhaps too busy in taking the Chilotans' gold away from them, but had they taken fifty times as much still the Chilotans were incomparably the gainers by the interchange, even if it were only their happiness in this world that was to be counted. They knew how to live like human beings: their spirit-haunted cousins to the south did not.

It was almost midnight before they managed to carry Captain Cheap up from the waterside, but these Indians nevertheless hurried out and killed a sheep in order to feed their guests handsomely, and this was an act that their guests appreciated to the full, no men more so. They ate steadily until the moon set, and then they slept for hours and hours – they slept until noon the next day. Since then they had been eating with very little interruption, pausing only now and then to assure the Chilotans of their warmest gratitude, regard and esteem.

But even they had their limits, and now, in the warm and drowsy evening, by the light of the fire (the icy wind roaring outside), they rose one by one from the table, and, bowing to their hosts and the company, crept slowly to their deep, fleecy beds, where they lay torpidly blinking at the flames for a few minutes before sinking into the uttermost depths of sleep.

'What?' said Jack, hovering on the edge of insensibility.

'I have a duck,' said Tobias slowly, with his eyes already closed, 'a duck. Three parts of a duck in reserve. Under my pillow.'

Chapter Fourteen

THE BLINDING WHITE GLARE of the sun beat down upon the broad Plaza Real, the heart of Santiago, and the fountains in the brass basin that gleamed in the middle of the square made charming little rainbows, most refreshing to the eye. It was a noble square, splendid, busy, animated and magnificently surrounded, and this was fitting, for from the governor's palace on the north side don José Manso (soon to be viceroy of Peru) ruled the whole of Chile, from the tropical aridity of the Atacama desert right down to the sodden island of Chiloe in the south, while from the cathedral and the episcopal palace that filled the west side, the bishop governed the spiritual affairs of the longest diocese in the world. A great many people – Spaniards, half-castes, Indians of many nations, and here and there a negro slave – moved in and out of the council-chambers, the law-courts and the highly-decorated prison; a great many moved up and down the wide, stately cathedral steps; and a great many who had business with neither the bishop nor the governor walked under the shop-lined arcades that ran along the bottom of the square and provided a grandstand for the bullfights with which the Spaniards, then as now, so strangely celebrate the major feasts of the Christian calendar.

It was a scene of tremendous animation – people, horses everywhere, mules in scarlet harness, boys from the Jesuit school in red capes, a delegation of Araucanian chiefs shining with barbaric splendour, more horses, a great deal of noise, and above all the naked blaze and reverberation of the sun. And yet one had but to turn out of the Plaza Real, past the Dominican church, past the barred windows of the house of the Holy Office (commonly known as the Inquisition), to find oneself in broad, silent streets so lined with trees that one walked in a green shade. The streets cut one another always at right-angles, but apart from this regularity one might have been in the outskirts of a country town, for the houses (all low, because of the earthquakes) were built far apart, and most of them were surrounded by garden walls, over whose tops waved more green branches: almost no buildings were to be seen.

In the patio of one of these houses, near enough to the Plaza Real for a confused hum of its activity to carry through the orange-scented shade, stood Dr Gedd, an elderly Scotch physician. This gentleman, having remained loyal both to his forefathers' religion and to the house of Stuart, found himself a proscribed outlaw in 1715. He had the whole world (or at least the Catholic part of it) before him, and he had a certain amount of money in his pocket: he therefore selected the finest climate in the available world and came to Santiago, where he had spent the last twenty years healing the Spanish rulers of Chile and growing cactuses on his patio. He had flourished: so had the cactuses. There was scarcely room for the gardener in his own garden – huge opuntias threatened him with their innumerable spikes at every turn; just above his head a towering cereus broke into dangerous branches; under his feet, obliging him to walk with a doddering, tip-toe step, uncounted mamillarias stood in tiny pots. But in spite of his exotic surroundings and the Spanish wig on his head, Dr Gedd remained very much a Scotchman. He spoke Castilian with the unmistakable accent of Auchtermuchty, and he now stood poised in his spikey paradise listening with a smile to the tentative howls of a bagpipe from within.

To him now there entered, by a small private green garden door reserved for friends, don Juan de las Matanzas, a jolly Spaniard with three chins and a sky-blue coat, who insinuated his bulk through the barbed perils and let himself down, gasping, towards a seat. Instantly he leapt shrieking to his feet, and Dr Gedd ran for the nearest pair of tweezers – there were many pairs scattered about the patio for the relief of visitors. 'Those were my spinosissima cuttings,' he said reproachfully. 'But do not apologise – do not apologise.'

The bagpipe howled again. Don Juan started nervously, but the machine had been explained to him before, and, recollecting himself, he spread out a handkerchief upon a bare, safe stone step and sat upon it. 'And is that instrument often played in Scotland, don Patricio?' he asked. The doctor nodded. 'Then,' said don Juan, his eyes already vanishing with the force of amusement, 'I do not wonder that you left your country. Ha, ha, ha, ha,' he went on, rocking to and fro and beating his quivering thighs, 'I wonder you stayed so long.'

'Now, now,' cried Dr Gedd testily, 'that's mirth enough for today. Have you nothing better to do than insult my exile, for shame? What have you to say?'

'What a flow of spirits!' said don Juan, wiping his eyes, 'what ready wit! – I am an agreeable rattle, am I not? But I have come to tell you that your heretical friends are being looked after. I have a packet from Valparaiso with all sorts of news, and Ramon informs me that the captain-general's letter to the governor, telling him to send them there, was received last month.'

'Where are they now?'

Don Juan spread his hands. 'Who can tell?' he asked. 'His Excellency of Valparaiso may have read the letter by now, or he may not. He may read it next month, and act upon it as soon as Saint Isidro's day: but, on the other hand, he may not. And, my dear friend, if he never thinks of it again, it might be just as well. I have a letter from don Miguel Herrera, of Chiloe, in the same packet, and he tells me that one of the young fellows is a sorcerer and that another of them is a libertine. Listen. "The ugly small heretic cured Dona Maria of her inveterate trembling palsy by removing three asps and a toad from her body. The large yellow-haired one trifled with the affections of the rector's niece to such an extent that she had to be locked up when they embarked for Valparaiso. He also did so horribly blaspheme that there was an earthquake, which broke, in my house alone, three blue plates, by casting them from a shelf." Don Patricio, you have quite enough to do with your countrymen,' said don Juan earnestly, nodding towards the curious sounds of Captain Cheap and Mr Hamilton preparing for Hogmanay, 'without mingling yourself with libertines and sorcerers, heretical at that.'

Dr Gedd paused, as well he might: and here perhaps it is necessary to observe that the captain and the remainder of the crew of the *Wager*, having reached Chiloe, gave up the idea of warlike operations against the Spaniards, and surrendered very willingly. They were received as prisoners of war by the governor of the island, who at

Captain Cheap's pressing request sent a boat away southward which presently returned with Mr Hamilton. They were soon let out of prison, and the kind people of Chiloe, overlooking the fact that these were national enemies who, but for misfortune, would have seized their shipping and perhaps burnt their towns, invited them for long visits in one house after another while the administration, in its meditative Spanish way, decided what should be done with them. It was at this time that Tobias, strong in Mr Eliot's doctrine, performed the cure with which he was reproached, in the town of Chaco, where Jack had also earned his uncomfortable reputation as a blasphemer. They were both staying with a family in which there were a great many daughters – very cheerful girls – and one day an Indian friend, passing by, called in to show them his most recent, proudest acquisition – the printed and coloured likenesses of various saints. The girls, who were all perfectly well brought up in the manner of the country, kissed the saints as they passed them round.

'I suppose you are too great a heretic to kiss them?' said the eldest girl.

'Yes,' said Jack, and added a rather foolish laugh – ha, ha.

Instantly there came a fearful clap and crack as of thunder, but worse: the ground twitched beneath them: flying dust rose everywhere. It was an earthquake. Everybody ran out of doors, cursing Jack and trampling upon one another unmercifully. The tremor did not last long and it did no great damage, but it cast a damp upon their visit, and it tended to make Jack extremely nervous. He never mentioned a saint again without particular civility and an anxious glance aloft.

But none of this made him half so nervous as the dreadful things that happened to him in Castro, the other town. Here they stayed with the parson, a very amiable old gentleman who was looked after by his equally amiable sister, a widow much valued by all hands for her mutton pies; but she had a daughter, a strong young lady with a moustache and a singularly aggressive way of champing on her pipe. Most of the women of Chiloe smoked a pipe, but few with the zeal of Señorita Marta; it was said that whenever she was in a rage, smoke would pour from her ears. She decided that she would marry Jack, who was really quite a good-looking fellow, now that he was fed again – pink, cheerful face and a bright blue eye – and she sent her uncle to tell him that he must be converted at once, so that the match could be announced without delay. It is impossible to describe Jack's sufferings for the remainder of his stay in Castro: his face grew wan, his eyes grew dull, and he could scarcely eat more than five meals a day; and indeed he never (or hardly ever) smiled again until they were aboard the ship that was to carry them to Valparaiso, and even then he waited until they were well out of sight of land.

At Valparaiso Captain Cheap and Mr Hamilton, who had kept their commissions and who were therefore known as officers, were sent up to Santiago, received by don José, and paroled, with liberty to live where they chose – in the event, with Dr Gedd, who hurried to offer them his hospitality as soon as he heard of their presence in the town. It is a very remarkable fact that they should have kept their commissions throughout all their complicated miseries: but it was usual then, for according to the rules of war as it was fought at that time, any officer taken without his king's commission could be hanged as a pirate. As for Jack, Tobias and Campbell, they had nothing to show – the midshipmen because they had never had any papers, and Tobias because he had lost his – and they were therefore treated as ordinary seamen. Captain Cheap (who, as he recovered, changed out of recognition) tried to explain the peculiar status of midshipmen in the Royal Navy as soon as he reached Santiago, and he pressed hard to have them released; but nobody paid much attention to him – the officials had the whole of Chile to look after, and although some of them were quite amiable, it seemed to them that it would be time to look into the question in a year or two, or perhaps three; and in the meantime the young fellows might very well stay in Valparaiso – the more so as they did not sound at all desirable.

'In my opinion,' said don Juan de las Matanzas, picking a spine from his leg with sedulous care, 'it would have been better if you had never worried don José about it at all. They would be far better in Valparaiso. Sorcerers and libertines, don Patricio, my dear, are far better in Valparaiso.'

'I wonder where they are now?' repeated Dr Gedd.

'A hundred to one they are still in Valparaiso,' said don Juan, 'and I think that an unofficial word to my cousin Zurbaran will keep them there.' He spoke not from any ill-will towards the prisoners, but from the warmth of his friendship for Dr Gedd, who had several times impoverished himself by his generosity and who, at this time, was far from rich – only his more honourable patients paid him, for he had never pressed a debtor in his life, and fully half his visits were among the poor.

But don Juan was mistaken. The governor of Valparaiso was an avaricious old man; he was quite blind and very near his tomb, but he was as grasping as ever. It had appeared to him that these unwelcome prisoners of war might possibly fall to his charge, that he might not be reimbursed for the few mouldy potatoes that he allowed them, that this might last for years; and he had seized the first opportunity of being shot of them. Within an hour of receiving the order to send the captives to Santiago he had begun working upon a plan for doing so without expense, and now the same brilliant sun that shone upon the Plaza Real beheld them toiling up the Cuchillo pass, singing vehemently, as they urged on the beautiful shining mules, that 'they were tarpaulin jackets, huzzay, huzzay', and that, in consequence, they would still love the billows, by night and by day, the dear little billows, by night and by day.

They were nominally subject to One-eyed Pedro, the muleteer, but Pedro's train consisted of one hundred and four mules, all laden with valuable goods from Valparaiso to Santiago, and nearly a quarter of them new beasts, unaccustomed to his direction; he had no time to be playing the turnkey. The journey had not begun at all well: Pedro had been called to the governor, had been told that he must take the prisoners to Santiago, and that he should have nothing for his pains, because prisoners of war came under the same heading as official parcels, which he was obliged by law to deliver free. He was to have nothing for their sustenance on the road, either. 'They can fast perfectly well for five days,' said the governor. 'They are accustomed to hardship. A mere five days is nothing to them.'

Pedro had set out, therefore, with a certain tendency to hate his charges: but he was a good-natured man under his dark, murderous exterior, and the official parcels showed such zeal in pursuing the more brutish and uneducated mules and bringing them to order that before the first day was over he was reconciled to their presence. Their way led over high passes and broad plains, and in the plains the mules – the new and wanton mules – strayed regularly from the dutiful band which followed their godmother, a little old yellow mare with a bell, and in the narrow roads among the rocks the dutiful mules retorted upon the others by biting and kicking them. There was plenty of scope for helpfulness; they exerted themselves, and Pedro's esteem for them grew day by day. In the evenings, when they lay, full-fed by Pedro's kindness, wrapped in their ponchos round the fire, he would tell them of the nature and antecedents of each of his mules, about mules in general and his life as a muleteer.

Now they reached the top of the pass; the narrow path cut into the worn rocks gave way to an open space, and there below them stretched the broad, dun plain, with a silver river winding through it, and far over, against the great snow-topped wall of the Andes, the city of Santiago.

'Santiago,' said One-eyed Pedro, shaking his head at it with disapproval.

'Shall we get there today?' asked Jack.

'No,' said Pedro, 'we shall not. Not until tomorrow morning. And if I had my way, we should never get there.' He drew Jack aside, and very earnestly assured him that the city was a place of iniquity and false dealing, extravagance, vice and folly; the pleasures of the city were nothing to the pleasures of driving a well-conducted body of mules – there was no life as happy and innocent as the life of a muleteer, healthy, with excellent company and variety of place; and Jack promised quite well in the trade. It was Pedro's duty, he said, to deliver Jack and his friends to the governor: but as barefoot sailors of no importance they would certainly be set at liberty, and then Jack must not think of remaining in Santiago, but should repair at once to the muleteers' inn, where Pedro would engage him, at seven pieces of eight a month and his victuals, but Jack to find himself in ardent spirits. 'Any time,' said Pedro, moving forward to guide the yellow godmother on the way down to Santiago, 'any time at all.'

And 'Any time,' he said, patting Jack as if he were a nervous mule, when he left his charges with the sentry outside the governor's palace in the morning. 'Remember what I say,' he called, turning as he went away across the courtyard and laying his finger along his nose to indicate private understanding. 'You and the ugly one – any time.'

'His Excellency wishes to see you,' said a secretary in a black coat. 'Wait here.'

'Strike me down,' said Jack, as they stood uneasily on the black-and-white squares of the marble hall, looking at a most imposing flight of stairs. 'I wish that we had been able to wash this last week, and that we had a comb among us.'

'A poncho covers a great deal,' said Campbell, as if he were trying to convince himself. There was much truth in what he said, however. A poncho is a large piece of cloth with a hole in the middle for one's head – it is not unlike a tent, the wearer being the pole – and it hangs down in every direction, concealing, in Jack's case, a very, very old pair of sailcloth trousers, mostly hole, and a little wrinkled shirt that had once belonged to a Jesuit, a gentleman whose charity was larger than his person; the poncho, being long, also covered Jack's bare and horny feet, rather more like hooves than Cousin Brocas, who prided himself on the elegance of the family leg, would have wished.

'Toby,' said Jack, 'you would oblige me infinitely by taking off that villainous wool thing.' The Portuguese nightcap, though hardy, was now in the last stages of decay; but Tobias was gliding about the chequered floor at this moment, to see how many moves a knight would need to go from A to B.

'Good morning, gentlemen,' said don José, appearing suddenly through a small door behind them. 'I am happy to welcome you to Santiago – most happy – could wish that the circumstances were otherwise – are you all well, all quite well? – you must have suffered cruelly – shocking privations – misery – wet, cold, frightened.'

Jack had not stayed this long among the Spaniards without having learnt to put a thing handsomely. 'Sir,' cried he, 'our sufferings are a trifling price for the honour of seeing Your Excellency and the pleasure of seeing Your Excellency's dominions.'

'Just so,' said Toby.

'Very good – excellent,' said don José, who spoke in this way partly because his mind skipped along at a great rate and partly because he thought such a language more suitable for foreigners than a continued flow. 'All over now, however – you have come into port, and may roll up the sails until the end of the war – the end of the present misunderstanding. And my advice to you, young

240

gentlemen, is to enjoy yourselves as much as possible until you can be exchanged – youth time for enjoyment, festivity – *nunc pede libero pulsanda tellus* – and Santiago is an excellent place for it.' With this he bowed, dismissed them and sent an officer to guide them to Dr Gedd's house.

Dr Gedd appeared to be as happy to see them as if they had been an immense acquisition to his household; Captain Cheap and Mr Hamilton welcomed them heartily; and Paquita, the housekeeper, cook and general organiser – a negress from Panama, as nearly spherical as anything can be in this imperfect world – laid on an unfailing supply of fish, flesh and fowl. Her mission in life was to feed others: hitherto her vocation had been sadly thwarted, for Dr Gedd was content with bread and a bowl of broth – he was a remarkably abstemious man, to Paquita's fat despair. Captain Cheap and Mr Hamilton had pleased her, as being men of reasonably keen appetite, but Jack, Tobias and Campbell surpassed her fondest hopes; here was walking greed, gluttony in person three times represented, which could be relied upon to eat everything in view, and to rise by night to go questing about for cold meat, a dozen hard-boiled eggs, a basket of pears. In some houses they might have been an embarrassment and a burden; but not in this. Dr Gedd's patients did not always pay him, but there was none so devoid of grace that he did not bring a present – roses, lilies, a handsome fish, some particularly beautiful peaches, a ham, potted ferns; and sometimes the courtyard behind would be half-filled with kids, lambs, little swine and even calves – all presents, and all, until now, wholly and entirely unwanted.

But a keener delight by far awaited them in Dr Gedd's house – news, much more detailed news of the squadron. Already, in Chiloe, they had heard that the English were on the coast; now they learnt that the *Centurion*, the *Gloucester*, the little *Tryall* and even the *Anna* pink had all come round, that they had refitted at Juan Fernandez, and that they were now playing Old Harry with the Spanish shipping. All this news came from people who had been captured by the squadron in various prizes – passengers travelling up and down the coast – and who had been set free whenever opportunity offered. They were all most generous in their praise of the commodore; there was not one who did not acknowledge that he had been well treated, and the reputation of the Royal Navy (very fortunately for the prisoners) was as high as ever Mr Anson could have wished. One reason for this was the force of contrast: the only English to have reached the Pacific coast before were pirates and buccaneers (Narborough excepted), and their behaviour had often been so wickedly, monstrously cruel that the name of the nation alone filled people with horror and dread. To find that the English could conduct themselves like human beings was therefore a wonderful relief to the Spaniards when they were captured, and in their eyes a strange, angelic light appeared to float about the head of the commodore, and even about the bulky persons of his crew.

And now more news had come: the *Severn* and the *Pearl* were not lost, but only disabled; they had put back, and had reached the coast of Brazil in safety, if not exactly in comfort. But, on the other hand, of all the powerful Spanish squadron not one single ship had yet been able to round the Horn for the defence of the Pacific: they had lost the *Guipuscoa*, their 74, the *Hermiona*, 54, the *Sant'Esteban*, 40, and a twenty-gun sloop in the attempt; and the *Asia*, the flagship, lay, a dismasted hulk, in the River Plate. Only the *Esperanza*, of fifty guns, could be patched up well enough for a further essay; she was now at sea, presumably somewhere south of latitude 60, and the Spanish admiral, with many of his officers, had come overland to await her arrival in the Southern Sea. It was they who had brought the news, a few days before Pedro reached Santiago with his charges.

'They have walked here,' said Captain Cheap, with marked satisfaction, as he told them about it all. 'Not that I blame Pizarro, you understand: but it does not allow the Spaniards to crow over us.'

So they had very good, reassuring, comforting news of their friends – news that also tended to restore them in their battered self-esteem – as well as unlimited good food and soft lying, in the world's most agreeable climate: it seemed that they were doomed to obey the orders of the enemy, to enjoy themselves as much as possible. Then, in an unusually brisk turn of fortune's wheel, all was changed; where there had been gaiety there was consternation; bitter repining took the place of carefree song; and Dr Gedd's house became a place of angry mourning.

'What is the matter?' asked Tobias, as Jack came running into the stable-yard, his poncho flapping with his haste and pale despair on his countenance.

'Don José has asked us to dinner,' cried Jack furiously.

'Very civil in him. Shall be most happy,' said Tobias, helping a pair of turtle-doves to arrange their eggs.

'To dinner to meet the Spanish admiral and his officers,' said Jack. 'Oh, strike me down,' he cried, with a low howl, 'to think of appearing at such a do, in front of the Spanish navy, in this rig. Toby, you are a mighty philosophical cove, but I do not think I can bear the humiliation. Nor can the others. They are all dreadfully moved.'

Even in this century, when clothes mean comparatively little, it is very disagreeable to find oneself in an ordinary jacket when everybody else is in tails: at that time men's clothes were gorgeous, costly and important; and the chasm between a poncho and the proper dress for an official dinner was immeasurably vast.

Ceremonial clothes were nowhere cheap, and in Chile clothes of European cloth and cut were exceedingly expensive. Dr Gedd was far from rich, and he was known to have lent all his loose money to an apothecary on the edge of insolvency. They were already under such great obligations to him that they could not increase them; and in any case he was away for the next few days, which made the thing materially impossible.

They walked gloomily out into Santiago, spreading melancholy abroad in the quiet, tree-lined streets, and Jack by way of overcoming any philosophy that might linger in Tobias' mind, explained to him, at considerable length, that it would on the one hand be totally impossible, unheard-of and even cowardly to refuse the invitation; and, on the other, quite unspeakable to accept it. For his part, Tobias would have been content to go in a sack, or even (the weather being what it was) nothing at all; for he had both a humbler and a prouder mind than Jack – humbler in that he did not suppose that anyone would notice him at any time, and prouder in that he did not suppose that he could be improved in any way by gold lace and taffety. But he was very much concerned at Jack's distress, and he racked his brain to find some cure for it. 'Suppose,' he said, 'I were to teach doña Francisca's boy Greek, as she desired me to do, that would be six reals a week; and suppose she had the goodness to pay in advance . . .'

'My poor Toby,' said Jack, 'at that rate it would take two years' lessons for a coat for one of us. The boy would be a doddering greybeard before his Greek could set us all up in coats, waistcoats, breeches, shirts, shoes, wigs . . . Come this way.'

They were in the Calle de Santander, and two turns brought them into the Plaza Real. The crowd was beginning to thin, for noon was approaching, but under the shade of the arcade that bordered the south side of the square, opposite the palace, there were hundreds of people still. 'There,' said Jack, stopping outside a tailor's shop, 'do you see that? Quite ordinary broadcloth, Toby – just good enough for the country. *Eleven pieces of eight a yard.* Oh strike me down,' he cried, and stepping back in the violence of his indignation, he fell into the arms of a very splendid Spanish officer.

'Sir,' he said, recovering his balance, 'I beg your pardon.'

'Sir,' said the Spanish officer, withdrawing to give himself room for the complex pacing and sweeping necessary to a high Spanish bow, 'I beg you will have the goodness to accept my excuses. Guiro.'

Jack responded with what elegance his poncho would allow (not very much), and having exhausted his stock of Castilian civilities, merely smiled.

'Guiro,' repeated the other. 'Manuel de Guiro.'

'Do you think he is swearing at me, Toby?' whispered Jack.

'I think it is his name,' said Tobias. 'I believe it is a form of introduction: try saying your own.'

'Byron,' said Jack, without much conviction, and at once the Spaniard's face, which had grown a little sombre, brightened: he presented himself to Tobias in the same manner, and invited them to drink chocolate with him. They never let slip any opportunity of nourishment, and accepted in unison.

'I am the seventh lieutenant of the *Asia*, Admiral Pizarro's flagship,' he said, as they sat down. 'I believe that we are to have the honour of meeting you at don José's on Saturday.'

'In effect,' said Jack, 'don José has had the extreme – what shall I say?'

'Benevolence,' said Tobias.

' – the extreme benevolence to invite us.'

Don Manuel noticed the lack of enthusiasm: he gazed at Jack and Tobias and said 'Ahem.' After a short pause he said that he was particularly happy to have encountered them, and that he had intended to call at Dr Gedd's house in any case, because he felt a strong inclination to offer them his services. His mother and his two sisters had been taken by the *Centurion* in their voyage from Callao to Valparaiso (his family lived in Chile); and they had been restored to their friends quite charmed by their adventure. 'They expected to be murdered, of course,' said don Manuel, 'but it seems that the officers were put out of their cabins to make room for them, and the midshipmen taught Maruja, the small one, how to knit, and sent her ashore with a tame penguin. She continually speaks of them – the aspirant don Augusto Keppel, the aspirant don Guillermo Ransome, the aspirant don Pedro Palafox.'

'Ha, ha,' cried Jack, quite shining with delight, 'so the mouldy old swab has survived. Sir,' he said, returning to Spanish, 'you could not have given us greater pleasure.'

'You are a most amiable and deserving creature,' Tobias assured him, shaking him warmly by the hand. They now fell into an easy and unrestrained conversation, and don Manuel told them of three months he had spent in England – he had been in one of the first Spanish men-of-war to be taken, and he had had to wait until the Spanish captured some English officers before he could be exchanged. He said that until he had been able to make some arrangements with a neutral merchant, he had been painfully short of money: it was, he thought, a very usual experience; and it was certainly a very disagreeable one.

Yes, said Jack, it *was* unpleasant, infernally unpleasant. 'And,' said he in a low voice, shifting his chair nearer to don Manuel's and privately nodding towards Tobias, who had fallen into a brown study, 'it is all the worse, because that fellow there, do you see, is so vain. The thought of being obliged to present himself at the palace dressed as he is makes him quite wretched.'

'I entirely sympathise with your friend,' said don Manuel, looking compassionately upon the unconscious Tobias, 'I can imagine nothing worse – would prefer a dozen battles. And yet I should never have supposed that he paid any attention to dress. He has none of the air, if I may say so, of a man of the world.'

'Yet it would amaze you to know how his mind is taken up with lace, brocade and embroidered waistcoats.'

'Very well,' said don Manuel, 'we must not let the poor gentleman suffer any longer.' And with this he offered Jack two thousand pieces of eight.

'Come sir,' said Jack, half rising, 'it is scarcely handsome to make game of us – if I knew Spanish well enough,' he added in English, 'I would tell you it was a mighty scrubbish thing to do, after such candour; and if I could afford a sword, I should call you out.'

'It is a sum that I happen to have by me,' said don Manuel, 'in a box. And I have no use for it, I assure you: you would put me very much in your debt if you would accept it,' he said, placing his hand upon his heart in a very graceful manner. 'It may help to keep you in little pleasures until you are exchanged,' he added, with a sincere benignity that carried entire conviction.

Jack was not accustomed to swallowing his words, but he did so now, and he did it handsomely, acknowledging his obligation to the utmost extent of his Spanish. Then, his eyes gleaming with a variety of strong emotions – among them relief from impending humiliation, but even more pleasure at don Manuel's magnanimity – he called Tobias out of his stupor, saying, 'don Manuel has offered us two thousand pieces of eight: it is the noblest thing I ever heard of.'

'Ay?' said Tobias. 'You are very good, sir,' – inclining his head towards don Manuel – 'but do you see that man with serpents, near the brass fountain?'

'Come, Toby,' cried Jack, 'do not be clownish, if you please. Two thousand pieces of eight. Think. Reflect.'

'What are these pieces of eight you are always talking about?' asked Tobias, withdrawing his eyes reluctantly from the throng about the snake-charmer. 'Eight what?'

'Eight reals, booby.'

'Oh.'

'Do you know what Dr Gedd's best horse cost?' cried Jack, much provoked by this lumpish stolidity. 'It cost four pieces of eight. Do you know what Paquita pays for a sheep? Four reals. Don Manuel offers us five hundred horses, four thousand sheep – an immense herd. An't you amazed, Toby?'.

'Why does he think we want four thousand sheep?' asked Tobias, peering with some curiosity at the Spanish officer.

'Oh, bah. You must excuse my companion, don Manuel. His parts could never have recommended him at any time; but now, with his sufferings, he has grown quite beastish. For my part . . .'

'Or such a great many horses? One or perhaps two apiece would be enough,' murmured Tobias. 'Five hundred would be ostentatious – excessive.'

'For my part,' continued Jack, taking no notice, 'I shall be happier than I can express . . .' and he went on to suggest various arrangements, such as a draft upon London, or a letter of credit to an agent in Lisbon.

But although a sudden, brisk comprehension was not always characteristic of Tobias when his mind was engaged elsewhere, yet nevertheless understanding did seep in, given time, and now he interrupted Jack by rising up, and with the greatest solemnity he addressed don Manuel in the following terms, 'Sir, you will allow me to say, that you not only reconcile me with your nation, but you oblige me to think more highly of mankind in general: sir, you may turn the pages of your Plutarch from the beginning to the end, without finding a more shining example of humanity to a captured enemy. Sir, we are told by Herodotus – we read in the learned Josephus . . .'

Don Manuel, being of Mediterranean origin, was accustomed to eloquence, but the spate of Tobias' gratitude (once it started to flow) quite stunned him, particularly as most of it was in Greek and nearly all the rest in Latin (all one to don Manuel).

'Oh,' said he, faintly, escaping in a pause between Hermippus and Agathemeros, 'it is just that it might serve to make your stay more agreeable until you are exchanged. Gentlemen,' he said, taking his leave, 'your servant.'

'Don Manuel,' they cried, sweeping their ponchos in the dust, 'yours – most humble and obliged.'

Chapter Fifteen

UNTIL they should be exchanged. It was an expression that was always coming up at first; as often as the words *when we are exchanged.* 'I shall not classify my molluscs until we are exchanged,' said Tobias. And 'When we are exchanged,' said Jack, 'I shall send don Manuel an English repeating watch. English repeating watches are the only tolerable repeating watches, it seems.' 'The lower reptiles may stay in your bedroom until we are exchanged,' said Tobias. 'They may be a little crowded, but it is not for long.' And Jack said, 'There is no point in being foolishly economical – it is not as though we had to make the money last. We shall soon be exchanged, and then we shall have a fresh supply – how delightful. So I believe I shall buy Juanita's brother's chestnut mare after all, and tell Sanchez to make me a long black velvet cloak with a crimson lining, for the carnival. This will be a great saving, in point of fact, as it will also serve for doña Isabel's party.'

Yet time went on; the months followed after one another; the oranges in the streets and gardens changed from green bronze to gold and were followed by heavy-scented flowers again: the orange-flowers dropped, the oranges formed and still the prisoners were there, a part of the permanent scenery of Santiago. Nobody noticed them in the streets any more, whereas at one time the belief that Englishmen had tails provided them with a train of idle boys, and even of people old enough to know better; and for their part they no longer noticed the intense fieriness of Chilean cookery that had once rendered them speechless and scarlet through long dinner-parties.

They began to mention exchange less often – indeed, they hardly thought of it for weeks on end. Tobias helped Dr Gedd in his morning rounds, botanised and collected in the afternoon, and in the evening applied himself to Spanish: Jack spent his time in a wholly useless and dissipated manner, rising late and going out almost every night to the parties, assemblies and balls that enlivened Santiago throughout the whole year, except in Lent, or making prolonged visits to friends who invited him to taste the delights of the Chilean countryside. He paid no attention to his Spanish, which, although it became very fluent, remained totally inaccurate; but, on the other hand, he learnt to handle the lasso, to smoke long green cigars and to dance the fandango until the morning sun put out the candle-light.

France entered the war. Captain Cheap and Mr Hamilton became uncommonly excited when this news reached Chile, told one another that they had always foreseen it, called upon all hands to support the statement and to listen to their further predictions. Captain Cheap interrupted the long and circumstantial account that he was writing for the Lords of the Admiralty (an account intended to hang any surviving mutineers, for although he had changed in many ways he remained bitterly vindictive towards the authors of his miseries) in order to send strong remonstrances to don José about the length of their captivity and their right to be exchanged, and for several weeks they lived in excited anticipation.

But gradually this faded away, and in time they heard the news of the distant battles with the calmness of the inhabitants of another sphere. Campbell, whose mind had turned very much to religion, became a Catholic, and moved away to Lima, in Peru; and on almost the same day as his departure they heard that the *Centurion*, half the world away by now, had taken the great Acapulco galleon, bound for Manilla with an enormous treasure aboard – a million pieces of eight, said some, and others, better informed, said nearer two. Tobias got into sad trouble with the Inquisition for carrying Mr Eliot's theories rather too far, in the shape of fourteen white mice and a young female owl, all from the one patient: he came so close to the stake that he smelt of singeing for weeks after, and Dr Gedd was obliged to dispense with his assistance. 'Go and stay with the Mendozas for a while,' he said. 'You can find where the condors nest not far from there, and you can take the opportunity to bring your friend into a more serious state of mind – he is but a poor flibberty-gibberty loon at present, I'm thinking. Runs aboot at random with no thought of his profession nor the cultivation of his intellect.'

No sober person could approve Jack's course of life, which was both frivolous and dissipated: yet had it not been for Jack they might never have been exchanged at all. Don José had a daughter, a plain girl, unreasonably proud, who had recently (to the great relief of the nuns) left the convent in which she had been educated: her name was Luisa, and there was no one in Santiago good enough for her. That is to say, none of the younger officials or officers who attended the governor's levees and who depended on her father would do at all; but she made an exception in favour of Jack, who naturally differed from them in every way, and she distinguished him by a great deal of notice. He had no intention of engaging the young woman's affections, but he was naturally polite and amiable; he also considered that a high degree of gallantry was called for, in foreign parts; and presently Luisa supposed herself to be afire with a high romantic passion.

Don José got wind of this somewhat later than he could have wished: he read an intercepted note, sighed at his daughter's spelling and the banality of her sentiments, and frowned at the nature of the message. His powers were very considerable indeed: he had but to give the word for Jack to be hanged by the neck, to be filled with leaden bullets, or to be separated from his head by means of an axe. He rather liked Jack, however, and he thought Luisa far too tiresome and silly a girl for such extremities: yet, on the other hand, he valued his domestic peace; and within half an hour of reading Luisa's note he had taken his measures. A messenger rode, with a cloud of dust behind him, northwards to Peru, galloping through the heat of the day, galloping by moonlight – fresh horses – poste-haste over the burning desert – post-haste in the name of the King – fresh horses – letters for the viceroy himself – letters for the viceroy at Lima. 'Dear me,' said the viceroy, leaning back in the viceregal throne and putting the letter (which was very private) into his breeches pocket, 'dear me, who would have thought it?'

Spaniards, if very much goaded, can act almost as quickly as reasonable beings, and that very afternoon the *Lys*, a French frigate lying in Callao, the port of Lima, received new orders just before she sailed, requiring her to put in at Valparaiso, to take aboard some prisoners of war, who were to be exchanged. Grumbling, the *Lys* cast off her moorings, worked out her new course, and in time appeared off the Chilean coast. As soon as she was signalled, don José sent Luisa to stay with her aunt Lopes for the week-end, invited his captives to dinner, told them that although it wounded him to the heart to lose them, they must be gone by dawn, as a French ship happened to be passing by Valparaiso, and it would go against his conscience not to give them the earliest possible opportunity of reaching their native land, their homes and their dear ones.

'How strange it is to be afloat again, Mr Hamilton,' said Tobias.

'Yes,' said Mr Hamilton. 'I had thought . . .' he began, but paused. They were on the quarter-deck of the *Lys*, watching Valparaiso vanish as the frigate stood out westwards for Juan Fernandez on a fine southerly wind that flung the brilliant spray over the foc's'le. Around them the French crew argued passionately about the fore-topgallant sail: the second captain thought it should be reefed; the bo'sun, the helmsman and some of the sailors who happened to be standing by assured him that it would not look pretty reefed; a lieutenant said that in his opinion it ought to be taken in altogether, and one of the cooks warmly supported him; the first captain had no views on the matter at all, being a landsman, but he said somebody really ought to wash the deck – it was positively black.

'I had thought,' said Mr Hamilton, moving round the gesticulating form of the bo'sun, 'that I should enjoy it more, however.' They exchanged a haggard look of mutual comprehension, and as the *Lys* rose and sank again on the sickening roll they hurried speechless to the lee-rail.

The *Lys* was a stout, seaworthy vessel; but she also had some of the qualities of a slug and a sea-going pig. She never went faster than six knots at any time – her masts would blow out before she would do better than this very moderate pace – and whenever she found any sort of a sea, she lay down in it and wallowed. This was not entirely her fault, for she was much overloaded with hundreds of chests of bullion; but she could never have been termed a graceful sailer. She had plenty of opportunity for showing off her little ways, for there was a great deal of sea between Valparaiso and the Horn, and she traversed most of it twice, wallowing steadily all the time:

she had to do it twice because she sprang a leak very low down in the forepeak some days out from Concepción, where they had loaded cattle for the voyage, and she was obliged to put back all the way to Valparaiso to repair it, arriving in the middle of February, with all hands, including the passengers, pumping day and night.

By March, when they set out again, the best time for passing the Horn had already gone by, and although rounding that terrible cape from west to east was a very different thing from beating into the perpetual western gales, yet it could not really be described as a picnic. The Horn treated them to twelve distinct howling storms, of a kind that they knew only too well, and they had every reason to congratulate themselves upon being aboard a very solid, well-found vessel: they should have been very thankful, but man is an ungrateful beast, and they were shrilly indignant about the cold and the snow – the snow indeed was unreasonable, pouring in from the south-west in such vast quantities day and night and night and day that it filled the bunt of the sails and loaded the *Lys* so that she grew even more ponderous, in spite of continual shovelling. Their indignation was rendered none the less shrill by the fact that all their clothes were designed for the climate of Santiago: a very light velvet cloak with a crimson lining is a charming garment for sauntering about in an orange-scented garden in the moonlight, while you gently thrum a guitar, but it is a wretched thing to wrap about you in 60° S when the air is full of flying crystals of ice – particularly when the said cloak is so threadbare as to be almost transparent in places. Don Manuel's noble loan had run out long ago, for the very good reason that Jack had spent it much too fast; and for these months past they had been limited to their official prisoner's allowance of four reals a day.

The snow not only made them precious cold, but it also deprived the *Lys* of a vitally important supply of fresh water. The day after they had made their final departure from Chile it was noticed that although they were admirably well provided with maritime stores and with solid food, they had forgotten to take in their water. This may have been due to the national prejudice against the use of anything but wine, but it was more probably caused by the strange ideas of discipline current aboard:. the average Frenchman is very strongly persuaded that he knows best, and the *Lys*, with a crew of sixty, had fifty-nine commanders – the sixtieth man being dumb from birth. The singular outcry that accompanied the *Lys* on every stage of her journey amazed and dumbfounded the Royal Navy: but they were obliged to admit that the frigate had come round the Horn, had somehow reached her destination and was now in the act of repeating the process backwards – a remarkable example of the care of Providence. Yet the French way of leaving everything to the higher powers did not always answer. 'Blue belly!' cried the second captain, in his native idiom. 'Sacred blue! Name of a pipe! You have forgotten the water, my faith!'

'It was not me,' said the lieutenant sulkily. 'Besides, there is some that was overlooked from the voyage out. And anyhow, you know how it rains off the Horn: we shall spread a sail and catch as much as we need.'

So on the second day of their voyage they were put to short allowance – a quart a head – and they waited confidently for the rain. But snow, though beautiful and very highly picturesque indeed, is not rain. Philosophically it is all one, perhaps, but you cannot fill a triple tier of water-casks with a blizzard – it is not feasible. They therefore rounded the Horn on a quart a day and began to work up northwards on the same allowance. They kept far, far out to sea, for both captains and the entire crew had a mortal (and very understandable) dread of falling in with the land, and they did not have so much as a shower all through April, nor a drop of rain in May. The winds were kind, the *Lys* waddled northward at her usual mad speed day after day, a steady creep that might carry her a hundred sea-miles in the twenty-four hours, and the weather grew continually warmer. The daily quart seemed to shrink as they came up to Capricorn, and between the tropic and the line thirst checked the garrulity of the crew to a shocking extent. They reached the equator at the end of May, and after a very hoarse, though protracted discussion it was decided that it would be impossible to reach Europe without a fresh supply, and that they must therefore bear away for Martinique.

This decision was reached with the help of everyone aboard, including the prisoners and the passengers, who, in the prevailing atmosphere of free and democratic discussion (liberty and moral equality and a weakness for making speeches flourished in France

253

long before the Revolution), could not refrain from putting forward their views and sentiments. One of the passengers was don Jorge Juan, who, with some French academicians, had been carrying out philosophical experiments in Peru, measuring degrees of the meridian: he and Tobias pressed very strongly for a detour to Martinique; and there can be no doubt that their advice was influenced by their vehement desire to view the flora and fauna of the West Indies. Captain Cheap was of the same opinion. His advice was even more disingenuous, for he knew very well that there would be British cruisers abroad throughout the Caribbean. He knew that there was no area, outside the chops of the Channel, that was so rich in prizes, nowhere where the Navy cruised with livelier attention – nowhere more likely for the *Lys* to be taken. He had never come to a tolerable command of Spanish, let alone of French, so he bade Tobias translate for him; and he dwelt very forcibly and lugubriously upon the horrors of a death from thirst in the breathless heal of the doldrums.

Right or wrong the decision was taken: the quartermaster (who happened to be of the contrary opinion) was persuaded to alter course, and they steered west-north-west. At the very end of June they made Tobago in the morning, their first sight of land for three months and more – a hundred days of sea, rough, calm, foggy, clear, black with dead-white foam, pure sapphire blue, grey, glaucous and an infinity of colours between, but always fluid and always stretching to the horizon. After three months of sea, particularly when you do not see another ship in all that time, you begin to feel that water is the natural covering of the globe; you begin to doubt the reality of the solid world; and for this reason (as well as a certain reluctance to die of thirst) their landfall was intensely interesting. Tobago jutted black out of the sea, cutting the sky with a hard, ragged line, and the people of the *Lys* lined the side, staring at the island with as much satisfaction as the inhabitants of the ark when they first saw Ararat above the flood.

From Tobago they shaped their course for Martinique, two days' sail northwards: but somehow they could not find the island – it did not appear where they looked for it. This will surprise no landsman who, reflecting upon the size of the island and the immense amount of sea in which it is hidden, is amazed that any ship should ever reach it at all, rather than that one should miss: but it is always apt to vex a mariner, and the *Lys* bore away south-west by south in a thoroughly bad temper. It was thought that the currents had carried them eastward, but when, after a hundred miles, Martinique still did not appear, they decided that they had been mistaken, that they must have been set to the west all the time, and that the thing to do was to steer north until they found Porto Rico (too big to be missed) and start again from there. This they did, and having found Porto Rico they stopped for the night – a very sensible precaution, in Tobias' opinion, that might with advantage be adopted in the Royal Navy – and steered, the next morning, for the channel between Porto Rico and Hispaniola. Jack was walking on the quarter-deck, admiring the bright blue world and digesting a leisurely breakfast of fried barracuda; Tobias and don Jorge were arguing about mice, and Mr Hamilton was darning his stockings with military precision and a piece of llama's wool when Captain Cheap suddenly appeared. His usually greyish-yellow face was red; he had an extraordinarily furtive air. 'Do not display any emotion,' he whispered to Jack, 'but look – look.'

There was a barrel bobbing by the frigate's side, an empty barrel. It turned, light and airy in the breeze, and all at once Jack's heart gave a great thump – it was a beef-barrel from a man-of-war: there was no mistaking the familiar marks. 'I was so near to it below that I could not be wrong,' said the captain, 'and if we do not see a cruiser before the end of the watch you may call me a looby. That barrel has not been in the sea above an hour.' He looked up at the masthead – as usual, there was no look-out there – and he said, 'We must not arouse their suspicions – engage the officers in conversation as much as you can – I shall tell the others.' He walked off, humming loudly, with a very elaborate affectation of unconsciousness. Soon all the prisoners shared something of the same air; they were unnaturally gay, feverish and talkative; they kept stealing hidden glances round the horizon; and their captors looked at them with amazement and dismay.

Presently a little white fleck showed on the clear horizon: ten minutes later the fleck resolved itself into three – the topgallants of a ship, for certain, and a little beyond there was another. Jack's flow of talk redoubled, but he was running out of topics, and he had begun to grow very tedious indeed (though not as tedious as Tobias, who had pinned a lieutenant against the binnacle with an unending account of the domestic economy of the honey-bee) when a seaman, walking about the poop, happened to notice that there were two ships, top-sails up already, in their immediate neighbourhood. He gave the alarm, and now, of course, people hurried up to the mast-head in great numbers: from there it was quite obvious that the ships were men-of-war, a two-decker and a twenty-gun ship, and that they were in chase of the *Lys*.

The morning's breeze was failing fast; by noon it had died to a flat calm, and all the *Lys's* canvas (she had spread every stitch she possessed) flapped idly under the sun. In the first panic of the chase her people had determined to run the frigate ashore upon Porto Rico, but now a little reflection upon the character of the Porto Ricans had decided them to take their chance and run for it, north through the Mona Passage. Noon passed, and at four in the after-noon a wind began to sing in the rigging; the *Lys* heeled a trifle and the water gurgled along her side. The cruisers, away to the leeward, dropped hull-down over the horizon. But very soon they too had the wind; and now, as the sun declined, they came up so fast that it was evident that they could sail three miles to the *Lys's* two. The Frenchmen looked hopelessly at their pursuers, and the officers went to their cabins to fill their pockets with their most valuable pos-sessions: the men put on their best clothes, and as the sun went down in a blaze of crimson, a party of them came to where Jack and Tobias were standing in order to give them the nuggets and the little heavy soft leather bags of gold-dust that they had acquired in the New World; for although the English did not usually strip their lower-deck prisoners, they had never been known to let the smallest particle of gold escape them; and, the sailors said, they would rather their friends profited by their capture than people quite unknown.

The prisoners' most difficult task, in these last hours of the day, was to conceal their glee, and to watch, with a decent show of indifference, the steady approach of their freedom and deliverance. When the sun, with its customary tropical abruptness, dropped below the edge of the sea, the two-decker was hull-up from the quarter-deck of the *Lys*, and with her studding-sails abroad she was gaining so fast that half an hour would bring her within random shot. In the short interval of velvet darkness before moonrise the *Lys* altered her course and dowsed her lights, but in this faint breeze she had little hope of gaining any useful distance, and the prisoners, immovably on deck, expected to see the ships alongside at any moment of the night, to hear the warning shot, the English hail and the rattle of the French colours coming down.

'I suppose there is no danger of their going to sleep?' said Tobias, in the starlit night. No, they all said, very sharply, there was no such danger – the Royal Navy *never* went to sleep – did he not know that much, after all this time at sea? – how could he be so strange? – if he had nothing more sensible to say, he might save his breath to cool his porridge – and might as well go to sleep himself, and pass no further remarks.

Tobias followed their advice, and, having a clear conscience and a supple frame inured to hardship, he slept until daylight. He awoke wet with dew, and stared vacantly around for a moment: the sight of Jack pacing moodily to and fro brought it all back to him, and the sight of Jack's face told him what to expect. The broad Caribbean was as empty as could be; all round the horizon the blue sea was unbroken by the slightest glint of a sail. The *Lys* was alone, save for a turtle sleeping on the surface a little way off her starboard beam and a man-of-war bird high over the cheerful look-out at the mast-head.

The crew were in a charming flow of spirits; they skipped about the deck and carolled in the rigging like so many canary birds, and they were particularly kind and considerate to their downcast prisoners. The first captain broke out his last canister of coffee and sent some of it along to Captain Cheap with his compliments; the cooks (there were five aboard) did their best to allay Jack's disappointment with an extraordinary object called a *pouding anglais*. It was not very like anything known on land or sea, but it was very well meant, and it did at least, by its very mass, have a deadening effect. Jack laid down his fork and gave Tobias to understand that the whole thing did not signify, and that after all a French ship would carry them back to Europe just as well as any other – rather quicker, indeed, than if they had to stay aboard a cruiser and then wait about in Jamaica for a homeward-bound convoy.

Convoys, homeward or outward bound, ancient or modern, are

257

governed by a very curious natural law that causes them to blunder about over the surface of the ocean like a mob of half-witted sheep. Ships that behave perfectly well alone become over-excited in a crowd: the merchant captains lose their seamanship, the seamen forget that there is quite a difference between port and starboard and the vessels fall aboard of one another in the most stupefying manner. At one time, in the convoy from Martinique to France to which the *Lys* belonged, there were no less than eight all together in the morning, some with their bowsprits through the others' shrouds, some with their yardarms entangled, some apparently lashed together for mutual support, while the men-of-war fumed with impatience and fired whole broadsides to enforce the signal to make sail: and all the while a fast-sailing privateer from Jamaica hovered to windward to make prize of the stragglers.

Slowly across the Atlantic, fifty sail of merchantmen and five men-of-war, with tempers growing shorter every day. The French admiral ran one of the wandering captains up to his main-yardarm and ducked him three times, by way of encouraging the others to keep station, but nothing would answer, and by the time they made Cape Ortegal the poor admiral was as nearly speechless as it is possible for a Frenchman to become, from mere rage.

But it profits us little to contemplate the coarse sentiments of the French admiral: nor would it be improving, or even decent, to record his words when, upon dropping anchor at last in Brest road, his flagship was rammed smartly from behind by the heaviest of the West-Indiamen, and we shall pass them over, together with the dreary interval that the prisoners were obliged to spend in France before orders came down to allow them to go home in the first neutral ship that offered.

Behold them, then, upon the greasy deck of a Dutch dogger, in sight of Dover. 'No violence, Mr Byron, if you please,' said Captain Cheap.

Jack was scarlet in the face with anger, and he had a belaying-pin in his hand; but he fell back a step at the command. This was proof of a very high degree of self-control, for the Dutch skipper, having promised to carry them from Morlaix to Dover, and having been paid in advance, now had the brazen effrontery to say that wind and tide did not serve – that he was obliged to go on to the Lowlands.

'He is a false rogue,' cried Jack, who was never one for concealing his opinions.

'Let him be, let him be,' said Captain Cheap, who was too weak and ill to resist. He had never recovered his health, even in the sweet climate of Santiago, and since they had come into northern waters and the winter (it was February now) he had been very poorly.

The skipper blew a scornful whiff from his pipe and shifted the spokes of his wheel: Dover diminished in the distance, and the grey waves of the Channel came slopping aboard with the turn of the tide. Below, in an evil booth that reeked of old bait, Tobias and Mr Hamilton groaned faintly in unison. They had both been quite horribly sick the whole of the way up from Morlaix (which is in Brittany), and the dogger seemed to have been carefully designed to keep them in that condition indefinitely: it was a vessel of shallow draught, as broad as it was long, and it had a great well in the middle, meant for keeping fish alive – a sea-going pudding-basin that lurched, pitched, tossed and rolled every moment of the day and night, and smelt most abominably. 'Another hour, and it will be over,' said Mr Hamilton, for Jack had come below to tell them as soon as Dover cliffs had appeared.

'Another hour can just be borne,' said Tobias – 'perhaps.'

Jack walked up and down, in a towering rage: he was a long-suffering, good-tempered creature nearly always, but the Dutchman's insolent fraud vexed his very soul. Besides, they would have to find their passage from Holland to England now, out of a very thin purse indeed. Dover was gone, and even its cliffs were fading into the haze: a Swedish brig came past, very deep-laden; over towards Dunkirk a hoy beat into the wind with a great deal of fuss. The Channel was full of shipping – there were at least half a dozen other sails, near and far, to be seen from the dogger. Jack stared at them gloomily.

Suddenly his attention was fixed: to windward there was a ship that had just put about. None but a man-of-war on patrol was likely to do that, and Jack, running up the shrouds for a better view, saw that he was right: furthermore, she reminded him more and more strongly of the *Squirrel*, in which he had served. Five minutes later the varying positions of the dogger and the man-of-war showed him the unmistakable rails of the *Squirrel*'s head, and with a melodious howl he leapt down on deck. In a moment he had started the dogger's sheets and let them fly before the amazed Dutchmen could stop him.

Letting fly the sheets is a most emphatic signal: it can mean several things, and the *Squirrel*, with a natural curiosity, instantly bore down to know which. A boat came bobbing across, and at the hail 'Dogger ahoy,' Jack left the safety of the rigging. 'Dick Penn,' he called over the side, 'strike me down if it is not Dick Penn. Will you not take us out of this infernal old tub, and carry us into Dover?'

A very grim lieutenant came aboard, determined to know who this was who made free with his name – this very foreign-looking object who seemed to think that he could make game of the Navy. 'Why, damn your eyes,' he cried, with delighted recognition dawning in his countenance; 'it's Jack Byron, dressed up as a Don.'

Jack had had the poetical intention of picking up the first handful of English soil and cherishing it, but it was raining steadily when the *Squirrel*'s cutter landed them, and the earth was all chalky mud, with skim-milk-coloured puddles standing on it, so he was obliged to come ashore like an ordinary Christian. They stood shivering in their thin Spanish clothes while the seamen hoisted up the seven crates of birds, plants, serpents, fishes in spirits, dried bats and skeletons, and the pitiful little bundles of their own possessions. 'It will have to be a guinea,' whispered Mr Hamilton urgently.

'We cannot afford it,' whispered Captain Cheap.

'We must,' hissed Jack.

'All ashore, sir,' said the coxswain of the cutter. 'Thankee kindly, sir,' said he, pocketing the guinea and looking pleased. 'Cutter's crew is much obliged.'

All the stage-coach places, inside and out, were bespoke for the next many days, so they hired horses and rode as far as Canterbury by nightfall. In the morning it was decided that Captain Cheap, who had been scarcely able to sit on his horse by the end of ten miles, could not go on in that way, but would have to take a post-chaise. 'I knew we could not afford that guinea,' said the captain despondently. 'We cannot run to a post-chaise – I am sure of it.'

Now followed the paying of their bill for the night and a very minute and anxious calculating of distance, cost and available capital.

Their common purse would stretch to a post-chaise for Captain Cheap and Mr Hamilton, and what was left, exactly as if it had been worked out by a somewhat parsimonious guardian angel, was precisely the amount needed for horse-hire for Jack and Tobias as far as the Borough – that is to say, as far as the southern suburbs of London. Angelic nature, however, does not require material sustenance, and the angel had overlooked this point: there was horse-hire, but not the price of a halfpenny bun on the road.

'It don't signify,' said Jack. 'We have put up with rather worse than one day's fast, I believe. You don't mind it, Toby?'

'No,' said Toby, 'I don't mind it. But I wish I could feel sure that the carrier would take due care of my unborn whale: he seemed a man of gross and earthy understanding.'

Outside the inn the post-chaise set off, and the hirelings were brought round.

'French dog of a Turk,' shouted an ill-conditioned boy, as they mounted.

'I did not like their ugly foreign faces,' said the mistress of the Pelican, counting her spoons and looking after them. 'They might have murdered us all in our beds.'

It is true that by daylight, in an English country town, they presented a curious appearance: fashions differed very much from nation to nation, and the Spaniards at that time wore breeches and coats of an inordinate length; but even if they had not, the poncho that clothed Tobias would have attracted a great deal of attention.

'The little ugly wicked one is a native,' said the waiter.

'He is not,' said the ill-conditioned boy. 'He is a Popish priest,' and with this he threw a turnip. It struck the horse, the horse moved, and thus they left Canterbury, followed by the hooting of its inhabitants.

'You know, Toby,' said Jack, reining in at Harbledown, 'I promised I should make your fortune if you came to sea with me.'

'Yes,' said Tobias, 'and I am very sensible of your kindness in doing so, Jack. My molluscs, to say nothing of my annelids, are beyond anything . . .'

'Yes, but I meant in money,' said Jack, 'and I do heartily wish that I had made a better piece of work of it. Because, do you see,

if I had, we should not be afraid of that damned turnpike ahead.'
He pointed down the road to a little neat box, where at that moment
a horseman was paying his toll to the keeper. The guardian angel
had slipped again: he had brought them up through Patagonia; but
Patagonia had no turnpikes. 'There is no help for it,' said Jack. 'We
shall have to ride through them all.'

This they did, sometimes by low cunning – walking up as if to
stop and then suddenly spurring away – but more often by thundering along straight through, in spite of pressing appeals to stop
and pay. Sometimes they had to get round by going through the
fields, and twice they had to leap the barrier – a chancy thing to do
on an unknown horse. It was exciting at first, but rather unpleasant in
the long run, and at the last two pikes, Deptford and New Cross,
whose keepers were often plagued by Cockneys and had therefore
grown unnaturally alert, they were very nearly taken. But at length
it was over, and they rode through the crowded streets of the Borough to the George with thankful (though very hungry) hearts, and
there they left their horses. Now they were within that area of
civilisation that was served by hackney-coaches, and Jack hailed one.
He told the man to drive to Marlborough Street, and leant back
with immense relief on the musty leather-cushioned seat. 'Lard,
Toby,' he said, 'how surprised they will be.'

They rumbled over London Bridge into the City; the mist swirled
up from the river and blurred the lights. They crawled along past
the brilliant shops of Cheapside among a hundred other coaches,
and Tobias, coming out of a deep meditation, said, 'I am very
happy to tell you, Jack, that I have a satisfactory theory at last – a
comprehensive theory – an irrefragable theory.'

'I am glad you are so pleased,' said Jack. 'What is it a theory
about?'

'Tombs,' said Tobias, recognising the place where he had been
hunted down by the press-gang and pointing it out with mild
approval. 'Those tombs that we found are my *terminus a quo*, and I
conclude that the whole of the country south of the Chonos islands
is the Indians' Holy Land. They go there for religious motives, as
it were on pilgrimage: this explains their presence in such barren,
unpleasant regions, and their displeasure at seeing strangers – they
may have thought us unclean spirits. There were several different

tribes, but although they were so savage they did not fight. They did not kill us – they did not steal from us. All this points in the same direction – a peculiarly extensive local sanctity. And the fact that they carry their dead thither to bury them confirms it. Besides, those bloody ceremonies at which they howled all night and gashed themselves with oyster-shells were certainly religious.'

'A pretty rum religion,' said Jack.

'Not more so than burning people at the stake,' said Tobias, who still felt rather strongly upon this point. 'And we read in Strabo . . .'

'Marlborough Street,' called out the driver, pulling up.

'Ha, ha,' cried Jack, bounding out. He darted up the steps, and gave a great thundering double knock on the door. He was smiling to the widest extent of his face.

Slowly his smile grew less. He knocked again, and looked up at the windows: they were all shuttered, lightless, blind. He went round to the mews at the back, but there was no answer. The coachyard door was locked and barred.

'Drive to Little Windmill Street,' said Jack to the coachman, who was now growing anxious about his fare. But Mrs Fuller's house was no longer there; a new street had been driven through it, and everything was strange.

Jack was dog-tired, very hungry and cold; he felt that he could scarcely grapple with the situation, and for a moment or two his spirits were as low as can be imagined; but while he stood musing his eyes rested upon a shop-front that said William Boden Linen-Draper, or to be more exact, William Linen-Draper Boden, the linen-draper part being in the middle, in different letters. Suddenly the familiarity of the name and the shop pierced into his mind: the family always shopped there – Boden made his shirts.

'Wait a moment,' he said, and crossed the street. The coachman, convinced that he was going to be bilked, followed him closely into the shop, breathing on his neck. 'Mrs Boden,' said Jack, to a well-remembered face, 'how glad I am to see you.'

'Dear me,' said Mrs Boden placidly, without a moment's hesitation, 'how you have grown, Mr John. A fourteen neck by now, I do believe.' Nothing that Jack had heard – not all the English in the streets, nor the well-known London din – had made him feel so much at home; and this simple observation also wonderfully strengthened his faith in the stability of the universe. A moment before it had appeared to be toppling from its base.

'I have just come from abroad,' he said, by way of explaining his growth. 'And the house is shut up. Pray be so good as to pay the coachman, Mrs Boden – I have no money with me.'

'Why, of course the house is shut up,' said Mrs Boden wonderingly, as she gave the man his money, 'and has been, ever since Miss Isabella married my lord Carlisle. Such a wedding, Mr John: thirty-seven yards of Mechlin lace and forty-three of right Valenciennes, counting the bridesmaids. And then the lawn, cambric and baptiste – is this gentleman with you, sir?' she cried, breaking off at the sight of Tobias, who, having been put out of the coach, had wandered in out of the drizzle, looking not unlike a walking umbrella in his poncho – a lowered umbrella.

'Yes, yes. Where are they now, Mrs Boden?'

'Why, in Soho Square, of course. Her ladyship is giving a rout tonight.'

'Toby,' said Jack, steering him out of the shop, 'it is an astonishing thing, but the girls all seem to have grown up – married – most extraordinary. But then it was always understood that Carlisle should marry into the family. I don't object to him as an in-law. We must go to Soho Square, and find them there.'

Tobias stopped, very pale. 'He has married Georgiana?' he asked.

'No,' said Jack, 'Isabella. Isn't it funny? Cousin Frances wanted him to marry Georgiana – always said he was going to – but he has married Isabella instead. But it's all one, you know – it's all in the family.'

'Well,' said Tobias, who did not seem to think it was all one at all; and after a pause he exclaimed, 'Isabella! How I shall delight in seeing her. Do you think Georgiana will be there too?'

Jack, observing that all the girls might be at Medenham, as far as he was concerned, so long as supper was to be had at his brother-in-law's house, guided Tobias along Oxford Street and down Soho Street. 'Not that they are not dear girls,' he explained, 'and very near to my heart: but supper, do you see, is a great deal nearer, just at present.'

The fog was dripping from the railings of the square; thin black mud ran underfoot; in front of Lord Carlisle's house two flambeaux,

264

in holders either side of the door, threw a warm flaring light into the darkness, very welcoming. A few people loitered to stare up at the lighted windows: there was a sound of music, busy activity, a party in progress.

Jack knocked at the door, which swung wide at once.

'What do *you* want?' said the hall-porter, half-closing it again at the sight of such a strangely clothed, barely reputable pair.

'Isabella . . .' began the one.

'Georgiana . . .' began the other.

'Bah,' said the hall-porter, and clapped the portal to.

'Ha, ha,' went the little crowd outside.

'Come,' said Jack, 'we must do better than that.' He knocked again. To the intense delight of the crowd, the door opened with a vindictive suddenness that promised great things. But the instant the door was one foot ajar, Tobias, crouching inhumanly low, darted furiously in with such terrible impetuosity that his head, coming into contact with the porter's waistcoat, drove every particle of breath from that worthy's body, and left him gasping on the floor of his unguarded hall. Jack closed the door behind him, and they walked upstairs towards the big double drawing-room.

'Now, sir,' cried Lord Carlisle, looking suddenly out of a door at them.

'Ha, ha, brother,' cried Jack, immensely tickled by the situation. 'You don't recognise me. I wish you joy, however. Where's Isabella?'

'Is Georgiana here?' asked Tobias, fondly taking his lordship's elbow.

Lord Carlisle glanced down at his stricken porter, and again at the maniacs who had broken in, and he bawled for his footmen. But hardly had he ceased bawling before his bride appeared – a little quicker in the uptake, and a loving sister as well. Instant recognition, laughter, tears, joy, infinite surprise expressed and repeated indefinitely – a proper homecoming at last. In all this family turmoil, that drifted off vaguely to Isabella's boudoir, Tobias was somehow separated from Jack. He walked composedly into the drawing-room, where the dowager Lady Carlisle was entertaining a large circle of guests. She received him with tranquil complacency (she was a very well-bred woman) and introduced him to a Mrs Hankin, who had an empty chair by her. 'The gentleman is a great traveller,' she said.

'Indeed, sir?' cried Mrs Hankin. 'It is a vastly interesting thing, to travel. Pray sir, was you gone long? Was it an interesting voyage?'

'Tolerably so, ma'am,' said Tobias, stealing a piece of sugar from her saucer.

'The Grand Tour, sir?' asked his left-hand neighbour. 'Did you kiss the Pope's toe? My cousin Gardner kissed the Pope's toe. Did you pass by Pisa?'

'No, ma'am – a voyage by sea.'

'Oh' – disdainfully – 'only a voyage by sea. But in a voyage by sea you miss all the charming variety of travel – 'tis all one, by sea – a monotonous desert of water – I do not think that I should care for a voyage by sea. Surely, sir, there is no variety, in a voyage by sea, no diversity?'

'No, ma'am,' said Tobias, stealing another piece of sugar.

'The grand object of travelling,' said a heavy gentleman, 'is to see the shores of the Mediterranean. Sir,' said he, turning to Tobias, 'did you see the shores of the Mediterranean?'

'But, on the other hand,' said the lady, 'travelling by land is prodigiously dangerous. Cousin Gardner lost the wheel of his chariot, by the lynch-pin dropping out near Pisa – that was why I mentioned Pisa, sir; a very dangerous place – and was like to be thrown down, which could never have happened at sea. And in Florence, his pocket was picked.'

'No man will be a sailor who has contrivance enough to get himself into a jail,' said the heavy gentleman, in a booming roar, 'for being in a ship is being in a jail, with a chance of being drowned.'

'No, sir –' began Tobias, with equal positiveness, but at that moment Georgiana came into the room, sedulously attended by the Duke of Lothian and Sir James Firebrace. 'Ha, Georgiana, my dear,' he cried, starting up and throwing down a little round table and two gilt chairs, 'there you are at last. How very, very happy I am to see you,' he said, kissing her heartily. The duke turned red with anger: the knight grew pale with fury. 'Come,' he said, taking her by the hand and leading her to a distant sopha, 'come and sit by me, and let us talk of bats.'